It's Who We Are

by

CHRISTI

GW00385211

 On Call

To my darling Davy – for more than thirty wonderful years of love, laughter and support

First published in Great Britain in 2018

Copyright © 2018 Christine Webber

All Rights reserved. No part of this publication may be
reproduced, distributed or transmitted in any form or by
any means, including photocopying, recording, or other
electronic method without the prior written consent of the
author, except in the case of brief quotations embodied in
reviews, and other non-commercial uses permitted by
copyright law.

A CIP catalogue record for this book is available from the
British Library.

Cover design by Jessica Bell Book Cover Designs.

Published by On Call

Printed and bound in Great Britain by Clays Ltd, St Ives plc

Typeset by the BORN Group

ISBN 978-0-9954540-3-3

All characters and locations in this book – apart from all
those clearly in the public domain – are entirely fictitious.
Any resemblance to persons, living or dead, is purely
coincidental.

Acknowledgements

Writing a novel is just the beginning. The important stuff is done by a wide range of experts and I want to thank all of them for the fantastic work that they do.

Clays are a marvellous company who have been producing beautiful books for over two centuries. I am so delighted that they print mine; special thanks go to the wonderful Georgina Aldridge who heads up the indie team – and who is not only brilliant at what she does, but an absolute delight to work with. I am also deeply grateful to Helen Baggott for her painstaking editing and proofreading. I am trying to persuade her to live with me so that she can dispense her wisdom any time I need it – which is often – but her other authors will be pleased to know that she has resisted this offer. I also want to thank Jessica Bell for designing the perfect cover.

I am thrilled that the hugely talented and best-selling author Elly James has provided me with such a generous cover quote. Thanks so much, Elly.

Big thanks too to Daniel Knight of the BORN Group for his typesetting skills.

I would also like to mention the writers' groups that I could not do without: The Alliance of Independent Authors, Book Connectors, The Creativist Café and Books for Older Readers.

Finally, heartfelt thanks to all my friends and family who were very supportive of my last effort, *Who'd Have Thought It?* – I hope you will be equally kind about *It's Who We Are.* Particular gratitude is due to my great mate Helen McDermott for all her marketing prowess and determination!

Prologue

For a brief and bizarre moment, I think she's me.

The overhead lights on the station are flickering on and off – probably because of the storm outside – making the walkway beside Boots unusually dark. So I can't tell whether the shadowy images ahead are real people, or shop-window reflections.

My heart starts thumping as the figure strides towards me. I note that we're both wearing black trilby hats and long leather boots. But there the similarity ends. She's young; young enough to be my daughter. And she looks how I would *like* to look, and how – perhaps – I once did. She gazes at me. It's unsettling, so I stop and rummage in my bag for nothing in particular.

'Get a grip, Wendy,' I mutter. But then I reassure myself that weird notions are justifiable, given that less than an hour ago I called 'time' on my twenty-seven-year-old marriage.

I'm trembling. Probably the last thing I need is caffeine, but I walk into Costa Coffee and buy a Flat White to take onto the train.

*

Making my way back through the church, having shaken hands with various people at the front door, I try to avoid chatting with those of my flock who linger.

1

'Father Michael!' someone calls.

I'm aware that my response to this parishioner's news that she's now a grandmother is somewhat automatic. 'Jolly good! It'll be the christening soon then!'

Another woman of similar age presses a cake tin into my hands.

'How kind! Goodness, I'll be looking like a sponge cake soon!'

Someone else wants a meeting.

'Can we speak about it tomorrow?'

In the sacristy, I push the cake into the parish cupboard; it will cheer up the Finance Committee later. Then I tear off my vestments and race out of the building and round to the presbytery. Once inside the front door, I lean on it, breathing deeply.

It's a blessing that the curate and elderly priest who share the house are out, and that I have time to calm myself before this afternoon's meeting.

As often happens these days, my mind turns to Father Brian from my first parish. I find it hard to accept that at fifty-five, I'm older than he was then. One Christmas, over too many glasses of port, he had confessed how celibacy had become harder with age. 'It's easy when you're young and planning to change the world,' he had claimed, before expanding on his feelings of regret at the lack of a wife and family.

I couldn't identify with his feelings then, but I do now. Only yesterday, my arms felt painfully empty when, having baptized a baby, I handed him back to his family. Everyone else has partners, kids, grandchildren. Of course I feel valued, but only as Michael the priest, not Michael the man.

Araminta was at Mass. Every day, I long for her to be there. But, when she is, I go to pieces. One morning I was in such a state that I almost forgot the Gloria. I need to sort my head out. But how?

*

I hadn't realised that being selected as the local prospective parliamentary candidate for the Green Party would be such a big deal. I'm amazed that it's made the front page of the *Eastern Daily Press*.

Perhaps journalists are hoping for a 'family conflict' story. My father, after all, is well-known as a very right-wing Tory peer. Predictably, he's incensed with my decision. Marigold says he's had to take double the dose of his blood pressure medicine.

I'm relieved though that finally I've stood up for myself, and made it plain that looking after the family business isn't enough for me. It's not that there aren't challenges – especially with the EU referendum going the way it did – but my life had insufficient purpose and that's changed now.

I'm planning to promote Geoff, my second-in-command at Baldry's, which will free up some of my time. My father shouldn't mind; he's never believed I'm up to the job. I've often wondered why, when he retired, he insisted I take over – which meant leaving London and my job in publishing. He could have employed a proper business manager and left me in the capital doing what I enjoyed.

My mobile's ringing. It takes several seconds to find it beneath a mound of papers. I see from the display that Marigold is phoning me; my wife is a very persistent woman. She obviously feels she hasn't had her full say. Reluctantly, I press 'Accept The Call'.

'Philip!' She sounds furious. I swing my feet onto my desk. This will take a while.

*

I put down the teapot, to answer the phone. At the other end, Mum is full of a story in today's *Eastern Daily Press* about Philip Baldry becoming a Green candidate.

I hear myself make a harrumphing sound, which I realise confirms that I'm now officially old. Young people don't harrumph, do they?

'He always was an odious little prick,' I growl when she draws breath.

'Julian! You and he used to be such pals.'

'A very long time ago.'

'I never understood what went wrong.'

'I don't remember myself now.' This is a lie because I recall precisely why I ended our friendship.

We chat for a while – well, she talks, and I listen while doing some calf and hamstring stretches. I've got a worrying niggle in my left leg which probably means I pulled something at my class earlier. It's pointless going to the doctor about it. Last time I went, he just said, 'Well, if you must do ballet at fifty-six!' But I won't give it up. I've seen friends abandon active hobbies and become doddery overnight.

Somewhat surprisingly, my indefatigable seventy-eight-year-old mother suddenly decides she's tired and needs to lie down, and we end with me saying, 'Love you, Mum,' which I truly do.

I make my tea and sip it slowly while enjoying a large slab of fruit cake. Life is more leisurely these days. Too much so; the schedule of an ageing freelance singer tends to have more gaps in it than bookings. I've still got Extra Chorus jobs at Covent Garden, and I get some sessions on commercials and so on, but I worry that my voice isn't what it was. Fortunately, I'm still one of the best sight-readers in the business, so hopefully I'll keep going for a while. And, on the plus side, I have a new paid job as Musical Director of a good amateur choir. It's only one evening a week, but it's bucked me up no end. To be honest, Rhys, the young accompanist, is part of the attraction. Far too young for me of course, but still.

I've been thinking about new repertoire for the choir so I'm going out to Westminster Music Library shortly to look at scores. I'm sure most choral directors get their ideas off YouTube these days! But I loved that library when I was a music student, so it'll be a trip down memory lane. And there'll be more nostalgia later;

4

I see from the *Radio Times* that there's an old production of *Tosca* on the box later. I had a small role in that. It'll be good to see it again.

*

I'm tired, but then my daughter Hannah and I spent the whole of yesterday beginning the clear-up of my father's house. And I got up at the crack of dawn today to make breakfast for her before she caught an early train back to London.

After she'd gone, I went to Mass. Father Michael was saying it, but there was no opportunity to talk to him. I've no idea where the afternoon went, but this evening, I saw a patient for a 'farewell' session. She's much more confident than when she came to me nine months ago, and she said, 'Araminta, you haven't just been a therapist, you've been the best support of my life!'

Moments like that make the job worthwhile, though I do feel it's time for a change of career. But at the age of fifty-three, what can I do?

It seems cold after all the rain we had earlier and I wonder if it's too early yet to go to bed. It's at moments like this that I feel the full impact of widowhood. I heard Esther Rantzen on *Woman's Hour* one morning saying that since her husband died she's found plenty of people to do things with, but no one to do *nothing* with. So true. Still, I noticed earlier that *Tosca* is on Sky Arts. I pour myself a large glass of Rioja and curl up in an armchair to watch it.

One of the small parts is being sung by a rather rotund chap whose face seems vaguely familiar. The music is absolutely wonderful. As wintry evenings in late October go, this isn't a bad one.

Chapter One

The 9.30 train to Norwich stuttered once or twice as it pulled out of Liverpool Street station, but gradually gathered momentum, and by the time it passed London's Olympic stadium it was bowling along quite jauntily. Wendy removed her trilby hat and fluffed up her chin-length hair with her hands while peering down the length of the railway carriage. She could see no one she knew, but she sensed the presence of past passengers; this was, after all, a train-line populated with personal ghosts.

Three decades ago, before her career took her away from Anglia Television to the studios of ITN in the capital, she must have made this journey hundreds of times. Then, there had always been colleagues for company, but those days were long gone, as were some of the colleagues.

She felt unnerved by the events of her morning, and particularly disquieted by that preternatural moment when she had 'seen' her younger self walking towards her. Were she to describe it to her twins they would, she knew, giggle and roll their eyes at each other.

Her mind settled onto her lovely boys and she wondered how and when she would tell them about the divorce. Daniel's day had yet to begin at Harvard Business School. And Rhys, who still lived with her and Robert, had slept through the awkward last breakfast she had had with his father.

'But why *this* time?' Robert had pressed her. 'You know you're the only one who matters. You also know I've always been a bad boy.' As he spoke the last two words, he had attempted to put his arms around her and nuzzle the back of her neck. She had felt his look of puzzlement as she had shaken him off and continued making porridge for two.

'We had all this out last night,' she had replied, refusing to turn and face him. 'It's true that each affair has hurt slightly less than the previous one. But I'm worn out, Robert. I want to move on with my life.'

'Doing what?'

'Things that don't involve you.'

Did it happen quite like that? Or was she already rewriting her version of the trauma and imbuing herself with more poise and eloquence?

They were pulling into Chelmsford already. Defiantly, she rearranged her mind in a bid to eject Robert from it and to focus instead on her visit to her father.

Her heart gladdened at the thought of him. He had always been such an interesting, clever and honourable man. And now that he had to live alone, because of the dementia that had claimed his wife, he bore his unwanted singledom with fortitude. Wendy wrinkled her nose. 'Fortitude' was not a word she tended to use, but it was apt.

What, she wondered, would he think about the divorce? Better, perhaps, not to go into Robert's infidelities. What was the point when she had kept them secret for so long?

She had always found out, of course. At least she *assumed* that she had known about them all. Robert was hopeless at being discreet. Or maybe, at some level of his consciousness, he had contrived to leave a trail for her to uncover. However, the last one had come as a shock. Foolishly, she had believed that he had stopped 'playing away'.

Yesterday had been productive; she had spent it training a group of politicians to be more effective in the media, so that they could make their case on radio and television no matter what was thrown at them by wily interviewers. It was exactly the sort of job she had envisaged enjoying when she had set up her company, BS&T – short for Broadcasting Solutions and Training – nine years ago. In many ways it was as satisfying as directing international television news, but without the heart-thumping tension that accompanies live broadcasting.

BS&T had started slowly, but had become profitable by the end of the third year, and after that, she had taken the decision to branch into Europe. Surprisingly soon, she had landed a number of lucrative contracts with large corporations. Then, she had spotted a gap in the market for small businesses – and had produced a series of television training podcasts in nine different languages. She had had no idea these would prove so popular. The expansion had led to her employing an extra half-dozen young people from various EU countries, and she had been full of optimism for the future – never for one second expecting that the UK would vote to leave Europe.

Since the morning of June the twenty-fourth, everything had changed, and she felt a constant undercurrent of anxiety about what was to happen to her bright, enthusiastic employees.

With the working day over in Hoxton Square, she had taken the crowded Tube to Barbican station and then given into the urge for tea and comforting cake in the cinema café near her home.

The café had been crowded, but a woman moved her coat so that Wendy could sit down. There had been texts on her phone from a new client, as well as an email from her son in America, which she had replied to, with a smile. Then, she had scrolled through her Twitter and Facebook feeds while sipping her tea and eating a flapjack – gradually allowing the strain of the day to drop from her shoulders. She had even allowed herself ten minutes to read a chapter of *Radio Girls*, a novel about the early days of the BBC.

At six o'clock, some of the laptop-users around her had looked at their watches, and packed up and left. Meanwhile, the evening's filmgoers had begun to arrive. And in the midst of the comings and goings, she had spied Robert in the doorway, chatting animatedly with a young woman.

Spotting her, he had carved his way through the crowd to her table, the female with spiky pink hair and a fixed smile following in his wake.

'Darling!' He had kissed her rather too boisterously on the lips. 'What a pleasant surprise.'

She had looked enquiringly at his companion.

'I'm sure I've mentioned my researcher. Here she is.' He had produced her as if she were an assistant to his conjuring act. 'Mel – my wife, Wendy.'

'This is really spooky,' the younger woman had giggled. 'Rob was just talking about you.' The pitch of her voice had risen at the end of her sentence as if she were Australian. 'Isn't it spooky, Rob? I call that *really* spooky.'

Wendy had felt her smile freeze and her pulse quicken. 'You probably want to talk business,' she had said as she rose to her feet.

'Not for long,' he had answered. 'Let's go out for dinner. What about some tapas at Pedro's?'

'OK. I'm just going to pop to the loo then I'll go home. See you soon.'

In the Ladies, she had peered at her image in the mirror and, with a sigh, had extricated a raisin and a couple of crumbs from the cowl neck of her sweater.

'Nice!' Embarrassed at herself, and feeling suddenly messy and old, her tone had been heavily sarcastic.

For no good reason, when it would have been easier to return to her flat and put her feet up till Robert returned, she had brushed her hair and spritzed it with a pocket-sized hairspray, applied a hint of blusher, a generous coating of lipstick, and renewed her charcoal eyeliner.

Just as she decided she would pass muster, the woman who had made room for her earlier had pushed open the cloakroom door and commandeered the basin beside her. In their somewhat squashed proximity, the two of them had exchanged views on the day's weather.

'I don't know why I'm doing my hair, really,' Wendy had laughed. 'It'll be blown out of shape in no time.'

Her new companion had muttered something about how one had to make an effort, but then she had paused and stared at Wendy's reflection in her mirror.

'What?'

The other woman had shaken her head briskly as she blushed slightly and rummaged in her handbag. 'No, I shouldn't… I mean, would *I* want to know?' Her voice had been little more than a whisper.

Wendy had raised an eyebrow, feeling as though she were performing a close-up for the camera in a TV drama. 'Let me guess. You're wondering whether to tell me that as soon as I came in here, my husband was all over that girl like a rash. Is that it?'

'Pretty much.'

Wendy had swept up her belongings and smiled too brightly. 'Thanks.' She had sounded more dignified than she felt. But then, it was far from the first time.

As they approached Ipswich, she found herself haunted by memories of family holidays on the Suffolk coast. Robert may have had his faults, but he had been a wonderful father. She wondered if he was serious about Miss Spiky Hair. And if so whether he might live with her and even produce a new family. The thought converted her numbness into actual pain.

She had wanted children, but had been determined that her career should not suffer. So, producing two babies from one pregnancy had seemed a real bonus. Robert, on the other hand, would have liked a daughter in addition to their twin boys. Perhaps now he would get his wish.

Daniel and Rhys had been born alike, but not identical. More importantly, they were robustly healthy, which had been a relief since various health professionals had warned that having a first baby at 'her age' – thirty-seven – carried certain risks.

Just before returning to work, she and Robert had had the boys christened. Afterwards, they had hosted a party in their recently-purchased house on the outskirts of Dorking; a home with ample space for their expanded family.

Wendy had been the only adult not drinking at the loud and excitable gathering. She had mingled with various groups in different areas of the property till it had occurred to her that Robert was missing.

Eventually, she had gone looking for him. The hall had been empty but as she reached it, she had glimpsed the back of a guest, dressed in a bright red coat, disappearing out of the front door. Intent on finding her husband, it was only later that she had stopped to wonder who had left the party so early and without saying 'goodbye'.

She had run upstairs and put her head round various doors before trying their own bedroom.

The bed was rumpled, and the quilt and cushions which had lain on it had been flung to the floor. Robert, who had not noticed her, had been absorbed in pulling on his trousers and then, clumsy in his haste, struggling to fasten his belt. Even from across the room she could see lipstick stains and a smear of mascara on his face.

11

When finally he spotted her, his features had contorted with panic, and she had felt her own face pale with the realisation that something utterly impossible was happening. He had swallowed nervously. She had said nothing. Eventually, he had begun to assemble an explanation, but the words had died on his lips in response to her silence. Stunned, she had shrugged her shoulders and left the room. Somehow, she had been charming and civil to him until their guests had departed.

'I felt neglected,' he had confessed once they were alone. 'I know it's not very grown up. You're the one who had to give birth. I'm not proud of myself.'

'How long has this been going on?'

'A couple of months.'

'Unbelievable!'

'I'm sorry, darling!'

'Don't "darling" me,' she had snapped, before locking herself in the bathroom to cry.

Naturally, she had forgiven him. It was the first time. Becoming a father was obviously difficult.

Despite being 'terrifying' – as her colleagues tended to label her – she had never felt very confident as a woman. Robert was more obviously attractive than she was. But she was bright and successful, and he adored her quick mind, and always claimed that she had laughed him into bed. And each time she had learned about one of his conquests, he had persuaded her that it was a 'temporary fancy' and meant nothing.

It was not long before she had stopped weeping about his infidelities and learned to live with them – and they had remained together in their own type of harmony.

As the train slowed on the approach to its destination, her mobile rang.

'Dad! Yes, nearly in Norwich. I know that I'm early… Um, well, OK. Take it easy. I'll go out to the coast and see Mum first… Good idea. Tea in the city will be lovely.'

It was hard to accept that her father, at eighty-seven, was sounding older and beginning to slow down. Clearly, he was keener on an afternoon rendezvous than an earlier one. Perhaps he needed a nap first.

The rain had stopped, and it was sunny, cold and breezy when the train arrived in Cromer after its forty-five-minute journey from Norwich. A sudden gust of wind almost knocked her over. And for the first time that day she laughed.

She took a taxi to the Seastrand Nursing & Care Home where a smell of the lunchtime fish pie hung in the air. In the lounge, a member of staff was wiping the hands of an elderly woman while chatting to her colleagues who were clearing trays and rearranging furniture. No one was watching the television, which was blaring away in the corner. Most of the inmates – including her own parent – were asleep in their chairs.

Wendy sat down beside her mother, who failed to stir even when she took her hand. She watched the news for a while then surveyed the various residents in their slumber. Most were people she had seen before, but there was someone new. Something about him seemed familiar; perhaps she had met him when he was younger. Despite his age, he was a fine-looking man, and dressed in a smart Norfolk jacket, white shirt and mustard-coloured tie.

Turning back to her mother, she attempted to wake her. 'Mum. Are you OK today?'

There was no response.

After ten minutes, she left. She would come again tomorrow. Right now it seemed more appropriate that she should spend time with her father.

'And how is Robert?'

For a second, Wendy's knife hovered over the segment of scone she was buttering. She and her father were at the Maids Head

Hotel. And, as she had not had lunch, she was enjoying afternoon tea with no qualms about calories or cholesterol.

'He's fine.'

She should tell him that her marriage was over, but somehow this did not seem the right time. Her head felt strange, as though it was not quite connected to her, and the events of last night and this morning now seemed so surreal that she could not find reliable words to describe them.

'And Rhys?'

'Bless him. He's playing the piano for ballet classes at Pineapple Studios. He also accompanies quite a good choir. But I think he's going to have to make some career choices before long. Everything's so uncertain for kids nowadays.'

Her father smiled. 'He'll be all right. I'm lucky to have such clever grandsons. Of course, I'd love them even if they weren't bright, but it's a bonus.'

Wendy beamed at him. 'And Daniel adores Harvard, and he's very caught up in the US presidential election. He says it's a fascinating time to be there.'

'Is the idea that he'll help you run your business once he's got that Masters?'

Wendy gazed at her parent and reflected how his brain did not appear in any way to have aged with his body. She hoped she might take after him rather than her mother.

'He was quite keen before he went, but I think his horizons have widened now. He told me that lots of corporations offer jobs to students before they graduate. And I imagine that most of those are in America. So, I'm preparing myself for the possibility that he'll stay there for a while.'

Later, back at her parents' house in Hethersett, the hours flew by. She made supper. They watched an episode of *Midsomer Murders*, and her father guessed who had 'done it' long before she did.

By unspoken agreement, they did not talk about the third member of their tiny family. She had never understood why her father had selected a home for her mother in the north of the county when he lived south of Norwich. But distance did not keep her parents apart because he drove to see his wife most days and remained as devoted to her as ever. Indeed, he was so adamant that his place was by her side, that Wendy was unable to persuade him to visit her in London.

'We've been lucky,' he declared suddenly. 'Your mother and I had a good marriage. The best possible daughter...'

His conversations with her often followed this pattern and she always joined in, asserting that *she* was the lucky one to have had such wonderful parents. But this time, over their pre-bedtime hot chocolate, he expressed some regret.

'Of course, it would have been nice to have had another child. A boy perhaps. But it was hard enough producing you.'

She was suddenly alert to a confidence that had never come her way before. 'Really? I mean, you were still young.'

'Your mother was thirty when we had you. Not as old as you were when you had the twins, but old for those days. We were fortunate.'

The next morning, the two of them went into Norwich and meandered around. They had no need to go to a supermarket because her father took care of all his shopping online; a fact she related to friends and colleagues, often and proudly. However, she did buy him a cashmere pullover and a bottle of his favourite whisky.

Later, they lunched at Harriet's Tea Rooms in London Street, before she left him to go out to the nursing home again.

The Seastrand was playing host to a number of visitors when she arrived. Her mother was awake today and they sat together with Wendy chatting away about her sons in the hope of triggering some spark of memory in that impaired brain.

But there was nothing. No comment. No eye contact. So, it came as a shock when the old lady spoke – for the first time in several visits. 'What are *you* doing here?' she demanded. 'Fuck off!' Then she pulled her cardigan up over her face and resisted with considerable force when Wendy tried to pull it down again.

Rationally, Wendy was aware that she was dealing with a poorly individual who had lost her mind and who was not rejecting her personally. But emotionally, she *felt* rejected – particularly because her mother had never used bad language at home and had indeed reduced Wendy's pocket money as a teenager when she had once shouted 'Blast' having banged her knee on the table.

Her mother remained beneath her cardigan, leaving Wendy feeling exposed as well as ashamed by the vehemence of the outburst, so she took herself off to the visitors' lavatory to collect her thoughts.

She remained in the tiny room for a while, repairing her make-up, and when she did emerge, she walked the long way round, through another lounge filled with more elderly men and women and their visitors.

The new resident she had spotted asleep the previous day gave her a twinkly smile. Again, he was smartly dressed and quite dapper – wearing proper shoes rather than the slippers favoured by most of the other inmates, and a crisp, white shirt beneath a purple V-necked sweater, as well as expensive-looking black trousers. His female companion turned to see who had caught his attention.

The two women stared at each other.

'Minty?'

'Wendy Lawrence! Wow! And how lovely to be called "Minty". Takes me back to my youth. Everyone calls me Araminta now.'

They both giggled. 'I haven't seen you since I left Anglia in 1990,' Wendy said.

'God, is it that long? What are you doing here?'

'Visiting my mum. Is this your father?'

The man nodded and put out his hand.

'Gosh!' Wendy took his hand. 'Dr Yateman, you won't remember this, but way back before I knew Minty, when I was a little girl, you were my doctor – until I was about seven, I think, and my parents moved house.'

'I *do* remember, Wendy,' he answered. 'And I followed your career.'

'That's amazing.'

He raised his right forefinger as he said, 'You were my Number One!'

Wendy laughed. 'Would you remember my mother then? She's in the next room.'

Dr Yateman suddenly looked confused and somewhat agitated.

'Dad's only been here for a week,' Araminta explained.

'I see, well, Mum's been here for months. I'm afraid she doesn't know who she is any more, let alone anyone else.'

The old doctor's eyes flickered between his daughter and Wendy. 'Want to lie down,' he announced. He tried to stand up, but his balance was poor and he needed help.

Araminta put out her arm to steady him. 'Dad, you've not been awake long. I thought we were going to play Scrabble.'

'Tired now.' He seemed distressed. 'Come again soon.' Then he swivelled round to look at Wendy again. 'Will you come too?' he asked as he lurched forward, almost falling, and kissed her cheek.

Araminta looked embarrassed, then muttered something about him still being a ladies' man. She held tightly on to her father's arm as he headed, jerkily, for the door.

'I'll just get Dad settled,' she called to Wendy, over her shoulder. 'I don't suppose you'd like to go somewhere and have tea?'

'I really would! Give me a couple of minutes to say cheerio to my mother. Not that she'll…'

The two women nodded knowingly at each other.

Having established that neither of them had to rush, Araminta drove them along the coast to a tea room in a nature reserve.

'Do you mind me asking what's wrong with your father?' Wendy queried as they walked in and selected a table by the window. 'He's certainly more with it than my mother.'

17

'Well, he had a severe heart attack six months ago, but – against all expectations except his own – he rallied quite well. However, his memory was affected, though I sometimes wonder if he's as vague as he appears. But other parts of his body seem to be giving up. To be honest, I doubt if we'll ever understand exactly what his health problems are because he's always been adamant that when he was old, he wouldn't want what he calls "interventions". He signed something to that effect which his GP passed on to the home.'

'Difficult, isn't it, this ageing business?'

Araminta nodded. 'Funny thing is that sometimes he seems almost normal. He definitely meant what he said about following your career. When I finally got him and my mother to agree to me applying for a job at Anglia, and that was a hell of a business let me tell you, he became fascinated in what I was doing, once I started working with you.'

Their conversation focused then on their time at Anglia. They agreed that the age gap of some six years between them had been too large for them to have been close friends as well as colleagues, but they enjoyed recalling how much they had liked each other, and reminisced about the days when Araminta – having started as a copy-taker – became PA to Wendy when she was the main news director. Their working partnership had been disrupted only when Araminta had married young and produced a son.

'I think the last time we met, you brought your toddler in when you came to do a shift on the programme. I remember everyone volunteering to babysit him in the newsroom. You could see he was going to be a heartbreaker!'

Araminta looked up from stirring her tea. 'I still have a photograph from that day of Andrew sitting on your knee. It lives on top of my piano... You've changed your hairstyle. It suits you shorter and swept back, but then you always did have good cheekbones. Actually, you've hardly altered at all.'

18

Wendy guffawed. 'What nonsense. I'm going to be sixty next year! I'm a rather overripe size fourteen, and my hair would be quite grey if I didn't have all these bronzy highlights put into it.'

'Well, you look great. I, on the other hand, have changed a lot.'

Wendy made no comment. Araminta was too thin and had the look of someone who had suffered. Having been a vivacious young woman and a colourful and trendy dresser, she was wearing camel-coloured clothes that looked slightly too big for her, her hair – a paler shade of auburn than it had once been – was pulled back into a ponytail, and her tired-looking face was cosmetic-free.

'Tell me,' Wendy changed the subject, 'what's your son doing now? He must be, um, about thirty. And did you have any more children?'

Araminta used her fork to play with the slice of chocolate cake she had ordered, but did not reply.

Wendy stretched out her hand and stroked the other woman's arm. 'Have I put my foot in it? Sorry.'

'No, it's OK. The good news is that I have a lovely daughter, Hannah. She's working for a company who make programmes for Channel 4. She's living the dream... wants to get into television news... Got an Iranian boyfriend, who's a journalist on the *Financial Times*, and is not just brilliant but the most beautiful creature you've ever seen. But Andrew was killed. He was a passenger on his dad's motorbike – about fourteen months ago now. They both died.'

'Oh! I'm so sorry. I was going to ask about Simon.'

'Obviously it was sad about him, but it was devastating to lose Andrew. He had such a lot of living left to do, but there we go. I've been lucky really. I've had a lot of support from the local priest. Also, I suspect the fact that I'm a therapist these days helped me. All the training, it, uh, provides insight into how we think.'

Wendy nodded, unsure what to say. After a moment she murmured, 'I'm sure you're a very good therapist.'

19

Araminta looked thoughtful. 'I hope so. But I don't see many patients now. I cut back when the accident happened and haven't felt like building up my list again. Sometimes, I wonder if I could do something else. Hard though, when you get older.'

The two women fell silent, lost in their own thoughts but after a moment Araminta's expression brightened. 'You had twins, didn't you?'

Wendy paused. Normally she would have launched into a proprietorial account of how wonderfully attractive and clever they were, but it did not feel appropriate. She settled for: 'Well remembered!'

'And the seriously sexy Robert?'

'Ah!' Wendy exhaled sharply. 'Actually, we're getting divorced. And you're the first person I've told. It's a bit mind-blowing, though nothing like as cataclysmic as what happened to you, of course.'

'It's still a hell of a crossroads. Being single again is very odd. Your world shrinks. You don't mean it to, but it does. To be honest, when I was married with children in the house, I'd sometimes go out for a coffee, or to a yoga class, just to have time to myself. Now that I'm alone, I tend to stay home.'

'Well,' Wendy replied, 'I'm hoping to just throw myself even more into work. I never was keen on yoga!'

Araminta grinned at her former colleague. 'But it'll change you. I'm just beginning to see now how many options there might be. Partly, I think also that since the EU referendum, there's been a weird sense of everything being up in the air for lots of people, and a feeling that while everything's so… unusual… you might as well go for something different. I'm not putting it very well. Sorry.'

'Actually, you're expressing exactly what I feel.' Wendy's voice was low and slow. 'I've never told anyone this, but when I woke up on June the twenty-fourth and found we'd voted to leave the EU, for the first time in my life I felt that I didn't want to carry on living in the UK. Not sure I feel better about it now. It's very destabilising.'

'It is. I wasn't actually in good shape in June so I didn't vote. But I hate the limbo we're in now.'

'Me too. And it impacts on everything. Let's face it, breaking up with Robert has always been on the cards. So maybe it was the sense of uncertainty all around that gave me the courage to end it this time. But it feels like I've stepped off a cliff, and right now I've no idea whether I'm going to have a soft landing or end up seriously damaged.'

Chapter Two

Philip's phone rang as he left the television building. He paused on the steps and patted all his pockets till he located it.

'Philip!' It was Marigold.

He noticed that his hands were trembling. 'Sorry,' he said. 'I've just got out of the studio. Was I OK?'

'Your father's been on the phone. It's unforgivable what you're doing to him. He's ninety for God's sake. Why did you have to do the interview?'

'They asked me. And the party thought it was a good idea.'

'Well, he's appalled.'

'He never watches that programme; he always says that news from Norwich isn't relevant to his end of the county. So maybe someone tipped him off. I wonder who that could be?'

Marigold ignored his insinuation and continued. 'Can't you see how awkward this is for him as a Tory peer?'

Philip found a steelier tone. 'He'll get over it. And you will too. I'm sorry the *Eastern Daily Press* coverage upset you yesterday, and that you're distressed about the TV interview. But it'll all die down now. However, the fact is that I've been selected and I'll be standing in the next General Election – which won't even be till 2020 – so that's that.'

He was about to say 'goodbye' when he realised that Marigold had already terminated the call. Shrugging his shoulders, he pushed the phone back into a coat pocket just as a man wearing scarlet-framed glasses and a clerical collar walked up the steps towards him. They exchanged a smile as he moved to allow the newcomer to enter the building. There was something familiar about him, Philip thought.

His fingers were still shaking, he noticed, and he felt distinctly unsettled. Perhaps, since he was in Norwich, he should have something to eat, or go to a film. There seemed little point in rushing home.

He had been focusing on the television interview all day, but had not foreseen how anticlimactic he would feel afterwards. His mood was not helped by the inevitability of his father's response, or by Marigold being critical rather than supportive.

He felt disappointed. Lonely, too. What an admission.

Should he drive home now, as he had planned, to the house he had renovated and come to love? But surely that was where he felt loneliest of all. Quite apart from Marigold's brusqueness, they never had sex – at least not in any joyous, exciting and mutually agreeable way.

Occasionally, if she was feeling generous, she did allow him access to her body with a grudging comment along the lines of, 'Oh, go on then, as long it doesn't take too long.' But he felt that hardly counted. Indeed, he sometimes wondered if it was worse than no sex at all.

He jumped slightly as three younger people emerged from the studios behind him. One of the two women caught his eye.

'Mr Baldry! Hi, I'm Katie, the producer. We spoke on the phone yesterday. Sorry I didn't have a chance to chat to you before you went on. I watched you though. You were a natural!' She bestowed a sparkling smile in his direction.

Genuinely pleased, he murmured. 'Oh, thank you. Most kind. Delighted to meet you.'

'Are you waiting to be picked up?' she asked.

'God, do I look that desperate?' He laughed.

She seemed embarrassed. 'Sorry, I meant is a car coming for you?'

He smiled. 'I know. Apologies. I was just feeling at something of a loose end and wondering whether I should stay in Norwich for a bit before driving home.'

'Well, we're going to a pub in St Andrew's Street,' she said. 'Why don't you come?'

He could not join them. He was a different generation. He would be in the way.

'Only if you want to, of course,' she added.

Her two colleagues nodded and smiled encouragingly.

'Well, that's very gracious of you. Maybe just one drink.'

Suddenly, Katie's male companion decided that he ought to stay sober tonight, and her female friend asked, 'Do you mind if I back out too? Early start tomorrow.'

As they disappeared, Philip gazed helplessly at the producer.

'I'm sorry. Obviously, they weren't keen to include me. Don't feel that you have to go through with it.'

Much to his surprise, she grabbed his hand and pulled him down the steps and across the busy main road.

'It wasn't you,' she explained, as she released him from her grasp and started to walk briskly, despite the high heels of her neat little ankle boots. 'Ooh, it's chilly, isn't it?' She pulled her capacious coat more tightly around her without breaking step. 'They've ducked out because they think it's OK to leave now that I'm not alone. I don't blame them. They've been propping me up most evenings, letting me talk and cry. My boyfriend, Greg, left me six weeks ago. He got promoted and moved from Norwich to London and didn't even discuss it with me let alone suggest I join him. Bit of a bummer – especially when people queued up to tell me that they'd always known he was commitment-phobic. Thing is, I was pretty blinkered, but my excuse is that I'm thirty-five and desperate not to be one of those ball-breaking females who give their life to the industry for no good reason. I also want a baby. I kind of knew things weren't right, but I didn't *want* to know.'

As they reached the door of the St Andrew's Brew House, she stopped talking and burst into tears. Philip hopped from one foot to the other, trying to think of something sensible to say.

She flapped her hands in front of her face, whether in a bid to control herself or send him as far away as possible, he was unsure. And she was sobbing so hard that the words she was trying to utter made no sense.

In his indecision, he could almost hear his wife's voice hissing in his ear, 'For God's sake, Philip, *do* something.' So, he did. He put his arm around Katie's shoulders and propelled her into the hostelry, sat her down in a quiet corner, and bought two large brandies.

She remained tearful for another ten minutes, during which time he made sympathetic noises, and also found himself hoping that no one would think it was he who was causing this delightful damsel such enormous distress. He would never want to hurt her. In fact – and it was a most surprising sensation – he felt an urge to do her ex-boyfriend significant and painful harm.

Suddenly, she brightened and apologised. Then she sprang up, seized her bag and headed to the Ladies.

When she re-emerged, all signs of blotchy mascara erased from her lovely face, she insisted on buying them both another drink.

The red wine came in large-bowled glasses, almost filled to the brim, and worked like medicine on her mood. Before long, she was laughing and recounting how marvellous her friends had been, and how one of them had recommended a therapist.

'I've seen her a few times now.'

'Is it helping?'

I think so. Araminta – that's her name – is great. But sometimes it just, you know, comes over me again.'

Philip was trying to make his wine last, but Katie was a quick drinker. Any minute now he would, he knew, buy another round.

25

He would have to, otherwise he would look wimpish or mean, which would not do at all. The trouble was that already he was feeling slightly inebriated.

He played for time. 'Araminta's an unusual name, but – funnily enough – I knew someone called that, ages ago. She was the sister of a boy I went to school with.'

'Might be the same person then,' Katie said. 'She is quite...'

He realised that she had been going to say 'old'. And as he watched her, he perceived that she knew that he knew. Her complexion grew pinker and she smiled an apology.

Of course, Araminta – if indeed it was the same one – would be 'oldish' to someone of thirty-five. And he was older still.

'Anyway,' she was saying. 'That's enough about me. Why don't you get us another drink and then tell me how you come to be standing for Parliament.'

As he stood at the bar, waiting to order two more glasses of Argentine Malbec, he kept glancing over his shoulder in a bid to garner more details about his companion. She had a delightful nose. And big eyes – round ones, not feline-shaped like Marigold's. Looking up, she caught his gaze and grinned. This was like a dream; a very good dream.

Once seated again, he started talking about himself as Katie plied him with questions.

No, he had not lived all his life in Norfolk, though he had been born in the county and grown up there. His mother was Irish, so he had spent long holidays there. He had gone to Cambridge University where he had read English. Then he had worked in his father's company – selling and leasing farm machinery – for a couple of years, just to learn how it functioned and to get a grasp of business matters, but had then gone to London and built a career in publishing, which he had loved.

He also told her how, unfortunately, eighteen years ago, he had been forced to return to Norfolk because his father had decided to give up running Baldry's.

'It wasn't what I wanted, but we have a good life in Norfolk. I work long hours but that's what CEOs do.'

She nodded.

Then, in a bid to make himself sound more interesting and dynamic, he mentioned that he loved to ride around his grounds on his quad bike. This was definitely stretching the truth. For a start it was an ancient three-wheeler rather than a quad, though it was classed as an ATV, or all-terrain vehicle, and he rode it at most twice a year, and then as slowly as he could – being a cautious man by nature.

She did not look particularly impressed, so he moved on to his reasons for going into politics – telling her how he was desperate to add more meaning to his life, particularly in light of the referendum result.

He surprised himself with how much he was talking, and as he went on – and she nodded encouragingly – he experienced a rare and heady sensation that perhaps, after all, he was an interesting man.

'You're nice,' she said, out of the blue.

She was, of course, treating him like a father. But he recognised that his feelings towards her were anything but paternal. His pulse was racing, and he realised with a shock that not only did he want to protect her, he wanted to own her too. His eyes feasted on the shadow of cleavage that was visible beneath the low cut neck of her sweater before he forced himself to look away. He was being absurd. He should go. Right now. Before he made a complete fool of himself.

'I think I need a walk.' He spoke to break the spell and bring himself back to reality. Things like this never happened to him. Best to leave while he retained some dignity.

'Good idea,' she agreed. And she helped him into his coat, before pulling on her own flowing outer garment, clutching his arm and leading him to the slightly foggy street outside. Despite them both being wrapped up against the elements, he could feel the swell of her firm breast against him, and as they wandered down a pedestrian passageway towards the river, he stopped, turned towards her and brushed her lips lightly with his. He could hear his own breathing. She pulled away. Of course, she would. But then, her mouth sought his.

She told him that her flat was five minutes away. It took them a quarter of an hour to reach it because they kept stopping in doorways to kiss and touch and hold each other.

Once inside her tiny apartment round the corner from the Art School, he took fright and urged himself to leave. He knew that he was taking advantage of her; she was vulnerable, and lonely. But when he voiced his anxieties, she told him to stop worrying before posing a series of searching questions. Surely he was lonely too? Why had he looked sad on the steps of the studios? Why had he been reluctant to drive home? Why was he so hungry for her? Might it be that he was as devoid of love and passion as she was?

'What's your wife like, Philip?' she asked suddenly.

He was shocked at her directness. An honest answer would be disloyal to Marigold, but he did not disabuse the young woman he was cuddling of her rapidly developing theory that he was in need of comfort, just like she was.

'Any children?'

'A daughter,' he whispered.

And as they fell together onto her unmade double bed, that was the last that was said till, eventually, they lay entwined in the after-glow of the kind of passionate sex he had given up hoping for.

'Meet me again soon,' he urged her. 'Please.'

She nodded, and he crushed his lips to hers once more.

Inevitably, they indulged in more wine. Then, after another hour, he was amazed to find that he was ready for more sex. She clung to him and he emptied himself into her with a groan of ecstatic relief that did not sound like him at all.

They had one more drink and she fell asleep in his arms. Gently, he edged out from beneath her. As he straightened up, he stood by the bed for several moments, gazing at her in disbelief. Would it matter so very much if he stayed till morning? Resolutely, he covered her nakedness with the duvet and quickly pulled on his clothes.

Outside, it was freezing. His plan was to hail a taxi, but none passed him. So he strode down the hill to where his rimy car stood by the river, just as he had left it in what now felt like a previous life. It looked reassuringly solid and welcoming. He could shelter inside it. Nothing wrong with that. He started the engine and turned up the heater.

As he shuffled back in his seat, he caught sight of himself in the driver's mirror and was bewildered to see the usual fifty-five-year-old face looking out at him when he felt so different inside. Not for the first time, he felt a wave of gratitude that he had not inherited his father's Roman nose, long teeth and haughty expression. In fact, he reckoned that in certain lights, he looked relatively boyish. He also had a good head of hair; again, this was unlike Pa, who had been bald for as long as he could remember. His jawline was still firm too and though he had some wrinkles, he hoped they might pass as laughter lines. Katie had said that he reminded her of someone called Dr Mark Porter. But had she just said that to be kind?

The ice on the windscreen had melted and he peered out onto the empty street. It was two o'clock. The whole world was asleep. Norwich was frosty and deserted. And he felt fine. Probably the walk in the bitter wind had sobered him up.

Chapter Three

'I'm sloping off early,' Julian had whispered to the ballet teacher. 'I'm on a promise!'

Half an hour later, walking along Shaftesbury Avenue towards his flat, he reflected on how many lies he told these days.

Today's untruth had enabled him to leave the class before they practised little jumps. His weight had crept up recently and he hated his jubbly flesh, which was more evident when he leapt off the ground.

More commonly though, he lied because of anxieties concerning his voice. He had never had stage fright until recently, but he had learned that plenty of performers, including Laurence Olivier, had suffered crises of confidence as they grew older. But was that all it was? Or were his vocal cords showing their age? He used to smirk at older singers with their widening vibratos, but he could see now that it was no laughing matter. Nowadays, singing softly, especially in small groups, induced total panic. So, he turned down jobs, lying about the reason, and only took those where the music was atonal and modern, or where he would be part of such a large group that he could sing out and relax. Luckily, he was often booked for the Extra Chorus at La Scala and Covent Garden when they were performing large-scale Wagner or Verdi operas. He worried that his fabrications would be found out, but that particular anxiety did not keep him awake, whereas his fear of making a hideous sound did.

He looked at his watch. Nearly home. He could have some time to himself before going out to meet Rhys, the delectable pianist, who often played for ballet classes at Pineapple and also accompanied the chorus that Julian directed. He was going to buy the boy some supper, ostensibly so that they could discuss new repertoire before tonight's rehearsal. He could not help hoping that there might be a spark between them. But he knew he was being ridiculous. The boy was too young and – almost certainly – rampantly heterosexual.

He unlocked the narrow door to his apartment block and took the lift to his flat on the second floor. As he stepped into the spacious living room that overlooked the busy street below, he felt, as he invariably did, a sense of pride that he lived and worked in central London. It was an emotion that had sustained him for over thirty-five years, ever since he had escaped from the provinces to study at the Guildhall School of Music and Drama.

With the benefit of hindsight, he realised that during the mid-eighties – when, typically, he had recorded a backing for a commercial in the morning, sung on a film track in the afternoon and performed in an opera, or chamber concert, in the evening – he should have done that sensible 'baby boomer thing' and bought a property. Flats like the one he lived in, had been on sale then for £40,000. At the time, it had seemed a fortune, but if he had been more frugal he could have afforded it, and his failure to act then was a major regret now.

The truth was that he had elected to be a free spirit and a spendthrift; and he had indulged himself with drink, good food and travel; sex too – though that had often failed to live up to his expectations.

His greatest stroke of luck had been that he had stayed free of AIDS. He knew so many who had succumbed to it during those terrifying times in the mid-eighties, and who had not survived long enough to access the modern drugs that routinely kept people alive today. If only he had been as financially prudent as he had been fortunate, he might now be solvent.

Instead, he mused, as he pottered into the bathroom, removed his sweaty exercise clothes and took a swift shower, his savings were almost non-existent. Worse still, his landlord had put the flat up for sale, at £800,000. The only glimmer of hope was that it might not sell for ages – the housing market in London having been jittery since the referendum.

Julian sighed deeply as he wrapped himself in his bathrobe and padded back to the living room.

To lift his mood, he sat at his keyboard and accompanied himself as he sang a couple of Cole Porter songs. While he did so, he remembered the summer's John Wilson promenade concert when he had performed with the Maida Vale singers – a gig which had caused him no anxiety whatsoever, and had been sheer joy from start to finish. He sometimes wished he had done more musical theatre, but he had always put the classical scene first.

As he finished with a flourish, he decided he was due a little treat. His delight as he savoured a slice of Patisserie Valerie cheese-cake was orgasmic. Unfortunately, once he had consumed the last crumb he not only felt slightly sick, but ashamed. So, he forced himself to walk into the bedroom, remove his dressing gown and view himself in the full-length mirror. His curly hair, with only a fleck or two of grey, was still plentiful, and his face had not aged too much. He moisturised lavishly of course, and he had fewer wrinkles than his thin friends, but the rest of him – especially his considerable stomach – was not a pleasing sight.

'Jules, dear boy,' he said aloud, 'your gluttony is showing!'

Resolving to do better, he dressed quickly, finishing off the outfit with a navy fedora hat and a flowing red scarf. He was no longer desirable or dashing, but he liked to think he retained a certain style.

'Don't even think about it.'

Julian swivelled his gaze from Rhys's departing figure and found himself looking into the beady eyes of the boy's mother. Her mouth was twitching in amusement but her stare was unflinching.

'I was just wondering where he was going,' he murmured, innocently.

'He likes to go across to the rehearsal room early and warm up his hands with scales and so on. But I'm sure you know what I'm warning you about. He's not gay, and even if he were, I'd want him to have magical experiences with someone of his own age.'

Julian wondered whether to be offended, but decided against it. Supper in Wendy's quirky apartment in the Barbican had turned out to be the best fun he had had in ages.

'Coffee?'

He smiled and nodded, and she headed off to the kitchen.

He had met Rhys as arranged, but the boy had suggested that instead of having a meal in the local pub they should join his mother for supper at home.

She had fed them coronation chicken, salad, fresh fruit and cheese – making no secret of the fact that Marks & Spencer had done all the work for her. There had been no sign of any wine or beer, simply sparkling water. That suited him. Alcohol tended to slow him down too much these days, and he avoided it when he was working.

Her flat, high in the sky, was impressive. Having always dismissed the Barbican buildings as brutalist, he was astonished by how much at home he felt. This would be an ideal base for him if only he had money.

Many of his friends' parents were dying off and leaving useful sums. But he had no such expectations. His mother had a state pension, and owned her home, but had no other assets. And he had not seen his father – once a public affairs specialist attached to the US air force – since he had returned to America, leaving nine-year-old Julian and his mother to fend for themselves. What an upheaval that had been. He had been moved from his preparatory school to the state system, and they had had to relocate to a council estate. Eventually, his unconventional parent, who had never married his 'Pop', had wed an insurance salesman for security and a semi-detached in Gorleston. When she died – and he hoped that would not happen for ages – the property would be left jointly to him and his younger half-sister, whom he barely knew and did not like. They would sell it, but his share would buy nothing but a broom cupboard in central London.

Wendy returned with their coffee. She was, he decided, not conventionally pretty but very attractive with her intelligent eyes and amused expression. She was also such an entertaining conversationalist that when eventually he glanced at his watch, he realised he was running out of time to get to his rehearsal.

'Oh God!' He jumped up. 'I know that Rhys could start the vocal exercises without me, but I oughtn't to be late.'

'It's my fault. I was enjoying your company so much. Sorry!'

'Not at all.' He felt hot and wondered if he was blushing. Something about her made him feel like a gauche schoolboy.

She rushed out to the hall, returning with his hat and scarf. 'Off you go!'

'I don't suppose,' he hesitated. 'I mean, do you sing? Why not come?'

It was her turn to look flustered. 'Oh no. I've got a date with a book – *The Gustav Sonata*. It's great.'

'Singing's much more fun.'

'No, I couldn't.'

'You called your son Rhys. You must be Welsh.'

'My mother was born in Wales, but what's that got to do with anything?'

'All Welsh people can sing!'

'That's ridiculous,' she retorted. 'But... oh, OK, I'll get my coat.'

He watched her throughout the rehearsal, beginning with the warm-up where he could see her giggling over her mistakes as the choir sang the tongue-twisting word 'Popecatepetl' on every note of each scale.

She laughed easily. And she was smart and sassy. In fact, she was the type of woman who had always appealed to him and would have loved to marry, if only his orientation had been different. Rhys had told him that his parents were divorcing because of his father's infidelity. How could anyone cheat on her?

They were working on Mozart's *Requiem* tonight and he was endeavouring to achieve a more balanced sound, which was difficult because the basses, who were plentiful in number, were swamping the half-dozen, somewhat weedy, tenors. But his gaze kept returning to Wendy. She had chosen to sit with the altos and was singing along, confidently. Probably, she was quite musical; Rhys must get his talent from somewhere.

After the rehearsal, most of the members adjourned to The Jugged Hare and he found himself surprisingly pleased when he realised that Wendy was among them. There was, however, a horde of chattering choristers between him and her. And, as always, he was hemmed in by a group of women of a certain age, all vying for his attention as well as for the 'privilege' of buying him a drink. He played up to his fans. After all, what choirmaster wants to lose members, even those whose older voices were in a far more parlous state then his? In fact, the membership had risen since he had taken over. Maybe that was not entirely due to his direction, but he did have useful contacts and had persuaded a trio of retired members of the Royal Opera Chorus to come along, which had boosted the sound considerably. It was just a pity that none of them was a tenor.

He could see that Wendy, nursing an orange juice, was pinned into a corner by a particularly boring male chorister. She was looking pained. Before long, she gathered up her bag and started searching for her coat.

Excusing himself, he declaimed, 'Darlings! Wonderful rehearsal. Best yet. Must go. Busy day tomorrow.' He really must stop fibbing, he told himself as he snatched up his music folder and hat and scarf, parted the crowd before him, and emerged slightly breathless onto the cold street just in time to see his new friend walking away.

'Wendy!' Fortunately, his voice could still stop traffic and she turned around. 'I'll walk with you.'

She waited for him to catch up. 'No need. I'll be back indoors in five minutes!'

'I know, but let me at least buy you a drink.'

'Would I sound very boring if I said I'd sooner we had one in my flat, then I can get out of these shoes?'

'Not at all. Let's make a detour to Waitrose and I'll buy a bottle.'

'I've got wine.'

'I'm sure you have,' he grinned at her, 'but you've already fed and watered me. This is my treat.'

Inside the store, he left her near the front door and raced around, picking up a box of Lindt chocolate truffles, a bottle of Rioja and a large bunch of yellow roses.

She giggled, and blushed slightly, as he presented them to her. 'Oh my goodness, you're far too generous. Come on, let's get back. It's freezing.'

Two hours later, she had had one glass out of their wine bottle and he had drunk several more while they had related to each other their life histories.

She had laughed on learning that his great love was ballet – doubtless unable to equate his size with his passion – and how he went to classes as often as he could. She had laughed on realising that they both came from Norwich. She had laughed too as she regaled him with stories of directing at ITN and when he had recounted tales of what could go wrong during opera productions. He had also told her how he sang a great deal of twentieth century music.

'Thing is,' he had explained, 'I've got a talent for sight-reading. I seem to have been born with it, and there are so few rehearsals allowed for recordings these days, that they need people who can get the notes right. I've never had the best voice, but having the knack of accuracy has taken me a long way.'

She had nodded, looking genuinely interested.

Eventually, they paused for breath before agreeing that another bottle of wine would be a bad idea and that they would settle for decaffeinated coffee.

As she returned with a cafetière and two mugs, she remarked, 'I used to drink a hell of a lot when I worked in television. But I can't handle it now. More than one glass and I really suffer!'

'I know the feeling,' he agreed.

'I suppose,' she ventured, as she handed him one of the mugs, 'that I was right about your orientation? You have such a coterie of female admirers at the choir that perhaps I got it wrong. If so I apologise.'

'No, you didn't get it wrong. I suspect they'd just prefer not to know I'm unavailable. They think because I'm a professional singer that I'm interesting!'

'Well you *are* interesting. And I feel like I've known you for years.'

'That's funny,' he said, 'I feel that too. Were you expecting me tonight? Was Rhys worried that I was going to come on to him and thought he'd be safer in Shakespeare Tower?'

She chuckled. Really, she had the most musical laughter of anyone he had ever met. 'As a matter of fact that wasn't it at all. I was half-expecting you, but that was because I knew Rhys was worried about me.' And then she sighed loudly, and her face became a picture of misery.

'Look, should I go? You look as if you could do with a good cry.'

She shook her head vigorously. 'Don't worry – that won't happen. I used up all my tears a long time ago. And I don't want you to leave, unless you want to.'

'Would it then,' he asked gently, 'be a help if you talked to me about what's wrong and why Rhys was worried?'

She told him then how when she had left ITN, she had formed a media consultancy company. And how, soon afterwards, she had brought in a friend to deal with the administrative side of the business.

'Her name's Francesca. I've known her for over twenty years. She's an accountant by training and is really hot on finance and contracts, none of which is my bag. So we complement each other.'

'Sounds good,' he said, encouragingly.

She nodded and explained then how unsettled Fran had appeared to be by the news that she was divorcing Robert, and how she had devoured every detail about his latest fancy.

'I thought it was strange, but I had other things on my mind. Getting a lawyer and starting the divorce process obviously, but also, since I saw my father last week in Norwich, I've been thinking a great deal about him and whether I should now work out a way to spend more time with him. So, earlier this week, I tried to talk to Fran about the future of the company, but all she wanted to discuss was Robert. It was weird. Anyway, when I went into the office this morning, she'd brought in a whole wodge of photos dating back to when my twins were babies. It turned out she had been at their christening, which I certainly didn't remember. But the horrific thing was, that in the pictures taken on the day, she was wearing a bright red coat.'

'And why is that significant?'

'The christening was the day I found out for the first time that Robert was cheating. I didn't know who the woman was, but just before I discovered what he'd been up to, I glimpsed the back view of someone, dressed in red, rushing out of our front door.'

'But maybe other guests were wearing red?'

'Not in the photos I saw. Anyway, I tackled Francesca about it. After all, why had she been so distressed that Robert had someone new? And it turns out that she's been his long-term lover since before that christening and on and off between his nubile students. And she's beside herself that he's finally free of me, but not – after all – going to marry *her*. You couldn't make it up.'

'It was brave of you to confront her.'

Her face brightened. 'I know! Wasn't it? Still, I think nature gives you confidence in later life – it's the one compensation for stuff like tired legs and wrinkles and growing fleshy side boobs that no longer fit into your bra!'

He grinned. 'Good way of looking at it. Next time I'm moaning about hair growing out of my nostrils, I'll remember that.'

A week later, because he was singing in the Extra Chorus for *Forza del Destino* at the Opera House, Julian invited Wendy to the opening performance. It was a modern-dress production in which he and his colleagues were decorated with fake tattoos and dressed in leather jerkins. When she met him at the stage door afterwards, she had the grace to say that he looked rugged, which cheered him up even though he knew she was just being kind.

They had dinner at Côte Brasserie, and Wendy said all the right things about the musicality and strength and togetherness of the chorus.

After the meal, they ordered tall glasses of hot chocolate and discussed the big news of the day – Donald Trump's victory.

'I thought I'd be seriously panicky if he beat Hillary Clinton,' she told him, 'but after the EU result, I already feel I don't understand the world I'm living in. This just seems another extension of that.'

'I think,' he remarked, 'I ought to tell you that I voted for Brexit, but only because my mum is one of those people who feel they're always going to be poor and that no political party bothers with them. I think lots of us voted "out" because of that. We wanted to make a protest, I suppose. I'm not sure it was the wisest thing, but we'll have to see. Trump, though, is much worse. And seriously dangerous.'

Wendy spooned cream topping into her mouth, then sighed. 'I rang my dad earlier, and he said that this year, for the first time, he's glad he's old. I think he voted for Brexit too, though I'd never ask him because he knows I'm so pro-Europe. But he said something about how he wouldn't be here much longer, and that he therefore couldn't really worry about it. Maybe that's what happens as you get nearer death, you realise that you don't mind bowing out, because you're no longer in sympathy with life as it's become.'

It was, Julian thought the next day, a real bonus to know Wendy – it was funny at times, soothing at others and always immensely stimulating. He felt almost as if he had fallen in love, except that he had no wish to sleep with her. Perhaps, he pondered, it was more like when you first go to school and make a friend who is unknown to your family – and you suddenly realise that the world is full of individuals who can become your own chosen people, because they're nothing to do with Mum and Dad. And you find yourself in this new club, which is grown-up and exciting. He had felt like that about Philip Baldry once, until that particular Speech Day at their prep school.

Julian had been proud of how his mother had dressed for the occasion. She had worn flowing, flower-power sort of clothes while all the other women were in neat suits that they called 'costumes', despite the fashion revolution of the 1960s. Her hair had been a lustrous magenta colour and so had her lips and nails. She had kept waving at him.

From his vantage point with the other boys on the stage, he had frowned, just slightly, to try to constrain her. But he had not minded much when she had paid no notice.

Philip, his best friend, had been sitting beside him.

'Who's that painted woman?' he had asked.

Julian had been shocked. 'That's my *mother*.'

'Ah…' Despite his youth, Philip had sounded world-weary. 'That explains it.'

'What? What does it explain?'

'Something Nigel said after the choir concert last week. He says your mother's a slag.'

'What's a slag?'

'A woman you wouldn't invite to your house for tea.'

Julian shook his head sadly. Almost fifty years after the event, that sentence still offended him. He glanced at his watch and decided to telephone his mother and try to establish why Philip had been so insulting all those decades ago.

She wanted to talk about her health. He wondered if he should make a note of these particular conversations. It was unsettling that over the past few weeks, instead of being her usual effervescent self, she had complained of being tired or cold or – like today – wanted to tell him that she had put on yet more weight.

Was it his imagination or had her voice altered too? 'You'd probably feel better if you did more exercise,' he suggested.

'No I wouldn't,' she retorted. 'I'm too exhausted. And I've never weighed this much, ever. But I hardly eat a thing.'

Having told himself so often that he did not overeat and that therefore his rising weight was an unavoidable, mid-life hazard, he decided not to get into that contentious argument but to change the subject to the main purpose of the call.

'Mum, d'you remember when I was eight or nine, I asked you what a slag was?'

'Not really. But I do recall when you were small, wanting you to stay innocent for as long as possible.'

'Mmmn. I asked you because another boy called you that.'

'Oh!'

'Sorry.'

'Well, it's a long time ago, Jules.'

'The thing is though, Mum, you were very unlike most people's parents. You were so lively and different. But did you, I mean, did you put it about a bit?'

'You're not getting all saintly in your old age are you? After all, you went through a pretty louche period yourself in the eighties!'

'I know. Don't answer if you don't want to.'

41

'You want to know if I slept with men other than Pop?'

'I suppose I do.'

'Well I did. I was a bit of a wild child. Happy memories!'

He grinned, picturing her as she had been when he was small. She could only have been twenty-one when she had him, but no one could have been a more demonstrative or loving mother. He had been very lucky until, several years after his father had left the country, she had got married. That had heralded a less happy period. But eventually, and obligingly, his greatly-disliked stepdad had died of the effects of smoking the pipe that had been clamped between his jaws for most of every day. After that, he felt his mother belonged to him again, just as she had in the old days. And because he rarely saw her in the company of his half-sister, he was not aware of having to share her.

'...Quite shocking, really. It was all over the local papers.'

Clearly, while he had been daydreaming, his mother had embarked on another topic.

'What was, Mum? Sorry.'

'God, you're getting vague, Jules. Your pal, Philip – ex-pal, I suppose. Remember I told you he was selected as the Green candidate for the next election? Well, after I spoke to you, he got done for drink-driving. Hell of a to-do. He resigned immediately. So, his political dream is over. Still, you're probably pleased.'

Strangely, he was not.

Chapter Four

Sunday lunch at the presbytery was over, and the three men who lived there were muzzily exhausted after a busy week and too much Chilean Merlot.

Michael found himself staring at the semi-retired priest who was snoozing, mouth open, in the worn leather chair, and then at David, the curate, playing a game on his phone.

Dear God, he thought. I'm living in the land of *Father Ted*!

It had been a challenging few days. There had been a suicide, which he had found particularly distressing – having spent hours over the past month talking with the young man who, eventually and nonetheless, had killed himself. And yesterday, there had been two weddings. Both couples had asked him to look in at their receptions. He had obliged, but as so often happened these days, his mood had dipped as the evening wore on, in response to his belief that he was the only person at either gathering who had no one to go home to.

For decades, he had loved being a priest. Now, increasingly he felt lonely and alone. Perhaps he should take a trip to Ireland? That generally restored his balance and humour.

The landline rang. He turned his back and allowed the answerphone to deal with it.

'You've been so kind,' the female voice said. 'So I wondered if you'd like to come for supper one night? My daughter Hannah's around this week, so that'll stop me boring on about me!'

He grabbed at the receiver. 'Araminta! Sorry, I'm here.'

'No, *I'm* sorry. This is your busy day. I'll call back.'

'Absolutely not. And, by the way, you're never boring.'

'I am, but it's kind of you to contradict me.'

His heart gladdened and there was a pause while he wondered what to say. Fortunately, she filled the silence.

'Well, please come. I don't remember if you spoke to Hannah at the funeral, but I'm sure you'll like her. I wish you'd been the parish priest when she was growing up. Your predecessor didn't impress her, I'm afraid.'

'Let's hope I can do better then! The only thing is, I might be going to Ireland...'

'Oh! Well, I'm sure you need a break.'

What, he demanded of himself, was wrong with him? She had been his first, and only, love, though she had never known it. And now, all these years later, he was back in Norwich where they had both grown up. For months he had longed to develop their relationship from a pastoral one into something more personal. Now she was giving him the chance to do just that. *Carpe diem,* he thought as he pulled his shoulders back before continuing. 'But it'd probably be better to go after Christmas when it's quieter. So, when were you thinking?'

They settled on Wednesday. It seemed a lifetime away and yet far too soon. He went through agonies trying to decide whether, just for once, he should abandon his priest's garb and wear something casual. But what? His mufti wardrobe was unimpressive.

When it came to it, he settled for a pair of 'work' black trousers, no dog collar but instead a white shirt unbuttoned at the neck with a black round-necked sweater over the top. He viewed himself in the mirror and smiled wryly at his monochrome outfit which was alleviated only by his trademark large, scarlet-framed spectacles, which – he reflected – were the only flamboyant thing about him.

Trying to ignore the churning in his stomach, he threw on the ancient heavy coat he reserved for the coldest weather and left the presbytery. 'It's just supper with a parishioner,' he reminded himself. But he was unable to silence the nagging voice in his head which warned that it was much more significant, and indeed dangerous, than that.

'Good to see you, Father Michael,' Araminta welcomed him as she opened the front door.

'Oh, please drop the "Father". I'm very definitely off duty!' He tried to stem his nervousness by gulping a deep breath.

She beamed at him before leading him through into the large, warm kitchen, which was dominated by a green shiny Aga and a worn but comfortable-looking paisley-patterned sofa. 'Red or white?' she asked. 'You're not driving, are you?'

'No, I walked. It only took fifteen minutes. It'll clear my head to walk home too and give me much-needed exercise!'

Was he talking too much?

He had been in the house before, shortly after Araminta's husband and son had been killed. But the scenario had been so tragic that he had barely registered the details of her home.

'I love this kitchen,' he enthused.

She grinned at him. 'It's my refuge – especially in winter. I only leave it to see my therapy clients in the basement, or to soak in my ancient cast-iron bath upstairs. That's one of my greatest pleasures!'

Michael felt himself redden slightly and dipped his head in the hope that she would not notice.

She looked amazing tonight, he thought as he raised his head again. Her hair was different; she was wearing it loose rather than tied back and it was glossy and swung attractively as she moved. And she was wearing a long red skirt with a matching top, which really suited her. Also, her lips were coloured bronze and she had sparkling stuff on her eyelids. He had never seen her look lovelier, which was heartening but simultaneously disquieting, because she seemed so out of his league. He had a slight paunch, his closely cropped hair, once black, was greying almost as rapidly as it was receding, his clothes were budget-priced, and he had so little to offer.

'Oh, here she is,' Araminta cried as a younger version of herself hovered in the doorway. 'You met Hannah, didn't you?'

The daughter, dressed in a black sweater and trousers and long boots, walked towards him with an outstretched hand and a smile as genuine as her mother's.

'I did,' he answered quietly. 'Not in happy circumstances though.'

'Yes, well...' Hannah's tone was determinedly bright. 'I'm glad you've come. It gave me an excuse to bully Mum into sprucing herself up a bit. Long overdue!'

He winced, fearing that Hannah was being too brutal. But Araminta was giggling at her daughter and did not appear to feel insulted. He was no expert when it came to family relationships. How could he be? He had hardly known his father, who had worked as an engineer in the Middle East from Michael's early childhood, and presumably stayed there – having written one day to say he was never coming home. As for his mother, though they were close, she would never have entertained the sort of joshing familiarity that was clearly the norm in this house.

He wondered what his mum would think if she could see him now, with the woman who – as a girl – might have diverted him from becoming a priest. Around the age of seventeen, he had tried to explain his feelings for Araminta. His mother had dismissed them. 'Passions come and go,' she had said, 'but you have a calling.'

'Actually,' he turned to Hannah, 'Your mother and I met when we were teenagers. But I doubt if she ever noticed me! She hasn't changed a bit.'

Araminta, who had moved to the Aga and was stirring something that smelled delicious, turned around.

'Really?' she asked. 'I mean, I'm not questioning whether I haven't changed, because I have – totally. I mean, *did* we know each other? I thought you came from Cambridgeshire somewhere.

46

Did you grow up here then?' Absent-mindedly, she topped up her own glass which was on the kitchen unit beside her.

He smiled. 'Yes. In fact, your brother Nigel and I were mates of a sort. So I came to your house quite often at one time, and I saw you in church and at youth socials and so on, but I was always too shy to speak to you. Anyway, I was destined for the priesthood, and when I was eighteen, my mum, who was a teacher, took a job at a school in Peterborough, which meant we had to move.'

'Fancy that!' Araminta peered at him more intently as if she were trying to peel away the years and reveal the youth who had been her brother's friend.

She turned to Hannah. 'Darling, take Michael into the sitting room and amuse him. I'm getting to a critical stage here and I don't want to muck it up!'

He felt much less nervous than he had anticipated, mostly because Araminta appeared genuinely pleased to have him there. Indeed, she seemed quite excited by the evening, and her mood encouraged him to hope that they might become close.

Suddenly, he realised that Hannah was wandering around the room, clearly unsure what to do with him. To help her out, he walked over to the baby-grand piano by the window and surveyed the family photographs on top of it.

'That's the last picture of my dad.' Hannah pointed to an image of a grey but fit man sitting astride a Harley-Davidson motorbike. 'He retired early. Heaven knows why. He used to claim that his back hurt after decades of bending over patients and peering into their mouths. Probably it did, though that didn't stop him doing private work in London. I personally think he was just fed up with the same old routine and wanted some fun. So that bike...' she gestured to the picture '...was about him living out his fantasies. Rather male-menopause stuff, wouldn't you say?'

Michael smiled at her, but did not comment, sensing that whatever he said might sound wrong.

'Anyway, he enjoyed it, even if it didn't go on very long.'

Michael changed tack. 'Who's that smiling lady in this picture with the toddler? She looks like you. Is she an aunt?'

Hannah shook her head then moved nearer to study the photograph. 'But I kind of see what you mean. She's even dressed like I am today! She was my mum's boss when she worked at Anglia. And the baby is my brother.'

'What are you two talking about?' Araminta entered the room, glass in hand.

'This woman. What was her name, Mum?'

'Wendy Lawrence. She directed the news programme. When Andrew was about a year old, I returned to Anglia part-time and occasionally I took him in with me. Someone must have taken that picture on one of those days... Wendy left Norwich in 1990, and we lost touch. But funnily enough, I met her a fortnight ago, for the first time since then. She was visiting her mother, who's in the same nursing home as Grandad. Look, darling, top-up Michael's glass, I need to check something in the kitchen.'

Hannah wandered over to the fireplace and threw herself into an armchair and gestured to Michael to take the one opposite.

'I'm glad you're here.' Her voice was conspiratorial. 'I know Mum's depended on you a lot. She seems to have got a lot better recently, and I think she's putting back some of the weight she lost after the accident. It's cool to see her entertaining again too. She was always good at it.'

'She's lucky to have you, Hannah.'

The young woman shook her head. 'I'm not sure about that, but I suppose you could say that the one good thing that's come out of all the tragedy is that she and I are even closer than we were before.'

Araminta, who had reappeared in the doorway, looked flushed and pleased. 'Yes, we are. And that's really lovely for me.' She swallowed before looking straight at Michael and saying, 'And another lovely thing has been your help and support – so thank you very much for that. Now, let's go to the dining room and eat!'

Later, walking home he reflected on how frequently over the evening Araminta had found words to thank him. Fragments of her appreciation wrapped themselves around his heart. He had desired her when they had both been teenagers, but there was so much more to her now. She was a wonderful woman, and so appealing. No wonder he had 'unclean thoughts' about her.

Hannah had turned out to be delightful too, he mused, as he reached the end of Bracondale and marched on towards the centre of the city. The thought had occurred to him more than once this evening that if he had followed his dream as a young man, and persuaded Araminta to go out with him, then Hannah, or someone like her, could have been his child.

Would he and Araminta have made a go of things if they had ever had the chance? Perhaps – especially as it was clear from this evening just how alike they were in so many ways, and how many interests they had in common.

They had both agreed, for example, how soothing it was to cook. They had chatted about their favourite TV chefs and found that they both idolised Rick Stein and Nigel Slater and Julia Child. And they had compared notes about their favourite dishes. Probably the only significant foodie fact he had not divulged was that he sometimes took recipe books to bed to read, because surely that was beyond 'sad', even for a celibate priest.

He had not expected the two women to be at the Winter Fair, but he spotted them while he was doing his rounds of the various stalls, and selecting items that he believed would remain unsold if he failed to give them a home. He had not seen Hannah since visiting their home ten days ago, but he had managed to talk to Araminta the previous Sunday. She had joined other parishioners for coffee after Mass, and they had gravitated to each other as the rest of the congregation had drifted away. He had flirted with the notion of asking if she would fancy a drive out to the coast for lunch. But inevitably, had bade her farewell after ten minutes and joined the other priests for a meal in the presbytery, as he always did.

With his mind still on Araminta, the customary diet of roast chicken and parish gossip had seemed less than absorbing and, pleading tiredness, he had gone for a nap in his simple, single room – plaguing himself with the belief that this was all he could expect from life until he died.

Araminta and Hannah were laughing over a vintage clothes rail. The urge to join them was powerful, but he forced himself to delay the pleasure, and to continue his perambulation around the tables dotted throughout the parish hall.

Gratifyingly, all his cupcakes seemed to have been sold. He had stayed up decorating them till two o'clock this morning. The woman who presented him with a Victoria sandwich at least once a week was in charge of the baking stall, and had assumed an injured air when he brought in his contribution.

'You made these yourself, Father?' she had demanded, querulously. When he agreed that he had, she had sniffed disapprovingly and tossed her head in such a way as to indicate that she was most insulted.

He considered pointing out that he had never *asked* her to ply him with cakes. Still, he was pretty sure she would stop now.

In the past half-hour, the room had become very crowded as people jostled to get a good view of the best bargains. Most of the pensioners, however, were seated on the chairs which lined the walls. Michael fleetingly imagined them, fifty years earlier, at a parish dance in the same hall. Norwich-born and bred as most of them were, a number of their life stages must have been acted out in this place. Surveying them today, it was hard to imagine a time when they might have stolen a kiss from someone they had lusted after in the congregation, as they danced the last waltz of the evening.

Now, with the bulk of their life behind them, they sat, necks jutting out of their collars – like ancient tortoises peering out of their shells – as they searched for others to talk to. Most of them had walking sticks, and a couple had Zimmer frames. A few had families living nearby and were part of a multi-generational group that came to Mass regularly. But far too many of them were alone, and about half of those lived in sheltered accommodation or care homes. Unlike him, the majority of them had not spent their entire lives as single people, yet they were lonely and isolated now. So, what hope was there for him? He had always assumed that he would end up in a house full of priests of varying ages and live out his life in service to the church. But any appetite he might once have had for such an arrangement had dwindled.

A couple of small boys chasing each other through the noisy throng barged into him. Michael laughed, even though one of them had trodden hard on his right foot.

'C'mon now, guys. Calm down. If you'd bumped into someone older than me, you could have killed them!'

'Sorry, Father Michael,' the bigger culprit apologised. 'Please don't tell Mum. She's shouted at me twice already.'

'Do me a favour then?'

'Anything, Father.'

'Jolly good! Go round to the presbytery and ask Father David to give you a big bundle of newsletters and come back here and give one out to everyone.'

They were gone before he had finished his sentence. The curate would probably be peeved, because now he would have to print off another batch of the weekly missive for the church tomorrow. But there were people here who rarely came to Mass except at Christmas and Easter, so it was an opportunity to engage them in the parish while they were buying the jumble and trying their luck at the tombola.

Thirsty suddenly, Michael began moving through the crowds towards the smaller adjoining room where they were serving tea and coffee. But on the way, he paused at the bric-a-brac stall where his eye was caught by a monstrous looking toilet roll holder

– a souvenir from Lourdes – which played 'Ave Maria' when you tugged at the paper. He was trying hard not to laugh as he offered two pounds for it.

'That's what Mum would call "naff"!' Hannah, though smiling at him, was clearly bemused at his purchase.

'Hannah!' He admonished her with mock severity. 'Don't be such a snob.' Then he added, as he had done frequently over the years, 'You have to remember that Catholicism is a classless religion.'

'Hmmn. Surely that doesn't mean it has to have no class whatsoever?'

Before he could respond, a youngish mother claimed his attention to talk about a forthcoming christening. He smiled, apologetically, at Hannah over the other woman's head. She grinned and made a gesture as if she were lifting a teacup, and he nodded at her, before turning his attention to his diary and picking a date when he and the congregation could welcome baby Ryan Patrick O'Leary into the fold.

Hannah was in the refreshments queue when he caught up with her. He had been hoping that Araminta might have found her way there too, but there was no sign of her. As if reading his thoughts, Hannah explained, 'Mum's running the tombola next door to give someone a break. She won't be staying long though, because she's had a text from some client who needs to see her, so she's going to fit that person in later.'

They were at the tea counter now, and as he paid, he congratulated all the helpers on their 'sterling work' and said 'well done' to about eight different people. He felt several pairs of intrigued eyes trained on him, and noticed a plump matron in a flowery apron nudge her friend as Hannah poured milk into his tea, and smiled up at him. If only they knew, he thought, that I wish she were my daughter, and that it's her mother I'm yearning for.

'Mum really likes you,' Hannah confided as they found a quiet corner and a couple of chairs.

'What?' He knew he looked astonished and embarrassed – and hopeful too – because he could feel his features betraying his thoughts.

'I don't mean… I just meant she sees you as a friend as well as a priest. She was terribly glad that she plucked up courage to ask you over for dinner.'

He forced himself to laugh, hoping that he was a good enough actor to hide his real feelings. 'I was glad she did too,' he managed. 'She's an excellent cook. That salmon dish was mouth-wateringly good!' Then he added, 'And it was great to spend time with you too. You're a breath of fresh air for me.'

'Well,' she went on. 'That's nice to know, because I was wondering actually if I could pick your brains?'

'Of course.'

'I'm helping with the big clear-out of my grandfather's house, because he's gone into a nursing home and he's not likely to come out of it. Thing is that his house – in Tombland – used to be the doctor's surgery as well as the family home.'

'I remember. He was my GP when I was small.'

Hannah laughed. 'That's amazing! Anyway, there's masses of paperwork in the house, including loads of old medical notes and diaries, and I've told Mum I'll go through them. As you know, it's not long since she had to deal with Dad's financial and business papers, and I thought doing it again for Grandad might be upsetting for her. But I'm wondering whether it's OK to read them? He's left a lot of records of his work and maybe they're important. Till he had his heart attack, he was pretty fit, so if all his stuff was secret, he'd have got rid of it. Right?'

Michael took a sip of tea to allow himself time to think. 'Not necessarily. Sometimes people know, intellectually, that they're getting older and that they should sort out their affairs, but they don't accept it emotionally. They assume they have plenty of time ahead, but then, out of the blue, something happens to them.'

'Hmmn. Should I ask him? Trouble is, I'm not sure he'll understand because Mum thinks his brain is deteriorating. But no one will investigate it, because his GP has some sort of document in which Grandad made it clear that he wanted no pointless interventions.' She swirled what remained of the tea in her polystyrene cup, watching it intently. 'It's hard to think that he's no longer very with it.'

'It's another loss for you,' Michael murmured. 'And you've had rather a lot of those. But I suppose, being a doctor, he would have more insight than the rest of us about what's useful when you enter what might be your final illness, and what's pointless or unpleasant.'

She nodded. 'I haven't been able to face going to the nursing home yet, but he's been there several weeks so maybe I should make myself do it. I mean, he could just suddenly die. And as he's not having a funeral, there'll be no opportunity to say goodbye afterwards, if you know what I mean.'

'No funeral!'

'Well, I gather there's no law that says you have to have one.'

'Still… is there some reason?'

Hannah sighed again. 'I'll tell you another time. It's weird, quite honestly. But I'm just wondering if I should go out and see him now as I've no idea when I'll be home again.'

'I'm sorry I haven't been much help.'

Was this what being a parent would be like? Wanting to solve everything but dismally falling short?

'But you have been,' she reassured him, as she jumped up. 'Would it be OK for me to have your mobile number? You're so easy to talk to.'

He smiled broadly, and quickly scribbled 'Michael' and eleven digits on a paper napkin, which he gave to her. She looked at him quizzically.

'I know!' he teased. 'You're thinking it's odd that I not only know my mobile number but that I want to write it down rather than do some digital exchange. It's called the generation gap!'

He laughed and she joined in.

'Thanks.' She reached up and planted a kiss on his cheek. 'If I leave now I can get a train out to Cromer.' She swept up her bag and left, taking her palpable energy with her.

Because so many people were keen to attract his attention, it took him a while to make his way back through the large hall towards the tombola. It was therefore not a surprise – though it was a disappointment – to discover that Araminta had gone. Still, he had been cheered by his conversation with Hannah, and he thought that probably it might seem acceptable soon to invite the two of them to dinner. Or even take Araminta out alone.

The Winter Fair was winding down, and he felt that it had reached a stage where he could quite justifiably ask Father David to take over and help the events' committee to count up the profits and put away the trestle tables.

'Jolly good!' he cried to everyone as he waved breezily and left the building to walk round to the presbytery and start writing his homily for tomorrow's Masses.

Before he had completed more than a couple of sentences, the front doorbell interrupted him. He was tempted to ignore it, but he thought that the curate might have sent some of the committee round with money or unsold goods.

He did not recognise the visitor; a man of around his age but taller, thinner and with more hair.

'Hello! I'm Philip Baldry.'

'Michael Chapman,' he said as he extended his hand.

'Sorry to bother you, but Araminta Allsop said you might be able to help me.'

Michael gazed at the stranger who had the air and assurance of someone moneyed and capable, but who also looked as if he had not slept for days. There was a slight tremor in his hands too, which suggested that there was much on his mind.

'Come in. Cup of tea?'

Philip nodded. 'That's very gracious.'

In the kitchen, the old priest had taken over the large refectory table, and was immersed in the racing pages of the Saturday papers. He would be saying the six o'clock Mass, and was unlikely to move before then, so Michael quickly made two mugs of tea and gave a vague wave at his elderly colleague, before ushering Philip away.

'Good man, yourself,' muttered the senior cleric, for no sane reason except that he was Irish and used the phrase to cover most eventualities.

'There's my study,' Michael suggested.

'Fine.'

They sat together, Michael at his desk and Philip in the one armchair.

'I almost bumped into you, Father, one evening some weeks ago when I'd just done a television interview,' Philip began.

'Really? Must have been when I took part in the debate on austerity.'

'You struck me as slightly familiar. Mind you, we're probably around the same vintage. Did you grow up in Norfolk?'

'I did. But I left in my late teens, and only came back relatively recently.'

Philip paused as he deliberated. 'Perhaps we were at the same school, but then I expect you were at a Catholic one, which I wasn't.'

Michael nodded. 'Yes, I was. Do you want to tell me why you're here, Philip – and what it has to do with Araminta?'

Philip took a deep breath. 'I'm having an affair and I can't think straight. On top of that, I had wanted a change of career, but that ended abruptly because I was caught drink-driving. Entirely my own fault. You may have seen something in the papers?'

Michael shook his head.

'Well,' Philip went on, 'Katie, the woman I've fallen for, is seeing Araminta for therapy. Now I don't remember her from my childhood, but it's an unusual name, so I'm pretty sure she was the sister of one of my friends at prep school.'

'Nigel?'

'Yes, Nigel!'

Michael smiled. 'I knew him too – through the church. I asked him once why he didn't attend the Catholic school I went to, and he said his father insisted he had a secular education. I expect you and I met at his birthday parties. Whatever happened to him?'

'We lost touch after prep school. However, a couple of years ago, my wife and I were in Barbados and it turned out that he owned the hotel. You wouldn't recognise him. He's got long hair and a bushy beard and walks barefoot about the place. He also seemed to have a harem of beautiful local girls and, I'm pretty sure, smokes a lot of wacky baccy.'

'He was always a bit eccentric. So, to come back to you, were you hoping to see Araminta for support?'

'Yes, Father. I went along an hour ago, when my um, girlfriend, was seeing her. But Araminta said there's a conflict of interest with Katie being her patient, and that's when she mentioned you as a possible source of help.'

Michael stood up. 'That's flattering. But, you know, Philip, I'm not really qualified to see you. I'm not your priest, and I'm not a shrink. And, to be honest, I've got a bit of a crisis of my own. So, I'm thinking that the best thing – if it's all right with you – might be for us to go and chat through it all in the pub.'

'Fine with me, Father!'

Michael stared at his feet. Did he want to be identified as a man of the cloth? Could he not, just for a change, be an ordinary bloke going for a drink with someone of a similar age who might become a mate? He straightened up and smiled. 'If you don't mind, I'd prefer you to call me "Mike". Now, let's go and get that pint!'

Chapter Five

'I think I'm pregnant!'

Araminta peered at Katie – a client who had wept throughout her early sessions because of the years she had invested in her ex-boyfriend in the misjudged assumption that he would provide her with high-quality sperm and long-term security.

However, at her previous appointment Katie had bounced into the consulting room and announced that she had 'moved on' and was sleeping with an older married man, and that everything was great.

But was it so great now? What must it be like, Araminta speculated, to be in your mid-thirties, and desperate to start a family? It had never been her problem. She had fallen pregnant at twenty-two. Far from being delighted, she had resented the baby in her womb – particularly as she had just started training as a vision mixer, and had plans to become a director, like her then heroine Wendy.

Of course, she had come to adore Andrew, but part of her had remained disappointed at losing the life she had planned.

Unlike her brother Nigel, who was a real rebel, she had done everything her parents had ever asked of her, including training as a secretary to 'have something to fall back on' if her ambition to 'get into television' came to nothing.

A nostalgic smile stretched at her lips as she recalled how once she had finally landed a job at Anglia TV, she had cut her hair brutally short, dyed it orange, and taken to wearing T-shirts with slogans, tight trousers and Doc Martens. She had also started dating Simon, who was twelve years her senior – relishing her unaccustomed role as a 'bad girl', and allowing herself a slight thrill at the discomfiture of her parents who were appalled at the age gap, and the fact that he had 'lived in sin' with women before. However, once she had discovered she was pregnant, their reservations about him had melted away and they had insisted she marry him, quickly.

'And,' Katie was saying, 'Philip's talking about leaving his wife, and us moving to London and living a bohemian lifestyle – as he calls it – in Shoreditch.'

Forcing herself to concentrate, Araminta asked the inevitable. 'And how do you feel about that?'

'Well, it's complicated because he's in such a terrible state.'

'I'm sorry I couldn't see him myself. But it wouldn't be ethical because of my duty of care to you as the original client.'

'Yeah, I get that! Maybe your priest bloke will help him.'

'I'm sure Father Michael will do his best. He's a wonderful man.'

Had she really said that? It sounded somewhat flowery.

Redoubling her effort to focus on Katie, she smiled and asked, 'Leaving Philip aside for a moment, how do you feel about the baby?'

'Well, it can't be an accident that I've been having masses of sex and not given a thought to contraception. It's as if my mothering instinct took over. But I hadn't actually considered that Philip and I might have a future.'

'You say he's very upset.'

'Yes, well,' Katie lifted her shoulders and then let them drop as she breathed out. 'I know it's a cliché but he's having a mid-life crisis. Obviously, he's not happy at home. And then there's his daughter.'

'What about her?'

'She's dead.'

'Dead!'

'He only told me yesterday. It was about seven years ago. Apparently, his house is set in large grounds, and there's a lake. How the other half live, eh? She drowned in it one hot day when she went swimming on her own. Philip's a pretty stiff-upper-lip sort of guy, but I'm sure he's never got over it.'

'You wouldn't,' murmured Araminta as an image of her son lying in the mortuary hijacked her mind.

'So, I think he's latched on to me as a fresh start for him.'

'People in mid-life do get sudden and strong feelings. They worry about whether they've achieved all they want, and whether they should be doing more exciting things while they have the time. And I suppose Philip now has the chance to kind of replace a dead child with a living one. Are his parents alive?'

'Yeah. Apparently, he's got an eccentric mother who owns a hotel in Ireland. We're supposed to be going over to meet her. But I bet she'll hate me. I mean she won't want him to get a divorce, will she?'

'Possibly not, unless she thinks his marriage is unhappy.'

'God, I don't know what to do. He's so into me. And I don't honestly feel that strongly about him.'

After Katie left, Araminta tidied up her consulting room and then wandered upstairs to the kitchen. The Winter Fair must be long over, she thought as she began chopping root vegetables for a pie. So where was Hannah?

She worked such crazy hours – it would be good if she would come home and relax before she had to return to London tomorrow evening for another long week. Television was a demanding industry. That much had not changed, even if so much else had.

In Norwich in the 1970s when she was growing up, there had been three main employers – Rowntrees, Norwich Union and

Anglia TV. There had been no contest in her mind about which she would go for. But she had had to battle for it, only to be forced to relinquish her dream after she had Andrew; filming away from home and emergency editing sessions had been an uneasy mix with motherhood.

She shrugged the memory away and rolled out some pastry, but then found herself thinking about Wendy. Her former colleague had said they should stay in touch. Perhaps now would be a good time to call.

Wendy answered her phone immediately, and soon the conversation was flowing as freely as it had a few weeks earlier when they had met at the nursing home.

'I've been wondering about your daughter,' Wendy said suddenly. 'I think you said she'd like to get into television news. Maybe I could help.'

'Really?'

'Well, I could at least talk to her. Give her a few pointers. I'll be in Norwich again in a few days, but I suppose Hannah's more likely to be in London then.'

As Araminta was agreeing how rare it was for her daughter to get home, Hannah appeared in the kitchen, swathed in her black and white striped faux fur, cheeks flushed, and carrying a loaded rucksack on her shoulders. She blew a kiss at her mother and retreated.

'Probably be easier,' Wendy was saying, 'if she and I meet in London.'

'That'll be the second generation of the family you've taken under your wing. I've always been grateful for the way you encouraged me. And, as I told you the other day, your influence smoothed things with my family no end, because Dad loved to hear about me working with you. Now it's my daughter's turn. Funny how things work out!'

Wendy laughed. 'Let's hope she's as talented as you were. Anyway, you and I must get together if you're free next week. I

61

want to introduce you to my new man! Well, that's not *really* what he is – he's more like a brother. But he comes from Norwich too and I'm having such fun with him. He's a professional singer and wildly gay, but that's great because there're no complications, are there? I know he's not going to try and get into my knickers!' She laughed again. 'It's strange how he's become so vital to me just when Robert's buggered everything up. Some things are meant to be!'

Araminta grinned as she put down the phone. Wendy had always been like a whirlwind when she was enthusiastic. It was interesting though about her 'new man', and something of a coincidence. For the first time, she allowed herself a tiny glowing sensation about her own male friend, though obviously it was different in her case, with him being a priest. Interesting though, she pondered. Both she and Wendy were natives of Norwich, and at a stage in their lives where all sorts of possibilities were opening up. Dr Jung would have called it 'synchronicity'.

When she arrived at the nursing home, Wendy and the slightly plump, jovial man were talking to her father, who appeared to be in sprightly form. Most days, he was quiet, morose and uncomprehending but this afternoon he seemed almost normal.

She watched from the doorway as he flirted with Wendy. Her right hand was clasped in both of his and he seemed in no hurry to release it. It was hard to hear what Wendy was saying, but the friend was louder.

'Interestingly, sir, I knew Nigel a long time ago. We were at the same prep school.'

At the sound of his son's name, her parent turned away and focused his attention on Wendy, kissing her hand till she looked slightly embarrassed.

Her father had always been tactile and energetically sociable. Araminta suspected that as an only child his boyhood might have been quite lonely, so maybe his love of having people around him was a reaction to that. Mind you, he had had a male cousin, Hilary, who had lived in Suffolk. They had been really close, and had remained so till Hilary's death a decade ago.

A movement in the corner of the room brought her back to the present. Her father's behaviour was becoming more erratic, like that of a child who is overtired because it's past his bedtime. He had tried to stand up, but fallen back in his chair, apparently having little understanding that his legs could no longer be relied upon. As she moved towards the group, she heard Wendy say that though she would love to see his room, maybe they could 'leave it till another day.'

'Dad,' she intervened, 'it's time for your sleep.'

'*Wendy's* taking me. I've got *two* rooms. Come and see!'

'Dad, stop it.' Araminta looked at Wendy and jerked her head in the direction of the door. 'See you in a minute,' she mouthed over her father's head.

Wendy and her companion withdrew, and she set about pulling her father into a standing position, trying not to strain her own back in the process.

He muttered something indistinct, but probably rude.

'You're a doctor, Dad. Behave like one.'

Fortunately, he forgot his petulance because the walk to his suite took all his concentration. It required considerable effort on her part too; her father's unsteadiness meant that he leaned heavily on her, and though he was slighter than he had been before he became ill, he was still quite a weight.

Once she had settled him in bed, she went in search of Wendy and her friend.

'I'm sorry I got him too excited,' Wendy apologised.

'Not your fault; he's always been a handful!' Araminta kissed the other woman and reached out her hand towards her male companion.

'Hello! I'm Julian Wilson.' His voice boomed in the small corridor and his face lit up with a beaming smile.

63

'Did you really know Nigel?' she asked him.

'A little. And I bet I met you when we were children – though you're obviously much younger!'

She laughed. 'Only a couple of years! But we probably did meet. I have a sense that I know you. Mind you, Wendy told me you're a singer and I sometimes watch televised operas. It's my new hobby!'

'I knew you were a cultured woman as soon as I saw you,' he declared.

Araminta grinned. And Wendy giggled before saying, 'Don't you just love him?'

Julian went on, 'I've certainly not had a major career. But a few weeks ago, I was on Sky Arts when they showed an old production of *Tosca*. I sang the small part of the Sacristan.'

'That's it! I saw you.'

'Fancy that! A viewer! Wonderful! Now, I'm going to buy you both a slap-up tea. What's the best place round here?'

The wine bar in the old shoe factory had been a favourite haunt for her and her late husband, but she had not mentioned that when Michael had suggested it.

He had been diffident when he had rung her, almost like a new client calling to establish whether she might be the answer to his problems.

'I really owe you dinner after the wonderful meal at your house,' he had said, all in a rush. 'I meant to reciprocate before, but the weeks fly past. Of course, you may be busy in the run-up to Christmas. I don't want to intrude.'

'I'd love it, Michael,' she had assured him, quickly.

'I... I... oh, you *would*. Really? Jolly good! That's splendid.'

She had put down the phone with a smile. No one was aware – she barely acknowledged it herself – how much she had enjoyed having Michael to dinner, or how she treasured her growing belief that he liked her as a person rather than just a parishioner. It was pretty pathetic, she knew, but being singled out by him to become more than just a member of his flock made her feel special. Of course, her supervisor – a wise and more senior therapist than she was – would have said, 'No one *makes* us feel special, Araminta. We *choose* how we feel.' Yet in this case, she believed that whatever was happening was beyond her control, and she was content to go with the flow and let what felt like an authentic – and unusually supportive – friendship develop in its own way. Mind you, she had to admit that she was helping it along. She had taken to going for coffee in the church hall after Mass, and enjoying how Michael always seemed to find time for a quiet conversation with her. And she had volunteered, along with half a dozen other parishioners, to augment the choir at Christmas, which – she had to admit – was more to do with hoping to bump into him rather than a desire to sing.

And now that they were together having dinner, everything seemed to be going wonderfully. She felt herself liking him more and more, and was delighted that he was relaxed with her, and that they laughed at the same things and that he was so attentive – pouring her water from the jug before her glass was quite empty and checking that she was warm enough. Maybe she could invite him for Christmas lunch, or was that too presumptuous?

'Norwich has changed so much, hasn't it?' he was saying.

'Sorry,' she apologised. 'I was thinking about Christmas! How rude of me… You're right. Norwich has changed, but then so have our habits. For one thing, people didn't eat out much, did they? My parents entertained at home, as my mother was a great cook, but I don't remember us going to restaurants except when we were away on holiday. However, my father's cousin Hilary, who was my godfather, took my mother and me out a lot. We had wonderful meals all over Norfolk and Suffolk. I don't know how he afforded it as he was a librarian and didn't make much money, but he was really generous and taught me so much about food.'

'That sounds lovely. My earliest memory of a restaurant was the carvery at The Royal for one of my birthdays. Mum was on quite a tight budget, but she was good at celebrations and occasions. I remember piling my plate high with the most delicious roast beef and melt-in-the-mouth Yorkshire puddings!'

Araminta laughed. 'You were a foodie even then! Were you an only child?'

'Yes. And I understand that my parents had quite a struggle to have me. My mother told me once that your father was very helpful when she couldn't conceive.'

'Really? I didn't know that he was your doctor.'

'Yes, back when he still had his practice in your house in Tombland. But after my father left us, we moved out of the city and had a different doctor. The only thing that didn't change was that we carried on going to St Mark's; we came in on the bus.'

'So that's how you knew Nigel?'

'Mmmn.' He topped up her glass. 'Which,' he went on, 'in a roundabout way reminds me that I've been meaning to tell you about Philip. So, he turned up after the Winter Fair that day, and to be honest I didn't really want to "counsel" him. Or feel responsible for him. I have enough of that with the parish!'

'Oh, Michael, I'm sorry. I should never have suggested he come.'

The priest smiled. 'No, no. That's not what I'm saying. I'm pleased that he came because I made a quick decision that things might work better if we kept them on a friendly basis, and it's turned out to be jolly good. In fact, it feels great to have a male chum who's not a priest or a parishioner, and it's happened rather naturally, because he knew your brother Nigel too, and it seems we'd met as children. Small world isn't it? Or is it just that everyone seems to know everyone in Norwich?'

The waitress arrived with their main course. They had both opted for grilled swordfish. 'Mmmn,' Araminta beamed at Michael. 'Now that smells fantastic... and just the right amount of hollandaise sauce, and... mmmn... chorizo as well. Interesting!'

'You sound as if you're on *MasterChef*!'

She blushed. 'Sorry, I just love trying to work out what professionals do with food, don't you?'

'Absolutely. And what I love even more is eating it!' He patted his stomach. 'As you've probably noticed.'

'You're not overweight, Michael.'

'I am a bit, but not as bad as some of my colleagues. Catholic priests are prone to derive their pleasure from cigarettes, booze, or food. Sometimes all three. I try not to be a cliché. At least I don't *smoke*. But,' he toyed with his wine glass for a moment, 'celibacy has a lot to answer for.'

There was silence. She suspected that he felt he had overstepped the mark. Shared too much. Been too frank. What could she say to help him? He looked slightly embarrassed, and was focusing far too intently on the nest of al dente vegetables that lay between them.

'It must be difficult,' she managed.

He raised his head and stared straight into her eyes, and in that moment she realised that his comment had been intentional, and that he was grateful that she had not ignored it.

'It wasn't, originally,' he explained.

'Funny, if I'd ever thought about it, I'd have imagined that celibacy as a young man, when your sex drive is at its height, would be the most difficult period.'

He revealed then what Father Brian – the senior priest in his first parish – had confided one Christmas, about feeling lonelier with age, and wondering if the sacrifice of not having a wife and family had been worth it. And then he told her how isolated he had felt for the past few years, especially since his mother had died, and how he had almost not come to St Mark's because he had considered taking a sabbatical at that time.

'I even spoke to a bishop in another diocese about it. He told me to pray, which I did, and said that the sense of aloneness would pass once I stopped grieving for Mum, which it didn't.'

'That sounds very miserable. But presumably, you have relatives and friends?'

'No relatives. Mum came from the south-west of Ireland and though she had a couple of older brothers they – like loads of others

– went off to America and she lost touch with them. And my father was brought up in care and never knew his original family. Of course, there are friends. Other priests, mostly. However, I have no one to call my own – that's the big thing – and I often feel so lonely, I think other people must be able to smell it on me.'

'That's terrible, Michael. I'm so sorry.' Then, keeping her voice as calm as she could she queried. 'But are you saying this isn't just about loneliness – it's also to do with not being able to have a partner?'

He nodded. 'And if I were going to do something about that, my whole life would have to change.'

She knew that she looked shocked. 'And is that on the cards? That you feel so strongly about what you haven't had, that you might have to… break your vows… secretly perhaps, or even have to leave the priesthood?'

He put down his knife and fork and stared at her. 'I do… think about… all of that. But it's terrifying.'

'I can imagine,' she murmured.

'Thanks. I, uh, have wondered for a while whether I could discuss this with you.'

'Of course.' Unaccountably, her heart was racing and she felt nervous and unsure about what to say. 'I mean you've helped me such a lot. And I *am* a therapist. Anyway, it's what friends are for, isn't it?'

He looked slightly puzzled before agreeing that it was.

Smiling brightly, she said, 'I can't thank you enough for bringing me here, Michael. I haven't been for ages. And I love the food, don't you?'

He nodded but looked away.

Her mind went into a spin. *Oh God, I've stopped him talking about what he wanted to say. He looks sad now. What did I do wrong?*

*

Feeling too restless for bed, she rang Hannah. The conversation was difficult because her daughter was in a noisy restaurant and talking against a background of booming music and loud friends.

'You went out with Michael? Like, on a date?'

'No! He's a priest! Absolutely not. But we are becoming good friends.'

'What?'

'Friends. We're becoming good friends.'

'Well, so long as it's *just* that.'

'Of course it's just that.' She could hear her own voice rising in frustration. This was a very odd conversation. Why was Hannah being so strange? Perhaps she was drunk. 'Anyway, sweetheart, I hope you're having a good evening. Is Najid there?'

'Who?'

'Najid. Your dishy boyfriend.'

'Oh, no. He's, um, busy. Look, Mum, I better go.'

'Maybe we'll speak tomorrow?'

'Yes. Night, Mum.'

Araminta sighed as she put the phone down. Then she sighed again, and though she had had quite enough to drink – and she was always planning to cut down, aware that she had drunk far too much since Simon and Andrew had died – she decided she needed more wine.

'At least I don't drink spirits,' she reassured herself as she walked into the kitchen and poured a generous amount of Shiraz into a tumbler, before sinking into her old sofa.

She had looked forward to tonight. *Too* much perhaps. And it had been going so well, till something she said, or did, had made everything awkward. But what *was* it? She could not be entirely sure and the amount of alcohol she had consumed was probably not helping.

Suddenly, she felt very warm – so warm that she wondered if perhaps she was having her first hot flush – as it occurred to her that Michael may have meant that he would like to break his celibacy with *her*. Surely not though. It was inconceivably vain of her to even imagine such a thing. So why did she suddenly feel tingly and fluttery and excited?

It was ridiculous. And mad. Had Hannah seen something in her demeanour with Michael that she had failed to perceive in herself? If so, that could explain her attitude on the phone. Becoming intimate with him would be a despicable thing to do. It could never be a harmless fling. And he must not jeopardise his vocation. It was unthinkable.

Katie turned up for her appointment and immediately confirmed that she was indeed pregnant. She looked it too; though, in reality, her baby must be about the size of a pea. There was a glow about her, and a certain softness.

'And,' Katie went on, 'Philip's telling his wife. *This* evening. And I'm not sure it's a good thing because suppose I don't love him enough and he breaks up his marriage for me?'

'Well, he's a grown-up. And it's his decision.'

'I suppose so. I think your priest guy Michael feels that his wife deserves to know, and that it's better that *he* tells her than that she finds out another way.'

'Yes, that sounds like the kind of thing Michael might advise.' Her voice was as quietly calm as her increased pulse rate would allow. 'I'm sure he'll have given it a lot of thought. After all, when there's a baby to consider it changes everything.'

'Mmmn. To be honest, I'm terribly glad that Philip's in touch with Michael. It was a good idea of yours. They seem to lean on each other. Philip says Michael's going through some sort of crisis himself.'

'Well,' Araminta interjected quickly, 'as I've said to you before, many people go through big emotional changes in mid-life.'

'Yeah, Philip said Michael really wishes he'd had children. So maybe he's a bit sentimental about my baby. Or wants one of his own! That would be a bit bizarre, wouldn't it? But of course men can go on fathering kids till they're ancient! Whatever's going on, the two of them have become really good mates. They're on the phone to each other all the time.'

Change the subject, Araminta urged herself. It's not relevant to Katie or her feelings, or her child.

'Weirdly,' Katie continued, 'I think Philip's worried about Michael. And in a strange way, I think that concern has kind of helped him. He says that our relationship is simple compared with what might happen to Michael. Mind you, he's not sure if Michael's actually got a woman in his life or whether he's just thinking about it, but apparently someone called Hannah has rung him a couple of times when he's been out with Philip, so maybe it's her.'

'Hannah!' Araminta's heart thumped in her ears.

'Yeah. Actually, Philip talked to her – by accident. He was in a pub, with Michael, who'd gone off to get some drinks or something, when a mobile phone on the table rang and because it had the same ringtone as his, he answered it before realising it was Michael's. Anyway, it was this Hannah, and they ended up having quite a chat. She wanted to know all about him, as well as Michael and how long they'd been friends. You don't do that, do you, unless you're seriously interested in a bloke? Philip said she sounded very young and bubbly.'

Araminta felt a trickle of cold sweat run down her spine and there was a dizzying swimminess in her head.

'Are you all right?' Katie was sitting forward in her chair, staring at her with a bewildered expression.

'Yes.'

'You're not ill, are you?'

'No, not at all.' Araminta blinked and forced herself to focus on her client. Then with a massive effort she added a lie that seemed justifiable in the circumstances. 'I've been rushing around today and didn't have lunch. Sorry.'

'Oh that's all right then. I thought perhaps you were upset about Michael. I mean you and he know each other. So, I don't suppose you'd be keen on him giving up the church and marrying some babe half his age. Probably be a disaster!'

Chapter Six

'Don't leave me, Philip!' Marigold screamed before throwing herself forward onto the polished dining table, and wailing like one of the Arctic wolves he had seen in a recent documentary.

It was not what he had expected.

All the way home in the taxi, he had felt secure in his longing for Katie. They had met after her day at the studios had ended and had gone together to 'their' pub, where she had drunk cranberry juice and he had nursed a pint of cloudy cider. He would have liked to have been invited to her flat, which had come to represent a unique amalgam of safety and sexual passion, but Katie was booked into an evening session with Araminta. He knew it was unreasonable of him, but he was jealous of anyone she wanted to spend time with. So, in a bid to bind her to him more closely, he had announced that this evening he would ask his wife for a divorce.

'Really?' Katie had looked shocked. 'Don't you think we should wait and see if we're still so attracted to each other in a few months?'

'What are you saying?' He had tried, and failed, to suppress the panic in his voice. 'That you don't want me to be there for you and our child?'

She had kissed his cheek, but offered no verbal reassurance.

He had rehearsed his confession in the back of the cab. It had seemed straightforward. After all, Marigold had not been interested in him for years. Surely, so long as he provided generously, she was unlikely to mind much. In fact, he had reasoned, the news might come as a relief.

He had asked the driver to drop him at the entrance of their grounds, and had buttoned up his coat and pulled his scarf tighter before walking up the long gravel driveway past the coach house and on to the main building. Various security lights came on, and in the temporary illumination, he had stood and viewed the beautifully proportioned property – imagining in that moment what it was going to feel like to give it up. Hunsford Hall, with its mellow stone and landscaped gardens, had been an enduring love affair, despite Emily's death here. He had bought it – a ramshackle and derelict apology for its former self – when he had returned to the county to do his duty in the family business. It had taken over a year to restore its fine structure and transform it into a warm and comfortable family dwelling.

Could he abandon it? He had to. Already, he could picture another home, and a new life full of warmth, companionship, love and sex. If he failed to grasp what was on offer now, he would regret it for ever.

'Emily, darling, it's Dad here. I won't be leaving you, just the house. You do understand, don't you?'

A gust of wind had blown through the tree above his head. He had felt her presence, but would never tell anyone that he was in touch with his deceased daughter. Not Mike. Not Katie. And certainly not his wife.

He had not planned to eat dinner with Marigold, but the meal was ready when he arrived home, and he felt it would have been churlish to have ruined it, just so that he could get his 'speech' off his chest.

The rich and fruity game casserole had been delicious and restorative. He had then opted for cheese rather than pudding, and had enjoyed a slab of Somerset cider-flavoured Cheddar with Stornoway sesame-seed water biscuits.

This was what his wife did best. She had been reared for it, having been educated at the sort of English boarding school where time had stood still, and the 'gels' had been trained to be wives and hostesses rather than career-women.

Her choice of music over dinner had been appealing too – Chopin waltzes played by Claudio Arrau. Marigold believed that watching television while dining was vulgar so they never did so unless there was an evening rugby game he was desperate to see – and when that happened he knew that she felt unsettled at his disregard for her 'house-rules'.

Suddenly, her howling quietened sufficiently for him to make himself heard. 'You don't love me, Marigold,' he pointed out. 'And you rubbish me all the time. I'm fifty-five. I can't live like this any more. I need to make a new life while I can.'

'I'll change,' she sobbed. 'I realised something was wrong. You've been quiet and remote for weeks. But I never meant to lose you.'

Mystified, he marched out of the dining room and along the hall to the little room they called 'the snug', where he poured himself a large brandy and added soda to it from the old-fashioned syphon. Somewhat as an afterthought, he poured another for Marigold. He sank into his favourite well-worn leather chair and sipped his drink wondering whether she would join him, or whether he should do the decent thing and go and talk to her. But he had spent most of their married life placating her and grovelling for attention. It had never worked before.

After a few minutes, she appeared in the doorway. She had dried her eyes and brushed her hair. She spied the brandy glinting in its Waterford glass. 'Is that for me?'

He considered asking who else it might be for, but merely nodded.

'Are you in love with her?' she whispered.

He nodded again. 'She makes me feel young, Marigold. I need that.'

'I *have* been awful to you,' she murmured. 'I suppose I wanted to punish you.'

'Punish me! Why would you want to do that? I adored you. If I could, I would have made love to you every day of my life. Your body's always had total power over me.'

'But maybe you've loved my body rather than me. I've often thought that. And of course everything changed when we had Emily.'

Philip sighed at the memory of the dark days of Marigold's severe postnatal depression when she had hated the baby, hated him and hated life. He had booked nurses to look after her and Emily, and taken charge of much of the cooking, even though he had been chronically overworked in his publishing job. Could he have been kinder? Perhaps. But he had doted on his daughter, who had been the sole compensation in the sorry mess. And because Marigold had been in no fit state to breastfeed her, he had given the baby her bottles whenever he could. She was his golden girl – so like her mother to look at, but adoring, and adorable.

'And by the time I recovered,' Marigold went on, 'you and Emily were in a little clique of your own. I never got a look in. And then, just when life seemed worth living again, you decided we had to come to Norfolk.'

'I didn't want to. You know that.'

'Agreed. But you never asked what I felt. I'd lived in Kensington all my life. All my girlfriends were there, and my brother. Everything I liked and understood.'

'Come off it, Marigold. Your parents had a place in the country. You went there for weekends and holidays and did all those gymkhanas.'

'But I was a town girl at heart. My life fell apart when we moved here. Flat Norfolk. East winds. A house miles from anywhere.'

'But you run everything so well. I thought you loved it.'

'That's the trouble, isn't it? I never told you, because my upbringing taught me that my only value was in making a suitable match and being a wife and hostess. And because I wasn't allowed to have more children, sex had no meaning for me, so I avoided it. More than that, I suppose I felt that denying you access to my body was my only weapon.'

Against his will, his voice rose. 'Oh, you've had plenty of other weapons, Marigold. Look at how you rubbished me over my intention to stand for the Green Party. You were hardly the meek compliant wife then, were you? And you're always siding with Pa instead of me, and making me look small in front of him.'

'Well, that's because I believe in *family* and because your father values my opinion and listens to my views. He understands me, actually, in a way you never have.'

'He *does*? Well, that takes the bloody biscuit because he certainly never understood me!'

Marigold drained her glass, placed it carefully on an occasional table and began walking towards the door. But, as she drew level with him, she paused, then, leaning over, she took his head in her hands and planted a passionate kiss on his lips.

He found himself rising out of the chair with his mouth still clamped to hers, and wrapping his arms around her. Instinctively, he pulled her even tighter to him, feeling the fullness of her ample breasts pressed into his chest. Her smell, her curves, and the little mole on her right cheek sparked off his customary longing and he felt the first stirrings of arousal which he was aware she could not fail to notice. How little she had to do to rein him in, he thought. He could have her now. That was obvious. And every nerve in his body seemed to be screaming at him to carry her off to bed. But, summoning all his determination, he broke away and stepped back. Her eyes were bright and she was breathing heavily. Was her expression one of triumph? He rather thought so.

'It might be best,' he said, as steadily as he could manage, 'if I sleep in my dressing room.'

She shrugged her shoulders and left. As he sat down again, he could hear her clearing up in the kitchen and then padding from one room to another. There was a pause and a slightly scratchy noise on the parquet floor in the hall, then the sound of her footsteps as she climbed the stairs.

Despite a health warning in his head about liver damage, he walked over and poured himself another brandy before wandering aimlessly around the room, pausing here and there to look at the framed sketches of Norwich which decorated the Farrow and Ball 'Card Room Green' walls.

His head was spinning with confusion. Even though they had just had a more honest conversation than they had had for years, neither he nor Marigold had mentioned Emily's death. It was a barrier between them – a barrier neither of them seemed able or willing to surmount.

Settling back in his chair he found himself thinking again about his dead daughter, and also about how much he loved this house – and yet he yearned for a whole new life with Katie, and to be free to tap into her comparative youth and passion. And there was a baby to consider now. That was another thing he had not mentioned to Marigold. She had been sterilised after Emily, at the suggestion of her psychiatrist, who had cautioned that were there to be another pregnancy, more mental illness could follow.

Now, he could start a new family. Doubtless Marigold would consider that unfair.

He would like to confide in someone, but it was too late to text Katie or to call Mike. He felt his eyes close as he struggled to work out what he should do now. A repeat of the odd scratchy sound puzzled him. It was an old house though, full of creaks and groans. But then he felt a familiar shove against his right knee and opened his eyes to see his two chocolate Labradors vying for his attention. They were normally shut up in the boot room at night and, despite their maturity, were quite skittish at this unexpected freedom. He reached out and patted one, then the other, and as their tails wagged in unison, his eyes misted with tears. The dogs had been bought for – and named by – Emily, but after her death it had been he who had walked and enjoyed them.

Marigold must have let them out. He almost chuckled at her cleverness.

'She's not going to fight according to Queen's Rules and Regulations is she?' he murmured to Hagrid and Dumbledore. Not her style at all!'

He met Michael mid-afternoon the next day, at the entrance to a riverside pub in Thorpe St Andrew. It was near enough to the presbytery for the priest to walk to it, but far enough away to make it unlikely he would be interrupted by parishioners. After weeks of cold, grey, wet weather, the day was warm and sunny, and they opted to go for a stroll by the water.

'So, how are you?' Michael asked.

'I'll tell you later. What about you? Any more thoughts about staying – or not – in the priesthood?'

'Plenty of thoughts. No decisions.'

As usual, Michael did not name names. But he did talk at some length about his deliberations, and went as far as confirming that he was now sure that he was in love, and that he had broached the subject of his celibacy with the woman in question.

'Well done, Mike!' For the first time in their burgeoning friendship, Philip gave Michael a manly but affectionate punch on the arm.

'I'm not sure I got it right though. When I told her that I'd wanted to talk about this for some time, she muttered something like, "well that's what friends are for" and I didn't know if she was just embarrassed or whether I'd completely messed up and failed to impress upon her that I have deep feelings for her and want us to be physically close.'

'Hmmn. Difficult. So, will you talk to her again?'

'I must. But I don't know when. Anyway, that's enough soul-exposure for one day. We're really meeting about your crisis not mine. Are you ready for a drink?'

As soon as they were settled in the pub at a table near the fire with glasses of Pinot Noir in front of them, Philip launched into a soliloquy outlining his mixed emotions, his longing for Katie, the wish for a new life, bewilderment that his wife wanted to fight for him, and the pull of their shared history. Michael listened, without interrupting, while Philip went on to tell him, for the first time, about Emily's death.

'How dreadful that must have been,' Michael sympathised, his voice barely above a whisper. Then he stood up and leaned over the table to put his arms around Philip.

Philip managed a gruff 'Thank you.' But he was relieved when his friend sat down again. He would like, he thought, to be the sort of man who was more at ease with closeness from male friends. But he had never learned how. His father had always avoided kissing or cuddling him, and back in his youth, school friends had never hugged each other.

'Thank you,' he repeated as he looked closely at the priest, and noted his warm and concerned expression. 'Her death was... it was...' he sighed audibly, 'unbelievably shocking.'

'I'm sure.'

They sat in silence for a moment, then Philip sat up straighter and changed the subject.

'I've found myself thinking about Christmas. My father always has his sister to stay or goes to her place in the Cotswolds, so I never have to consider him, thank goodness. But Bro, as I call him – my wife's wacky brother – generally comes to us, and he and I go out and get mildly pissed on Christmas Eve before going to the cathedral for the midnight service. Then we take a taxi home and put the world to rights. And the next day, Marigold always produces magnificent food, and is usually in good spirits. But if I leave for Katie, it'll never be the same again... Sorry, I seem to be going on and on.'

'No you're not, and I'm sure it's time that you shared these things,' Michael responded as he swept up their empty glasses and headed to the bar.

In his absence, Philip checked his phone; nothing from Marigold, or Katie, but two texts from Geoff, his manager.

'Thanks, Mike,' he smiled as his friend returned with more wine. 'I suppose you hear this kind of story all the time?'

'Variations of it. Usually there's more acrimony – fisticuffs occasionally!'

For the first time that day, Philip laughed. 'I don't think violence is Marigold's style. She's not the kind to cut one arm off all my suit jackets or dump my possessions in a skip, or put poison in the porridge. She's been pretty admirable, actually. For one thing, she made a great breakfast this morning and acted as though nothing had happened. But then she said she's booked herself into a spa so she can lose a stone in weight. It's ridiculous, she looks fine as she is. Why couldn't she have been horrible, snappy and sarcastic like I thought she'd be? That would have been much easier. I've got to see Katie now and I hardly know what to tell her. We're supposed to be going to Ireland tomorrow to see my mother. I just hope she hasn't changed her mind about coming.'

'Why would she?'

'Well, something she said yesterday evening made me wonder if she's quite as serious about me as I'd assumed.'

'Phil, I'm sure she is. She's pregnant. Maybe her emotions are unpredictable. Not that I'd know, but don't women become a bit hormonal?'

'I don't think Marigold did. Well, of course she became extremely up and down *afterwards*, psychotic in fact. But she sailed through the pregnancy. If anyone expressed any concern for her, she used to say, "I'm pregnant not poorly"! She's tough.'

He noticed Michael studying him.

'What?'

'I was just thinking that maybe the last chapter hasn't been written on your marriage.'

Philip shook his head. 'Once we both get used to the idea, we'll be better off without each other.'

'How will you feel if she finds someone new?'

Philip picked up his wine glass then put it back on the table without drinking from it. 'I'll be glad for her,' he declared loudly. 'Anyway, there's a baby on the way now, so I have responsibilities that don't include her.'

Sitting in the vast lounge of her hotel, Philip could hardly believe how well his mother had received his news that he was to be a parent again. Not only that, she had taken an instant liking to Katie. And as they ate their way through a mountainous afternoon tea, he noticed that his mother kept patting her, as if she were a favourite pet.

Suddenly, she chortled loudly. 'This is going to take Miss Marigold down a peg or two!'

When both Philip and Katie looked bemused, she added, 'I never liked her; she's *very* snooty!'

Philip grinned. His eighty-four-year-old mother had always spoken her mind. She was descended from a Norman family who had lived in Ireland for centuries. Perhaps there was some Celtic ancestry in her genes somewhere, but he doubted it, and he knew that she was one of those people who are laughed at indulgently by the indigenous population and categorised as 'More Irish than the Irish'!

When he had been in his mid-teens, and his parents' marriage had fallen apart, she had returned to the Republic, reverted to her maiden name of Fitzhenry and set about renovating an extensive property not far from the family home where her ageing father lived in solitary splendour – her older siblings having departed many years previously for Australia.

She had opened a dress shop in nearby Ballynakilty, which had more than paid its way, and had invested her 'marital pay-off' as she called it, very wisely. Then, fifteen years ago, when her extremely ancient father finally died, she had inherited a substantial sum from him, as well as his large country house and grounds, which she had set about turning into a sumptuous hotel.

Philip had worried about her adding on fifty extra bedrooms, a large swimming pool, and a conference suite, but everything she had planned had prospered. In fact, the hotel was doing so well that he and Katie could only stay for three nights because the entire complex was about to be taken over by a rich Irish-American for his daughter's wedding.

'Jaysus,' gossiped his mother in a not entirely convincing country brogue. 'They're spending a *fortune*. And sure, hasn't the daughter been married twice before? Mustn't she just love the taste of the wedding cake!'

Upstairs in bed, after their tea with his mother, he lay beside Katie replete with mental and physical satisfaction.

'Marvellous!' he exclaimed before gently brushing her hair away from her forehead, and kissing her tenderly on each eyelid in turn. 'You're a miracle worker, Katie. My cock thought his best days were over, but you've breathed new life into him.'

She opened her eyes. 'Isn't it wonderful here? I must just look properly at this bed and see why it's so comfortable.'

'What are you doing?' He didn't want her to move and spoil the mood.

'Yes, oh my goodness, that's it!' She was pulling the sheets away from round his feet. 'That is amazing. Instead of a normal mattress protector, there's like a whole plump duvet under the bottom sheet. No wonder it's so soft and cosy. Can we both give up our jobs and come and live in this hotel and let our child run around the grounds?'

He smiled at the thought which, even in his post-coital bliss, he knew was impractical. 'Maybe.'

'Oh, thank you.' She bounced up and down on the bed and kissed him enthusiastically.

'Wait. No, I mean, probably not.'

'We'll think about it later,' she decided. 'Let's go down for dinner. I'm starving.'

'How can you be after all that soda bread and fruit cake?' he joked.

'I'm eating for two, remember. Anyway, I've never stayed anywhere as smart as this in my entire life and I don't want to miss a thing!'

Chapter Seven

While he was waiting for the kettle to boil, Michael scrolled through the texts that Hannah had sent after the Christmas Fair. He had kept them, feeling a sense of connection through her to the new existence that he craved.

Paradoxically though, whenever he thought about a different life, he felt guilty that the brotherhood of priests no longer sustained him. He was certain that all his colleagues felt spiritually and emotionally supported by each other, so what was wrong with him?

Hannah's original message had explained that she had tried to talk to her grandfather about his medical diaries, and having done so – despite his vagueness – had decided to read them.

Over the next couple of days, she had communicated that many of the entries were written in a weird sort of shorthand. In a later text, she had asked him for the translation of various Latin medical terms. As his knowledge of that language was entirely ecclesiastical, he had ended up googling them, but that had not stopped him feeling heartened that he had been of use to Araminta's daughter.

Strangely, after a week, Hannah had stopped contacting him. He had wondered whether to ask why, but decided against it even though, absurdly, he felt bereft.

Meanwhile, Araminta continued to dominate his thoughts. He wished that he could tell Philip about her.

Not for the first time, he felt grateful and amazed at how quickly he and Philip had established such a good relationship. The affirmation he received from the other man generated a welcome sense of fellowship and comfort. However, despite their closeness, he knew he must resist revealing the identity of his secret passion; with Araminta being both Katie's therapist and Nigel's sister, it felt almost incestuous.

On the other hand, he was going to have to do something about offloading his whirring thoughts. His brain felt as if it was going to burst out of his head. He should probably 'man-up', as his curate was fond of saying, and tell Araminta exactly what she meant to him. But she had only been to Mass once since they had had dinner together, and had rushed away before the closing hymn, so he had not been able to speak to her.

However, today he had learned that she was among the volunteers who were going to join the choir over Christmas, and that extra rehearsals were scheduled, beginning with this evening. So, he had rung the organist and asked him to bring everyone to the presbytery after their practice for mulled wine and mince pies. But would she come? And could he contrive to see her alone?

The day dragged and his mood fluctuated wildly. On top of that, the old priest was furious about the arrangement, because Michael had not entered the 'booking' into the presbytery time-table forty-eight hours in advance.

'It's your rule, Father Michael,' the supernumerary pointed out in an aggrieved tone. 'And I was looking forward to watching the football on the big set in the lounge. But now it'll be crawling with chatty parishioners, won't it?'

'Sorry – yes, it will. But they're all going to spend lots of time over the next week, learning and singing all that music. I felt we should show our appreciation.'

'Well, I can't fault your argument,' snapped the elderly man. 'I just want some peace and quiet sometimes.'

'I'm sorry,' Michael repeated. And he was. He was also ashamed that he had hinted at altruism when his motive had been entirely selfish.

Araminta did come to the presbytery. Initially, he forced himself to keep his distance though he tried unsuccessfully to catch her eye. Why was she talking endlessly to the organist and laughing at his pitiful jokes? In the end he could restrain himself no longer and walked up to her to enlist her help in clearing up the empty glasses. Even as he asked, he recognised that it was a thoroughly bad move.

In the kitchen, she searched around for a pair of rubber gloves and donned them, then launched into the washing-up without looking at him. He stood, unsure what to do or say, before reaching for a tea cloth in a bid to help, and also to stem the worrying hostility that was emanating from her.

'So, are you all right?' he ventured.

She nodded, her gaze focused on her task. But then she said, 'Lovely meal the other night, Michael. Thank you.'

Immediately, he felt brighter and bolder. 'Um... you know my confession to you that evening. I suppose this isn't the place or the time really, but are you OK with what I said?'

Araminta nodded but said nothing.

Nonplussed, he searched for a way to get the conversation going. 'How's Hannah?'

Araminta turned to him, and peeled off the gloves. 'I gather you and she are in touch.'

'Ye-es.'

'Often?'

'Well, a bit.'

'Do you want to tell me why?'

'Oh – well... I'm not sure I can. It may be private to her.'

Araminta looked very flushed suddenly, and she shot him a look that he hoped was not as furious as he perceived it to be, then she shook her head and ran out of the kitchen.

Stunned, he stood rooted to the spot, then as he heard her cry 'Good night' to someone and slam the front door, he picked up one of the clean glasses and went in search of red wine.

He was on his fourth black coffee of the morning, nursing a pounding headache, when Philip rang to say he was back from Ireland. They agreed that as it was such a beautiful day, they would meet for lunch at the coast and settled on Blakeney.

Was it unfair though, Michael asked himself, to be taking time off today? They were terribly busy. More people died in mid-winter. Many became depressed. A larger than normal number of the congregation wanted to come to confession before receiving Christmas communion. There were also school carol services to attend, and more homilies than usual to write and deliver. However, he had given up on sleep at two this morning and tackled a mountain of paperwork, so perhaps he was entitled to a break. He had also sent the old priest back to bed when he had appeared in the kitchen – blearily – at half-past seven.

'I'll say the early Mass,' Michael had insisted. 'It's the least I can do after ruining your football.'

He asked Father David to hold the fort for a few hours, telling him simply that he had to go out on an emergency. The young man loitered in the hall, while Michael slipped into his coat.

'Is there anything I should know about?' queried the curate, in a slightly sarcastic voice.

'I don't think so,' Michael replied in as breezy a tone as he could muster.

Father David was very keen on phrases like 'collaborative approach' and 'team player'. And as he drove away, Michael recognised that he was failing to be the type of priest that the younger cleric favoured. Was this another sign that it was time to give up?

He groaned audibly as, for the thousandth time, he remembered Araminta's anger of the night before. What had upset her? Could it have been to do with Hannah and the diaries? What a mess he was making of everything. And drinking so much after their encounter had been both stupid and immature – surely at fifty-five he should know better.

He headed off the ring road, in the direction of Cromer which, though not the direct way to Blakeney, was the more scenic. In contrast to the traffic nightmare of the city roads, there were few cars heading north on this December day and Michael felt his shoulders drop and a certain amount of tension leave his body, even though his mind continued to mull over his current crisis.

Had it all begun three years ago, with his mother's death? Originally, he had thought so, but now he wondered if his growing sense of isolation and loneliness had predated that. Whatever the truth was, he had felt utterly desolate once she had died. He had put this down to grief at losing the only relative he knew, and had sought help from Cruse Bereavement Care in the hope his panic and sadness could be contained.

Then, out of the blue, he had been invited to become the senior priest at the church of his childhood, and he had moved here, full of hope that a change of scene would cheer him up and reboot his ministry.

It had worked for a while as he absorbed himself in his new and large parish, and brought himself up to date with the changes that had occurred in Norwich since his teens.

He had, however, been aware of a wave of loneliness that would inundate him from time to time. One of the worst instances had been when he had returned from leading a school group to Lourdes. Having been surrounded for an entire week by bright and engaging teenagers, he had been unable to stop weeping once it was over and he returned to his single room in the presbytery.

But then, his general sense of aloneness had found a new focus.

Araminta had turned up, shocked and distraught to ask if he could put together a funeral for the two men in her life. She had explained that neither her son nor her husband had been religious, but that she wanted them to have a proper 'send-off' with music, poetry, and plenty of ceremony. Throughout the discussion he had waited for her to recognise him, but she did not.

Had his heart started beating faster that first day? No, but he had been disturbed sufficiently by their meeting to sleep only fitfully for the following night or two – aware that some soul-stirring process was beginning from which he was not prepared to retreat, even though he knew he should.

After that, it seemed to him that every time he saw her, his feelings grew. He had – and he knew it – a penchant for people in distress and had always liked himself better when providing solace to those who needed it. But something totally different was happening with her. Soon, his longing to see and help her became addictive, and he kept engineering ways in which he could. He felt almost like an alcoholic who could stay off drink so long as there was none on offer, but who was compelled to quaff himself senseless whenever he got so much as the whiff of a cork.

Still, what could he have done? She had needed his support. And somehow, he had deluded himself into believing that he was coping with his emotions.

However, over the past few weeks, as their relationship had morphed from a professional association into a bonding friendship, his desire for her had become overwhelming.

He would explain all this to Philip, without mentioning Araminta by name. Phil was more worldly than him. Perhaps he might have some answers.

Before long, he reached Blakeney, parked the car, stepped out of it and breathed deeply. There was a frost in the air, but the sun was shining and the sky was startlingly blue.

Looking around, he could see no sign of Philip so he wandered into the Blakeney Hotel. Hungry suddenly, and realising that he had not eaten since lunchtime the day before, he studied the menu. His spirits rose as he decided what he would order once his friend arrived.

Outside again, a taxi drew up and Philip, plus two bounding chocolate Labradors, emerged from it. The dogs charged towards him, and he bent to fondle their ears and pat them before they raced off again.

'So, they're Hagrid and Dumbledore. Aren't they beautiful?'

'They are!' Philip smiled and punched him playfully on the arm. 'God, it's grand to see you. How are you, my good sir?'

'I was dreadfully hungover earlier, but I'm better now. Lots to talk about.'

'Me too. I've been to Ireland, as you know. Mother loves Katie.'

'That's good, isn't it?'

'Yes and no.' Philip's face took on a rueful expression before he continued. 'Look, shall we walk before we eat and you can tell me what's been happening?'

The Labradors darted ahead, running around in circles for a moment or two and jumping up at each other. Then they scampered back to Philip who patted each of them in turn, before they dashed away, far into the distance. How easily pleased dogs are, Michael thought enviously.

Striding out on the Norfolk Coast Path towards Cley, and trying to keep up with Philip – who was clearly much fitter – he sensed a sudden freedom in his mind, and began to empty the thoughts and anxieties that resided there into the bracing north Norfolk air. The only detail he withheld was Araminta's identity.

When he had finished, Philip gave him a searching look and suggested that it was 'high time for lunch'.

They retraced their steps pausing only to watch three birds – which Philip identified as a redshank and a pair of curlews – feeding on the mudflats.

Once in the hotel, Philip found a porter to mind the dogs, and – despite the presence of various groups of pre-Christmas revellers enjoying lunch – settled the two of them at the best table overlooking the estuary. As he often did, Michael marvelled at his friend's 'old-money' air of assurance.

'Wine or beer?'

Michael shook his head. 'Definitely not! This drama is turning me into an absolute lush. I must stop it. I've seen far too many people medicate their stresses with alcohol to know that it's a very rocky road.'

Philip nodded. 'I won't drink either.'

Michael protested. 'I don't want to inhibit you.'

'You're not. When I lost my licence, I thought the worst thing would be the lack of easy mobility. But I'd no idea how unhealthy it would turn out to be! Knowing that I can't get behind a wheel has turned me into even more of an old soak than usual. I need some booze-free days. Especially after Ireland!'

Michael laughed.

'Ah!' Philip nodded as the waiter appeared. 'Sparkling water, please. And I think we're in a go-state for the food...'

'I picked earlier.' Michael exchanged a grin with Philip, before giving his order of fish soup, seared calves' liver and colcannon potato cake.

'And I'll have the seafood plate followed by the cheese soufflé.'

'Now,' Michael paused till the waiter retreated out of earshot. 'Tell me all about you. I've monopolised the conversation long enough.'

'OK,' Philip agreed as he poured water into two tumblers packed with ice and slices of lemon. 'But I wish I had some advice for your situation. I can't imagine what it must feel like for you. I mean, it's your whole career... your calling...'

Michael winced. 'Bit of a bugger really.'

'That's rather strong language for you! But who could disagree?'

Their first courses came, and they started chatting generally about the church and the preparations for Christmas, and Philip's staff party and how many days the business would be closed over the festive period. However, as the main dishes replaced their starters, Michael looked across at his friend. 'Go on then – what happened in Ireland?'

'Well, my mother's fallen totally under Katie's spell, and I certainly never saw *that* coming. She's treating her like a favourite doll. Not only that, I noticed she gave her an envelope stuffed with euros. It looked like the whole night's takings from the bar. I mean, *I* can provide for her. I *will* provide for her, so God knows what that's about. I suppose my mother's thrilled to be having another grandchild, but it's a bit strange.'

'And how does Katie feel about your mother?'

'She seems to adore her. On the last night, when I wanted us to leave the dining room, and have some, you know, time on our own, Katie actually told me not to be so boring, and the two of them carried on chatting for ages. And she kept going on about how wonderful the hotel was and how she didn't want to leave it and how three days there wasn't nearly enough. And on the plane home she hardly spoke to me because she was engrossed in a book about the south-west of Ireland. I almost feel I don't know her.'

He took a sip of water before continuing. 'When we first met, she couldn't get enough of me, but since she learned she was pregnant, she doesn't seem nearly so keen. You'd think, wouldn't you, that she'd be looking to me to take care of her and make everything right? But I don't get that impression at all. I'd hoped though that she'd be all over me in Ireland, while we were away from everything here. It started well, and we made love after tea on the first day, which was wonderful, but she didn't want to do it again.'

'Are you sure you still want to be with her?'

'Of course! But everything's confused. My main desire, and I'm not proud of this, is that I'm desperate to make up for lost time, and I felt quite peeved yesterday that I wasn't getting any sex. Don't tell me that's childish and petty, because I know. But time must be running out for me to have a rollicking love life. I've always been hopeless with women. Not, I must stress, because of a poor libido. Quite the reverse; my ever-present sex drive has made me feel like I've been chained to a lunatic since I was thirteen. Part of the trouble was that once I met Marigold in my

92

twenties, I was mad about her to the exclusion of everyone else. Unfortunately, my feelings were entirely unrequited and she got engaged to a viscount. I couldn't compete with that! However...' Philip paused and his face took on a brighter, almost gleeful, expression '...he suddenly dumped her and quickly married an American heiress who was prepared to pour money into his crumbling estate. Marigold was pretty humiliated, so I proposed. I knew she married me on the rebound but I thought it would be OK. Unfortunately, her lack of interest continued. I don't think she ever fancied me, so – and apologies for being this blunt – I've pretty well had to manage the DIY way.'

'You're not the only one,' murmured Michael.

A waiter appeared to clear away their plates.

Philip froze till the man had gone. 'God, do you think he heard? I don't know what's come over me. I've never had this frank a conversation with anyone before.'

'Nor me.' Michael studied the tablecloth for a few seconds. Then he looked Philip in the eye. 'But, to be honest, as a virgin, I welcome it. I'm a total dunce when it comes to all this stuff.'

'Poor chap. I can't begin to understand what a celibate life must be like.'

'Well, my zest for the priesthood kept me going when I was younger. As I told Araminta the other day, it's now that I can hardly think of anything else.'

'*Araminta?*'

Michael felt himself redden. 'I decided to confide in her. We're... friends.' He glanced at his watch. 'I must get back.'

'Sure.' Philip looked around for a waiter and made a little signing gesture in the air.

'Let me get it?'

Philip shook his head. 'You do it next time.'

'You always say that. I know I'm on a pitiful salary but I'm probably not as poor as you think. I've actually got some money stashed away that my mother left me.'

'I'm doing it.' Philip was firm. 'It's the least I can do.'

Michael shrugged, but he smiled too. 'Well, allow me then to give you a lift. I'm not sure exactly where you live but it must be pretty much on my way.'

As they drove, Philip commented, 'I didn't really know Araminta when we were kids. She was a bit younger. But I must have met her, being mates with Nigel.'

Michael quickly seized on Nigel as a handy subject to divert them from dangerous territory. 'Were you best friends with him?'

'Not at all,' Philip replied. 'We weren't even in the same form. And to be honest, I wasn't good at friendships. Probably it's that "only child" syndrome. One grows up interacting mostly with adults.'

'Exactly so. I know I did.'

'Oh, I didn't realise you were an only child too. So were *you* close to Nigel?'

'No, we just went to the same church. I don't think he even liked me. But for some reason I often got invited to his house to play. And his dad was very friendly. In the early days he used to give me a half-crown whenever he saw me. But in my teens, the amounts increased. Once he gave me a fiver! I had assumed he did the same to everyone, but Nigel got quite cross once and said something weird about his dad having a soft spot for me.'

'That *is* strange.'

'I don't mean to suggest he was a paedophile or anything.'

'No, I know you don't. But interestingly, the old boy used to single *me* out to chat to as well. He wanted to know everything about me and what I was doing and what I wanted to do when I grew up. He never gave me money, but I do remember Nigel getting pissed off about it… Oh, next turning and, here we are.'

As Michael drove up the long drive, and the impressive old house came into view, he grinned. 'So, this is Hunsford Hall. I don't feel so bad about you having bought lunch now!'

They drew to a halt and immediately the dogs began thrashing the back seat with their tails, and making high-pitched appeals to be allowed out of the car. Philip reached behind him to open the back door for them – and with a rush and a couple of excited barks, the two animals scrabbled out of the vehicle and disappeared swiftly round the back of the house.

Both men stepped out of the car and exchanged a handshake and then the briefest of hugs.

'You'll keep your Labradors whatever happens, won't you?' Michael asked.

Philip, standing in front of his magnificent home, seemed to sag slightly as he replied, 'I really hope so.'

'We'll both sort things out,' Michael assured him, in the confident tone he usually reserved for his parishioners. Then he jumped back into his ten-year-old Volvo, turned it in a large circle on the gravel driveway and headed towards the road.

'Mike!'

'Hang on.' Michael had jerked awake, and reached for his mobile when it rang, but he was struggling to escape his dream, in which he had been breaking down a door because Araminta was imprisoned behind it. He sat up and fumbled on the bedside table for his spectacles.

'Philip?'

'Mike, sorry if I've woken you.'

'Why are you whispering?'

'I've done something terrible. Marigold came back last night from her break at the spa. She looked fantastic. I went to sleep alone in the dressing room and that was an effort, I can tell you. But she came in and got into bed with me and one thing led to another, and, oh God, I fucked her. And it was great. But I am such a heel. I mean she's pottering around now, singing, and probably thinks everything between us is fine. Meanwhile, I've got a girlfriend whom my mother approves of, which is a bloody miracle I can tell you, plus a baby on the way. Jesus! Sorry, but this is chaos.'

'Take it easy. You're not the first person to have had sex with a partner you're preparing to leave. I hear this all the time. But when are you seeing Katie again?'

'Later this afternoon.'

'Are you going to tell her about Marigold?'

'No! Do you think I should?'

'Probably. Just as, probably, you should tell Marigold about the baby.'

'No!' Philip shouted again. 'I couldn't. Oh God.'

'Think about it. We can chat later.'

'OK. By the way, how are you?'

'Well, you know...'

There was a pause, before Philip ventured, 'I think I've guessed who you're in love with. It's Araminta, isn't it?'

'What! Why do you think that?'

'I let you believe yesterday that I'd swallowed your line about you confiding in her as a friend. But I didn't buy it because you've often said I'm the only person you talk to. It must be her. But that's *great*. She's a fine woman, and she's single, isn't she?'

'Yes, she's a widow.'

'Marvellous! I was afraid it might be someone unworthy of you – possibly silly and younger. In fact, I thought her name might be Hannah because someone of that name called you a couple of times when we've been together.'

'Hannah! Absolutely not! It *is* Araminta. But I should *never* have said her name. Trust you to work it out.'

'Sorry. Anyway, go for it. You love her. If you let her go now you'll always regret it. And if you have to stop being a priest as a result, well, you're a bright man, you'll find another career. I'll help you!'

Despite his panic, Michael felt as though an unseen spirit had wrapped him in a comforting blanket. Philip was his friend. He was a *good* friend. He was going to *stay* a friend.

'Oh God, Marigold's coming upstairs. Talk later.'

Michael threw back the bedclothes and leapt out of bed. He showered. Dressed. Breakfasted. Tackled his emails. Printed the newsletter with the details of all the Christmas Masses on it, and all the while kept checking his watch until – finally – it was nine o'clock when he picked up the phone.

It was answered after two rings.

Michael cleared his throat, announced who he was, and began to speak the words that were going to change his life forever.

Chapter Eight

Though she was aware that she was torturing herself, Wendy clicked again on Julian's Facebook timeline.

There were even more pictures now of the previous night's event, featuring a pride of gorgeous gay men looking as though they spent half their lives in the gym and the other half moisturising.

Irrationally, what upset her most was the stunning décor of the Chelsea house where the party had been held.

When she and Robert had moved into their Barbican flat, she had fantasised about creating a classy interior with the odd, interestingly obscure painting on an occasional wall, a ceramic pot here and there, and maybe a piece of roughly hewn sculpture on a pedestal in the hallway. Instead, the apartment had become overstuffed with books, gadgets, CDs, sheet music and a piano that sounded fine but looked as if had served time in a rough public house. Having assumed that Julian had found her home charming if not impressive, she could see all too clearly now that he knew people who had far more style.

One of the images pictured her friend with a blissful smile and his arm around a muscly man with an extraordinarily smooth face. She told herself that Julian's expression was not proof that he had gone on to have sex with the guy. But even if he had, what of it? He had never made any secret of his orientation; never promised her his exclusive attention.

She remembered her father's disapproving comment after she had introduced him to Julian. They had had tea at the Maids Head Hotel in Norwich, and – as the three of them had laughed and gossiped together – she had felt warmly content that these much-loved men were getting along so famously. But after Julian left them, her father had put down his teacup and declaimed, 'He's queer of course so he's never going to marry you!' Then he had signalled for his bill, and paid it – pleased, she imagined, to have said what he felt he should.

She had chosen not to tackle him at the time, but the following morning she had explained to him that she had always known that Julian was gay, that they were simply good friends, and that she had no need of a husband, but just wanted to have fun.

And there had been a lot of fun. But maybe they were too involved. She felt furiously jealous – but hated herself for it – that he had been to such an elegant and 'upscale' soirée without her, even though it was plain from the pictures that it had been an all-male affair. Had her contact with him been as healthy as she had presumed? After all, they had quickly developed a habit of meeting most days. Perhaps being with him so often had prevented her from properly processing not only her sorrow at the end of her marriage, but also her outrage at Francesca's treachery.

She had worked from home as much as possible in recent weeks to avoid having to talk to Fran. And she had kept putting off dealing with the divorce. Seeing Julian had been like taking a happy pill – enabling her to forget the unpleasantness of her personal circumstances. Soon, she must respond to the mounting number of texts from Robert and the lawyers – and she would. But not yet.

Now she had to go out to meet Minty's daughter in Covent Garden. Probably it would be fine when she got there. But right now, most unusually, she felt tired. However, she must not let the young woman down. Or Rhys, who was performing later in a nearby charity carol concert.

Surveying the customers in the crowded tea room, she quickly spotted Hannah, who was seated at a table in the corner, waving exuberantly.

'I feel I've known you forever,' Minty's daughter told her. 'I've grown up with a photo of you and my brother on the top of the piano at home. It was taken before I was born, but you look just the same.'

Wendy chortled. 'Sweetie, if only that were true!'

'I mean it though. There's something about you that's no different. And funnily enough I now see something that Michael mentioned.'

'Who's Michael?'

'Hasn't Mum told you about him? He's a priest who helped her a lot after Dad died. They've become friends.'

The expression in Hannah's eyes seemed vaguely troubled. Wendy was about to ask what was wrong when the waitress appeared at her elbow.

Hannah opted for fruit tea.

'Shall we eat something too?' Wendy asked.

'They do this amazing cake here,' Hannah's eyes shone as she described it. 'It's chocolate, with cream, zabaglione and fresh fruit in it.'

'Sounds marvellous,' Wendy agreed. 'Two of those then!' She grinned at the waitress. 'And I'll have a pot of English breakfast.'

The beverages came quickly, and the two women smiled at each other across their individual teapots.

'Tell me more about your priest friend,' Wendy encouraged her young companion.

'Well, when he came to supper, we were looking at all the family pictures, and he asked if you were a relation. I said "no" but I can kind of see why he thought that. And, I know this may seem odd but, about two months ago, I passed somebody in the passageway by Boots at Liverpool Street station one morning, and I thought she looked familiar. And I wonder now if it was you?'

Wendy suddenly noticed the hat that lay on the chair beside Hannah, and she felt her eyes widen as she turned to look more intently at her. 'Oh my goodness. I remember that day very well. The weather was atrocious, and I was in a very strange mood as I'd just told my husband that I wanted a divorce. I was going to Norfolk to visit my parents, and when I saw you, it was as if I was viewing my younger self walking towards me. It was a weird sensation. I know that's rather off the wall.'

Hannah reached across the table and patted Wendy's arm. 'No, I don't think it is. It was very stormy, wasn't it? Felt a bit apocalyptic! Most of the lighting in the station was on the blink. But I remember looking at you and your hat – which was like mine – and your boots, and thinking I must somehow know you. I didn't connect my thoughts with the photo till now. Actually, that makes a lot of sense.'

'In what way?'

'Oh – not quite sure yet, to be honest.'

'Are you always this enigmatic?' Wendy giggled.

Hannah laughed. 'Possibly. I was just kind of thinking how often people might be linked to passers-by, if only they knew it. Probably lots of us are connected in ways we'd never suspect. I mean, quite apart from you and me possibly looking a bit similar, or liking the same sort of clothes, there you were in the same corridor as me and you knew my mother really well, years ago. That kind of thing's a bit freaky, isn't it?'

'These are deep waters.'

'Mum has always said I'm very fanciful!'

Their food arrived. Wendy took one forkful of her gateau then beamed at her companion. 'Oh my, that is seriously good.'

'I know!' Hannah grinned.

'You've obviously been here before?'

'Yes, with Mum. I live quite near the Opera House. It was Dad's place. He'd retired from his Norwich practice but then started working for a private dental clinic in Wimpole Street – and he bought a flat so he could stay some nights in town. Anyway, after, um, the accident, Mum transferred the ownership of it to me. I think she hoped it would cushion the blow of losing Dad and Andrew. And perhaps it has – especially because I used to live in a crowded flat-share in Willesden Green and now I have my very own space, with no mortgage and no rent to pay. Best of all, and most unusually for a studio flat, it has a bath, and I love a soak in the tub at the end of the day!'

'Oh, so do I,' agreed Wendy.

Hannah chuckled, then began chatting about something else, while Wendy sat back and listened and enjoyed her. She had often wondered whether her life might have been different had she had a girl. Of course, mothers and daughters were not always close; but it would have been marvellous to produce a child who had turned out like this attractive young woman. Having sons was wonderful, but you never found out about things like hair or eyelash extensions, or what the newest way was to tie a scarf so it looked fashionable and not just as if you were hiding your neck. And would a daughter have left her alone at Christmas?

Probably one of the reasons she had been so upset earlier about Julian was that Rhys had chosen this morning to tell her that he was going to spend Christmas in Boston with his twin. It was understandable; she knew they missed each other. But to have one son in America over the festive season was bad enough. Two seemed like a hammer-blow. She imagined that Robert was paying for Rhys's flight. He would be spending Christmas with Miss Spiky Hair, so probably he had no reservations about both boys being away. Listening to Hannah, and hearing the hum of conversation of festive shoppers all around her as they merrily recharged themselves with tea, cakes and glasses of Prosecco, she felt suddenly very single and alone.

'So, do you think that's awful?' Hannah was asking.

Wendy felt herself blush. 'I'm terribly sorry. My mind was drifting. What were you saying?'

'That I seriously fancy my boyfriend's younger brother! It all started when I went with Najid – he's the boyfriend – to the O2 arena to see the Andy Murray final against Djokovic, and his brother Farid came too. Afterwards, I couldn't stop thinking about him. Now, he's uh, helping me with some, um, research and we're spending lots of time together. And I'm avoiding Najid, which is very cowardly, I know. I'm supposed to be seeing him later, but I think I'll duck out of it. I haven't told Mum, by the way, because she adores Najid. Sorry, I'm going on and on. You're just so easy to talk to. Are you all right for time?'

Wendy looked at her watch, and then apologised and explained about the carol service at St Paul's, Covent Garden. Much to her astonishment, Hannah asked if she could come too. Then she offered to settle the bill which seemed both sweet and astonishing. Wendy refused, but was touched. Much as she adored her boys, she was pretty sure they never noticed that she paid for everything. Certainly, neither of them had ever suggested treating her when she was out with them. But here was this smart, funny, lively young woman, just a couple of years older than them, genuinely reluctant to accept her hospitality.

As they began walking along the cold, crowded windswept street, Hannah murmured, 'This is nice.'

'It is,' agreed Wendy happily. 'And we haven't even started to talk about your career. Your mum said you were keen to get into television news.'

'Yes. Just in the newsroom, though. I don't rate my chances of appearing on camera or anything. But there's so much competition for even the most basic job, as you know. It was hard enough getting the one I've got, which is just researching for a pretty dire game show.'

'I don't know what I can do exactly, but I still have mates at ITN. I could put some feelers out and maybe get you a meeting with someone.'

'But it would be awful if you went to all that trouble and they thought I was stupid or naïve or hopeless.'

Wendy stopped walking, turned to Hannah and spoke calmly but very firmly. 'You may not be right for them. They may have no vacancies. All sorts of problems might stand in your way. But I can assure you that no one meeting you will see you as anything other than intelligent, articulate and very able.'

Hannah's face broke into an enormous smile and she threw her arms around Wendy, apparently oblivious to the procession of people pushing by.

'Mum *said* you were always really kind and lovely.'

'I've always thought that about *her*,' laughed Wendy as she pulled away from the embrace.

'Come on,' Hannah said as she took Wendy's arm. 'We mustn't be late for your son!'

Hannah was quick to agree to Rhys's post-concert invitation to join him and his musical friends for a drink, but Wendy bowed out in favour of a quiet evening at home with a book. Paradoxically, having felt uncomfortably single earlier, she suddenly longed for solitude. But the carol service had generated welcome emotions of peace and goodwill, and she felt calm and happy.

She walked through Covent Garden, dodging all the revellers taking selfies in front of the huge illuminated stag and the Christmas tree, before carving her way through the back streets and out to the Aldwych to catch a Number 4 bus which would deposit her near her flat.

While she waited, she searched her handbag for her mobile. Julian had left a voice message, which made her smile:

'Soooo hung over. Been such a silly boy! It's another *Forza* night tonight, so am at ROH. All I've done today is post pictures on Facebook and drink coffee. Sorry to have missed you.'

No longer upset about Julian and the party, she wondered why she had been so exercised by it earlier. Sometimes she worried about how changeable her moods were. But recently, she had read a book about dealing with divorce, which had been reassuring about volatile emotions during a break-up.

Julian would almost certainly be on stage at the moment, so she texted rather than called him.

> Sounds like quite a party. I'm sure you must have enjoyed it at the time. I'll take a look at Facebook when I get home and see what you got up to!

That was dishonest, but she was too ashamed to reveal how much of the day she had pored over his pictures, or of how desperately she had minded that he had gone without her.

The bus arrived, and she climbed to the upper deck and found a seat, then reached into her bag for spectacles and her Kindle, keen to get on with her book. But as the vehicle slowed in The Strand's traffic, she found herself captivated by a group of laughing young lawyers, decked out in gowns and wigs crossing the road from the Royal Courts of Justice, and then setting themselves up to sing carols on the island in front of the illuminated St Clement Dane's church. After a moment, she could hear strains of 'Hark the Herald Angels Sing' and she could not resist humming along with them. What a good day this was turning out to be after all.

She heard the sound of the slap on Robert's cheek followed by his outraged howl and, as her fury abated, she realised that she had hit him.

'Bitch!' He spat the word at her.

She marched to the other end of her kitchen where she found an already opened bottle of Fleurie. Breathing heavily, she poured herself a generous measure which she gulped at before turning towards him, the glass held tightly in her trembling right hand.

'I apologise. I shouldn't have hit you, Robert. But then again you most certainly shouldn't have been here when I arrived. You were supposed to have given me your keys. And it's upsetting to see you when I'm not expecting it. OK, you had things to say, and I listened. I'm not sure if I'm sorry or not that Miss Spiky Hair has dumped you, but it doesn't alter the fact that we're getting divorced. So, it's beyond bizarre of you to think that I might want to take her place on the trip to the Seychelles. And pressing up against me and forcing your tongue into my mouth was not just inappropriate, it was disgusting.' She shuddered with distaste. 'You'd better go now, because I'll probably start throwing things at you if you don't. I hadn't actually realised till now how much I hate and despise you, and slapping you was so-oo satisfying, I might not be able to stop.'

Robert extricated his house keys from his jacket pocket and flung them onto the table before reaching for his coat and heading for the hall.

'Why don't you take Fran?' she called after him.

'What!' Robert reversed back into the kitchen. 'What the hell are you talking about?'

'Francesca. Your long-term, on-off lover. The one you had your way with in our bedroom the day the twins were christened, and carried on seeing in between all the other women.'

'You've lost your mind!'

'She *told* me, Robert. For God's sake, do you even *recognise* the truth? You've lived so many lies, I wonder if you do. But that woman probably loves you. She was certainly devastated to hear I was going to divorce you but that you had somebody else. By the way, has Miss Spiky Hair gone for good, or is it a temporary tiff?'

'None of your business! I had no idea you could be so vindictive and insulting.'

'Well you know now.'

She almost laughed at the look of disbelief on his face as he gazed at her, briefly, before turning and walking away. He slammed the front door and then there was silence.

For decades, she had lived in dread of the next infidelity. But she no longer had to do it. She had had her say. She had stood her ground.

Leaning against the fridge, she sniffed her wine in an attempt to calm her racing heartbeat. She was lucky. She had a future. She was solvent. Her marriage was well and truly over, and she was glad. So why could she not feel it?

Quickly, she found his details on her phone and called him. 'Where are you?' she asked.

'Downstairs – about to leave the building.'

'Come back for a minute.'

'Why?'

'I just feel we shouldn't end things this way.'

He would have to ring the bell. She paced up and down till he did.

Opening the door, she saw him with freshly objective eyes; a man who at this moment appeared crumpled and defeated and all of his sixty-one years. And for the first time she gained an impression of how he would look in old age.

Without asking him, she poured a glass of the wine she was drinking, and left it on the table near to where he was standing before returning to the other end of the kitchen and leaning again on the fridge.

He ignored the drink for a moment, then cautiously stretched out his hand to pick it up. She could see him debating whether or not to sit down. He decided against it, and stood, awkwardly, trying to catch her eye and assess her mood.

Suddenly, he cleared his throat and spoke. 'At the risk of making you even angrier, I think you should know that I've found you so intimidating and so bloody capable, that it emasculated me. I know that I've treated you appallingly. But I like romance, I like the chase. And I really, really like sex.'

'You think I don't?' she asked quietly.

'I'm sure you do in your own way.' He smiled and suddenly looked beguiling and boyish – a look she must not succumb to, though it was hard not to capitulate as she had done a million times in the past.

'I can be romantic and sexy.'

He shook his head forlornly. 'On the day we found that you were pregnant with the twins, I wanted to go to bed and treasure you and take my time making meaningful and caring love with you, but you were hell-bent on spending the evening talking about how we would manage them. I think you even drew up a business plan of their development and what it would cost, and how much external help we might need.'

'Somebody had to be practical.'

He went on, 'Sometimes we've had sex in the afternoon. Not often. But I would cheerfully have spent ages more in bed, having sex, then reading a poem maybe, enjoying a little snack and glass of wine, and then making love again, but you always sprang up eager to get on with whatever it was that drives you.'

'Well, why couldn't you ever just think – that was really good, but there are loads of other important things to do? You always seemed to be wanting more, and wondering how soon you could do it again.'

'That's how men are.'

'Really? *All* men?'

'Probably.'

'I suppose mistresses make time for the sort of elongated sex you have in mind? But isn't that just part of their job description? After all, they're not bringing up your children, or providing meals three times daily, or organising the laundry, or sorting out when people should be going to the dentist.'

'I used to ask what I could do to help, but you always said that if I had to ask it wasn't worth telling me and that it was quicker to do it yourself.'

Wendy blushed as she heard her own words recited back at her.

'And you know,' he continued, 'recently, I tried one night to cook a romantic dinner and I lit candles – but I could see you thinking that I hadn't put quite enough mats on the table and that the wax might drip on the polished wood. I would always assume that that kind of thing wasn't important so long as the mood was right, but you'd be thinking that the gesture wasn't worth it because of the mess it would leave.'

'You make me sound…' she took a deep breath as she searched for a suitably damning phrase, 'heartlessly functional.'

'I'm not making excuses for my infidelity,' he mumbled, almost to himself. 'Not really. But maybe I'm offering one or two reasons.'

He drained his glass and placed it carefully on the table. Then he took a step towards her, but she shook her head.

'I suppose I needed to hear all that,' she whispered, 'though it made painful listening. Still, there are women out there who will doubtless indulge all your romantic gestures, and I will carry on somehow – probably by being the controlling, capable and pragmatic being that I am.'

Thrusting his hands into the pockets of his coat he had not removed, he studied the tiled floor. 'I love you, Wendy, in my own inadequate way.' He sighed. 'But you're right that we have no future.'

'I've loved you too, Robert,' she murmured. Then with a bolder tone, she added, 'This is a better ending. But could you go now?'

Chapter Nine

Julian winced as he lowered himself into the hot bath, holding his breath as he waited for the warm water to ease the discomfort.

It was five days since the party, but he had not fully recovered. Was he never going to learn? Never going to stop allowing himself to be used by men who inflicted severe pain while pursuing their own pleasure?

He sighed. The soreness would disappear soon, but his sense of shame would linger.

Perhaps he could confide in Wendy. He would see her tomorrow at the choir's Christmas concert. However, despite her being so liberal and worldly, he feared that sharing such sordid details might shock her.

The magnificent church of St Mary Magdalene in Little Venice turned out to be a wonderful venue for the concert. Everyone was in festive mood, and the chorus had added touches of glitter – tinsel, sparkly brooches, colourful cufflinks or diamante earrings – to their uniform of black suits or dresses.

The sound was sublime too. The sopranos' voices floated upwards, apparently effortlessly, and filled the roof of the late nineteenth century church with exquisite melody. Even the tenors sounded passable. He was singing with them this evening; as a baritone, his voice added substance and tone to the middle and lower notes. Fortunately, he had no nerves about this performance, and even though he had had to resort to falsetto on a couple of the higher passages, he felt his contribution was improving the balance of the chorus.

Some of the members had asked him if he minded that he was not conducting the concert. But he had no illusions about his baton technique. He was good at rehearsing his singers – getting the notes into their heads, helping them listen to each other so they were more aware of pitch, and showing them how to breathe correctly so that they sang the phrases more musically. However, when it came to all that 'waving your hands about' as Wendy called it, he lacked style and confidence. So, he had persuaded the committee to bring in a talented young woman from the conducting course at his alma mater, the Guildhall School. He had also suggested booking a small chamber orchestra from the conservatory, as well as four singing soloists.

'They won't expect to be paid though, will they?'

The question had come from their Chairman, a hedge fund owner, and therefore – Julian surmised – someone who was worth millions and had never been asked to work for nothing. Other committee members had weighed in, keen to elaborate on what good exposure it would be for these young musicians to be performing with them – and how they could invite agents and friends, and how indeed 'it might lead to something'.

Julian had listened, biting his tongue to prevent himself from launching into a furious tirade about money and the arts. Eventually, he had taken a deep breath and stated, quite quietly for him, that 'exposure' did not pay the rent or put food on your table, and that he would resign unless the chorus paid a small fee to all the students taking part.

One or two of the committee had had the grace to look shame-faced at his stance, and there had been some muttering along the lines of, 'Of course. Point taken.'

It was true that many of the choir were pensioners who were not – if appearances were anything to go by – rich. But the younger choristers included bankers, doctors, and heads of HR departments; individuals who would have no clue what it was like to be a freelance artist. It felt good to have struck a blow for fellow musicians as well as for decency and common sense. Even better, all these youngsters were doing a great job.

He closed his score on the two sections of Bach's *Christmas Oratorio* that they had just sung. The evening was rushing by. Rhys, who was playing the harpsichord in the orchestra, was taking a bow. Julian caught a glimpse of Wendy, radiating maternal pride.

They embarked now on a selection of carols, and then finished the concert with a very fast rendition of 'The Twelve Days of Christmas' which generated enthusiastic applause from the audience, and even a whistle or two despite the ecclesiastical environment.

Wendy lifted her glass and smiled at him across the tiny table in the crowded Italian restaurant they had found near St Mary Magdalene.

'A triumph, Julian! You must be very proud.'

He felt himself grow pink at her praise. 'I'm certainly pleased. And for the first time this year, I feel festive!'

'Are you keen on Christmas?' Wendy queried as she chased a plum tomato round the plate before finishing her *insalata caprese*.

'Not specially. I always spend it with Mum in Gorleston. My half-sister and her monstrously dull husband and charmless son usually drop in around teatime on the big day, and we all make a pretence of liking each other so we can get through a couple of hours in a civilised manner.'

Wendy burst out laughing.

'What?'

'Just the expression on your face! They can't be that bad.'

'Perhaps not,' he agreed. 'But my mother getting married to Mr Insurance Salesman when I was a teenager changed my life for ever.

He was gross; always patting her bottom and making lustful growling noises.' Julian flapped his hands in the air as if that might magic the memory away. 'Awful, awful, awful. Families, eh!'

'I used to have what I thought was a perfect family.' Wendy's voice was so unusually soft that he had to lean forward to hear her.

He nodded.

She continued at the same volume. 'And everyone came to our house in Surrey for the festivities. On Christmas mornings, before it was light, I used to try to get more sleep, but end up laughing at the sound of the twins scampering along the landing, issuing instructions to each other in stage-whispers that they mustn't wake the grown-ups. There was lots of food and board games and charades. Both sets of the kids' grandparents came, and all got on very well. Back then, my mum was a terrific grandma. Rhys in particular adored her.' There was a catch in Wendy's voice which she attempted to hide by clearing her throat then picking up her glass of water and drinking from it.

Julian pushed his empty plate out of the way and reached across the table to take her free hand in his, reminding himself that this Christmas was going to be different from all previous ones for her, and that he must support her.

'I was wondering...' her voice intruded on his thoughts '... whether maybe you and I should live together?'

He knew he looked stunned. He *was* stunned. He also knew that she had noticed.

Attempting a laugh, she apologised. 'Silly idea. Sorry. I think I'm getting a bit maudlin. I don't know what came over me.'

He escorted Wendy homewards by Tube and insisted on walking with her from Barbican station to her apartment block. Then he turned west and made his way through Smithfield Market and on along Holborn, avoiding Christmas merry-makers who spilled into his path from time to time, urging him to have a drink, or to give them money or – in one case to – 'just piss off, you posh git'.

He had laughed at that. 'Posh' was not a word he associated with himself, though perhaps his long woollen coat – purchased at enormous expense in Milan a couple of years ago – and his flowing red scarf and fedora marked him out as affluent.

'If only they knew,' he muttered to himself.

As he opened the lift gates at the second floor, he noticed a letter sticking out from under his front door. Bending to scoop it up, he felt a pulse drumming in his right temple as he realised that it must come from the landlord, because the postman had no access to individual apartments. His fingers shook as he shut the door behind him, threw off his outer clothes and tore open the envelope. Was this the notice to leave the property?

Not daring to unfold the A4 sheet of paper which would reveal the message, he took a couple of deep breaths and then, bracing his core, executed a couple of *demi-pliés*, immediately feeling old and ridiculous because he had had too much to drink and wobbled so badly that he almost toppled over.

He wandered into the kitchen. There was a half-empty bottle of cheap Prosecco in the fridge, so he poured himself a glass, even though it had lost its sparkle.

'Bit like me,' he mused, in a voice tinged with distaste.

He drained the glass before unfolding the note.

There was momentary relief – the landlord was taking the flat off the market because purchasers were 'thin on the ground' during the post-referendum uncertainty – followed by renewed anxiety as he read on to discover that the rent would rise by £350 a month. Finding that amount of money would not be easy. Perhaps he would be forced to leave.

He would sleep on it, he decided.

Unfortunately, his brain refused to stop buzzing, and the longed-for oblivion never came. What, he pondered, had Wendy meant about living together? Had she mentioned it because she was particularly lonely or upset? She had told him about her husband's unexpected visit to her place, but had seemed quite calm about it. She was distressed, not unnaturally, about Rhys announcing at the last moment that he was spending Christmas in Boston with his twin. And he knew that though she had always planned a visit to Norfolk for part of the festive season, it felt like 'second best' to spend the entire holiday there. But would any of that have prompted her to suggest they move in together? Surely she had no intention, or hope, of turning him heterosexual? He liked her so much. Loved her, probably. But his orientation was not going to change now.

The biggest concern of course was money. Did she know how little he had?

His heart could not help leaping with hope at the possibility that Wendy might solve his financial turmoil. But he felt disgusted with himself to be thinking that way... degraded by that notion... unworthy of her... a parasite. How had mid-life become so complicated? The answer had to be that he had never planned for it.

Eventually at six o'clock, having managed only a fitful snooze or two, he abandoned his bed and stood at the window, looking down on the street below. He took some deep breaths and then raised himself on tiptoe – both ankles locked together – and balanced. He managed thirty seconds without difficulty.

'Not bad, Jules. Not bad at all,' he said cheerfully. But then he caught sight of himself in the mirror and his mood plummeted. His wiry curls were all over the place and too long because he needed a haircut. His stubble looked anything but 'designer'. His velour dressing gown had a stain on its lapel. His leather slippers had seen better days and he was overweight. The reflected image shook its head at him in despair.

His mobile phone, still attached to its charger by the bed, warbled with an incoming text. Who on earth was awake at this hour?

I know u r planning to go to Norfolk 2day. Was going tomorrow, but now think I'll go today myself. Can we travel together? Would 11 am be a good train? I can get tickets.

115

Was Wendy, like him, anxious that there would be awkwardness after last night?

He texted back: *Lovely idea! Thanx so much. Love, Jx*

In the end, he was almost late. Relaxed and cheered by her message, he had watched *BBC Breakfast* while eating toast and marmalade, and fallen asleep. It was gone ten when he woke, and he reached the station with only five minutes to spare.

Wendy was at the barrier and together they jumped on the train which was excessively crowded. Both of them were weighed down by carrier bags crammed with presents, and she was trying to wheel a large suitcase through gangways not quite wide enough for it, while the rucksack he was carrying kept falling off his right shoulder and hitting passengers who were already seated.

A group of inebriated young women – sporting slightly wilted pink bunny ears – were opening bottles of cava.

Wendy looked over her shoulder at him and raised her eyebrows. Had it been such a good idea to catch this train, he wondered. There were so few empty seats and he certainly had no wish to be near this exuberant party.

One of their number screeched. 'Good riddance to that bastard, anyway – he promised me a bottle of champagne if I gave him a blow job outside the club. But afterwards just buggered off. Can't fucking trust anyone, can you?'

Julian could see Wendy's shoulders shaking as she stoically pushed her way to the end of the long carriage, and then through several more.

Eventually, in a First Class compartment they came to a halt. Everyone was silent apart from one family group comprising an elderly couple and their grandchildren.

Wendy indicated two seats facing each other with reserved tickets on them. He felt weak with relief.

'This is such a treat,' he murmured. 'What do I owe you?'

She shook her head. 'My shout, Julian. It's the least I can do. Life has been so much pleasanter for me since I've known you.

I'm sure if we hadn't met, I'd have found all the stuff with Robert – and Francesca – much harder. Also, I've found I adore singing, thanks to you. Last night's concert was wonderful. Honestly, you're just magic!'

Julian looked around the railway carriage. Almost all their fellow travellers were absorbed in laptops or tablets or Kindles. Most of them were sporting earphones. How private could their conversation be? He decided to risk it.

'You know what you said about living together?'

'Yes. Sorry. I've been worrying about that all night.'

'Me too. Well, actually not worrying so much as wondering.'

'About our different orientations?' she asked.

'Yes, but more than that. I've got virtually no savings, just a few ISAs which have hardly made any interest in years. I've earned reasonable money, but I've spent it as I went, on clothes, parties, living right in the centre of London, and far too many Tom Merrifield limited prints and sculptures. And now I'm earning less, and the couple of pensions I've got are barely worth having. It's my own fault. I can't tell you how many savings schemes I've started – only to cancel them when I felt hard up because I'd bought something I didn't need! And of course my state pension won't pay out for ten years yet. But a freelance singing career isn't something you can do for ever. The voice ages. Fashions change. So, it's not a good picture. But presumably you've got loads of dosh. How would that work? I don't want to sponge off you.'

'I'm not interested in your money!' Wendy giggled.

'No, obviously I realise it's my body you're after!' He roared with laughter and one or two of their fellow passengers looked up from their gadgets to smile in his direction.

'Seriously, Julian, money doesn't matter much to me.'

'That's because you've got plenty! Your father doubtless worked hard all his life at Norwich Union and had a generous salary and got a good pension. Without being crass, I guess you'll inherit quite a bit from him. Your own career has been massively successful too. You're sensible and prudent...' He stopped. Was he sounding envious or even a touch bitter?

She nodded. 'I'm probably not as well off as you think. I've had to shore up my business a couple of times, though it's doing fine now. And no one emerges from a divorce better off, do they? I suppose I was just thinking of us being company for each other. This year has been so bizarre that none of the usual rules seem applicable. I guess I want some fun and companionship, but also some certainty.'

'Well, I'd like those things too. But you can't get away from the fact that I'm a bit of a wastrel really.'

The way he described himself generated more giggles. He then went on to explain about his mother's poverty, and expanded on his confession about his spendthrift ways and his regrets over never having bought a property.

'We all make mistakes. Certainly I have... Anyway, you might yet meet the love of your life and if that happens, you'll want to live with him, not me!'

'Not a cat in hell's chance!' Julian pulled down the corners of his mouth into a dramatically mournful expression before grinning at her.

'You might,' she insisted. 'I – on the other hand – have done with all of that.'

The serious discussion, punctuated with peals of slightly suppressed hysterical laughter, continued for the rest of the journey as well as through lunch in a small Cypriot taverna near Norwich station.

'I just have such great times with you,' Wendy reiterated as they sipped tiny cups of sweetened Greek coffee at the end of a simple but delicious meal.

'That goes double for me,' he said. 'So, here we are! It's Christmas, or almost. What are your plans?'

'Just to spend time with Dad. We'll go and see my mother, of course. Then, on Boxing Day, my friend Minty has invited me to lunch. You liked her, didn't you? Why don't you come? Or do you have to go back to the Opera House?'

'Oh no. It's wall to wall *Nutcrackers* there! I'm not working again till January.'

'Well, I'll text you the address, as long as you think your mother can spare you. Invite her too if you like. I'm sure Minty wouldn't mind.'

Julian considered the suggestion.

He idolised his mother. But did he want to involve her in the unexpected turn that his own life had taken? And might she get the wrong idea about Wendy and decide that he fancied her? Despite all his protestations that it could never happen, she had always said that she would love to see him settled with a nice girl. And suppose she drank too much, which was a possibility if she were nervous? He did not want her to embarrass herself, let alone him.

Wendy was studying him with a quizzical expression.

'Have I told you before how like Celia Imrie you are?' he asked. 'Did you see her in those *Best Exotic* films with Judi Dench? God, she was marvellous.'

Wendy chuckled and said that she was flattered but nothing like as attractive as the actress, and somehow the subject of his mother was forgotten – or perhaps expediently dropped.

The restaurant staff pressed glasses of Greek brandy on them, and another half an hour went by while Julian drank both of them. Finally, they parted – and made their respective ways out of the city, to their elderly parents.

He got a shock as he approached his mother's house. Instead of a beautifully decorated fir or pine in her window, there was a spindly, sparse, slightly lopsided fake tree in its place. He then registered that the net curtains looked limp and grey and when he stepped inside he noticed that the house seemed to have acquired an 'uncared for' smell since his last visit.

His mother was much altered too. She was dressed in a non-too-clean track suit which was too small for her, and she seemed slightly vague and helpless, and not at all ready for his arrival. He hugged her tightly, overwhelmed not just by anxiety about her current state but his fear of the void that would claim him when she died. And there was something else; a hot sensation of guilt at what a snob he had become and how he had not wanted Wendy to invite her on Boxing Day.

'You look tired, Mum,' he said. 'Sit down, I'll make us a cuppa. I bet you've worn yourself out shopping and cooking. Busy time of year, isn't it? Christmas Eve tomorrow! We'll have a ball!'

In the kitchen, he opened the fridge, and felt renewed alarm when he saw that it was almost empty. Above it, a cake tin contained only mouldy Mr Kipling apple pies, and the ginger biscuits in the old-fashioned barrel had gone soft with age. Still, they were better than nothing, so he put them on a plate before warming the pot and making the tea. He reached for two mugs and opted to wash them before use, as they were stained and sticky to the touch.

While the tea brewed, he pushed open the door that led from the kitchen into the garage. As ever, it was a mess of recycling bins and cardboard boxes and old photo albums and a bicycle with one wheel missing. But the big chest freezer, which was normally stocked to capacity, appeared not to have been opened for weeks. Certainly, when he lifted the lid, there was no frozen turkey within, or side of pork, or bag of sprouts, or tubs of cranberry sauce and brandy butter.

Never mind, he said to himself, but then he sighed, because he *did* mind; everything he had always depended upon suddenly seemed fragile, and he had not truly realised until this moment how quickly it might disintegrate.

When he returned to the living room, his mother was asleep in the chair. He woke her, gently. As she opened her eyes, they were filled with bewilderment. But then, she shook her head as though rejecting her initial reaction, searching for a more appropriate response. After a few seconds, she clutched at him and called him 'my boy', and normality was restored.

Later, they watched *White Christmas* on the television and he rustled up a couple of omelettes and filled them with a mixture of tinned tomatoes and a few dried herbs – and, as a side dish, served a heated-up ready-meal of cauliflower cheese, which he had found at the bottom of the freezer.

'This is nice, Jules,' his mum murmured with a nodding smile. And in many ways it was.

The next day, he wondered if his mind had exaggerated her problems. She looked quite sprightly, and when he said he thought they ought to go shopping, she replied that of course they should because it was Christmas the next day and somehow she had neglected to do anything about it.

She was keen to go to a superstore near Yarmouth, but the thought of hundreds of people stocking up their trolleys to bursting as if they might never eat again filled him with queasy distaste.

'Let's shop locally,' he suggested. She agreed, though insisted upon him driving her car despite the fact that they could easily have covered the distance on foot.

'Too much to carry,' she explained. 'I'm not as young as I used to be.'

Julian decided not to comment, but he noted that this was the very first admission from her that she was feeling her age. It had to come some time, he supposed.

An hour later, they had purchased wine, mince pies, Christmas pudding and cake from the Co-op, a large basket of fresh fruit and vegetables from a farm shop, and a joint of beef – for a change, they said, as all the poultry at the butcher's was either sold or earmarked for customers who had ordered it weeks ago.

'This is the best way to shop,' his mum announced, as though it had been her idea. 'Support local industries, that's what I say!'

He managed to secure them a table for lunch in the restaurant at the Pier Hotel, where a starter of delicious crispy whitebait followed by a huge steak and ale pie and a half bottle of wine raised his spirits.

'I've just remembered,' his mother said, 'I've got tickets for the panto this afternoon at the Pavilion Theatre. Not sure I want to go now though. I'm terribly tired.'

She did look exhausted. Having begun the meal with relish, she was now pushing food around her plate as though she had insufficient energy to convey it to her mouth.

He ordered coffee from the waitress. Perhaps that would wake her up.

'What's the panto?' he asked in an over-ebullient voice. 'Such a good idea. Haven't seen one in years.'

'I forget. Have a look, Jules – the tickets are in my purse.'

He did what she asked. '*Aladdin*! My favourite!'

'Mine too. Widow Twanky's just like me – bringing up a boy without a man in the house.'

He was confused by her train of thought. Perhaps she was too. She fell silent and he watched her as she allowed her eyes to close. In repose, her facial features no longer looked like her; not the 'her' that he carried in his mind. They were heavy, and old.

Stretching out his hand to stroke hers, he found her fingers were icy to the touch. Maybe, he thought, I should get her to a doctor. But surely that would be difficult to arrange on Christmas Eve.

The coffee arrived and, much to his relief, his mother seemed to rally. Indeed, he perceived that she recognised that she was not acting normally, and seemed to be making a conscious effort to sit up straighter and be her usual self.

'You know, Jules,' she volunteered, as she spooned sugar into her cup, 'I've often wondered if I should tell you why Pop left. It must have been difficult for you. Probably I should explain things while I still can.'

His anxiety levels rose again. Did she think that she was dying?

'What do you mean, Mum?'

She gazed at her cup and said nothing more for a while. He could feel his pulse quicken as he watched her. There were huge circles under her eyes and folds in her face that until recently had not been there. Surely she was not seriously ill? If she had cancer, for example, would she not be losing weight rather than gaining it?

'Pop was a good man,' his mother began, with a faraway expression in her eyes. 'But he was too regimented for me. We didn't have much in common apart from sex, which he was quite good at. But politically, we were worlds apart. And, he was too sporty. Remember how he used to take you out to the park and try and coach you in baseball, and you didn't want to know?'

Julian had little memory of his father. But his mother's words evoked an almost forgotten feeling of unease. Of course, even then, his whole focus had been on music and dance. He had loved singing in the school and church choirs, and going to his weekly ballet class in which – in those pre-*Billy Elliot* days – he was the only boy. He remembered now that Pop used to call him a 'sissy'.

'We always knew that at some point Pop would want to go back to the States,' she continued. 'Early on, I was excited about going too. But later I went off the idea. Anyway, I was a naughty girl!'

His mother suddenly seemed to shed about thirty years as her eyes sparkled and her lips pouted. Julian beamed at her. This might be a very odd conversation to be having in a crowded restaurant, but it seemed to be doing her good.

'Were you unfaithful to him?' he asked.

'I'm afraid so. I started going out to dances when he was on the base working late. The woman next door used to keep an eye on you. I never met anyone serious. It was just a bit of fun. But then I did a really silly thing...'

'You're sure you want to tell me this?'

123

She nodded. 'The posh school Pop sent you to always had lots of stuff going on that parents could go to. And at one concert, I bumped into Dr Richard Yateman, whose son, it turned out, went there too. But the thing is, years before that, I'd had a fling with the doc, when I was a barmaid in a pub he used to come into. Anyway, we were chatting, and I mentioned that it was my son who'd sung a solo in the last piece. Richard congratulated me, and I said something like "Well maybe he gets his talent from you!". We had a giggle and that was that. But his little boy, who was running around, had heard our conversation, and though he probably didn't understand it, he told his mum and there was an argument. And then Pop wanted to know what was going on. All a bit embarrassing. I was only having a laugh. There's no way that Richard was your dad. But things went badly downhill at home after that. And soon afterwards, Pop said he was going home to South Carolina.'

Julian picked up a tumbler of water from the table in front of him and drank it dry. He had had no idea of his mother's connection to the old doctor. But the son, of course, would have been Nigel Yateman, who had been Philip's friend. It was obvious to him now that soon after the concert, Nigel must have told Philip about the incident, and that that was why Philip had called his mother 'a slag' – and why, as a consequence, he had fallen out with his very closest mate.

He had no recollection of having met Dr Yateman before seeing him recently in the Seastrand nursing home. The old chap was still stylish, and it was easy to see how dashing he might have been in his youth. Fancy his mum having had a liaison with him. Life was full of surprises.

Suddenly, she slumped sideways. Having recounted the story of her past in such a lively way, the problems of the present were reclaiming her.

He paid the bill and then urged her into a standing position. The pantomime might cheer her up.

Inside the theatre, he bought a programme and pressed it into her hand then propelled her past a group of jostling children buying Aladdin magic lamps from the merchandise stand and finally got her seated, just before the curtain went up.

'This'll be good, Mum,' he murmured as the music started. And it was. It was just a pity that she slept throughout.

Chapter Ten

So looking 4ward to lunch on Boxing Day. Can I bring
Julian? He's spending Xmas with his mum in Gorleston.
Also, looking 4ward to seeing Hannah again. Wx

Wendy's text gave Araminta a welcome if temporary lift. She
was filled with trepidation about Christmas. In fact, ever since she
had made the hideous discovery that Michael appeared to be
pursuing her daughter, she had longed to crawl under a duvet
and hide till the festivities were over.

After her dinner with him at the beginning of the month – and
what a long time ago that seemed now – she had fantasised about
spending Christmas evening with him, eating wonderful food,
sitting before an open fire and cosseting him after his busiest time
of the year. She blushed with mortification now at such audacious
imaginings. The truth was, she realised, she had grown too fond
of him, and had allowed herself to imagine that he might care for
her too, because that was what she wanted to believe.

The doorbell rang. It was time to get into 'therapy mode'. She
had agreed to see two patients today – even though it was Christmas
Eve. Katie was coming later, but first she had taken on a new client.

The middle-aged man, who had been abandoned by his wife,
slumped into the chair opposite hers, tears streaming down his

face. She made him a mug of tea, but he was barely able to lift it to his lips because his hands were trembling so violently.

'At what point,' he sobbed, 'did she find my penis inadequate?'

Oh, here we go, Araminta sighed inwardly. Heartbroken women always discussed how their partner had never listened to them, or had failed to be emotionally supportive when the children were small. But the men inevitably focused on their sexual territory and equipment.

'I expect her new lover has a much bigger cock. They're probably "at it" all the time. She says she's never been so passionately in love before. That can only mean he turns her on more than I did.'

This was not the moment to disagree. What her heartbroken patient needed was for her to mentally hold his hand and accept – with him – the enormity of what he was suffering.

Katie was very different. She burst into the consulting room, all smiles, and keen to discuss the details of her trip to Ireland.

'So, it was good then?' Araminta smiled encouragingly.

'Fantastic! Philip's mother is a grand old Anglo-Irish lady, and phenomenally rich – and she adored me! We stayed in the gorgeous hotel that she owns. It's called The Fitzhenry. How cool is that? It's her maiden name!'

'And how are things going with Philip?'

'Um, OK.'

'You don't sound very sure.'

'Well, I haven't seen a lot of him, and when we have met, I haven't felt like going to bed with him. Work's been crazy at the studios. And he's had stuff to do like his staff party and drinks with clients. But he still seems seriously keen on me, though after we got back from Ireland, his bloody wife managed to seduce him. He admitted it, because he felt he should. He's too decent for his own good, really. Thing is, you can't get over the fact that there's a huge age difference. And another problem is that he's a bit needy – which isn't attractive. So, I've got a plan! As I said, his mother loves me – so much so that she'd like me to go and live with her, and to be honest, that's very convenient for me, because I've been looking for a way to get off the television tread-mill for a while. I know it sounds self-indulgent, but hey, I fancy a bit of pampering and Irish comfort.'

'Well that certainly would be quite a change.'

'I'll say! Nora – that's her name – and I have been in touch since I got back and she says I could learn the business and help her run the hotel. So, she's sent me an air ticket to Cork for Christmas, and booked and paid for a taxi the other end to the hotel. And I'm going to go tonight on the ten o'clock flight. I can't imagine what Philip's going to think. We agreed that he'd spend one last Christmas at his home. Someone called Bro – that's his brother-in-law – is coming, and that seems to matter. Funny what ties people into the past, isn't it? I'm afraid I lied and said I was going to see my mum, so he doesn't have a clue that it's *his* mother I'll be with, let alone that it might be a permanent move. Is that awful? Thing is, I'll never get another offer like this. And I never did fancy the bohemian lifestyle in Shoreditch he kept going on about.'

Araminta listened, trying to empathise with her client, but failing. She knew from what Katie had told her in previous sessions just what emotional upheaval her married boyfriend had been going through. She had the impression that he was a man of integrity, not generally given to putting himself first, but now desperate to have a new life with his younger girlfriend. Basically however, it seemed that Katie had got what she wanted from him – a baby – and that she saw him now as dispensable. Mind you, there had been absolutely no mention of the child today, which seemed odd.

'Well,' she replied with a bright tone that sounded false in her own ears, 'sometimes solutions present themselves in ways that we never expected.'

'You can say that again,' laughed Katie. 'The other weird thing is that Greg got in touch.'

'Greg!'

'Yeah, my ex. He texted out of the blue. Can you believe it, after what he did to me? Still, as it happens, he's flying to Scotland this evening from Heathrow, so as we'll both be at the airport, we're going to have a coffee at the terminal. It would be romantic if it weren't so bloody odd. Anyway, I think I better cut this short now. I need to go and pack.'

'OK. I'll invoice you for this month's sessions at your Norwich address, shall I?'

'Oh! No, I'll pay now. I've got loads of cash from Nora.' Katie pulled a bulging envelope from her pocket.

'They're euros.'

'Oh yeah, sorry. It won't matter, will it? You can use them on your next holiday. It'll just help me.' And so saying Katie peeled off several large denomination notes and thrust them towards her. 'That should more than cover it,' she declared airily, before sweeping up her coat and leaving.

Araminta did not follow her to the door, but remained seated. She felt disappointed. Worse than that – though she was resisting the mood because she was sure it was an overreaction – she felt insulted. Having money virtually thrown at her felt degrading. Maybe this was what prostitutes felt like when a client, having taken his pleasure, paid as swiftly as possible without a thought for the sensibilities of the woman who had serviced him. Somehow, she must keep a sense of proportion even though, right now – and devastatingly – she felt nothing but despair.

'Do I want to carry on with this job?' she asked aloud as she forced herself out of her chair and began filing away her notes.

When she had had two children at home, being a therapist had been the perfect occupation, but as her circumstances had changed, she had changed too. And now this last session with Katie had seemed so dreadful, that she felt disinclined to continue. One thing was certain, she would never see Katie again. If the younger woman needed further help, she would refer her to a colleague.

It was somewhat liberating, yet an anxiety at the same time, to be considering a change of career. What she really longed for was to be back in television, or at least to have a job where she was with people, and could organise schedules and travel. But could that possibly happen at her age? She needed to think things through properly, and now was hardly the time, while she was so consumed with distress about Michael and Hannah.

As she walked up the stairs from the basement, she acknowledged that there was another pressing problem – one she had, quite frankly, been in denial about – which was the necessity to make money.

Before he died, Simon had raided his pensions to buy the Harley-Davidson and various other gadgets he saw as necessary for his retirement, so the proportion of what should have filtered through to her after the accident had been reduced considerably. He had also re-mortgaged their house in order to buy the London flat, which – after his death – she had given to Hannah, without mentioning how it had been financed.

So, here she was, rattling around in a four-bedroomed house that she only partly owned, with no viable way of making a decent salary, and living well beyond her means. Her only gesture towards economising had been to lock her car in the garage when the tax and MOT had become due recently, and to use public transport.

In the kitchen, thoughts of Michael drifted into her mind. Tomorrow, assuming that she was right about him and Hannah, she was going to have to look and act as if she was happy for them both. She hoped she could rise to the challenge.

Unutterably tired suddenly, she stretched out on the old sofa and fell asleep.

*

The tree, a Nordmann fir, which she had decorated a few days ago, looked stunning with its silver glass ornaments that shimmered in the firelight. She hoped it would conjure up some seasonal magic for Hannah.

Her daughter had texted while she had been asleep. It was obvious that she was excited about a traditional Christmas at home, and also about her 'amazing news' which she could not wait to share.

So, it had to be true. It would be Hannah and Michael from now on.

What *was* her lovely daughter thinking? Knowing all too well how large the twelve years' age gap had seemed between her and Simon, she could not conceive of how huge thirty years must feel.

Naturally, she could see what was propelling Michael. He regretted that he had spent his life as a celibate and was childless, and was obviously biologically driven to find a partner with whom he could make babies.

A phone call from Hannah interrupted her thoughts.

'Darling, where are you? Is your train delayed? I know Christmas Eve travel can be hell.'

'No, Mum, it's all cool. I've... erm... Look, I hope you don't mind but I've decided to stay at Grandad's. I, uh, I spoke to the cleaner and she's away over Christmas and I thought suddenly that it might not be a very good idea to leave the house empty with no one popping in. You know how boisterous it can get in Tombland with everyone drinking. That's OK, isn't it?'

Araminta shook her head in disbelief. What fresh hell was this? Perhaps Michael was there, in her father's house.

'Mum?'

'What? Oh sorry. Yes, fine – if it's what you want. Are you coming to Midnight Mass?'

'That's not really me, is it? So, I'll see you for a late lunch tomorrow after I go over to see Grandad.'

'You're going out there in the morning?'

131

Hannah's tone was patient. 'Mum, you said you'd be at St Mark's, so it makes sense for me to go while you're busy with that.'

'But how will you get there? There won't be any trains.'

'Don't worry, I've made arrangements.'

Araminta let her head drop back as she looked up at the ceiling, trying to work out how to continue this conversation as if everything was entirely normal, which clearly it was not. 'OK. Well, don't be too upset when you see him, he's fading fast – at least that's how it seemed the other day.'

'Don't worry, Mum. Have a lovely evening.'

It was gone nine. Time to have a bath and get ready, but first she really needed a large courage-inducing glass of wine. She just had to get this Mass over with. Then the one in the morning, and – somehow – negotiate the next couple of days. After that, perhaps she could get away somewhere.

She chose a tumbler rather than a wine glass for her Rioja.

You're still drinking too much, Mum. I told you about it before.

It was only when she was very tired or overwrought that she imagined her late son talking to her. Perhaps it was when she missed him most. She missed his girlfriend too, who had dealt with her grief by going travelling after Andrew's death, and had ended up staying in Australia. Perhaps if things had been different, they would still be together. Married even – and possibly thinking about having a family. Maybe that was the worst part of bereavement – the never-ending 'what if' about a future that had been cut off before it could happen.

The Mass with all its celebration and joy was over. Araminta pushed her way out of the still crowded church, wishing various people 'Happy Christmas' as she went. Michael was at the front door, shaking hands with everyone in sight. She avoided him. 'Jolly good' she heard him say, and despite her dejection she smiled at his trademark phrase. Sneaking a look at him, her heart automatically contracted with pity as she saw how exhausted he looked.

Turning away, she began walking as fast as she could towards her house. It was raining and not at all like the cold crisp weather people hoped for at Christmas. A drunk lurched towards her, but just as quickly staggered backwards and steadied himself by grasping someone's front gate. He meant no harm.

Her umbrella almost blew inside out, so she collapsed it and relied instead on the hood of her duffle coat to keep her dry. Soon she could sleep, and in the morning she would put on a bright face, sing in the choir, cook, entertain, pretend to be happy for her daughter and Michael, then do her Boxing Day lunch, and after that, her time would be her own. Perhaps she should go and try to repair her relationship with her brother? Barbados at this time of year would surely be a tonic.

She had been so deep in thought that she was surprised to realise how near she was to her home.

Someone was running. That was what had disturbed her. It could be nothing to do with her, unless it was a mugger who had spotted a woman walking on her own. Don't turn around, she told herself as she reached the front door and, after a couple of attempts, managed to get her key into the lock. Breathe deeply. You're almost indoors.

'Araminta!'

She swivelled towards the voice. Michael, breathless and very, very wet, stood panting on her front path.

'I had to see you,' he gasped.

'It's almost one o'clock,' she whispered as she pushed open the front door and reached for the light.

'I know.' He adjusted his voice to her volume. 'And I was going to leave it till after Christmas. But I can't. We have to talk now.'

'Look, I gather you have exciting news, but tell me tomorrow.'

'I don't know what you think the news is, but I need you to hear the truth now.'

Against her better judgement, she stood back to allow him to enter the house. 'You're very masterful,' she said. To her horror, she realised that she sounded flirtatious, which was completely, and embarrassingly, inappropriate.

He closed the front door behind him and then removed his spectacles before reaching into a pocket for a handkerchief to wipe the lenses. As he put the glasses back on his nose, he looked straight at her and mumbled. 'Please don't mock me.'

She was shocked. 'Michael! I would *never* do that. What a thing to say. Come on, we'll go into the kitchen.'

The warmth hit them as they walked in and they scrambled out of their wet coats and abandoned them on a chair near the door. Without asking what he might like to drink, Araminta picked up two wine glasses from the draining board and filled them with the remains of the bottle of Rioja she had been drinking earlier, then headed for the sofa.

As Michael sat down at one end of it, he looked nervously at the door which was ajar. 'Is Hannah here?'

'No – she's at my father's house. I rather imagined you'd know that.'

'Why? Why would I know that? Oh Lord, this is such a mess. I think you think something that is *so* not true that I can't believe you would think it.'

'That's quite a convoluted sentence and I might need a moment to untangle it,' she remarked as the great heaviness in her chest seemed to shift slightly.

'OK, this is hard, but just listen. Sorry to be bossy. The first thing to say is that tomorrow's mid-morning Mass will be my last one as a priest.'

'What!'

He nodded. 'I don't know exactly what I'm going to do but after the upset with you that night at the presbytery, and then talking to Philip, I came to the conclusion that I couldn't go on in the church. It would be wrong. But I want you to know that I still believe, very powerfully, that the gospels' message offers us the best way of living a good life. However, despite that, I feel I can no longer deal with the demands of the priesthood. I've been struggling with desperate loneliness for ages, but then I fell in love, and that changed everything. And though that love may not be reciprocated and may indeed not work out, I have to try. And that's why I'm here. You think it's Hannah, don't you? That I'm turning my life upside down for her?'

Araminta avoided his gaze but nodded.

'Do you *really* think that's likely?'

She looked up and caught his eye, then – with a shamefaced expression – slowly shook her head.

'Well, thank goodness for that.'

'Amen,' she said without thinking. 'Sorry, but I've been trying to get my head around you becoming my son-in-law.'

'You're an idiot,' Michael laughed. 'A very lovely one, but completely barmy. I've been trying to tell you for months that I love *you*. Now, I don't expect you to feel the same but I thought – before things went wrong – that we got on well, and I wonder if you will at least let us meet up and see each other in a different light and let me try…'

Araminta put down her glass on the table in front of them. Then she reached for his hands and held them tightly in hers. After a moment, she took a deep breath, leaned towards him and kissed him lightly on his lips. 'I love you too,' she whispered.

Somehow then, they found themselves in each other's arms kissing, hugging, laughing and crying all at once. Eventually, he pulled away.

'Darling, Araminta.'

She removed his glasses, which had steamed up, and kissed him again before wiping them on her skirt and handing them back. 'You can call me Minty, you know. My old friends do.'

'No. I've always loved you as "Araminta". I couldn't possibly call you anything else.'

She beamed at him, and they stared into each other's eyes as if they were searching for a clue as to why this miraculous moment was happening to them. 'By the way,' she said, 'Happy Christmas!'

His smile lit up his entire face, and then he laughed and kissed her again.

She pulled away suddenly. 'Oh – I haven't bought you a present.'

He took her hands in his. 'Darling girl,' he whispered. '*You* are the only gift I've ever really wanted. And all I want from you is your help in getting me attuned to a completely different way of life. For a start, romantically, I'm a total novice. I've rarely kissed a woman – and till just now, hadn't attempted it since I was nineteen! Also, and I blush to tell you, I've never had sex, so if we ever progress to the bedroom you're going to have to be very patient.'

She felt her own cheeks redden, but then suggested, 'We could progress there now if you like.'

'Araminta!' He looked shocked and she worried that she had gone too far but then he smiled. 'Sorry, but I think we should wait till I've said my last Mass.'

'Of course. But are you really giving up? I mean, that is a huge thing. What will you do?'

'I'm going to try not to think about the future until I've had a rest. But unlike some other priests I've known, I've decided against joining the Anglican ministry. I know that would have given me a role, but I've always been a Catholic and I'll die one too.'

'I understand that… I'll help you… I've been so unhappy, Michael. I… I grew more and more desperate for your love, but I knew I shouldn't think that way – bearing in mind your vocation – and then it all seemed to be going wrong. But I worry if you know me that you'll lose interest. I mean, there are awful things about me. I didn't really love my husband enough, though I did hold it together, and we were good companions. But much worse than that, I hated getting pregnant with Andrew and having to get married at twenty-three. It felt like a trap, and it was ages before I bonded with my son because, partly, I resented him. No nice person would have acted that way, just because they couldn't carry on working in television.'

136

'You do beat yourself up, don't you? Some people in your situation might have refused to marry and had the baby adopted.'

'*Adopted!* He was my own child! I couldn't have done that.'

Michael smiled again. 'There's so much I need to know about you but the main thing I have to tell you is that I like what I know, indeed I love what I know, and I'm sure I always will.'

Araminta beamed at him. 'What now?'

'I must drag myself away – and believe me, I really don't want to – and go and get some sleep, and then make the best job I can of my last two Masses. Will you come to the eleven o'clock?'

'Of course. I'm singing in it, don't forget.' And suddenly she was enormously pleased that that was the case. Leaning towards him, she pressed her lips to his and felt the responding pressure and love and passion from him. Then she stood up and fetched his coat, and helped him into it before carefully tying his scarf around his neck.

Arm in arm they walked to the front door. As she opened it, he clung to her for a moment.

'Will you come for lunch?' she asked as she drew back from his embrace.

'I'd love to, but I can't. I must honour my commitment to the retired priests who always come to eat at the presbytery on Christmas Day.'

'Supper then?'

'Fantastic.'

'I'm not taking things too fast, am I? You do want to come?'

He raised his eyebrows in a comic expression. 'What do *you* think?' He chuckled, then stepped outside the door, grimaced at the pouring rain, blew her a kiss and sprinted away.

It was only as she returned to the kitchen and started rinsing their glasses that she wondered what on earth Hannah had meant about having 'amazing news'. Well, nothing could be more earth-shattering than what had just happened, she thought as a wave of absolute bliss swept over her with such dizzying power that she had to sit down.

Chapter Eleven

'Hey, Mum. It's a quarter past eight. Shouldn't you be getting up?'

Araminta struggled out of her deep slumber, and fought to free herself from the top sheet which had wrapped itself round her right arm. Then she sat up and attempted to look more awake than she felt, as she processed the fact that her daughter was indeed in her bedroom.

'Merry Christmas!' Hannah pushed the tray bearing a teapot, two mugs, a jug of milk and a plate of home-baked chocolate chip cookies onto her mother's lap, and then hugged her before bounding over to the window to open the curtains. 'Thankfully, it's stopped raining,' she said. 'It didn't feel at all Christmassy when we arrived. But there's a slight frost today and a blue sky.'

'Who's we?'

Hannah swung around with a huge grin on her face. 'That's the reason I'm here. I couldn't wait another minute to tell you. I've brought someone to Norwich with me.'

'Najid? How marvellous. Will he be OK with celebrating Christmas?'

'They celebrate everything! But it's not him. It's Farid… Sorry, I know I must look dreadful,' she turned to appraise herself in the dressing table mirror and flick a strand of hair behind her right ear, 'because basically, well, let's say there's been very little sleep, but it's been fantastic. I had no idea sex could be so mind-blowing! I can't wait for you to meet him.'

Araminta started to giggle.

'What's funny?' Hannah looked puzzled.

'I can't tell you,' she replied as she had a sudden vision of what might have transpired had Michael stayed overnight and her daughter discovered them together.

'You're very mysterious.'

'Not really. Sit down.' Araminta patted the bed beside her, before picking up the pot and filling the two mugs with tea, one of which she held out for Hannah. 'Now, who's Farid?'

'Oh – of course you don't know. He's Najid's younger brother.'

'Good heavens!'

Hannah giggled. 'I know! It was a bit awkward at first but it's OK now.' She reached for a biscuit. 'Mmmn, these are great.'

'You can't beat Nigella's recipes at Christmas! So, what's he like?'

'Wonderful! A doctor. Seriously clever. He wants to specialise in genetic medicine and he's taken a year out to do an MSc in something terrifically complicated to do with that. He's very ambitious and great fun!'

'And gorgeous?'

Hannah lowered her eyes and gazed at the leaf-green throw at the foot of the bed. Her dimples were much in evidence as she blushed and curled her lips into a satisfied smile.

Watching her, Araminta felt a stab of regret; something was different this time. Could this new man be a long-term prospect? More than anything in the world, she wanted Hannah to find happiness, but it was so sudden. His brother had been delightful but, quite clearly, had not thrilled her daughter in the way that his sibling did.

'Don't be sad, Mum. It's brilliant.' Hannah chortled. 'And he's taking me away for a little break, on Wednesday. I can't wait!'

'I'm not sad! Where are you off to?'

'Oh!' Hannah took a gulp of tea. 'Not sure. It's a surprise.'

Araminta beamed at her daughter. 'So, you're still coming for lunch today?'

'Definitely!'

'I suppose Farid eats turkey and drinks wine?'

'Of course. He was born and brought up here. His mother and father have been in England since they were students in the seventies – but because of the revolution in Iran in 1979, they never went back.

'Well, I'm very pleased for you, but I hope Najid's OK.'

'He's cool! So, I'm taking Farid out to Cromer shortly. We picked up a hire car yesterday so we can get around. I want him to meet Grandad before it's too late… Talking of being too late, hadn't you better get moving?'

'The choir doesn't sing at the 9.30. I'm not due there till mid-morning.'

'Oh, have another cup of tea then! But I must go. By the way, you don't mind if we leave right after lunch, do you? I know you usually have the neighbours in for drinks on Christmas evening, so you won't be alone. I want to introduce Farid to the crowd. They're nearly all home with their parents.'

'No, go ahead.'

Hannah had always kept up with a sizeable group of friends from her school days. They were quite competitive with each other, and she imagined that her daughter was eager to reveal her new boyfriend to them.

'Thanks, Mum. You'll be OK, won't you?'

'Of course.' She knew she ought to mention that Michael was coming and also that she had not invited any neighbours for drinks this year. However, while she was pondering what to say, Hannah leant over to kiss her in preparation for leaving.

'Your present's under the tree, but no peeking till after lunch!' Her daughter laughed as she disappeared out of the door.

'How exciting. What is it?'

The reply floated up the stairs. 'You'll have to wait. Love you!'

The exuberance of youth, mused Araminta as she felt – as well as heard – the judder that the front door made when Hannah slammed it. Her lovely girl had always been blessed with huge energy, but today she was even more effervescent than usual. In fact, the house seemed suddenly quiet and empty without her.

She sipped at her tea and then breathed in deeply and exhaled slowly. What an extraordinary few hours she was having. Yesterday morning, she had been engulfed by gloom. Today she had never felt happier.

Last night, she had sat for a while by the Aga, unable quite to believe that Michael's visit had taken place. Though she had been certain she was too excited to sleep, eventually she had climbed the stairs to her bedroom, and hummed carols to herself as she had removed her make-up, noticing as she did so that the haunted expression she had worn for the past few weeks had disappeared. Naturally, they had massive hurdles to surmount, but they had each other. What could go wrong now?

She had tried to read, but had had little appetite for the somewhat moody novel on her bedside table. So she had switched off the light and replayed her discussion with Michael till she had fallen into the contented sleep in which her daughter had found her.

Glancing at her watch, she worked out that she had a couple of hours to herself before leaving for Mass, which meant that as well as preparing the lunch, she could spend some time planning a special supper for Michael. Recalling how bouncy Hannah had been, she realised that she too had a lightness of being today that was generating the most exhilarating energy she could remember. I would so love to bottle this feeling, she thought. But there again, perhaps there was no need; if she was lucky, she might feel this good for the rest of her life!

Happy Christmas! R u having fun? Dad and I about to go to see Mum. Then going to the Country Club 4 lunch. Dad's booked taxis both ways! Very relieved. He's such a cautious driver these days. Makes me nervous! He's still better than me though! Looking 4ward to seeing you tomorrow. Will you come in by train? Shall we meet at Norwich station? W xx

Julian read the text twice. Thank God for Wendy.

His mother had been quite vivacious first thing but had now returned to her bed, pleading exhaustion. He had googled 'tiredness in older people' on his phone and had been confronted with a range of worrying possibilities including dementia. He knew that Wendy's mother had Alzheimer's so perhaps he should ask her how it had started. On the other hand, it was not a very Christmassy thing to do. He would leave it till tomorrow.

Yes, station – great. Have tremendous lunch. We're staying in. But had terrific food at the Pier Hotel here yesterday. Catering in Norfolk much improved since our youth! J xx

The doorbell rang. Surely his sister and family were not going to break the habit of a lifetime and turn up early. That would be a nightmare. Quite apart from having to make polite conversation for longer than usual, the joint of beef would never stretch to feed five.

A large black man with bushy, greying Afro hair, dressed in a Hawaiian shirt and sports trousers – and carrying a bunch of bronze chrysanthemums – stood on the front path.

'I'm Joe,' he announced in a deep, musical voice, 'your mother's newish neighbour. You must be Julian.'

Julian accepted the flowers and stood back, indicating that the visitor should come in, which he did, walking purposefully through the hall and into the kitchen with the assurance of someone who visited regularly.

Julian followed him. 'Mum's having a little nap. Coffee?'

'Thanks – if you've got time,' answered the guest as he seated himself at the kitchen table.

Julian placed his left hand on his hip as he answered, somewhat sardonically. 'Everyone has time at Christmas, don't they?'

'Are you talking about the days feeling extra-long when you have to spend them with family?' Joe's accent was an attractive blend of the Caribbean and Norfolk.

'God, am I that obvious? I'm bracing myself for my half-sister coming later. Have you got a houseful?'

'No. Both parents are dead. I've got a sister, older than me, but she's in Jamaica. I'm on my own now, since my partner left me.'

Julian was unsure what to say.

'Your mother's been very kind,' the stranger went on. 'She's lovely.'

Julian, who was engaged in pouring the coffee, turned to Joe and nodded. 'Yes, she really is.' He put sugar and milk on the table before handing one mug to Joe and cradling the other in his hands.

'Before you came yesterday,' Joe asked, 'how long was it since you'd seen her?'

'Not long,' Julian answered quickly. Did the neighbour think he neglected his mother?

'I was wondering whether you'd noticed anything different about her?'

'Well...' Julian hesitated as he asked himself whether it was fitting to confide in someone he had known for so few minutes.

Joe peered at him with an enquiring expression on his large, pleasant face.

'I wondered,' Julian began again, 'if I was imagining it, but she's put on a lot of weight, and she's tired all the time and not very organised, which isn't like her.'

Joe helped himself to a heaped spoonful of sugar and stirred it into his coffee. 'Well, I'm no expert, but I do work part-time at a local nursing home and I'm sure there's something wrong, and that she should see her doc and get some tests.'

Julian sat down heavily.

'Sorry,' Joe murmured.

'No, don't be. I'd come to the same conclusion and I—'

There was a loud noise upstairs. The men looked at each other, before Julian jumped up and raced out into the hall. 'Are you OK, Mum?'

'Yes,' she called. 'I think so. I want to take some old VHS tapes to the charity shop, but I've dropped the lot.'

Julian took the stairs two at a time and led his mother back to bed, explaining that the charity shop would not be open for several days and encouraging her to have more rest before lunch.

'Sorry,' he said as he returned. 'You're so right. I'll take her to the doctor after the holiday. Thanks for marking my card. You always know that your parents will show signs of age at some point, don't you? But when it happens, it's still a surprise. It's good she's got you next door!'

Joe nodded in a slightly embarrassed way.

'Look, Joe, what are you doing for lunch? Would you like to join us?'

'Oh, no. Thanks, but I'm working.'

'Today?'

'Someone has to,' Joe answered quite earnestly. 'And as one of the few members of the team who lives alone, I thought it should be me. Everyone's grateful. I'm pleased to be busy. And get double pay!' He drained his mug, and stood up. 'Must go. Say "Happy Christmas" to Vera.'

'Why don't you pop in tonight and have a drink with us and you can say it yourself?'

There was a slightly awkward pause.

'Only if you want to, of course,' Julian added to fill the silence.

Joe appeared to be considering his options. 'I do want to,' he replied, slowly. 'Gotta go now, though.' And without turning back, he walked to the front door and left, closing it carefully behind him.

*

At precisely twelve noon, the phone rang. Some things never change, thought Philip as he reached for it. 'Hello, Ma. Happy Christmas!'

She babbled at him about the hotel being full and the bar being busier than she had ever seen it. As he listened, he smiled, enjoying – as he always did – her relentless enthusiasm. With his other ear, he could hear Marigold preparing for the Christmas lunchtime drinks they held every year. He wondered if Bro would make it downstairs in time.

He and his brother-in-law had arrived home around one o'clock this morning looking, as Marigold called it 'rather the worse for wear' – after several drinks in The Glass House pub, prior to the midnight service at Norwich Cathedral. The festivities were following their customary pattern. It was as if some giant in the heavens had placed a sticking plaster of normality over the turbulence of the last few months.

'And, Katie is looking very well this morning!' His mother's voice was filled with pride and delight.

Suddenly, his mind was alert and his body tense in response to the reminder that, in fact, everything had changed since last year.

'Katie! Katie is with *you*?'

'Yes. Surely I told you I'd sent her an air ticket? I must have done. I'm just surprised you decided to spend Christmas at home with Miss Marigold. You'd be having a much better time here, I can tell you. I'm drinking Guinness and champagne out of a pewter tankard. It's fantastic! D'you know, I think I can just see a little bump in Katie's tummy now. Thrilling!'

The doorbell rang. 'Ma, I'm going to have to ring you back, sorry.' He replaced the handset just as Marigold sashayed towards him, heading for the front door. She paused for a second. 'My God, you look awful, Philip. Can you get the drinks?'

He watched as his wife ushered in the first of their guests, her voice uttering the same insincere pleasantries she had deployed every year since they had moved here. It had been her idea to reinstate the custom, started by his grandfather, of inviting 'the workers' for Christmas Day drinks. He sighed. It was hideously feudal. And he was quite sure that the company employees would have preferred to spend this time in the 'local', or with their families, rather than have to spruce themselves up and come along to please 'the folks at the big house'. But Marigold persisted with the ritual, and so the nonsense of fizzy wine, sausages on sticks, cheese straws and the patronising tone his wife reserved for individuals not of her class continued. It made him sick to his stomach.

He retreated to the kitchen and started to pour Prosecco into the glasses that Marigold had assembled on a silver tray. Then, after furtively looking behind him, he opened another bottle and drank straight from it. You're being childish, he told himself, but he needed anaesthesia, and he needed it fast. He had once sunk a yard of ale at a student rag week however, he discovered, it was harder to consume an effervescent drink at speed. Still, he persevered.

Why had he felt he should spend Christmas at home? He was unsure about that now but resolutely certain in that moment that next year would be different. With that thought acting as a protective barrier between him and the nightmare of the sixty minutes that was to come, he picked up the drinks tray and pulled back his shoulders. 'On parade!' he cried, in an exaggerated imitation of his father's voice and strode towards the sitting room.

Michael pulled on his white vestments. The vestry was bustling with cheery servers and readers who were creating a surround of sound, leaving him silent in the centre of it as he recalled his first Christmas Day Mass and decades of subsequent ones. Would there really be no more?

It was not that he regretted his decision. He had been awake all night after his visit to Araminta – exhilarated about his future and feeling more fortunate than he deserved to be. But now that it came to it, he felt disloyal about abandoning the priesthood. However, surely the church demanded too much of its own now that people lived so long? Even Popes could retire.

'What if it doesn't work out?' The Monsignor, whom he had approached to discuss his laicisation, had asked the previous week when they had met up. 'We both know how often people leave partners for someone else who turns out not to be so special once the passion is spent. You're turning your back on more than a marriage. Your priesthood spans your entire adult life. You don't know anything else. You've never lived as a lay person. You've had a built-in status. You might feel totally lost wearing an ordinary collar and tie.'

Michael had listened carefully to the senior priest's argument, but throughout several days of deliberations and meetings he had retained his overwhelming wish to be with someone special of his own, and to belong to her.

He was about to switch off his phone when, on a whim and to settle himself, he decided to text Philip. But his fingers were clumsy and when he read back his first three words he realised that the infernal machine had decided on its own interpretation of what he was attempting to say, and had spelled out: *Last evening massive.* He smiled at the way the predictive text had perfectly summed up the enormity of the night before. Erasing it, he carefully spelled out the correct version: *Last ever Mass. Speak later.*

Father David coughed and looked at his watch.

Michael nodded, and said, 'Right, let's go!'

Araminta wondered if anyone else would notice that she had eyes only for Michael. Looking at him, she reflected that no one would guess what momentous decisions were taking place, and what turmoil the parish's priest was going through.

He sang the carols as lustily as ever – the microphone picking up his pleasant light-baritone voice and augmenting it so that it sounded almost as if he were a soloist accompanying the choir.

He was especially good with the children when he invited them, and their new toys, up to the front of the church for his homily. He joked with them, as they jostled each other in their enthusiasm to show off the gifts that Father Christmas had brought. No one knew yet that he was bowing out of everything he did so well.

Surveying the crowds in the church, it was clear to her just how much the congregation admired him. Could Father Michael Chapman, everyone's friend, really relinquish this universal affection in favour of her love alone? And could she ever return to St Mark's, which meant so very much to her? Could he?

She allowed her gaze to roam around the wonderful old building as though she were a film camera; the Nativity scene with its crib and painted wooden figures, the festive red and white flowers, a little girl – dressed in green velvet – jumping up and down and clapping her hands at the thrill of the season, an arthritic gentleman who hauled himself into a standing position so that he could offer the sign of peace to those across the aisle from himself, and the berry-laden holly that decorated the window ledges. The beauty of it swept over her like a tsunami. And when the choir began to sing the Agnus Dei, she found that she could not continue after the first few notes because tears misted her eyes and choked her throat.

She chose not to join the communion queue, having come to a swift decision that it was not appropriate for her to receive the sacrament when she was about to help the priest administering it to break his vows.

The organ thundered into life with 'O Come All Ye Faithful'. Michael's voice was strong and true. Hers, by contrast, was wavery. She hoped no one else would notice.

Wendy watched as her father helped her mother to unwrap presents that meant nothing to her. All around, families affecting the same artificial brightness were going through similar rituals with their poorly relatives.

'Look,' the middle-aged man across from her said to his elderly father. 'Look what I've brought you. Aren't you a lucky boy...?' The words faded in the face of a blank, unimpressed stare.

Her mother was in a civil mood today. She seemed calmer in her husband's presence. Perhaps because he came so frequently, she had more concept of him being part of her life even if she did not know exactly who he was.

Suddenly, in the doorway, Wendy spied Hannah. The young woman was scanning the room – undoubtedly searching for her grandfather. She was accompanied by a tall, handsome stranger of Middle Eastern appearance. Wendy waved, and Minty's daughter ran over and kissed her, before turning to the older couple and saying, 'Lovely to meet you, Mr and Mrs Lawrence.'

Wendy's mother peered vacantly at the newcomer, but her father rose to shake hands with Hannah and nodded to the young man beside her.

'I'm coming to your mum's for lunch tomorrow,' Wendy announced, to fill the sudden gap in small talk. 'So we can have a chat then. Really looking forward to it. By the way, your grandfather's probably in the other lounge.'

'Thanks, Wendy.' Hannah smiled broadly as she backed away.

'That's Dr Richard Yateman's granddaughter,' Wendy explained to her father. 'Have you met him yet? We could go and say "hello" when you're ready.'

Her father turned back to his wife, and busied himself by draping a recently unwrapped warm and colourful scarf around her shoulders. He was so sweet with her – patting her shoulder gently and lovingly, and then squeezing her hand. Clearly, his love for her was undiminished.

For some reason, Wendy found herself thinking about Robert. She wondered what he was doing, and with whom. Francesca had suggested that they close their office till after New Year, which they had never done before, so perhaps Robert had, after all, taken his long-term, on-off lover away to the sun. She rather hoped that he had.

Eventually her father was ready to leave.

'So, shall we go and see Dr Yateman?' she asked again, feeling that it would be rude not to.

'Not today,' her father said with a firmness that surprised her. 'We don't want to be late at the Country Club.'

She felt she should have gone into the other room herself to see the old doctor, but her parent was making for the door, and since he was by far the most important reason for her being in her home county, she followed him.

The daylight had gone, Araminta realised, as she lit the candles on the table in the dining room ready for her supper with Michael.

Earlier, she had produced the lunch that her daughter loved and expected – roast turkey with all its accompaniments, and a proper flaming plum pudding. Hannah and Farid had been enthusiastic and complimentary about the food, but they had had the look of a couple whose only real hunger was for each other. Indeed, the air seemed to crackle with electricity every time their eyes had met.

Farid was not unlike his gorgeous brother, but his smile was not quite as warm and ready as Najid's. Still, he was tall, fit-looking and imposing. And he clearly adored Hannah. I will forgive him for not being his brother, Araminta had decided, so long as cares for my girl.

The sound of the doorbell brought her back to the present. She took a couple of deep breaths to steady herself, then – in a gesture she recognised as reminiscent of Hannah this morning – she paused before a mirror and flicked a tendril of her shoulder-length hair behind her right ear.

Michael, shoulders slightly raised, his hands grasped tightly round the strap of his large holdall, stood on the path, hopping from one foot to the other.

Araminta stepped back, making a welcome gesture with her arms as he entered, dropped his bag on the floor and closed the front door behind him before pulling her to him.

'Yes, we don't want the neighbours seeing,' she murmured against his shoulder, half in jest.

'Absolutely not!' His tone was deadly serious.

As he took off his scarf she noticed that he was not wearing his clerical collar. He caught her eye. They smiled at each other, shyly.

In the kitchen, they fell into an easy routine – Michael rinsing the mixing bowls and utensils she had been using, then polishing glasses while she finished preparing her version of Jamie Oliver's five-spice duck salad.

'I hope this'll be enough for you.' Her voice sounded diffident. 'I've assumed that, like me, you've already eaten a pretty large lunch.'

She felt him move to stand behind her and wrap his arms around her waist, and as he gently nuzzled her neck, she allowed herself to lean back against him. It felt such a tender and 'belonging' moment that her eyes pooled with tears.

He turned her to him and kissed her lips.

'I ate far too much earlier, so a light meal would be perfect. We don't even have to bother with pudding if you don't want to.'

'But I've made a pear and cranberry crumble.'

'My favourite!' he announced.

'Really! I thought I'd just made it up – using what I had to hand in the kitchen!'

Michael laughed, a big, booming, masculine sound that filled her with gladness. 'Well, I'm sure it *will* be my favourite, and unique, for having been the first dessert in our life together.'

The whole meal, though informal, had an intensity and significance about it, and they both remarked how the food they had eaten together would remain in their memories for ever. Interestingly, they drank little alcohol.

151

As if they had discussed this change in their behaviour, Michael remarked, 'I've done an awful lot of drowning my sorrows.'

Araminta nodded her understanding. 'Me too. But I hope that now we'll have fewer sorrows to drown.'

'Far fewer,' he agreed as he raised a glass of sparkling water to toast her.

They continued to eat in companionable silence; there was, after all, a lifetime ahead to talk.

Eventually, she brought up the subject of St Mark's.

'Who's going to tell the congregation?' she asked as she offered him a second helping of crumble which he grinningly accepted.

'I've written a special parish newsletter. There's no mention of you obviously, just a few paragraphs about physical and spiritual exhaustion and a decision to take a break to review my position. I'm afraid that I have to ask you to keep our relationship secret for now.'

She laid her left hand over his right one. 'Whatever it takes… The best part of my entire life is beginning right now. I'll be patient. But, can't we tell *anyone*?'

They both laughed. 'I am just so, so overwhelmingly grateful that I have you,' he murmured. 'How about we confide in one person each?'

'OK. Who will you trust with it?'

'Philip. He's the best friend I've ever had. And that – may I say – is all down to you sending him to me because of his emotional crisis.'

Remembering Katie in their last therapy session blithely recounting how she was going to spend Christmas with Philip's mother in Ireland, and – somewhat derogatively – describing him as 'needy', she murmured, 'A crisis that continues, I suspect.'

Michael nodded. 'Can I invite him for lunch tomorrow? I know you're planning a Boxing Day meal?'

'Of course,' she answered, glad that she had decided her sessions with Katie were at an end, which meant that socialising with Philip would no longer be a problem.

'And who will you tell?'

Araminta looked pensive. 'The obvious person would be Hannah, but I feel it might be too much for her to cope with at this stage. Probably better to let her get used to you being around more, and to us being friends. I don't suppose she even has a clue that you're planning to stop being a priest. So, I think my friend Wendy would be best. She was my role model when I worked in television, and then we lost touch for twenty-five years or so. To be honest, I'm thrilled to have her back in my life. You'll meet her tomorrow.'

He nodded. Then – as if their moves had been choreographed – they rose and cleared the table, loaded the dishwasher, opted for a pot of decaffeinated coffee, and headed towards the sitting room where the air was suffused with the fragrance of the Christmas tree.

Michael took it upon himself to puff up the dying embers of the fire with the giant bellows he found by the hearth, before adding kindling and then larger logs, as the flames flickered into life. Standing back, with a contented expression on his face, he regarded his handiwork. 'How lovely to have an open fire. It's not the sort of creature comfort you have in a presbytery.'

Araminta walked towards him and put her arms around his neck, then standing on tiptoe, she reached up and kissed him very passionately. He wondered if she could hear his heart beating; to him, it seemed as loud as the percussion section of an orchestra.

'Thank you for being here,' she murmured as she pulled back. 'You are my dear, darling man and I wonder now how I've managed to get through life without you.'

Should he tell her, he wondered, just what she had always meant to him?

He risked it, confiding how he had yearned for her as a teenager and how his mother had had some inkling of his feelings, but had insisted that he had a vocation and then moved him away.

'It took me years to forget you, even though I did want to be a priest.'

She hugged him again before pushing him gently into a large armchair by the fire while she went back to the kitchen to collect the coffee. Having poured them both a cup, she picked up a box of Swiss chocolates from the foot of the tree, tore off the cellophane wrapping and offered it to him.

'I've got a very sweet tooth, I'm afraid,' he confessed.

'Me too!'

As they both giggled, he put his cup down on the occasional table beside him and took a deep breath, then nervously adjusted his spectacles.

'I said last night that I'm a novice when it comes to relationships – though I think somehow that just actually being around each other may be easier than I imagined, even though I've had to be very self-sufficient till now.'

How adorable he is, she thought, as a warm bubble of gladness rose in her chest.

'But,' Michael continued, 'to be blunt, when it comes to actual sex, I'm afraid that I won't have a clue. I mean, I've had to study diagrams in a book just to be sure about where everything is, and I don't suppose every woman is quite the same as a drawing.'

He paused because Araminta had choked on her coffee and was laughing and coughing simultaneously.

'Are you OK?' He hoped he did not look as anxious as he felt but she was giggling and motioning that he should continue.

'Thing is, in the presbytery, we kept a few fairly graphic self-help manuals, like *The Book of Love*, which we used to loan out to couples whose marriages were in trouble in the bedroom. It was the only way we could help really, because as celibate priests we were hardly qualified to advise.'

Araminta clutched her abdomen, trying to stifle her giggles.

'What's funny?' he asked, but he too began to snigger.

She shook her head, unable to speak.

'I suppose it does sound mad that we had to give advice on "intimacy" when none of us had ever had any. Well, I think one old priest in my early days claimed to have had a racy past, but I'm not sure I believed him. Most of the clergy I've known have been the sort of boys who were good to their mothers and never got beyond a bit of hand-holding with girls. A number of my colleagues have been gay of course, and I suppose they might have had more practise, but would that have been much help to hetero-sexual couples who were failing to provide each other with satis-faction? I doubt it.'

Araminta could feel mirthful tears rolling down her cheeks. She tried again to compose herself, but when she saw Michael's brooding expression, another peal of laughter rang out.

'I'm sorry,' she apologised. 'It's probably nerves. It's just I've never had such an explicit conversation – not even when I was training as a therapist – and certainly never with someone I loved.'

He stopped then, and leapt to her side and cradled her to him. 'Thank you for saying that. I love *you*, Araminta. And you're right, this is funny. And you'll laugh even more when I tell you that this week I've reread a couple of those books to educate *me*! So, I've kind of mugged up everything I could find about female anatomy and arousal and I hope I'm going to be able to, you know...'

Araminta put her finger to his lips. 'I actually think,' she whis-pered, 'that you've done more than enough theory and that it's time to retire upstairs and try the practical!'

He nodded, though continued to look apprehensive. 'Great idea. But I just hope...'

She interrupted him firmly, but with a smile. 'We're going to take it gently and just explore what we want to do and what feels right, and it's all going to be fine.'

And it was.

Later, lying spent and saturated with sensations of deep delight and profound attachment, she reached for his hand and grasped it tightly.

'How was it, Michael? Worth waiting for?'

'Like flying on a magic carpet,' he murmured.

Chapter Twelve

'Who's Julian Wilson?' Hannah asked.

Araminta was in the kitchen, on the phone to her daughter, explaining who was coming to the Boxing Day lunch.

'A great friend of Wendy's. You'll like him.'

'So, it's her and this Julian guy, and Michael?'

'Yes, and Michael's friend, Philip.'

'Really?' Hannah sounded very surprised. 'Do you mean Philip Baldry?'

'Yes.'

'Wow! I spoke to him on the phone one day when I was trying to get hold of Michael. Well, fine. So, that's it. No neighbours or other friends?'

'No.' Araminta felt slightly discomforted by Hannah's precise questioning, not least because it highlighted how insular her life had become.

In the past, her social network had been dominated by Simon's dental colleagues and their spouses. Was it her fault or theirs that they had failed to keep in touch? How quickly one can become isolated, she thought. But then she smiled as she remembered that everything would be different now.

'Cool! Sounds good,' Hannah said. 'See you later! Love you. Bye.'

As Araminta put her phone down on a nearby worktop, she realised that Michael was watching her from the doorway.

'Talk about feeding the five thousand!' He nodded towards the buffet that had appeared while he had been upstairs hiding any evidence that he had stayed the night.

'I may have overdone it for only seven people!' she giggled as she returned to a large apricot-stuffed ham which she was glazing with a tangy, mustard sauce.

'Let's just say I hope you like Christmas leftovers as much as I do!' Michael eyed the spread before him: turkey and raspberry salad, home-baked bread, a whole Stilton and a slab of Gurney's Gold Norfolk cheese, a colourful fruit salad, a sherry trifle, and a coffee gateau covered with swirls of cream and toasted almonds. 'You're a marvel! Oh and...' he reached into a trouser pocket and drew out a tiny velvet-covered box. 'I forgot yesterday with everything else that went on, but I bought you these.'

'But...'

'No buts. And please change them if I've got it wrong because I've never bought a woman such a personal gift, apart from my mother. And that was obviously rather different!'

She gave his arm a squeeze. 'You shouldn't, especially when I haven't bought anything for you yet.'

As she opened the box she gasped with pleasure as she saw the amber earrings set in silver. 'They're gorgeous, Michael. What wonderful taste you have.'

She hugged him tightly, as if afraid that if she let go he might disappear. Then she released him so that she could remove the plain gold studs she was wearing and replace them with her exquisite present – aware, as she did so, that this was another moment from the beginning of their relationship that she would cherish.

Michael gazed at her. 'They suit you beautifully,' he whispered and reached for her hand and brushed it with his lips.

Her eyes held his for a moment, then she grinned. 'They'll all be here soon, so make me keep my mind on the party!'

He laughed.

'Now, would it better, do you think, for everyone to come and serve themselves out here? I was thinking of carting all the dishes into the dining room, but it might be easier to move the people rather than the food!'

He nodded his agreement, delighted to be consulted. This was how, at his most hopeful, he had imagined his new life might be.

'I don't see why you have to go out for lunch, Philip,' Marigold's voice took on an unattractive whiny tone. 'Why aren't I invited? Is this all about *her*?'

She refused to use Katie's name.

'No. I'm having lunch with my friend who's the priest. He's going through...' Philip stopped, unsure what to say; Norfolk was such a small county when it came to gossip. 'He's not been well. Why don't you do something with Bro before he leaves? You've hardly spoken to him since he arrived.'

'We're not very alike, you know.'

'Even so, you're the one who's always going on about "family".'

She shrugged.

'Look,' he continued, in a more conciliatory tone, 'as we'll be on our own tonight, shall I take you out to dinner, or should we have a quiet, early night?'

She sighed as if the decision was all too much for her. 'We can decide later,' she muttered before walking away.

He stood where he was in the hallway, attempting to make sense of what was going on. Marigold had surprised him with her determination to keep their marriage intact. Indeed, for about a week after she had returned from the spa, she had appeared to want him as much as he had always wanted her. This had coincided with Katie being 'overrun' with work at the studios – and with her keeping her distance even when he had pressed her to meet up. 'I've gone off sex,' she had told him blithely. 'Probably something that happens in early pregnancy.'

Unsure then about everything, and unable to have any meaningful conversation with Michael – who had been locked in meetings about leaving the priesthood – the view of his future had vacillated inconclusively between life with Katie or Marigold.

Partly, he felt he owed it to his wife to stay with her. And there was no doubt that he had – at least initially – enjoyed their new closeness, beguiled, as he was still, by her beautiful body. However, before long he had suspected that her efforts were calculated and artificial, that her loud orgasms were faked, and that, despite trying his best, he failed to arouse her.

It had always been the same. One night during their first year together, she had said, 'I prefer a G & T to sex any day' – and the shocked disappointment he had experienced in that moment had seared an indelible memory into his brain. Was it his fault? Did he have no technique? Smell wrong? Bore her?

The ring of the doorbell interrupted his reflections. He shook his shoulders vigorously in a bid to shrug off his gloomy thoughts. Once he got to Araminta's he would be able to talk to Michael, which would help. And meanwhile, in the taxi, he would call Katie. He had not been able to reach her on Christmas Day, but she was a bit scatty at times and had probably let her phone battery run down. However, they could have a long chat while he was being driven to Norwich. Once she came home again, he would know what to do.

As soon as the Yarmouth train stopped at Norwich station, Julian leapt from it, negotiated the ticket barrier at the end of the platform, and rushed towards Wendy, his bulging rucksack bouncing on his back as he ran.

'Hello, you!' he cried and swept her into such an enthusiastic hug that it lifted her off the ground.

Giggling as he set her down, she wrinkled her nose and sniffed, reacting to the peppery lime fragrance that emanated from him. 'Gosh! You smell gorgeous. Present from Mum?'

'No. To be honest, that would be out of her league on a number of levels. It's some self-indulgence that I bought in a shop in Burlington Arcade. I felt it was rather me!'

She laughed. 'And what's in that rucksack?'

'Something for you.'

'Oh my goodness.' Wendy looked genuinely embarrassed till he added, 'And bottles of cheer for our hostess.'

'No wonder you haven't got any money!'

He looked slightly rueful till she reassured him that she was jesting. 'You're a big-hearted fellow,' she went on. 'Too much so for your own pocket, but I wouldn't want you to be different. How about we grab some coffee before we go and meet the others?'

'Great idea,' he enthused, before propelling her towards one of the cafés on the concourse, finding her a chair, and queueing for two cappuccinos.

Once seated himself, he watched Wendy's grateful expression as she swallowed her first sip. They smiled broadly at each other before falling into a discussion about the events of the previous day. Julian seemed especially keen to talk about his mother's neighbour.

'He's Jamaican – and he's got this mellifluous speaking voice, with an accent that's a mixture of Caribbean and Norfolk. And to look at, he's a bit like Sir Willard White. D'you know who I mean? Wonderful singer. Anyway, it's good Mum's got him next door.'

Then he asked Wendy how her mother had been and listened carefully to her response, aware that he was looking for clues which might explain his own parent's behaviour.

'It must be pretty soul-destroying when you see her,' he ventured.

Wendy nodded, before taking another gulp of coffee. 'But lunch with my father was lovely, and then, when we got home, we played Monopoly like we used to when I was a child, and we watched *It's a Wonderful Life*. The only problem was that I felt bad that

I'd been regarding this Christmas less than enthusiastically, once I'd learned the boys would be away. But honestly, I wouldn't have missed it for the world. Somehow, just being with my dad seemed to put right some of the madness of this past year. And it made me appreciate more than ever, the love and stability he's given me. I just hope he's got plenty of years left.'

Wendy closed her eyes tightly for a second and breathed deeply. 'Sorry,' she said, and she took Julian's hand and squeezed it.

'Emotional time, Christmas!'

She grimaced but then grinned. 'You can say that again. How's your mother?'

'I was going to ask you about her, actually.' And he proceeded to outline how his parent looked older and had gained a lot of weight, and lost her normal energy and ability to organise. 'Do you think she's got dementia? I mean, does what I'm telling you sound like your mum when she first got ill?'

Wendy cast her mind back before speaking. 'Not really, no. And I haven't a clue what those symptoms might mean. She ought to see a doctor.'

'Definitely. I'll take her. But right now, having got that off my chest, I'm going to throw myself into today and stop worrying. Joe said he'd pop in on her while I'm away.'

'Good! So, can I give you your present now?'

His face lit up as she handed over a carrier bag from Aspinal of London with a professionally wrapped Christmas gift inside it.

He looked genuinely overcome. 'Can I open it?'

Inside was a black soft calf leather washbag with a monogrammed silk lining. He smoothed out the wrapping paper it had come in, and spread it over their table before laying his new present down to examine it. Clasping his hands over his chest in a gesture of pure delight, he flashed Wendy an excited smile before picking up the bag and sniffing it reverently.

'This is what's called inhaling pure luxury,' he chortled. 'It's fabulous. How well you understand how I'd like to live!' He

161

jumped to his feet, then reached over the table and planted a kiss on her cheek.

'What a pleasure it is to buy you a present,' she reflected.

He raised an enquiring eyebrow.

'I think I told you how my husband believed me to be utterly practical and businesslike, but I've always had a love of beautiful things. And to be honest, I've never really had anyone in my life before who understood that, or wanted them.'

'Well you've found someone now!' He laughed, then picked up his rucksack, reached inside it and pulled out a Fortnum and Mason carrier bag. 'Happy Christmas!'

Beaming, she opened the bag and found two parcels. She tore the wrapping paper off the larger one to find an embroidered Christmas stocking containing a selection of small jars of old-fashioned sweets: rhubarb and custards, pear drops, aniseed balls and jelly babies. There were also boxes of marzipan fruits and crystallised peppermints. And nestling right in the toe, was a pink candy mouse.

Her eyes glinted with joy. 'This Christmas is turning out to be the most fun I've had in years,' she declared, and she blew him a kiss before unwrapping the second gift – an elegant bowl of gold-leaf dusting powder with an accompanying puff.

'I *love* this,' she screeched, and the couple of elderly women at the next table looked across and laughed.

'You've got a good man there,' observed one of them. 'Hold onto him.'

Julian turned to them. 'I'm going to hold onto *her*,' he declaimed. 'You wouldn't think we'd been married for thirty years, would you? I love her as much as I did the day we were wed.'

'Aw, tha's lovely,' the other woman joined in.

Wendy smiled and wished them both 'Happy Christmas' before gathering up her belongings in one hand, pulling Julian to his feet with the other and marching him across the concourse and out of the station where she burst out laughing.

'You are entirely mad. But thank God for you. Now, are we going to walk or get a taxi?'

'Walk!' he insisted, as he pushed his present from her into his rucksack and slung it on his shoulder. 'One of the things I hate about Christmas is the lack of exercise. I did get out yesterday, when Mum was asleep, and had a little cavort on the beach. Everyone else had a dog or children with them, so I felt a bit of a prat. And then a small boy came along and wanted to jump around with me, but his mum shouted: "Leave the strange man alone, Jacob. He can't help it". But hey, I have to keep moving. I mean, look at me. I'm portly. What would I be like if I didn't exercise?'

'I must make a New Year's resolution to get active. You put me to shame.'

'You could come and do ballet.'

'No I couldn't! I have no coordination. That's why I'm a lousy driver. It's a mystery to me how I managed all the technology in television because I'm noted for not knowing my left from my right. But I will do something… I can't bear the idea of running. Perhaps I could swim.'

'You need something weight-bearing though, to maintain your bone density.'

'Goodness,' she responded. 'I had no idea you were such an expert.'

They carried on discussing the merits of tennis, yoga and Pilates, and were just embarking on a discussion about the Thames Path National Trail – and whether they could walk it together – when Wendy realised that despite believing she was familiar with every street in Norwich, they were lost.

Philip rang the front doorbell. He felt worried that Araminta might find it awkward to have him to lunch, because of Katie being her client, but he was keen to meet her again and to thank her for directing him towards Michael.

As she opened the door and welcomed him into the house, he said, 'I'm sure you won't remember me.'

'But I do! I don't get many callers who look as distinguished as you!'

He gave her a shy smile. 'I'm so grateful to you for connecting me with Michael. He's become such a great mate. Thanks very much for inviting me. How is he?'

He thought she blushed slightly as she shut the door on the frosty air and took his coat.

'Pretty wonderful!' she answered, softly. 'Go and join him, he'll be so pleased you've arrived.' She pushed open the door to the kitchen and ushered him in before rushing upstairs to change.

The two men, initially awkward, exchanged a tentative hug and then a rather more enthusiastic handshake before stepping back to take stock of each other.

'So?' Philip began.

Michael smiled broadly. 'She's left us alone so I can confide in you. We agreed we'd each tell one person what's happened, and you're my choice, obviously. I've done everything I said I would do. I've said my last Mass. I smoothed things with Araminta – for some reason she'd decided that I was interested in someone else, but she... she loves me.' His voice trembled slightly as his face took on an expression of incredulous wonder. 'So, at the moment, I'm staying here. But no one must know what's going on. Not even Araminta's daughter, who you're going to meet soon.'

'And have you, you know, done the deed?'

Michael nodded his head but averted his eyes. 'I have – and it was wonderful.'

'Welcome to the club. From now on you're probably going to spend your entire life wondering when you can do it again!'

Michael grinned as he gathered up some dirty dishes and a couple of forks and put them in the dishwasher. 'Shall we have a drink? And you can tell me your news.'

'Excellent idea,' agreed Philip as he followed his friend through to the sitting room. 'You seem to fit right in here. But it's funny to see you without a dog collar. I suppose I'll get used to it!'

'Well, so far that's the only part of my fashion statement that's changed. I need to buy new clothes, as I only have black sweaters and trousers. And most of my shirts are black too. Hopefully, I'll develop some sort of civilian savvy eventually!'

He uncorked a bottle of sparkling rosé and poured them both a glass. 'Cheers!'

Philip took a sip, nodded his approval and then, with his free hand, reached into an inner pocket of his Norfolk jacket and drew out a cheque.

'This isn't a very imaginative present, Mike,' he said seriously. 'But you need to find your feet and I can afford to help you. This should buy some clothes and a holiday – which in my view, you really need.'

Michael took the cheque and looked at it, then looked again. 'I couldn't possibly!'

Philip turned his back, sensing that Michael was about to try to press the cheque back into his hand. 'Listen, I'm sure you know about the widow's mite, and how she was a good person because, despite having so little to give, she donated all she had. Well, from the point of view of what I'm worth, this isn't very generous at all.

'At least delete one of the noughts?' Michael suggested.

Philip smiled. 'Nothing doing! I go through life being of little assistance or value to anyone, so please allow me to help. It's the least I can do, especially since I'm going to need to bend your ear about my crazy situation.'

The doorbell rang.

'Well, no amount of advice is going to compensate for your generosity, but thank you. Now, before we get interrupted, tell me what's going on.'

*

Having divested himself of his outdoor clothing, embraced their hostess and presented her with two bottles of Veuve Clicquot, Julian found himself being pushed through a door into a large sitting room where two men, standing in front of the crackling log fire, were deep in conversation.

Unusually for him, he felt awkward, so he wandered over to the grand piano to look at the photographs on top of it. Almost immediately, he spotted one of a younger Wendy, with a toddler on her knee. And there were several of Araminta alongside two children, and a man he imagined must be her dead spouse.

'I'm terribly sorry...' said a voice behind him. 'We were so busy chatting we didn't hear you come in. I'm Michael Chapman.'

Julian turned and took the outstretched hand. 'Julian Wilson. I'm Wendy's friend. Pleased to meet you... Love your spectacles... Very Elton John!'

Michael chuckled. 'I wish I could afford his hair transplant! Let me get you a drink. This,' he gestured towards his glass on the coffee table, 'is something Araminta is championing. Local sparkling rosé!'

'Sounds festive. Sorry if I interrupted you. I was, uh, kind of "encouraged" into here by Araminta and Wendy. I think they had some chatting to do.'

Michael nodded happily and handed a glass of wine to Julian, then indicated his companion. 'And this is...'

Julian gasped in astonishment as the other man turned towards him. 'Good God – Philip Baldry.'

Philip hung back looking apprehensive before, somewhat diffidently, moving towards Julian. 'We used to know each other,' he explained to Michael.

'Yes, we did,' Julian concurred, his sonorous voice filling the room. 'But then we fell out badly. And I've got something to say about that.'

Michael indicated that Julian and Philip should sit in the two chairs by the fire, then he walked over to a bookcase and perused its contents.

'You don't have to...' Philip began.

Michael turned. 'I think I do. Clearly you have some history to revisit. So carry on. I'd leave the room, but I don't want to disturb Araminta. I know she wants to run something by Wendy.' And with that, he selected a book and meandered across to a seat by the Christmas tree.

The other two men looked awkwardly at each other before sitting down.

Julian took a deep breath. 'Listen, I want to apologise.'

Philip looked perplexed. 'Whatever for? It's I who should apologise. I've wondered about you so often. I'm pretty sure it was my fault you were expelled.'

'Expelled? I wasn't expelled.'

'But that day in the playground.'

'When we had a fight after Speech Day?'

'Yes. The Head saw me with a bloody nose and asked around and found out who I'd been fighting with. I promise I never told him, but for some reason you and I never spoke again. And soon after that, you left the school. I asked our form master what had happened to you, and he said you'd been expelled.'

'Well, I wasn't. All that happened was that my father, who was attached to the American air force, went back to the States and, as my mother had no money, I had to leave the prep and go to a state school.'

'But why were we fighting, Julian? We were such good mates.'

'You called my mother a slag.'

'Did I? How appalling. I'm dreadfully sorry.'

'Don't you remember?'

'Not really.'

'Well, you did. But you said that Nigel had told you. Thing is, I had to ask you what that meant, and you said a slag was a woman you wouldn't invite to your house for tea. So, maybe you didn't know either!'

The two of them stared at each other, and then Julian chuckled. 'What innocent kids we were. But this weekend, funnily enough,

167

though it's not so much comedic as tragic – given how we fell out – I discovered that my mum had once had a fling with Nigel's dad, and very unwisely had flirted with him after one of our choir concerts. I gather that Nigel was running around at the time and overheard what went on. There were some heated exchanges I think and probably someone called Mum a slag and he just repeated it to you.'

'My dear chap. What a waste of all these years.'

'But why would they say I'd been expelled? Mind you, it does sound rather glam!'

Philip grinned as he saw emerging before him the boy who had been his trusted companion and the one person in all of his life who had been guaranteed to make him laugh. 'Don't you remember how they were at Bevingham? They prided themselves on their long waiting list. Probably it didn't fit with their image to have someone leave of their own accord!'

'Do you know,' Julian said, 'when you smile, you're quite like the dishy doctor, Mark Porter.'

'Really? Someone else said that a couple of months ago. But I hadn't a clue who she meant!'

'He writes for *The Times*. And appears on the telly!'

As the two old friends chatted on, they started giggling like their nine-year-old selves and Michael took the hilarity as a sign that he could recharge their drinks.

Julian raised his glass at the other two and then asked, 'Are the women joining us?'

Michael drew up another chair and sat down. 'Yes, I expect they'll be in soon.'

Julian nodded. 'When I left them they were busy comparing notes about clothes. Wendy's wearing leather trousers, and it turns out that Araminta bought an identical pair the other day, and then it transpired that Araminta's wearing a dress that Wendy owns in another colour. They're both Modern Rarity addicts!'

'What's that?' Philip asked. 'Sounds like some sort of art movement!'

'It's a new design-label by John Lewis for older but trendy women,' Julian explained.

'How do you know?' Michael and Philip chorused.

'Don't you read the fashion pages?'

All three of them guffawed as Julian wondered whether he should own up to the fact that actually he did.

Araminta led Wendy into the kitchen and offered her a glass of rosé. Then, with slightly embarrassed merriment they exchanged gifts.

'Do you realise, I haven't bought you a present for a quarter of a century?' Wendy reflected. 'Honestly, you might not like it. Give it away if you don't.'

'Give away a Jo Malone set! Are you mad? It's fabulous. But then you were always incredibly generous.'

'Nonsense,' Wendy replied. 'Look, thanks so much for inviting me today. I've been dreading Christmas but it's turning out brilliantly.'

'I'm glad. It's exactly the same with me.'

'Goodness!' Wendy suddenly noticed the huge spread. 'How many people are coming?'

'Just us – I may have overdone it a bit! But Hannah and the boyfriend are dropping in at some point and she can eat for England. I decided not to invite anyone else as I wanted to be surrounded by people who really matter. Does that make sense? It's been such a funny old year... I hope Julian didn't mind being bundled into the sitting room. It's just I wanted to talk to you.'

'No, he'll be fine. I want to talk to you too. You first though. Mmmn, this is nice.' Wendy took another sip of her wine.

'Locally made. So, listen, you're going to meet Michael in a minute.'

'Michael?'

'Yes. He is, was, my priest.'

'Oh yeah, Hannah mentioned him.'

Araminta nodded. 'Well, the thing is, he's... well I suppose you could say, he's had a big emotional crisis and, uh, he's taking time out from the parish to think things over.'

'Poor man, is he having a breakdown?'

'No! Well, I don't think so. He just wants to stop being a priest.'

'Well, it's lovely that you're helping him. Typical of you.' Wendy's tone was warm and affirming.

'There's a bit more to it, but it's really confidential. I know I can trust you.' Araminta looked round for the wine bottle, feeling a sudden need for more alcohol.

'Whatever it is,' Wendy reassured her, 'I know you'll be a great support to him.'

The kitchen door swung open and Julian appeared. 'I've been delegated to come and ask if we three discarded blokes could possibly have some sparkling water? We thought we should pace ourselves! Michael said we shouldn't disturb you but Philip and I overruled him!'

Araminta motioned to him to help himself from the fridge before saying to Wendy, 'Shall we continue this later?'

Smiling, arms around each other, they followed Julian into the sitting room.

'Now,' Araminta said, unable to suppress the pride in her voice, 'I'd like you to meet my friend, Michael Chapman.'

Wendy smiled at him. 'Are you doing OK?' she asked quietly.

He nodded. And as she looked at him she thought what a kind face he had – and that there was something about him that seemed to her to mark him out as a good man.

'And this,' Araminta took her by the arm, 'is Philip Baldry.'

Wendy looked up into the brown eyes of her fellow guest, her lips twitching into a tentative smile. 'Hello. And where do you fit in to this...' she searched for a suitable word, '...quintet?'

He grinned at her choice. 'I met Araminta first, albeit briefly, and she suggested I talk to Michael about something and he and I have become great pals. We're a couple of old crocks really but

170

we prop each other up! And, just now, I met up with your friend Julian, which is marvellous, because he and I were best friends at school a million years ago!'

'Really?' Wendy's eyes sparkled as she turned her head from Philip to Julian who was chuckling away. 'Small world, isn't it?'

There was a pause then Wendy noticed the photos on the piano. 'Gosh,' she walked over to survey them. 'Minty, is the picture here that you told me about? Oh, yes, it is! Your lovely boy on my knee. Thirty years ago. Heavens!'

They all crowded round the piano to look.

'Who plays this wonderful instrument?' Julian asked when they had finished viewing the images.

'Not me! It belonged to my father,' Araminta explained. 'He used to play really well. But soon after we moved here, when the children were small, he offered it to us. Unfortunately, though both kids took lessons, neither of them stuck with it.'

'Well, come on, Wendy,' Julian suggested. 'You play a bit, don't you?'

'Not in public!' She looked aghast.

'I'm sure you're quite good really – young Rhys must get his talent from someone.' He turned to Philip and Michael. 'Her gorgeous son is a wonderful musician.'

'Why don't you give us a tune?' Wendy suggested.

With a cheery shrug, Julian settled himself on the piano stool and struck up a few chords before launching into 'Anything Goes'. He sang along to his own accompaniment, with a complete mastery of all the tongue-twisting internal rhymes. One by one, the others tried to join in – with varying degrees of success. Wendy had had no idea that he could play the piano so well, but she suspected that this was a party piece he had long ago perfected. She of course, had heard his wonderful baritone voice on many occasions, but she enjoyed observing the others as they realised what a professional they had in their midst.

With a final trill and a flourish of runs, he was finished and jumped up and bowed extravagantly to the other four as they applauded him. Michael even whistled.

Araminta looked at her watch. 'Heavens! It's gone two, is anyone hungry?'

The five of them agreed that they were and made for the kitchen, where they admired the buffet and proceeded to load their plates amid squeals of discovery and enjoyment.

'Such a great kitchen,' Philip commented as he stepped backwards bearing a piled-high plate.

Araminta grinned. 'Shabby chic, I think you'd call it.'

'That beats designer chic any day!' Philip replied. 'I was brought up by my mother to view the kitchen as the heart of the home. I did my homework by the warmth of the Aga. Mum used to keep a pot of Irish broth on the hot plate and I would help myself.' He looked wistful.

'Doesn't sound as if you have that kind of a kitchen now,' Wendy ventured.

He shook his head. 'My wife's more of a "bespoke" and "luxury" sort of woman. She favours German engineering and a kitchen where you can't find anything because it's all housed behind identical cupboards – and where there's no seating apart from a couple of uncomfortably high stools. Still, she means well.'

Julian and Michael raised their eyebrows at each other, clearly sharing Philip's lack of enthusiasm for his wife's choice.

'Actually, I think this is the nicest kitchen I've ever been in,' Michael murmured.

As he spoke, Araminta stepped sideways so that her back was directly in front of him and, with a shift in her balance, she leant against him. He felt a sigh of satisfaction escape his lips, then – as he looked up – he noticed that Wendy was watching them. She smiled and turned away.

He must be more careful, he told himself. Wendy almost certainly now knew the truth about him and Araminta, but apart from Philip no one else must. Reluctantly but resolutely he walked to the other side of the room to talk to Julian.

'Sounds like you and Philip were very good mates as kids.'

'The best.' Julian nodded. 'Funny really, because our backgrounds were so different. Didn't matter then. And I don't think it would matter now. It's the bit in the middle we all seem to screw up. How much of our life do we spend trying to meet and consort with the right people, the useful people, the people of influence?'

'That's quite a challenging question,' Michael mused.

'Yup.' Julian grinned. 'Now, is that Gurney's Gold over there? I love that. Can I get you some?'

'This lunch is going to play havoc with my waistline!'

'Is that a "no" then?' Julian's expression was full of mischief.

Michael chuckled. 'Perhaps today's not the right time for restraint!'

The two men edged past Wendy and Philip, who were deep in conversation, and sliced into the cheese.

Araminta cleared away a couple of dirty dishes, humming slightly as she went. She was aware of a deep sense of contentment as she looked around this group of noisy people who were all connected in various ways, but who had had such different careers and experiences. She was particularly pleased to see that Philip appeared to be relaxing. Knowing what she did about him, and about how he was being treated by her client Katie, she felt protective of him. He seemed such a quiet, dignified but somehow sad individual and had the air of an abandoned dog in a rescue kennel who was hoping that someone might want to take him home. Still, he seemed very interested in what Wendy was saying, and he was chatting back. Perhaps he would be all right.

Meanwhile, Michael and Julian appeared to be bonding over their love of food. She watched as each of them sampled a different type of bread and discussed their choice.

Suddenly Wendy pinged her fork against a glass.

'Can I have a bit of quiet and decorum?' She giggled before reassembling a serious expression. 'As probably the oldest person here, I'd like to point out that we're making a heck of a racket! Honestly, our parents – alive or dead – would have a fit!'

Everyone laughed.

'Seriously, all I want to do really is to thank Minty for this wonderful lunch. As most of you know, I've had a rather turbulent few months. I haven't decided yet whether or not it's been good to get all my personal changes over during a period which has seen unprecedented political disruption! Been crazy though, hasn't it? And I'm aware that others here are facing their own various challenges, and I just want to say that I sympathise, and also that having dreaded Christmas, I'm having the best time, in the best company!'

Julian cheered and Philip raised his glass in her direction.

'And I also want to say,' she went on, 'that I would never have thought when I was young that we'd be like this in mid-life. Noisy, boisterous, still working hard, trying to make a difference, changing our lives and, I don't know, being so alive and vital. And, above all, making new friends, or finding how much old ones matter. I'm not making sense really...'

Michael interrupted. 'Oh yes, you are. Perfect sense.'

Julian piped up, 'Absolutely. You're describing it so well. And actually, we are pretty amazing!'

Philip raised his glass. 'A toast to Araminta for having us!'

'Araminta!' they chorused.

She beamed at everyone. 'Thank you all so much. I kind of feel like we're a family – but a family who all *like* each other!'

Julian roared with laughter and performed a little tap dancing step. 'How aptly put!'

And suddenly, they were all hugging and kissing as though it were midnight on New Year's Eve.

'Mum!' Hannah who had been trying to attract her mother's attention from the kitchen doorway, called out. But no one saw or heard her. She shouted again, and waved her arms above her head. Michael noticed her and smiled, and then signalled to Araminta that she should turn round.

'Oh, hello, darling.' Araminta tried to make herself heard. 'I didn't know you'd arrived.'

'I'm not surprised,' Hannah cried. 'I could hear you all from the street. I'd no idea it was going to be such a party. Can we join in?'

Chapter Thirteen

'I don't exactly know how to begin,' Hannah announced, her voice breathily excited. 'But as we arrived, I heard Mum say something about you lot being like a real family who all get on really well together! And that's fantastic, because I have some amazing news which is going to affect most of you. And I really hope you're going to love it.'

'Sounds intriguing,' Araminta laughed. They had all helped themselves to more of the lunch buffet, and had then moved to the dining room, where Michael poured each of them wine, or water, or both.

Hannah and Farid had been the last to join them, lingering in the kitchen for a while, having what Michael perceived to be a very intense conversation. He hoped all was well. Hannah was such a lovely girl. It was probably too soon for his feelings to be 'fatherly', but he certainly wanted the best for her.

Once in the dining room, Hannah had sat at one end of the long table and Farid at the other.

'Yes,' Hannah continued in response to her mother's comment, 'it *is* intriguing. I've been working on it for about a month now. But it only really took shape when I involved Farid. So, if you're ready, I'll start.'

'That sounds like something they used to say on *Listen With Mother*,' Wendy remembered.

'Yes,' Philip agreed, with a nostalgic smile. 'Are you sitting comfortably? Then I'll begin...'

'My mum and I listened too.' Michael joined in. 'I suppose everyone of our vintage did. Now there's so much choice I don't suppose you ever get the whole nation glued to one programme. Shame really.'

'Right, here goes,' Hannah said as soon as there was a lull in the older people's reminiscences. 'When my grandfather went into the care home, I volunteered to clear up his papers. I thought it was something I could help with. And I suppose, having always been close to Grandad, I thought it'd be interesting to find out more about him. Well,' she paused dramatically. 'I couldn't have begun to guess how very interesting it would be.'

'Are we going to like this?' Wendy's question reflected her sudden sense of foreboding that Hannah's speech would not end well.

'I'm sure you will,' Hannah's young voice burbled. And despite there being an uncertain and slightly bemused air in the room, most of them found themselves smiling at her enthusiasm.

'To be honest though, it will be a shock. But I think the fact that you all get on so brilliantly will mean you'll be thrilled in the end. There's just one thing – what I'm about to say doesn't have anything to do with you, Julian. So, I don't know how the others feel about you being in on the conversation.'

'Well, he's not going to leave.' Wendy's tone was the one she had deployed over decades to quell any argument in the febrile atmosphere of a news studio. 'He's our friend. He's been invited for lunch. He's an absolute dear...' She looked around at the others, suddenly unsure. 'That's what I think anyway.'

'Me too,' Michael spoke up, and Philip and Araminta exchanged glances then nodded their agreement.

Hannah took a deep breath. 'OK, well, here's the thing. Before the days of IVF and pioneers like, uh, Patrick Steptoe and Robert Edwards...' She glanced at Farid. 'Did I get the names right?'

'Certainly did,' Farid nodded and smiled at her.

'Cool – yeah, before test-tube babies and so on, there wasn't much help for couples who couldn't conceive. But Grandad was interested in helping them.'

Wendy knew she looked bewildered and could see the same expression etched in the faces of her companions.

'And what I've learned from the diaries he kept at the time,' Hannah continued, 'is that Grandad realised people were pretty ignorant about when conception was most likely to occur, and therefore often didn't have sex near enough to ovulation to get a good result. He wrote in the diaries that many couples would have sex every Saturday night, but have no clue that the woman was never ovulating then, because – say – her ovulation always fell on a Wednesday or whatever.'

'Gosh, that's interesting,' Wendy commented, and the others nodded their agreement.

'So,' Hannah continued, 'he monitored women carefully and got them to take their temperatures daily, so that they knew when they were ovulating. Obviously, there were no commercial ovulation kits back then, but it appears he had quite a lot of success with couples – simply by advising them to have sex at the right time of the month for them.'

'That's fantastic.' Araminta beamed. 'I love the idea that he helped people to have babies. I wonder why he never told the family.'

'Well,' explained Hannah. 'That was just the first phase of his work, and it was ages ago – back when he was a junior partner to a much older GP who, at that time, owned the Tombland house and practice. And from the entries in the diaries, it's clear that the senior doctor was uneasy with what Grandad was up to – particularly when he moved on to his next idea, which was to inseminate the women, with their husband's ejaculate, on the day they were ovulating.'

Philip sat forward. 'My word – I imagine that *was* somewhat controversial.'

Hannah nodded. 'Grandad's belief was that he could achieve a better result for the couple if the sperm was projected straight through the cervix and into the womb rather than having to swim up there from the vagina – especially as he'd started looking at the husbands' semen samples under a microscope and found that some of them were pretty poor.'

'Are you saying that some of us here were conceived with your grandfather's help?' Michael asked. 'That's quite something.'

Suddenly the atmosphere lightened again, as a burst of excited chatter broke out.

Hannah smiled at them. Only her mother realised that her daughter's smile was a nervous one and that she kept licking her lips – a gesture which had always indicated stress or uncertainty – and that she glanced continually at Farid for reassurance.

'There's more, isn't there?' Araminta asked when she could stand it no longer.

'Yes.' Hannah threw her a grateful glance. 'Grandad seems to have convinced himself that he was doing ground-breaking research. He even tried to get a paper published in *The Lancet*, but they weren't interested. He was quite bitter about that, it seems. So, he looked for a way of increasing his success rate. And he hit upon a new method, but we can only find a record of one baby who resulted from it at that time – in 1957. And then he appears to have put the whole thing on hold.'

'Why was that?' Philip asked.

'Well, Farid says that even allowing for Grandad's enthusiasm, he must have realised that what he was doing was illegal – and don't forget he had his boss in the house keeping a watchful eye on him.'

There was a stunned silence.

'What changed then?' Araminta's voice sounded fearful.

'Well, the old doctor retired, and Grandad raised the money to buy both the house and the practice. It must have been a very hectic time, because he became the only practitioner. But in the summer of 1959, he started his project again. And it looks like he continued it till he knew that he was going to be a father, and Uncle Nigel was on the way.'

'But what was the project?' Wendy demanded. 'And are you implying that *I* was the first baby? I'm assuming I'm the only one here who was born in 1957.'

'Yes, I believe you were that baby,' Hannah replied. 'And as I uncovered this information in the diaries, it was a big shock to me to find that I knew you – because by the time your name came to light, Mum had mentioned that you and she were in touch again. So, you were the first one conceived when Grandad took things further.'

'What do you mean by "further"?' Wendy's voice rose in pitch. 'I mean, in those days, what could he do?'

'Well, this is the hard bit to get our heads around. Basically, what he did was to mix some of his own sperm with the husbands' ejaculate.'

There was an audible intake of breath but Hannah pressed on. 'As I said, Wendy, you were the first one but – after a break – others followed. And among them were Michael and Philip.'

'What!' Both men spoke as one.

Hannah nodded. 'I know it's a lot to take in…'

'It certainly is,' Philip interrupted her. 'And I don't know about the rest of you, but I need to take this slowly.'

He extracted a leather-bound diary from an inside pocket of his jacket and flicked through the end pages till he found a blank one.

'Right,' he said. 'I'm going to make notes. So, Wendy, when were you born?'

'March 1957.'

'And it appears,' Philip clarified, 'that you were the first baby to result from Dr Yateman's peculiar method. What was your father's name?'

'Arthur Lawrence,' she told him, in a whisper.

Philip nodded as he wrote. 'So, it seems that either Arthur's sample, or Dr Yateman's, fertilised your mother's egg and produced you. Fifty-fifty chance then.'

'Except,' Farid contradicted him, 'we know that some of the male patients that Dr Yateman assisted had very poor sperm.'

'OK,' said Philip. 'But surely there could still be a chance that Arthur Lawrence is Wendy's biological father?'

'I suppose so,' Farid conceded.

'Right,' Philip looked around the others before continuing. 'So then after a break, by which time Richard was in practice on his own, he started treating would-be parents again, by mixing his sperm in with the semen of the male partners – and injecting it into the female ones. And you're saying that two of the couples he treated in this way were Michael's parents, called…'

Michael supplied the names, 'Mary and Brian Chapman.'

Philip noted the details. 'And my parents – Nora and George Baldry. This seems to mean that three of us in this room were born as a consequence of our mothers being inseminated by a mixture of our fathers' ejaculate and Dr Richard's. Is that right?'

'Correct!' Farid answered. 'Which means there's a possibility that any or all of you might be Richard's child.'

Suddenly, Dr Yateman's words to her in the nursing home resounded in Wendy's ears. "I followed your career… You were my Number One." She leapt to her feet. 'I don't believe this. It's disgusting, and morally repugnant. The only comfort I have is that I'm so like my wonderful dad that I can't possibly be anyone else's child.' And with that, she rushed out of the room, knocking over a chair in her haste.

Araminta jumped up to follow her, but Philip pulled her back.

'I know that you and she are friends,' he counselled softly. 'But you're the doctor's daughter, and she may not be ready to talk to you right now.'

Then he looked across at Michael whose face, normally quite healthy in colour was ash-grey, and in that moment, he recalled their conversation before Christmas about Dr Yateman favouring the two of them, and encouraging Nigel to invite them to his parties, and giving Michael half-crowns. And he realised that Michael was thinking the same thing.

He was upset that Wendy was distressed and that Michael looked so gloomy, but to his great surprise he could not suppress a flutter of excitement in his chest at the thought of being Richard's son, and Michael's half-brother. However, in the next moment, he remembered Araminta, and a thunderbolt seemed to explode in his head as he grasped the possibility that Michael and she – now lovers – might also be half-siblings.

'You'll all get used to the idea,' Hannah's tone was determinedly cheerful. 'I mean, you all like each other. It'll be marvellous to find you've got brothers or sisters you never knew about. You might even end up all living together in one big house when you get old!'

'Shut up, Hannah,' Araminta screamed. 'I know you mean well, but everyone came here today believing that they knew who they were, and this has changed everything. You have absolutely no idea of the possible consequences.'

'Mum!' Hannah burst into tears and ran to her mother looking for comfort.

There was none. Araminta lifted her arms in a weak effort to reach out to her daughter, only to feel them drop helplessly to her side.

Farid stepped in and pulled Hannah into his arms. 'Come on, babe. It's OK. But this kind of stuff – people's genes – it's hugely important to them. They need time to think. We should probably leave. Why don't you go and get your things?'

Once she had left them, Farid reached for the shoulder bag that had been on the floor beside him and produced from it several buff-coloured packages which he explained contained DNA kits. 'Obviously,' he went on, 'I knew that Hannah was planning to talk to all of you about her findings, so I came prepared. I'm aware that you're in a state of shock, but if you want to know for sure whether or not Richard is your father, we have the means to determine that information. And if you want me to, I can take your swabs.'

'Seems reasonable,' Philip responded softly. 'What would happen after you take them?'

'I'd send the swabs and paperwork to an outside source; unfortunately, it would be impossible to put them through my own lab at the hospital. You'll find that inside each envelope, there's a form for you to fill in your personal data, your address – so they can send your results – and also your credit card details so you can pay for the test. That's about it. Of course, none of you may want to do it, but the offer is there.'

There was a heavy silence in the room.

'I don't want to overload you with information,' he continued, 'but for completeness I should tell you that Hannah and I took her grandfather's DNA yesterday. So that bit's done.'

'You did *what*?' Araminta screeched at her daughter's boyfriend. 'That is so wrong. Even if he gave you consent, he probably didn't know what he was doing. What were you thinking?'

'Hannah was concerned to get on with things. She's worried that he may not live much longer and that anyone who turns out to be his biological child may want to meet him.'

'Unbelievable!' Araminta bellowed as she turned and strode over to the window.

'It seems somewhat uncanny,' Michael commented, in a slow, almost sarcastic tone, 'that all the babies Richard Yateman created by this most questionable method are here today. I mean, we don't know for sure that any of us are his children, but if we are, wouldn't it be a hell of a coincidence if we all knew each other, and we were the only ones he'd manufactured?' His voice cracked as he finished the sentence.

'But you're not the only ones,' Farid countered. 'After Dr Yateman started his infertility treatment again in 1959, his diaries suggest that he treated six women. Your mother and Philip's were two of them. Out of the other four, only two got pregnant. And both women had girl babies.'

'I see,' Michael murmured. 'So are you going to do anything about them?'

'Well, women can be difficult to trace because they usually, unlike Wendy, change their names when they marry – and sometimes nowadays that happens more than once. We haven't tried to track them down yet. In fact, we decided that if any of you are Richard's offspring, you might want to make the decision about them yourselves.'

Philip and Michael looked at each other but said nothing.

'We know one thing for sure,' Farid continued. 'Richard stopped this project by the end of 1960. You see, he got Barbara, his wife-to-be, pregnant in the autumn of that year. They married quickly and Nigel was born in July 1961. Obviously, Richard must have realised that having his own son changed everything, in that there could be incestuous implications in a small city. But what might have finally clinched it was that we found a letter in his files from the GMC, dated late 1960, informing him that a male patient had made a complaint about him. Whether it was to do with the infertility treatment is unclear and it doesn't seem to have amounted to anything. But it would certainly have worried him.'

Hannah appeared at the door. 'Wendy's in the kitchen. She looks terrible. And she wouldn't answer when I tried to talk to her. I think someone should be with her.'

She had barely finished speaking when Wendy reappeared. She noticed the pile of padded envelopes on the table.

'What are they?' She glared at Farid.

Nervously, he explained about the paternity tests.

'Good! *I* want to be tested,' she announced. 'I know for sure I'm my dad's daughter and I want this nonsense cleared up as soon as possible. Are you going to take Dr Yateman's DNA to check for any matches?'

'He's done that already,' Araminta's voice was weary as she continued to stare out of the window.

'You'll go far, young man,' Wendy snapped.

Farid lifted his shoulders defensively.

'Sorry,' Wendy said. 'That came out all wrong. I just meant that you're efficient and driven. As for you, Hannah, though this has been a most upsetting tale, you delivered it... very cohesively. I just hope you're completely wrong about everything. Now, Farid, let's go to the bathroom or somewhere and get this bloody thing done. How long till we get the results?'

'I'll courier the samples to the company first thing on Wednesday when they open after the holidays. There may be a backlog after the Christmas break, but you'll get them quite quickly.'

'A couple of weeks then?'

'Probably sooner.' Farid turned from her to his girlfriend's mother. 'I was wondering, as an extra check, if we should get you and Hannah tested too?'

Araminta continued to peer out of the window and replied without looking at him.

'Hannah can do what she likes. I'm not interested. I know I'm Richard's child. Even though right now, I really wish I weren't.' She rotated and gazed at Michael who attempted a stricken smile in return.

'What about us?' Philip turned his attention to Michael. 'Do we want to know?'

'Not really. But what we've heard today can't ever go back to being unsaid. We would always wonder.'

Philip nodded. 'OK, Farid, it looks like you've been volunteered to take all our samples.' As he spoke, he walked over to Michael and hugged him, then turned to Araminta and drew her into an embrace.

Hannah watched them all, with a helpless look in her eyes. 'I'm going to the car,' she whispered to Farid. 'I'll wait for you there.'

Wendy watched her go, then – her voice heavy with sadness – she said, 'I think she's just beginning to understand the enormity of what she's done.'

Farid swept up the DNA kits and left the room and, after a glance back at her companions, Wendy followed him.

Philip sank back into his chair. He gazed at the ham and the cheeses and bread and salad still on his plate, and seemed to consider continuing with his lunch, before pushing it away.

'This may not be the time,' Julian said, then stopped. The other three looked at him in surprise. He had been so quiet, and they had been so involved in their own discovery, that they had all but forgotten he was there.

'What?' Philip asked. 'Sorry, old chap. This jolly lunch has taken a distinct downturn and none of it's to do with you. Not quite sure how to rekindle the conviviality of Boxing Day. I don't suppose you want to play us another tune?'

'I doubt if this is the right moment,' Julian responded. 'But can I just run something past you? You know, before lunch, I told you that my mother had once had a fling with Araminta's dad? Well the thing is, it was before I was born. But not *long* before. Do you get what I'm saying? I'm just wondering if the man I knew as my father – a guy I had nothing in common with – was perhaps not my dad at all. And that I might be Dr Yateman's son... I know it's a bit of a longshot, but I really felt a strong connection with him while I was playing his piano earlier. And I mean, he was musical and I'm musical. And I really liked him when I met him recently. Stranger things have happened. So, would you all mind if I asked Farid to test me too?'

'Why not, Julian?' Araminta snapped. 'What's one more addition to this weird family?'

Julian shrank from her bitter tone. He noticed that Michael turned and put his arm round her. Worried that he was being insensitive, he fell silent. But he was filled with hope that Richard could be his father, and that he might be related to some of this great group of people. Araminta, of course, was bound to feel put out at her father's antics. But surely she would get used to it.

Unable to help himself, he said, suddenly, 'What a turn up!'

Michael gazed at him blankly, but Philip gave him a sideways grin. 'Has there ever been a more surreal day in our lives? After more than forty years, we meet again, and then this. Personally, I see no reason why you shouldn't join the DNA testing brigade.'

Julian nodded vigorously. 'Right you are,' he said, trying to hide his excitement as he strode out of the room to find Farid.

Philip watched as Michael took Araminta's hand and whispered something to her that he was unable to hear. He could feel a sense of devastation emanating from the couple, and he racked his brains for ideas of how he might help or comfort them.

But, without any warning, a tiny fragment of memory detached itself from its hiding place in some outer wing of his brain and bubbled into his accessible mind. It was connected with his mother, ages ago, having explained to him how a doctor had given her a magical injection which, nine months later, had turned into Baby Philip.

That conversation – which had probably taken place, like many of their fascinating chats, over the kitchen table while she fed him soda bread or potato cakes – had never, to his conscious knowledge, been revisited.

The words, so clear in his mind, were entirely commensurate with his mother's attachment to fantasy and romantic language and, noticing that Araminta and Michael were still deep in conversation, he slipped out of the dining room to ring his parent.

His mother said that she was in her office, catching up with some accounts, and she began relating the day's events, and how she wished he was there too. But as she drew breath, Philip mentioned the injections, and she went very quiet. He pressed on, reminding her of what she had told him as a boy, and then he asked if Dr Yateman could possibly have been the doctor who had treated her.

187

'He was, yes,' his mother answered.

'And, do you know what was in the injections?'

'Oh,' she sighed loudly, 'do I have to spell this out, Philip?'

'I'd be grateful if you would.'

'Well, 'twas your father's stuff. You know. His *white* stuff... Don't make me say anything else.'

'It's OK. Thanks, Ma. I get the picture. But, how did you come to see a GP in Norwich? I mean, we lived in the north of the county, and as far as I recall we always had a private doctor.'

'Ah, well now, that was all down to Our Lady of Walsingham,' his mother explained. 'And sure it was a miracle.'

'Really?'

'It was, yes. I'm certain of it. One day, I went to the shrine, in the Slipper Chapel in Walsingham. Even though I come from a Protestant family, I somehow knew I had to go there. Your father and I'd been trying for ages to have a baby. It was getting desperate. By then, he and I didn't get on at all. But while I was there, I met another Irish woman, who'd recently become pregnant after a long time trying. She was at the shrine to give thanks. We got talking, and when I explained my situation, she told me about Dr Yateman. I remember it as though it were yesterday. She and her husband had had to have three lots of injections before she conceived. I was lucky. It only took one. But it changed my life forever, thanks be to God. And thanks too to Mrs... uh... wait now, it's on the tip of my tongue... Mrs... Charlton... no... Champion, no... Chapman. I think that was it. Chapman.'

'Chapman! Are you sure?'

'Yes, I am, yes. Is that all you wanted to know?'

Philip was so taken aback that he could hardly speak. 'Yes,' he managed. 'Thanks.'

'OK, my treasure. Happy St Stephen's Day. Better get on!'

In a daze, he walked back into the hall and bumped into Michael.

'I'm just going to have my swab taken,' said the former priest. 'Needless to say, I'm hoping against hope that my father was not one of the blokes with non-swimming sperm. Have you been tested already?'

'No, I'll come with you.'

'By the way, when we fill in the form, could I put down your address, as I don't really have one now?'

'Of course you can… Listen, perhaps I shouldn't tell you this because you'll probably regard it as another nail in the coffin of your hopes – but I just rang my wacky old mother, because I suddenly remembered her telling me about a doctor who gave her a magical injection, which created me. And it all happened, she's just told me, because she met a Mrs *Chapman* – who one might assume was your mother – at Walsingham. They got talking, and your mum, who was newly pregnant, recommended Dr Yateman. Can you believe it? So, I might not be here had it not been for your mother, and perhaps neither of us would have been born without the old doc's methods. This has got to be the most bizarre day of our lives, don't you think?'

Michael stood swaying in the hallway as if someone much larger had punched him; his facial expression one of incomprehension mixed with incredulity. Then he cleared his throat and whispered, 'It was the best of times, it was the worst of times…'

Chapter Fourteen

Julian had prepared a cold beef salad for his mother's evening meal, and was trying to encourage her to eat it. After a while, he switched on the television so that they could watch Agatha Christie's *Witness for the Prosecution*. But by ten she was desperate to go to bed.

He tried to persuade her to stay up for a while longer, feeling as though his festivities were dwindling away to nothing. More than that, he did not relish being alone with his memories of the afternoon. Had he been crass and uncaring towards the others at Araminta's house? He hoped not, but it was an anxiety.

'Mum,' he initiated a new conversation. 'You know what you said about Dr Richard – and how nice he was?'

She looked at him blearily. 'Do we have to rake this up again, Jules?'

'Sorry, but do you think, that he *could* have been my father? You said yourself I was nothing like Pop.'

She sighed loudly. 'Long time ago, son. It doesn't matter now, does it?'

He wanted to scream that it very definitely *did* matter but he bit his lip.

'Go on up, Mum. You're tired. I think I'll see if your new neighbour wants to come over for a drink. You wouldn't mind that, would you?'

Joe answered his door immediately and invited Julian to step inside.

'Well, I'd never have expected this,' Julian laughed as he gazed around at the colourful furniture, several large-scale wood carvings and a cabinet full of highly polished pieces of wood of different sizes and varieties.

'I used to be a carpenter,' Joe volunteered. 'Had my own business.' He opened the cabinet and invited Julian to examine his work.

'God, this is fantastic. You could charge people to come and see all this!'

Joe looked pleased. 'That bit you're holding is Lignum Vitae – literally, the wood of life. You find it in the Caribbean mostly. I brought it back from Jamaica. Feels soothing, doesn't it? But at the same time, it vibrates with energy.'

Julian found himself staring at Joe with fresh eyes. Who would have thought that this gentle giant had such a creative soul?

'We could have a drink here?' Joe suggested.

Julian paused. He would have liked to remain in this unusual setting, feeling – as he did – strangely comforted by it. 'Maybe another time,' he answered. 'I think I ought to be home in case Mum needs me, though she's probably out for the count now.'

Joe smiled and reached for a thick sweater to cover his floral shirt. 'Not a problem.'

Philip was sprawled in his favourite old leather chair in the snug. Marigold had long ago gone to bed, giving no indication that she was keen for him to join her. And, possibly for the first time since he had known her, he had no appetite for her body. There was too much else to think about.

He tried to recapture the effervescent nature of Araminta's party prior to Hannah's appearance. What a day it had been. Not yet quite used to having as close a friend as Michael, he had been amazed at how pleased he had been to see him again.

As for Julian, bumping into him after more than four decades had been a massive stroke of luck. Not only that, but finally, he had been able to extinguish his long-held fear that he had been responsible for his friend leaving their school. To be together in the same room as both Michael and Julian had been an extraordinary experience.

But then the jovial mood of the day had been torpedoed by Hannah's revelation. Why had she done it? She was obviously a bright and good person – an optimist of the kind that was much needed in the world. But her naïve fancy that he, Araminta, Michael and Wendy would be thrilled to find themselves related had been wildly simplistic.

Despite knowing he would suffer for it, he walked over to his drinks table and poured himself a generous measure of brandy.

The oddest thing, he mused as he returned to the comfort of his armchair, had been what he had learned during his phone call to his mother. And once Wendy and Julian had left, he and Michael had gone over it in detail.

'It's astounding to think that our mums met, by chance, at Walsingham,' Michael had said. 'And that my mother may be responsible, in a way, for your existence.'

He and Michael had gone on to try to understand Dr Richard and his motives. But after a while, though he would have been happy to continue talking for hours, he had sensed that Araminta and Michael needed to be alone.

Their despair was palpable. He, on the other hand, felt strangely elated at the possibility that he might be Richard's son, and a sense of rightness and relief that the remote, critical man he had believed to be his father, might not be his parent after all.

Keen to learn more about Dr Yateman, he had called his mother again after he had left Araminta's house, but she had launched into an account of the latest bit of excitement in her own life, which was that some film star he had never heard of had booked an entire floor of the hotel for her birthday.

Eventually, he had asked if he might speak to Katie, but yet again, she had been unavailable. Every time he had rung over Christmas she had been asleep or out walking. What did his mother make of their lack of contact? Perhaps she assumed that he and Katie were talking regularly on their mobiles. But Katie had not answered his calls or texts since she had arrived in Ireland. Initially, he had felt utterly woebegone by her inaccessibility, but now he was surprised to find that – though it was only three days since they had had any kind of conversation – he was feeling somewhat disengaged from her. Her treatment of him seemed more dismissive than he deserved.

By contrast, just before she had left Araminta's house, Wendy – a woman he had met for the first time only a few hours before – had sat down beside him and asked how he was feeling after Hannah's 'bombshell'. It was obvious that she herself was devastated, so her concern for him had been touching.

They had exchanged mobile numbers. 'In case I need to talk to someone who understands this chaotic mess,' she had explained.

It was four a.m. He hoped that, unlike him, she was asleep. But perhaps he could text her in the morning.

'Are you awake, Michael?' Araminta's whisper was barely audible, as she had no wish to disturb him if he had fallen asleep at last.

They had discussed the situation endlessly, from the moment that Philip, the last guest to depart, had left. And every time their words dried up, they had clung to each other, like victims trapped on the rocks as an angry sea engulfed them.

At bedtime, she had made Horlicks, and they had both had a hot bath, then she had sprinkled their pillows with lavender oil. But for hours after they had switched off the lights, she had lain awake, aware from the sound of Michael's breathing that sleep was eluding him too. What was Hannah's news going to do to his plans, his mind and his future? She must have slept eventually, but now, at 5.15 she resigned herself to the miserable realisation that she was so wide awake she might as well get up.

193

Could she ease herself out of bed, without disturbing Michael? She lay still for another ten minutes trying to breathe deeply against the knot of panic that had taken up residence in her stomach. Somehow, she must persuade him that all would be well and that they could still, somewhere – and in some way or another – be together. Anything else was unthinkable.

She felt him snuggle closer to her. 'Araminta,' he whispered. 'Are you awake, my darling?'

At 5.30, Wendy abandoned all attempts at sleeping and put the light on for company.

After returning to her father's home, she had made a spirited attempt to appear normal and positive, but she was aware that her performance had been less than convincing; inside, she had felt like a character in *Doctor Who*, reduced by a malevolent alien to a pile of rubble.

Previously, her only real worry concerning her father had been that one day he would die. But having to contend with the probability that a rogue sperm had cast her adrift from him, his history, and his name was infinitely worse.

Who am I? she asked herself again and again. *And how can I continue if I'm not the woman I've always presumed myself to be?*

Earlier, she had plucked various Marks & Spencer packs from the freezer and prepared a dinner she had had no wish to eat. She had focused as best she could on talking to her father, but every now and again, had made some feeble excuse to fetch something from the kitchen, where she had gasped in lungfuls of air in an attempt to calm herself.

He must have realised that all was not well, though he had made no comment till he was about to go to bed. Then he had muttered something to the effect that she did not seem to be quite her 'bright and breezy self'.

She had apologised, whereupon he had embarked upon his habitual warning that she worked too hard and that, for the good of her health, she should take things easier. 'After all,' he had remarked, 'you are going to be sixty next year.'

'I know, Dad,' she had forced a smile. 'Don't remind me!'

Stretching out, she tried to cleanse her mind of all unwelcome thoughts, but after thirty seconds, she found herself recalling her confidence when she had declared to the others that her father must be her real parent because they were so alike.

Now, the more she thought about Hannah's revelations, the more perturbed she felt. Everything Dr Richard had said to her during their two meetings haunted her, especially: 'You're my Number One'.

She almost wished that she had never bumped into Minty and never resurrected their friendship – because if she were to be deleted from her father's family tree, and forced to accept that half her genes had been donated by someone other than him, she had no idea how she would reconcile her old self to her new one.

And, she realised, as another sweep of panic stole over her, there were other considerations. Julian had often asked where Rhys's musical talent had come from; something she and Robert had wondered too – though at least her son had Robert's looks and her sense of humour. But Daniel was not just super-bright, he bore no resemblance to her or her parents, or anyone in Robert's family either. At school he had shown prodigious talent in science and maths, and a teacher at one parents' evening had joked that 'every class should have a Daniel'. However, another master had said, somewhat cynically, that Daniel had a most original way of thinking, and that, 'He'll either be a genius mathematician or a master criminal!' She and Robert had laughed politely. It did not seem funny now. The possible link between her boy and Dr Richard's unorthodox mind processes and behaviour was too unsettling.

She turned on her side, rearranging the bedclothes around her. For a moment, she thought that sleep might come at last, but then her legs started twitching. Perhaps she would feel better if she got up and made some tea.

'Who'd have thought it, eh?' Julian murmured as he rolled to the side of Joe's bed with a contented sigh.

Joe lay, breathless, beside him, a huge smile illuminating his large face. 'It's been such a while. I was too quick and not very good.'

Julian took the other man's huge hand in both of his. 'Not true. You were gentle. Kind. Loving. And actually,' he grinned, 'very arousing. And I can't tell you what a change that was. I have a tendency to go for beautiful men who treat me badly.'

'Are you saying I'm not bootiful?' Joe spoke in an exaggerated Norfolk accent.

'Actually, you have a special beauty.' Julian's voice warbled slightly with emotion, which came both as a surprise and an embarrassment to him. But he persisted. 'It's very real too, and not manufactured in one of those poncy gyms in the city. You're a bit like your woodwork. Pulsating and true. Cor – get me... I'm not usually this poetic. Thing is, I hadn't even spotted that you were gay. Must be losing my touch!'

'I've never been anything else – but being a "batty boy" in Jamaica was bad news. Still is. So, I came to Britain in the early eighties, and not long afterwards I met my partner and that was real good for a long time.' Joe reminisced with a faraway look in his eyes. 'But once he retired, I think he was worried that he might die without having had enough nookie. So, he started hanging around trendy clubs, had facial fillers, hair weaving... all that jazz. I used to worry, but gradually I saw it as pathetic. D'you want a drink?'

'No, I'd better get home before Mum wakes up. It was just as well that we came over to your place once we got going!'

'I know. I'm a noisy old bugger, aren't I?' Joe grinned.

Julian kissed him lightly on the cheek. 'I hope we can do it again,' he ventured as he moved towards the door. In the absence of a verbal response, he paused, nervously, on the threshold and turned.

Joe saluted him and smiled. 'Me too.'

'I'd like to go for a walk,' said Michael.

They were sipping tea in the kitchen. It was still dark, and their continuing ruminations were leading them nowhere.

'Mmmn,' Araminta murmured. 'Me too. It would be OK if we lived by the sea. I've always thought that it seems perfectly normal for people to wander along a beach at virtually any hour. But I'm sure my neighbours would think I'd lost the plot if I want walking along the street here at…' she checked her watch '…6.15 on a winter's morning.'

'I'd love to live by the sea,' he murmured.

'Then that's what we should do.' Suddenly, Araminta felt a tiny glow of optimism and she ferreted around in her brain for other thoughts to nurture it, much like one might seek out paper or dry twigs to coax a recalcitrant flame into a viable fire.

'We could,' he agreed. 'We were always going to need to find somewhere away from here and – in my case – a new occupation too, if we were going to be together. From that point of view, I suppose nothing has altered.'

'Exactly.' Her voice was firm. 'If we do turn out to be half-siblings, who needs to know? You're not going to change your birth certificate. At the moment, the only person who's aware that we're together is Philip. He's not going to spill the beans. Or argue that what we're doing is immoral or illegal.'

'There's Wendy.'

'No, actually, there's not. I didn't find the right moment to tell her.'

Remembering Wendy's half smile when Araminta had leant against him at the party, he said, 'I suspect she may have guessed.'

'Well, even if she has, she's unshockable.'

'What about Hannah?'

'She need never know.'

'Darling girl, of course your daughter must know if we're living together. We can't compartmentalise our lives to that degree.'

She sighed noisily. 'Well OK, but we don't have to tell her if you do turn out to be one of Dad's scientific successes. Farid insisted everyone should get their results sent directly to them so they could keep them private if they wanted. I know you all agreed that you'd share them. But that doesn't have to include Hannah.'

'I don't know what to think.'

'I know.' She nodded, then pulled him closer and planted a kiss on his cheek.

He gave her hand a quick squeeze. 'I love you, Araminta.'

'Good.' Her face relaxed into a smile. 'Because I love you too. We'll sort this. Bit of a bastard though, isn't it?'

She peered at him as he sat, slumped and motionless. How gaunt and exhausted he looked. What must it be like for him? He had finally taken the enormous decision to leave the priesthood, only to find the track ahead strewn with insurmountable hurdles.

Suddenly, he sat bolt upright. 'I think I should go to the presbytery and load up the car with all my stuff. Philip said I could store my belongings with him till I get settled.'

Araminta, unaware that her lower lip had begun to tremble, asked, 'How long will you be gone?'

'Till lunchtime perhaps. Will you be all right?'

'Of course,' she answered, though a pulse of panic started beating wildly in her neck.

Michael reached for her hand again and kissed it. 'I'll go in about half an hour then,' he said as he disappeared upstairs to shower and dress.

She wandered around the kitchen, which was still a mess of dirty plates and dishes with remnants of the Boxing Day lunch congealing upon them. Several times yesterday she had begun to clear up, but her attempts had been half-hearted and all too readily abandoned every time either she or Michael had sparked off a renewed conversation about their future.

It seemed somewhat pointless, in the face of this emotional earthquake, to worry about landfill sites, or whether any of the food lying around was fit to be frozen or must just be thrown away. But there was a kind of comfort to be had in following customary routines. So she scraped all the salad and vegetable remnants into a large bucket and took it outside to the composter. Back indoors, she surveyed the baskets of bread. It was too late to freeze any of it now. Everything seemed such a waste.

Blinking back tears, she wandered out into the hall and spied Michael's coat hanging on the hat stand. She gasped as if someone had punched her in the stomach, and almost fell over with the visceral assault of grief on her body. In a daze, she slipped into the garment and sank down onto the bottom step of the stairs and began to wail.

He would leave her now. He would do the moral and upright thing. And there would be no more possibility of Michael and Araminta – the loving couple who would enjoy life together companionably and joyfully into their dotage. She could smell him on his coat, and for a moment she was reminded of the days after her son's death when her only comfort had been to sit in his bedroom and sniff his sweaters. She had endured the death of her husband, the demise of her son, but she could not, would not, lose her new love.

'No!' she screamed. 'No, no, no. no.' Then she toppled off the step and lay weeping, on the floor.

She felt him raise her up and pull her to him. He rocked her to and fro as if she were a child having a nightmare.

'Darling! It will be all right.'

'But it won't. You'll leave this house and once you're in the presbytery, the priesthood will reclaim you, and you'll feel that all this is a judgement on you. Then you'll decide that you must do the right thing and disappear from my life – and you'll fly off somewhere remote, and then email me saying it would never have worked. I can't risk it. Please don't go.'

199

'Araminta, look at me,' his voice had a desperate urgency to it and she immediately pulled a hand free from his coat, clumsily wiped her eyes, and raised her gaze to meet his.

'What?'

'I'm far too selfish to live without you. I've felt overwhelmed by loneliness for so long, but now I don't and that's because of you. I've no idea how we're going to sort this. But whatever we do – change our names, go to the other side of the world – we're going to be together.'

'Michael, I know that right this minute you mean what you say, but I can't envisage our future. And I'm terrified that once you walk out of my front door, you won't be able to imagine it either.'

'I promise I won't let you go.'

'Well, please don't leave me here,' she whispered. 'Please don't.'

He led her back into the kitchen and sat her down on the old sofa then walked to the other end of the room and made a fresh pot of tea.

Could she rely on him? Could they survive? Could they, if they had to, live with their secret, hoping forever that no one would discover it?

'I think we should go away,' he said as he pressed a mug of strong tea into her hands. 'Today.'

She nodded.

Swiftly, they dismissed the Caribbean as being too frivolous for their present mood, decided against the north Norfolk coast because it was too near, almost elected to go to Brighton but wondered if it might be less restful than they wanted and somehow came to the conclusion that Ireland was the best destination.

'My mother was from Dingle,' Michael said. And suddenly the decision was made.

Wendy's father disturbed her thoughts. 'What are you doing up, poppet? It's only seven o'clock.'

She elected not to tell him that she had been downstairs for over an hour, and had not slept at all. 'I know. I woke up early. There's tea in the pot.'

'Good,' he smiled as he sat down at the kitchen table. 'Any chance of some toast and marmalade?'

His hair was wild and bushy, and brushed the collar of his tartan dressing gown. He was so familiar. So solid. So true.

'Can I talk to you?' Her father's voice was tentative.

She nodded but did not turn, choosing instead to busy herself with the toaster and the teapot. He was probably going to ask what was upsetting her, and she could not decide what to tell him.

'Aren't you having any?' her father asked as she presented him with two rounds of wholemeal toast and his mug of tea.

'Bit early for me to eat. You know I've never been a morning person.'

They grinned, each suddenly caught up with their own memories of her growing up in this house.

Then, in a slightly swaggering tone which she put down to embarrassment, he said, 'Presumably, you don't need money... I don't want to pry, but I assume that even with the divorce, you're comfortably off and don't need me to leave this house to you?'

Wendy knew she looked bewildered. Had she, without realising it, communicated to her father that she may not be his child, and had that sparked off a decision to leave his assets to someone else? Her head started to swim from lack of sleep and the tensions of the previous day. She stared hard at the floor and dropped her head slightly, breathing deeply, in a bid to regain control.

Her father held out a slice of toast. 'I think you'd better eat something.'

She nodded and took a mouthful, trying not to reveal that the thick-cut marmalade he adored was not to her taste.

'Sorry to land all this on you at this hour,' he said. 'But there never seems to be a perfect moment to discuss my plans with you, and this seems as good a time as any. The crux of the matter is

201

that I can't stand your mother being in that nursing home. I know you think she doesn't have a clue what's going on, but I'm not convinced. And in her right mind she'd have hated us to be parted, and to be reduced to sitting all day watching TV programmes she'd never have picked when she was well. And the final straw was Dr Yateman being there. I could see you thought I was rude on Christmas Day not speaking to him, but he reminds me of a time I'd prefer to forget.'

'What do you mean?' She tried to swallow the panic in her throat. What did her father know? How *could* he know anything? And if he did, how could it have remained a secret all these years?

'I told you recently,' he explained, 'that your mum and I had some difficulty in having you. This was long before test-tube babies and the like, so we were grateful when Dr Yateman suggested to your mother that we might have more luck with a more direct approach than nature can provide. Sorry, it's a tad embarrassing. But it involved using the husband's... semen, and injecting it directly into the woman's womb to increase the chance of conception. Luckily, it worked, and you came along. But there was a bit of me that felt less of a man because of it. I felt I should have been able to get your mother pregnant the normal way. And when I found Yateman was in the same home as your mum, it disturbed me. I don't know why. It just did.'

Wendy exhaled loudly, having unconsciously held her breath during her father's explanation. This was a better outcome than she had feared. Her father knew about the technique that had given her life, but not about the doctor's personal donation.

'What are you planning, Dad?' she asked gently.

'I'm going to move your mother to a new development where couples can be together. We'll have our own apartment, but Mum will go down to the communal nursing home during the day and just come back at night. The staff will get her ready for bed, so it won't all fall on me. It's very expensive though, so I'll be selling this house. But we'll be together and I won't have the expense of an independent life, or all that travel to see her.' He pushed himself up from the table and walked over to a pile of papers on the dresser and rifled through them till he came upon a glossy brochure which he presented to Wendy. 'The complex is called Wherry Haven. It's out in the country, near Holt. And the apartment is furnished, which makes life easier, though of course I can take personal belongings – clothes, books, photos, things that matter...'

Wendy blinked as she looked at the brochure. Living there would be her idea of hell but clearly, her father saw it in a positive light.

'We'll have enough money to see us through,' he went on. 'And there may well be savings left over that will come to you, but I just want to be sure that if we live long enough to use up all our reserves, you'll be OK?'

She leapt up and hugged him so tightly that he eventually begged for air. 'Do it, Dad. I know you want to be with Mum. But I can't help feeling it's going to cramp your style. I mean you can go out any time you like here. You've got friends...'

'It won't be a prison, Wendy,' he interrupted her, manifestly relieved to have discussed his plan.

He was still handsome, she realised. Still sharp. Still her lovely dad.

'I'm going to carry on driving for as long as I can,' he continued. 'But the truth is when you get to my age, few of your friends are still around, and those that are, don't get out much. The estate agents came last week and want to put the details of the house online tomorrow. So, are you happy about the plan?'

'Of course, Dad. It's a splendid idea.'

He smiled broadly. '*I* think so. Now, why don't you go up and try and get another hour's sleep? Then later we could drive out to see Wherry Haven, and have lunch somewhere and pop in on your mother.'

After having a bath and making them both breakfast, Araminta threw a random assortment of clothes and toiletries into a large suitcase, dressed herself in a warm 'walking' outfit and shoes and

– once it was eight o'clock – phoned the experienced, senior therapist who acted as her supervisor. She expected to have to leave a message, but the other woman was an early riser and listened carefully as Araminta asked her to take over her caseload because of a 'family crisis'.

She could hear her voice betraying just how shaky and tearful she felt, but her colleague simply murmured, 'Absolutely,' and then, 'Of course you can't work at the moment,' before adding, 'I'm happy to have a few extra clients. To be honest, I could use the money right now.'

Araminta sighed with relief. Now all she really had to do was to make contact with Hannah.

Darling, sorry yesterday didn't work out as you'd planned. But everyone will be all right in the end. Just to say I've gone away. We'll speak after your holiday with Farid. Have a brilliant time. I'm going to turn off my phone for a few days. Lots of thinking to do. Loads of love, Mum x

Finally, she tackled the remaining mess in the kitchen – sweeping all uneaten food into large bin bags which she crammed into her wheelie bin.

They called a taxi, which took them to the presbytery and she went for a walk while Michael packed such worldly goods as he owned into his old Volvo.

Within an hour, they were on their way to Philip.

'And once we've offloaded all this,' Michael announced briskly, 'it'll be Ireland next stop!'

To her surprise, Wendy did manage to sleep for a couple of hours. And then she lay in bed for a while longer, surveying her bedroom as if for the last time.

On occasions, she had wondered if she might return to Norfolk, but her inchoate thoughts had never crystallised into a decision to live in this house. At the back of her mind, she had imagined that she might one day suggest that her father leave his property to her twin boys. But somehow that conversation had never taken place. And now it was too late.

Her phone warbled with a text from Philip.

Just wondering if you're awake? Do you think, if it turns out we're related, we'll find we have similar tastes? Never had a sibling, so not sure how alike brothers and sisters are. Shall we try an experiment?

Wendy found herself smiling. Philip was an unusual person and she had liked him very much at their first meeting. He had seemed quick-witted and sophisticated, but strangely lacking in confidence. Quite an endearing combination.

A sort of quiz do you mean?
Yes.
Go on then!
OK. Spendthrift or saver?
Both.
Dinner party for six, or large party, standing up nursing drinks and canapes?
Dinner.
Dutch Masters or Impressionists?
Mmmn – used to be the latter, but I think Dutch Masters now.
Theatre or cinema?
Both – but specially theatre, I suppose.
ITN, Sky or BBC News?
I used to direct programmes for ITN!
I knew. Michael told me.
Bit of a trick question then! I should say ITN but truth is they're all good.

Organised or disorganised?

So organised and capable that my departing husband told me he found it emasculating.

Ouch!

I know!

I shouldn't be flippant about all this – specially because you're upset – but on this evidence, there's no doubt that we're related! Maybe talk later?

I'd like that.

And she would, she realised. It was something to look forward to.

Chapter Fifteen

Walking holiday or five-star luxury?

Wendy paused before answering Philip's latest text. She was, she realised, trying to impress him – which seemed somewhat pathetic – but she did not want to appear stupid when it was obvious how clever he was. If he did turn out to be her half-brother, she suspected that they might develop a healthy sibling rivalry.

Would like to say 'walking' but love luxury too! Have often wondered about those organised trips in France or Italy where you ramble all day but stay in fabulous places at night, and then have all your gear transported to next location so you don't have to carry it, and can take plenty of luggage including all the right shoes!
Sounds perfect.
Doesn't it? OK – here's a question: Mondays or Fridays?
That's tough. When I worked in publishing, I'd have gone for Mondays. I couldn't wait to get to work. I wish it was true now!
I've always been a Monday person. I adored getting back to school after the weekends and I've always loved having a

career. I suppose I'm someone who looks forward, not back. I'm not very sentimental or nostalgic. Boring isn't it?

Not to me. How are you going to spend today? Are you OK?

Better than y'day, mostly because I managed five hours' sleep. Hope to get hold of Julian. I tried every way to contact him y'day, but didn't get him. Feel bad that I was offhand with him on Boxing Day. He's such a great mate. Later, going out again to Dad's new place, and we're taking more of his stuff. It's all a bit weird and sudden. What are you doing?

Going to office. Some staff will be in now bank holiday's over. I'll cycle. Do me good! Will you give my best to Julian? Terrific to meet him after all these years. We used to be best pals. Btw, is there a wife?

No, he's gay and single.

Ah. I hope he's happy. He was always so good to be around.

Still is!

Can I text later?

Please do.

I don't want to be a bore.

You couldn't be.

You don't know me!

'Dear heart!'

'Julian, is that you?'

'How many other blokes call you that? Don't tell me you've been two-timing me.'

Wendy laughed. When Julian had not responded to her messages the day before, she had convinced herself that he must be cross, so his call came as a welcome relief.

'I'm afraid I was awful to you on Monday. Frankly, it's a bit of a blur now. But I'm really sorry.'

'Don't be ridiculous. I thought I'd offended *you*, so I didn't like to call – and unfortunately, I didn't receive your messages till this morning because my phone was dead and my charger had given up the ghost. These things are beyond me. But my, um, the new, uh, neighbour is good with technology and he bought me another one as soon as the shops were open. So, I'm all tickety-boo now! But also, this morning, I took Mum to the doctor and we were there for ages. Still, great news! He thinks she's got an underactive thyroid. She's got to have a lot of tests and so on, but…'

'Is that good, though?'

'Well, it's a hell of a lot better than dementia or cancer. He says she's a classic case, and that once they get the medication right, she'll be more like her normal self quite soon. I can't tell you how much of a relief…' His voice cracked.

'I'm sure,' Wendy murmured soothingly. 'That's marvellous.'

'How are you now about Dr Yateman?'

Wendy exhaled sharply feeling her fringe lift off her forehead as she did so. 'Bit better, I suppose. We should meet and talk. Maybe we could all get together, though I think maybe Minty's away. I texted her a couple of times but she hasn't replied. I hadn't really thought much about how it might affect her – after all, she knows for sure who her father is. But I suppose finding that he may have sired several other children must take some getting used to.'

'I should say so.'

'Before I forget, Philip sent you best wishes. He's really chuffed to have met up with you again.'

'Awww. Me too. Had you met him before Monday?'

'No, but we've texted a lot since. I think he wanted to see whether siblings are really alike in their tastes – assuming that's what we turn out to be. Being an only child, he's curious about it. I suppose I am too, though I'd do anything to ensure that my own father really *is* my father, if you get what I mean.'

'What a peculiar time this is.'

'You're right,' Wendy replied with a smile in her voice. 'But it's not all bad, is it? Even I'm beginning to see that.'

In his office, Philip felt that he was getting in everyone's way. His role, as he saw it, was in networking with clients, and encouraging them into new deals. He was a good listener, regarded as an honourable salesman and, he acknowledged, not unpopular among landowners and farmers throughout the UK and Europe. But no one wanted a meeting between Christmas and New Year, so he was reduced to wandering around in an attempt to look as though he were as much in command as his title of CEO suggested.

He had begun to wonder if he would feel morally bound to give up all claim on the business if it turned out that he was not Pa's son. The ramifications of Hannah's discovery were only just beginning to occur to him. He assumed it was the same for the others.

Reaching for his mobile, he was about to text Michael when he remembered that both he and Araminta had said that they were going to turn their phones off while they were in Ireland. Wondering what to do next, he stopped and gazed out of the window.

The freezing fog that had clung to the landscape earlier had lifted, revealing a Titian blue sky. Would it be so dreadful to go home now? After all, in terms of work, the days between Christmas and New Year were pretty pointless, and it would be good to get some exercise. As a gesture towards conscientiousness, he checked with his staff that there was nothing of use he could do, and then cycled home to pick up his dogs and go walking.

As always, being active enlivened him, and he strode energetically around his own grounds and the neighbouring fields. The dogs bounded back to check on him from time to time, but mostly raced ahead to chase rabbits, or scrabble and sniff at the earth and stick their big heads into the entrance of tiny burrows. It was one long, joyful investigation for them, and they never tired of it, even though they must have walked this route several times a week for the whole of their ten-year lives.

He stopped by a stile and leant against it while he texted Wendy again.

Are you around? Hope this isn't too personal, but have you told your father what we learned on Monday?

She replied immediately.

I thought about it, but decided not to. Are you thinking of broaching it with yours?
Yes. But dreading it, as we don't get on.
Gosh. Well, good luck with that.
Thanks. I'll need it.

As he walked back to the house, he wondered what form any communication with Pa should take. They were both hopeless at talking on the phone to each other. They were either stilted and polite, or – more usually – Philip found himself on the end of a barrage of criticism. And often, when he did brace himself to put in a call, he was given the impression that he had chosen 'a bad moment'.

Writing would be easier, but as his father refused to own a mobile phone let alone learn to text, and had no clue about emailing, this would require him to use Royal Mail. But could he compose the letter, he wondered, in his laptop and just print it out and sign it? Better probably to handwrite it, since it was a matter of such personal importance. Whatever he did would probably be wrong.

This is so symptomatic of our relationship, he sighed. Why should a man be so uneasy about contacting a parent? Thank God that dealing with his mother was different in every way.

It was still just about light, and on a whim he decided that he would put off communicating with his father a while longer, and take his motorised trike out for a spin. Since he had told Katie about the three-wheeler all-terrain vehicle, he had never so much as unlocked the shed that housed it.

He started up the engine and edged the vehicle out onto the courtyard and then drove it, really slowly, around the large paved area in front of his stables and other outbuildings. Really, he should give it more of a run and take it into the meadow, but the sun had long gone down, and honour was satisfied in that when eventually he talked to Katie, he would be able to say he had been riding it.

Back in the house, he turned his attention once more to communicating with his father. He had business stationery in his study, but that did not seem appropriate, so he went in search of something more suitable in the morning room. Sure enough, in Marigold's antique writing desk, he found a selection of Smythson correspondence cards, and selected one with a red lined border and a matching envelope lined in scarlet tissue.

'What are you doing?' Marigold stood in the doorway. She was dressed in a fur hat and winter coat.

'I beg your pardon?'

'You never come in here.' Her words were barked out in the form of a rebuke.

'That may be so,' he replied slowly, 'but I didn't know I wasn't allowed in. When was that decided?'

'Well, those are my things. It's private.'

Philip sighed. 'Sorry. Is it OK if I just have this card and envelope?'

She shrugged, and then stood back to let him walk out into the hallway before swiftly closing the door as if he were a tiresome child who had strayed into a part of the house reserved for grown-ups. He felt she would have liked to lock the room and spirit away the key.

'Right,' she announced. 'I'm off.'

'Where? It's dark now.'

'I'm driving to London, Philip, I *told* you,' she responded with a well-practised tone of resigned despair.

He did not believe that she had. 'When will you be back?'

'Not sure. It's Cordelia's sixtieth birthday. Various things going on.'

'Who's she again?'

'Don't you ever listen to anything?'

'Sorry – are you staying with her?'

'Good God, no. Her children will be there. I'm staying with Bro. Must go!'

They did not kiss, though he did walk with her to the front door and watch till her rear car lights disappeared from view.

He had no excuse now not to write his letter, but first he wandered into the kitchen and made himself a cup of instant coffee rather than bother with the elaborate espresso machine that Marigold favoured.

There was nowhere comfortable to sit, so he headed for his study. Would he mind, he asked himself, if Marigold came in here and borrowed his stationery? He was unsure. Certainly, he did not encourage people to visit this room. And he restricted his housekeeper's interference to once a fortnight, which drove Marigold mad. But then, he was always irritating her.

He felt unsettled by her attitude earlier. Naturally, she was entitled to privacy. But what had she got to hide? And if she was still keen to rescue their marriage why was she so abrupt with him most of the time? He found himself revisiting her protestations that she loved him. How heartfelt were they? Certainly, she was vehement about not wanting to lose him, but was that more to do with pride than love?

Then there was sex – or lack of it. None had been on offer during Bro's visit, because she had claimed that he might hear them. It had seemed unlikely. After all, the three-hundred-year-old walls in their part of the house were almost two feet thick. And her favours, so lavishly bestowed on him for seven surreal nights before Christmas, had not been reinstated now that they were alone again. Did he mind? Not really. Initially, the week of

213

passion had been a thrill, but it had ended up as a pretty vacuous experience, devoid as it was of warmth and kindness.

'Damn it,' he shouted to the empty room. 'Am I so undesirable? So unlovable? So uninteresting?'

He reached for his mobile phone and rang Katie. As it had for days, it went straight to voicemail.

'Katie,' he said in a much less appeasing tone than usual. 'Ring me back, please. I want to hear how you are and when you're coming home. And I want to talk to you about us and the baby.'

Finally, when he could think of no other diversionary tactics, he put pen to paper.

Dear Pa. I trust you had a good Christmas. I hope you're well. Sorry to spring this on you, but I need to ask you something. You and I are not alike at all. Has it ever occurred to you that I may not be your biological son? Apologies for asking. Yours, Philip.

'So, what do you think?' Michael stepped out of the car, zipped up his waterproof jacket and gazed, with a broad smile on his face, at the miles of sand around them and the frothy waves beyond. 'This is Inch Beach. They filmed *Ryan's Daughter* here. Other movies too, I think. I haven't been back since my gran died when I was about eleven. Mum and I used to come over every summer till then. Wonderful, isn't it?'

Araminta nodded enthusiastically, then sniffed in the salty air. 'Marvellous.'

They laughed with relief and hugged each other – aware that somehow there had been a flick of a switch in their brains to a brighter setting.

'The king is himself again,' Araminta declaimed.

'What?'

'I think it's a line in *The Madness of King George*. It just came into my mind. For days, I've been struggling to feel like me, and coming here seems to have done it.'

Their journey had begun with them unloading all Michael's possessions into a barn in the grounds of Philip's house. From there they had driven through the day to Holyhead, where they had caught a ferry to Dublin. They had opted to spend a couple of nights in the old city, in the comfortably traditional Wynn's Hotel, where they had talked endlessly, slept poorly, but eaten well.

On the second evening, they had left their sanctuary to go to a production of *Juno and Paycock* at the Abbey Theatre, which they had both agreed was excellent, but hardly an antidote to their misery.

However today, their drive across country to Dingle had begun to feel like an adventure instead of a cowardly escape, and now, their spirits rose even more as they broke away from their embrace and ran, giggling along the sand, stumbling slightly when the wind gusted and caught them unawares.

They settled into a brisk walk for half an hour or so and then turned back. There was a café right beside the car park and with a strong breeze behind them, they almost fell into it, ready for a hearty meal.

Standing on the platform at Cromer station, having been dropped there by her father, Wendy dug her hands deep into the pockets of her warm coat and wished that she had worn a hat.

For the fourth day in a row, the two of them had packed boxes of books, CDs and clothes at the Hethersett house, loaded them into the car and conveyed them to the new flat at Wherry Haven. Her father was focused on one issue only – accomplishing his move as quickly as possible. Clearly, Wendy had realised, he had signed a contract long before confiding in her. And much to her amazement, she had learned earlier that her parents would start sleeping at their new place tomorrow, on New Year's Eve.

Her father had always been a very determined man, and age had not dented that particular characteristic. She loved him for it, convinced – all over again – that he must be her biological parent. After all, she was businesslike and decisive and driven, and she must have inherited those traits from him.

The train was late, so she paced up and down to keep warm and to stave off the bleak sensation she felt at the prospect of the sale of their family home. It seemed to signify the end of her father's active life, even though he had been anything but inactive since telling her of his plans. But, she realised, she had vaguely expected her mother – whose useful existence certainly seemed to be over – to expire at some point, either from her dementia or perhaps a bout of bronchitis, leaving her father more time to spend with her, in London, Norfolk, or on holiday. But he had made it plain that he saw Wherry Haven as his last home and that he would die there, whether or not his wife predeceased him.

She was stunned by how much she minded. The other disappointment was that she had assumed they would spend New Year's Eve together. Perhaps they could still, but it would hardly feel the same as being with him in Hethersett. She could, of course, go home to London, but the flat would be empty, and Julian would not be in the city because he was staying in Norfolk till next week to help his mother... Neither of her sons showed any inclination to come home... Minty was not answering calls... Hannah was away...

Life had changed so much, so quickly. Was it possible that she was lonely – she, a woman who had always prided herself on being productive, positive and pragmatic? How had that happened?

She shook herself impatiently; she must 'buck up'. Soon, she would be back at work and everything would feel more normal.

A text from Philip pinged into her mobile.

What are you up to?
Feeling sorry for myself, waiting for a Norwich train on Cromer station.

Ten seconds later, her phone rang.
'Wendy.'

'Hello, Philip.'

'Look, I don't know if this would suit, but I don't live that far from where you are. If you get a train to Sheringham instead of back to Norwich, I could pick you up and we could come back to my house. It's almost teatime. My wife's away but I'm sure I could rustle up something.'

'You don't have to take pity on me because I'm in a soulful mood!'

'I'm not. I've walked the dogs – twice. No one needs me at my business because it won't chug back into life properly till the third of January. I'm just pottering around, and feeling somewhat moody myself, so you'd be doing me a favour.'

She was certain that he was just being kind, but the thought of his company was cheering. So, she took the train to Sheringham as he had suggested, and half an hour later, after hurtling at hair-raising speed through narrow winding lanes in a taxi, they drew up outside Hunsford Hall.

'Beautiful house,' she breathed as he unlocked the front door.

'Yes,' he agreed. 'It is now. It was a wreck when I bought it!'

He took her coat, and then led her into the kitchen while he put on the kettle and went in search of cake, opening a series of cupboards till he happened upon the tins he was looking for.

'Have a potter around and see where you fancy sitting,' he invited her.

'What would your wife think if she knew you were giving free rein to a strange woman in her house?'

'You're not a strange woman – you're probably my sister! And she's not here and has given no indication of when she's coming back. Go ahead. I'll be interested to see which room you choose!'

'By the way, thanks for meeting me at Sheringham in a taxi. Don't you drive?'

'Ah, I forgot you don't know. I'm ashamed to say I got done for drink-driving – in October. Totally my fault!'

'You don't seem the type,' she smiled at him. 'I had been thinking that perhaps you're a terrible driver, and that that would be another indication that we're related. I'm the world's worst! I hate to admit it because I like to see myself as someone who can tackle anything.'

'I bet you're not as bad as you think. You're obviously brilliant at most things. Perhaps you're just a little *less* brilliant at that.'

She giggled. 'Nice try. But way off beam. I'm hopeless. My twin sons wouldn't even get in the car with me once they were old enough to have their say.'

'Hmmn. I like to think I'm quite a good driver.'

'There you are then. We're not siblings after all!'

He followed her as she explored the spacious ground floor. The dining room seemed too large. She rejected the morning room too; though she refrained from saying so, she disliked the formality of it – and the silver-grey décor and powder blue chairs seemed wildly impractical. Suppose she had mud on her shoes and dirtied the carpet, or spilt her tea on that pale and immaculate furniture? It did not bear thinking about.

She almost settled on the sitting room with its trio of Edward Seago watercolours on the tastefully neutral walls, but nearby, she found a small, windowless room, painted in quite a masculine shade of greyish green, and dominated by two comfortable-looking leather chairs.

'What about here?' she turned to him.

'Good idea. The snug – my favourite room!'

He left her there, but returned almost immediately with fruit cake and two mugs of tea. 'Now, tell me everything about you!' he said. So she did. And when she had finished, she asked him to do the same and learned about his father, his marriage, Katie and his dead daughter.

It was gone six o'clock before they – temporarily – ran out of topics.

'What about a drink?' he suggested as his eye went to the nearby trolley. 'Brandy?'

'Lovely – just a tiny one.'

'So,' he commented, as he handed her a heavy, wide-bowled crystal glass, 'neither of us has had a happy marriage.'

She sipped thoughtfully. 'I'm not sure that's true of mine. It had loads of ups and downs, but there was a lot of conversation and laughter, and Robert was a very good dad. Still is. But he was seriously over-sexed. And I'm not. In fact, I don't think I'm very good at it – not from what he said.'

Philip grimaced. 'I don't think I am either,' he remarked ruefully. 'Perhaps it runs in the family!'

The next morning, Wendy watched her father walk down the stairs as he prepared to take his leave of the family home. He looked very dapper in a grey suit with a blue shirt and tie, and highly polished shoes. He was excited, almost skittish, like a young lad going on a date. For the first time it occurred to her that he might still be capable of having sex. Could that be part of what this was about? And if so, was it right that her mother should be inveigled into such intimacy when her mind had gone? She shuddered as she tried to un-think the thought. It was not her business.

'Bringing in the New Year together,' her father said suddenly, 'will mean a lot to me. You don't stop wanting to be with your lifelong companion just because one of you is ill and you're both old.' He surveyed her very intently for a moment. 'Maybe I shouldn't say this, Wendy, but I hope you'll marry again, and that I'll live to see it. You deserve someone decent and honourable; someone who'll put you first and value you.'

'That's nice of you, Dad. But I don't think it'll happen.'

He smiled. 'We'll see... You're welcome to come over this evening.'

'Thanks, Dad. But I'll probably watch a film and go to bed early. I'm going to need all my strength to make decisions about the company once 2017 begins.'

He nodded. 'You'll be back soon?'

'Of course. You're sure about this move, are you? You'll be surrounded by ill and old people. It might slow you down, or depress you.'

He looked thoughtful for a moment, but then he smiled. 'I'm pretty old myself now. Perhaps I'm ready to wind down a bit!'

'So, what are we doing for New Year then?' Julian leant over and kissed Joe. 'I was hoping Mum would be better enough to stay up tonight but the doc won't give her any medication till he's got the blood test result so, realistically, she's going to be dead to the world by nine. I could come over here... and we could... you know...'

Joe laughed. 'We should definitely stay in. Going out is mad, and expensive. I was wondering if you'd like me to do a Jamaican buffet? It really soaks up the booze. Just a thought.'

'It's a good thought. Do you want it to be just us?'

Joe looked pensive. 'Not sure.'

'We could see if my friends Philip and Wendy want to come over?'

'Whatever you think,' Joe answered as he rolled out of bed. 'I'll make sure there's plenty of food.'

Julian looked at his watch as he squeezed into the small sofa next to Joe. 'I always think this is the longest sixty minutes of the year! When you've done loads of drinking, eaten far too much, and there's still an hour till midnight!'

'Let's do something with it then,' Wendy suggested. 'Some sort of game?'

'Could do. While we're deciding, does anyone want a mince pie? I know they don't quite fit with the Jamaican theme, but they're delicious!'

'Couldn't eat another thing,' Wendy sighed happily. 'I'm really full after all that jerk chicken, rice and peas and... what was that dish that looked like scrambled egg, Joe?'

He smiled. 'Tha's called ackee. It's a fruit.'

'Well, it was fantastic. You're a brilliant cook and it was so nice of you to invite us. Totally unexpected.'

'Unexpected! That's it!' Philip, who had been quiet for a while, spoke up. 'That's the obvious game for the end of 2016. Let's list everything in the last year that was unexpected.'

'That'll take us well past midnight,' Wendy laughed, 'but let's go for it!'

Immediately, there was a chorus of remembered UK and world events – many of the choices shouted simultaneously:

'Brexit.'

'Trump.'

'David Bowie's death.'

'And Terry Wogan's.'

'Alan Rickman too.'

'Oooh and Prince…'

'Theresa May becoming prime minister.'

'Boris not becoming prime minister.'

'Tragedy in Nice.'

'And Berlin.'

'Istanbul football stadium attack.'

'Jo Cox assassination.'

'Oh God,' Wendy broke in. 'No wonder so many people are saying they can't wait to see the end of this year. We must think of some good events that were unexpected, or we'll want to cut our throats by midnight. What about Ed Balls in *Strictly*?'

'Good one!' Julian nodded. 'And Andy and Jamie Murray both finishing the end of the year as Number One in the world.'

'But what about all the personal unexpected things?' Philip suggested. 'We've all had lots of those and I'm not sure whether it's easier dealing with the chaos in your own life while the whole world seems to have tilted off its axis, or whether it's worse. This time last year I'd never have guessed that I'd have an affair with a much younger woman. Or that when I told my wife, she'd decide she didn't want to lose me – despite having been… well, I don't want to be disloyal, but pretty offhand with me for as long as I can remember.'

The others stared at each other. 'This is rather serious territory,' Julian murmured.

'Mmmn, I know. And that's something else that's unexpected – finding people who I feel comfortable talking to. And another very good unexpected thing was meeting up again with my old mate on Boxing Day.' Philip pushed himself out of the chair and walked over and gave Julian a slightly awkward hug before sitting down again.

Joe picked up the jug of rum punch and waved it enquiringly in Philip's direction. But Philip shook his head. 'I think I've had more than enough of that,' he said slowly, 'judging by how unbuttoned I'm becoming!'

Wendy grinned. 'It suits you, Philip. You're a hell of a decent and nice man. You should be able to bare your soul to people you like and can trust. And for myself, I feel the same. Who'd have thought as one approaches sixty that one might renew old friendships and make such good new ones?' She gazed intently at Julian, and then Philip. 'Getting close to both of you has been a real bonus. It's totally unexpected but in a very good way.'

'And I suppose,' Julian paused, knowing he was on risky ground, 'the fact that we might all be half siblings… well, not Joe of course… is unexpected. To be honest, I'd love it if we were. But then my father and I never got on.'

'I'd like it too,' Philip agreed solemnly, 'for similar reasons. But poor Wendy,' he smiled across at her, 'I know it will be tough for you.'

'Well,' she said briskly, 'tonight is very cheering and one of the unexpected things about 2016 has been spending New Year's Eve here at Joe's place in Gorleston, especially since I didn't have a clue I was going to do that when I woke up this morning! So, I think what I'm learning is that there will be compensations. I certainly wouldn't mind being related to anyone in this room! Or Hannah and Minty either. Or Michael. It's just that I feel sick every time I think of what Richard Yateman did. Even though it may have created some of us who wouldn't have been born other-wise, I think his actions were deplorable.'

'Changing the subject slightly,' Julian said quickly, and he looked directly at Joe as he spoke. 'Something else has happened that's unexpected, but very good. I've been someone who's rubbished Norfolk since I left it and always compared it unfavourably to London. But if I'm honest, London hasn't always been so great. There's been heartache as well as fun. And one of the reasons for that is that I'm a hopeless picker of men. So it's totally unexpected for me to have not only enjoyed spending the festive season here in Gorleston, but to find that my mum's new neighbour is a kind and gorgeous man, who I fancy like mad!'

'That's wonderful,' Wendy responded. 'Even if you end up spending more time up here and abandon me in the big city!'

Julian beamed at her. 'Oh, I'll still be in London most of the time. I have to work, at least for as long as the voice holds out. Also, I don't think there'd be much in the way of ballet classes for adults round here, and I want to carry on directing the chorus on Thursdays. But I suppose I will end up spending more time here as Mum grows old. And probably you're also going to be here more, because of your father.'

She shook her head. 'I'm getting the impression that my father needs me less than I thought,' she murmured. 'It's weird actually. I'm as sure as I can be that he has no inkling I might be Richard's child and yet, since I learned about the possibility, there seems to be a different vibe between us. He's suddenly focused on a future that doesn't include me so much. It makes me feel as if he's... kind of peeling my fingers off the cliff that I've always clung to and that when the last finger is prised away, I'll fall... God, I'm getting really maudlin now. Do you think I could have some more water? I'm obviously more boozed than I thought.'

Julian blew her a kiss then reached for a large bottle of Perrier. 'Here you go,' he said as he poured water for her. 'I'd better have some myself. Anyone else?'

'Yes,' Philip and Joe spoke in unison. All four of them drank deeply and silence descended on the group until a ringtone from a mobile made them jump.

'That's mine,' Wendy cried, as she reached into her bag. 'It's my son, Daniel. I'll go and take it in the hall. Don't want to disturb you all.'

'Is she all right?' Philip asked Julian. 'You know her better than I do. She's such a lovely lady. How's she going to cope if Richard really is her father?'

'I don't know,' he responded. 'But we can both look after her.'

Philip nodded then looked puzzled for a moment as his own phone vibrated in his pocket. He extricated it and read the text. Then he read it again.

'Well,' he said. 'That's certainly a turn-up.'

Julian was wondering whether to ask him to elaborate when Wendy returned.

She looked at them all and then, somewhat unsteadily, walked back to her armchair and sank into it.

'My son Daniel has been offered an absolutely brilliant job in banking in Toronto when he finishes his MBA – in fact, he'll be working for them before the end of the course, by the sound of it. I knew he'd decided not to stay in America now Trump's going to be president, so I'd kind of thought he'd come home. But apparently, this is too good an opportunity to turn down, and he'll have to commit to it for at least a couple of years. But the other thing is that his twin is thinking of going too. God knows what he's going to do, but they've got plans, they said. They're so excited that I had to sound excited back, but, well, it's another unexpected change.'

Julian walked over and knelt beside her before giving her a cuddle. 'It seems that 2016 hasn't quite finished with us yet, even though it's only got…' he glanced at his watch, '…eight minutes to go.'

Wendy nodded and tried to smile but then noticed that Philip was staring at his phone. 'Are you OK, Philip?'

'I think so,' he answered softly. 'But something else unexpected... I'd tried to contact Marigold earlier after Julian invited us tonight, just to check she wasn't planning to come home for New Year. I left a message but she never responded. So I texted her brother because – on Wednesday, before she left – she said she was staying with him. But he's just texted to say she's not there, and that he hasn't seen her at all.'

'Are you worried about her?' Julian asked.

Philip sighed. 'Not really. I was just thinking that I must be the only man in the world who's got two women in his life, neither of whom wants to sleep or speak with him.'

'You deserve so much better,' Wendy assured him.

'Absolutely!' Julian agreed. 'And next year *will* be better. Let's have a glass of that champagne you brought. It's almost time for the chimes.'

The noise in the dining room of the hotel in Dingle was deafening as the partygoers raced around, wishing friends and strangers all that they might wish themselves while the band launched into a medley of traditional Irish music and song.

Araminta, dressed in the emerald green frock she had purchased earlier in the day, raised her glass, her eyes sparkling with merriment, and shouted over the hubbub, 'Happy New Year, Michael!'

'Happy New Year, my darling!' Michael responded. Then he reached across the table, and picked up both her hands before kissing each of them, lovingly, in turn. 'Thank heavens we came here. It's just what we needed.'

She leant towards him and kissed him on the lips, with no concern for who might see. 'You're right,' she agreed.

'Come on, you lovebirds!' A voice bellowed behind them. 'There are fireworks outside. You'd be sorry not to see them. They'll be grand.'

The red-faced reveller, bedecked with scraps of ribbon and sparkle from the party poppers that people had set off at midnight, swayed marginally as he exhorted them to join in the fun. But then, with a surprisingly strong grip, he grabbed Araminta's arm, pulled her to her feet, and started to drag her towards the door. Laughing, she looked back at Michael and shrugged her shoulders. He grinned and jumped to his feet and followed her.

The inebriated man, who introduced himself as Ronan O'Halloran, was right that the display was too good to miss. And when the last firework died, there was a collective sigh of disappointment.

Once back in the relative quiet of the residents' lounge, Michael offered to buy Ronan a drink, but he had already signalled for a bottle of champagne, which came quickly with four glasses.

'My wife'll be back in moment. I've no idea where she's got to.' He smiled broadly. 'I hope she hasn't decided that 2017 is the year to leave me. She'd be a hard act to follow and I'm not sure anyone half-decent would have me now!'

At that point a grey-haired woman, in a silver trouser suit, burst through the door.

'I've done it,' she announced.

'Done what, my treasure?'

'Come and see!' She turned her gaze to include Araminta and Michael. 'You can come too if you like.'

Along the corridor they stopped outside an empty room which housed a lectern in front of several rows of chairs. On the open door was a notice, scrawled in black felt-tip writing and somewhat inexpertly attached with Scotch tape.

NEW YEAR'S DAY
7PM
LECTURE
THE ROLE OF THE POTATO IN THE HISTORY OF
IRISH FAMILY PLANNING

Michael and Araminta looked mystified but then began to giggle. Meanwhile, Ronan roared with laughter and bent forward from the waist and slapped his right knee several times. 'Maeve,' he gasped, 'you're totally mad!'

'Amn't I, Ronan? Still, you surely knew that when you married me!'

'I did. But you're even madder now.'

They linked arms, and staggered slightly, almost falling against the wall, but righting themselves just in time. As they turned to retrace their steps to the lounge, Ronan explained that he was a part-time GP and that his wife was a family planning doctor.

'So, is she giving the lecture then?' Michael asked, trying to make sense of it all.

'Oh, Jesus, not at all,' Ronan laughed. 'There won't be any lecture. It's just a small little bit of fun. We'll be home by then anyway.'

Once they were all seated again, the older couple explained that they used to practise in Dingle but that they had given up full-time work, and now lived out in the country. They had, they said, been 'married for ever'. And they recounted details of children and grandchildren scattered round the globe, and how they had decided this year to spend the whole of the festive season, just the two of them, back in the hotel where they had met at a medical meeting in 1983.

'And how long have you been married?' Maeve asked Araminta.

'Oh, we're not. That's to say...'

Maeve laughed. 'You don't have to explain. But there again, as we're all on the lash, you can say anything and be reasonably confident we won't remember it tomorrow!'

Maeve and Ronan dissolved into giggles again.

'You look like a Kerry man, yourself,' Ronan turned to Michael.

'Well, my mother came from here, but she left in the early fifties to go to England to train as a teacher. She'd worked in the family pub but it closed down. I'm sure life was very tough.'

'It was, of course,' Maeve agreed. 'What was your mother's name?'

'Mary Moynihan.'

'Ah, well now, there was a Mrs Moynihan in our street when I was growing up. She had a daughter, who had gone off to Britain before I was born. I think I may have met her once when she came back for a holiday. I believe her husband died – I know she had a little boy she was bringing up alone. But I don't think it can be the same family because he became a priest.'

Michael felt himself redden.

'Oooh, my...' Ronan intervened. 'Sorry!'

'No, it's OK. Especially as you promised you won't remember anything in the morning! I am a priest – or I was. I celebrated Mass for the last time on Christmas Day. I'd thought long and hard about it. I couldn't go on. The loneliness became unbearable. I love this lady and I want to marry her.'

'And I say you should, for sure!' Ronan raised his glass in Michael's direction. 'I couldn't help noticing you earlier. You look made for each other.'

'Well, we have a lot of sorting out to do,' Michael murmured, half to himself, 'but I think we can do it here. We've even switched our phones off! We went to Inch Beach yesterday when we arrived, and we've arranged to rent a cottage there for a few weeks. We can move in tomorrow. It seems like a good place to get ourselves together.'

'It's perfect,' Maeve agreed. 'Sure, when I was younger, I did my best thinking while walking on that beach. I revised for my medical exams there too. It's grand.'

'I've never been to the west coast before,' Araminta told her. 'It's certainly gorgeous.'

'It is,' Maeve responded. 'Apart from the rain, but you get used to that.'

'Absolutely!' Ronan agreed. 'You could live here. We can keep a secret, can't we, Maeve? No one need ever know what you used to do for a living. And of course, with a mother from here, you'll easily get Irish citizenship when the UK leaves Europe.'

'Actually,' said Michael, 'I have it already. My mother always used to say it might be useful. And now it very much is!'

'And you can get married here. Though not in a Catholic church probably.'

'No,' Michael shook his head. 'Not, I think, without the Pope's dispensation or something similar. And that would probably take for ever.'

'Anyway, you don't need it.' Maeve's tone was emphatic. 'This is post-religious Ireland, thank God. Get married in a lovely hotel. There's one in Killorglin or, oh what's the fantastic place run by that eccentric woman... Nora somebody... out on the coast? The Fitzhenry! That's it! Fair play to her, it's out of this world!'

'I think that hotel's run by my best friend's mother! What a coincidence.' Michael laughed.

As Araminta gazed at him, a warm wave of belonging wrapped itself around her. How marvellous he was, she thought, and how beneficial this conversation was turning out to be. He seemed to have shed years suddenly, after all the stress and tension of leaving the church and the shock about her father. Perhaps living here would be viable. Was Michael thinking along the same lines?

'If we did get married, and live here...' she said quietly. 'I mean, well, we haven't discussed this at all, but, would we fit in?'

'Oh you would, yes. Yes, I'm sure of it.'

'I suppose we'd get to know people. Make new friends. It seems to me like everyone knows everyone in Ireland!'

Maeve thought for a moment. 'I'm not entirely sure that they do. But I think everyone knows *someone* who knows everyone!'

'Sounds good to me.' Araminta laughed.

'Yeah, it's great,' Maeve agreed, before adding. 'Mostly great... Nearly always... Of course, sometimes it's a complete and utter pain!'

Chapter Sixteen

Philip perched on one of the tall stools in the kitchen vowing never to drink again – or at least to avoid rum for the rest of his life. In the hope of soaking up all the alcohol in his bloodstream, he was ploughing through a hastily created concoction of three slices of fried bread, two fried eggs, a rasher of fried bacon, and a couple of fried tomatoes.

Surveying the mess of pans, crumbs and eggshells on the normally immaculate worktops, he hoped that Marigold would not choose this morning to return home.

He hoped too that his father would not opt to phone today. Ever since he had written to the older man questioning their genetic connection, he had been expecting a furious response.

Gingerly, he edged himself off the stool, topped up his coffee mug, cradled it in his hands and walked through to his study. As he sat down and switched on the computer, his mind returned to the party of the night before.

It seemed to him that he had never enjoyed a happier New Year. His only reservation was, that in the happy conviviality, he might have revealed too much about himself. He had discussed this worry with Wendy as they had travelled back to Hethersett in the early hours of this morning, but she had reassured him that all of them had shared personal thoughts and feelings, which was what real friendship was about.

'It's like os… os… uh… osmosis, that's it!' She had nodded triumphantly. 'Good mates speak and listen in equal quantities. Sorry – I sound like Pseuds Corner!'

Having dropped Wendy, he had dozed fitfully in the back of the taxi while the driver returned him to Hunsford Hall at the end of the night's circuitous journey.

'That's the best start to a year I ever had,' the cabbie had laughed as Philip had added a generous tip to the considerable fare. 'Love this job!'

Philip smiled at the memory. Shouldn't he himself, he pondered, be able to derive similar pleasure and joy from his own business?

'Buck your ideas up,' he exhorted himself as he clicked on his company's website. It would need updating with all this year's prices, plus the diary of conferences and agricultural shows they would attend. He left the technical changes to his IT expert, but he did enjoy writing the text for the site, as well as for the brochures they brought out every year. It was one of the few aspects of the job that he knew he was good at. It reminded him, he supposed, of his days in publishing.

Having mapped out a calendar of fixed dates, he felt that 2017 was beginning to take shape in his mind. But would everything change in the business world once the Brexit negotiations began? Geoff, his executive manager, was convinced that there was a better future and a bigger market outside of Europe. It was not a view that he shared.

As for his life away from work, it was impossible to envisage how the year might pan out. Was he going to find that he had brothers and sisters? Was he going to settle down with Katie and help bring up their child? Would he stay with Marigold?

'OK, let's try and get some answers,' he said decisively as he reached for his phone.

He began by texting his brother-in-law to wish him a happy New Year – and to ask if Marigold had been in touch.

A reply was quickly forthcoming.

Happy New Year to you! Not seen or heard from her. Sorry. You don't deserve this.

What did that mean? What was it that he did not deserve? After all, many people might consider that Marigold did not deserve to be married to someone who was having an affair with a younger woman.

But was he still having an affair? It was over a week since he had spoken to Katie. Over a week since she – without telling him – had travelled to Ireland.

He decided to call his mother.

She sounded tired; presumably, she had had a late night if indeed she had been to bed at all. For the first time in ages, she hinted that she would like him to live with her and help run the hotel. Whenever she had raised this in the past, he had pointed out – in as reasonable a way as possible – that he had a business as well as a wife in Norfolk. But this morning, the idea seemed strangely appealing. And after all, at eighty-four, his mother must be entitled to some support.

Tentatively, he asked how Katie was getting on, and whether she was proving helpful, but his mother changed the subject. Probably she was too exhausted to think beyond the immediate running of the hotel.

They chatted about other things and he told her about celebrating New Year in a small house in Gorleston. He was about to embark upon Marigold's disappearance when his mother interrupted him with, 'She's not really the girl I took her for.'

'Katie?'

'Yes, Katie.'

Should he say that he shared his mother's feelings? But Katie was carrying his baby. He had an obligation to be loyal.

'I'm sorry if that's harsh,' his mother apologised. 'I know she's going to present me with another grandchild, which will be lovely of course. But she's erratic and self-interested. It was totally mad here last night, and sure she was no help at all. Worse than that, she was out of her head on booze – and her pregnant as well. And this morning, she's gone to meet a friend, would you believe?'

'A friend? I never knew she had friends in Kerry.'

'Seems there's a lot we don't know about Katie.'

Maeve and Ronan smiled and waved energetically from across the breakfast room.

'I'm glad that we met them and got on so well,' Michael murmured. 'It's reassuring to know one can make new friends at our age, in a new place and in new circumstances. It's one of the things I've been worrying about.'

Araminta nodded. She had drunk too much the previous night and regretted it now – though the substantial porridge she was eating seemed to be settling her stomach.

'Let's not buy any booze for a day or two,' Michael suggested. 'My liver could do with a rest.'

She smiled agreement at him. Even though they had been together for just a week, she was aware of how often they shared the same thoughts. It was gratifying, she mused, as she tried to silence the voice in her head pointing out that maybe they were not alike because they were soulmates, but siblings.

For a while during the New Year celebrations she had managed to forget that they were anything other than a new couple, in love and delighted to be so. However, morning had summoned in renewed reality. But surely fate could not be so cruel as to allow her to feel this passionately for her own half-brother?

The Irish couple came over to say their farewells and to exchange embraces and mobile numbers.

'We hope you'll visit us soon,' Maeve said. 'I know you've just started your life together and you probably want to be alone. But even if the cottage you're going to is perfect, you'll go stir-crazy if you never see anyone else.'

Michael and Araminta thanked them and watched as their new friends wandered towards the door, conversing with various other guests as they went.

'We won't go stir-crazy, will we?' Michael whispered as soon as the other couple were out of earshot.

'Of course not!' she assured him, stroking his arm.

'I'm just thinking,' he went on, slowly, 'that maybe we shouldn't meet up with them before we know the DNA result. They're so friendly and open that it would be easy to confide too much. Seems to me there are things that we're going to have to keep to ourselves, because once said they can never be retracted or forgotten.'

Picking up a clean fork, she traced a pattern on the white starched tablecloth in an attempt to distract herself. She felt like crying but did not want to waste any moment of her time with Michael in being miserable. They had to stay positive. They belonged together. Nothing else mattered.

Many of the shops in Dingle were closed, but they found a small family-run store, and were able to buy sufficient items for a basic 'first-night' supper in their rented home.

'We can stock up properly when everything's back to normal,' Araminta said brightly. 'I'm looking forward to cooking for you.'

She stopped, aware in that moment that she had an almost infantile view of their stay in the cottage, as if they were children playing a game of 'mothers and fathers'. It was not exactly like that, because they both had a real desire to learn everything about each other, and to explore each other's bodies, but even so…

'Sounds good to me,' Michael remarked cheerfully, but she could see that he knew her mind was troubled and was grateful when he reached for her hand and held it tightly.

They were not due to arrive at the Inch property till two o'clock, so before they left Dingle, they ate lunch in a restaurant, which had a colourful board outside promoting Irish stew and local cheeses.

'It's so good that we came here,' Araminta announced cheerily, as she enjoyed the last morsel of Bluebell Falls goats' cheese on a home-made seeded cracker. 'For a start, I love the food! But I feel you belong here. And that, in time, I might too.'

'But do I belong here?' Michael demanded of himself as he mooched along the vast expanse of Inch Beach in the gathering gloom. 'Can I do this?' he asked the salty air. 'Am I good enough for her? How can I ask her to live a lifelong secret if we're siblings? What should I do for a living? What will she do?'

Two hours ago, when they had arrived at the cottage – which was situated a short walk from the beach – they had darted in and out of all the rooms like excited children. They had approved the kitchen and drooled over the breathtaking views. Laughing together, they had worked out how to light the wood stove, then they had made themselves tea and eaten slices of iced carrot cake, before trying out the television, which had hundreds of channels. They had also discovered a stack of DVDs. As Araminta had flicked through them, her voice had risen in delight: 'Oh, wonderful! *Casablanca... Sleepless in Seattle... Annie Hall... Tootsie... The Ladykillers... Chicago... Top Hat... Some Like It Hot...*'

He had grinned at her enthusiasm and she had beamed back at him with that broad smile which made his heart feel as though it was going to burst out of his chest. Moments later, he had raised her up from her kneeling position and kissed her gently, then more insistently before putting his arm around her waist and leading her to the bedroom where they had fallen on top of the plump duvet. They had made love hurriedly and hungrily – so desperate for each other that they had not undressed but simply pushed aside any clothing that impeded them – riding together towards the pleasure they craved. He had felt her passion pulsing around him just before exploding into her with an intensity that released the most powerfully thrilling sensations of his life.

'Oh my God!' Her breath had shuddered in her throat as she had tightened her muscles around him and pressed herself firmly against his body, before screaming out so loudly that it had astonished as well as delighted him. He had kissed her then, so hard that now his lips felt bruised, and they had hugged each other close till the waves of their mutual excitement had subsided.

Making love to her was everything he had yearned for. And if he had the strength and health, there was nothing he wanted more than to own her body every day of his life. But most of all, he needed her care and company and friendship. That much was certain. Nothing else was.

In the aftermath of their coupling, it had not taken long before his anxiety levels had risen once more, and the unanswerable, deeply troubled questions had begun all over again. Even if the DNA test turned out in their favour, might she tire of him? Or maybe he would find he was hopeless at being in a relationship. Perhaps he had been alone for too long to change. He had spent years as a solitary figure. Could he learn new habits so late in the day? And when you were a 'pair', should you do absolutely everything together, or was it acceptable to sit alone and read a book sometimes? Or was that the beginning of the demise of the magic, inexorably leading to them becoming the kind of couple who filled their days with different hobbies and friends because they no longer had anything to say to one another?

The truth was that he did not know. And it was only now he was with her, that he realised just how little he knew about anything.

Before leaving for his walk, he had wandered into the kitchen and watched as she chopped onions and tomatoes and broccoli in preparation for the frittata she was planning to cook. Trying to make light of his pressing need for personal space, he had reminded her of her assertion that one could walk on a beach at any time without being viewed as odd. Even so, she had looked at him slightly nervously as he spoke, and he had hated himself

236

for diluting her post-lovemaking euphoria. He did not want to be the person who could furrow her brow in that worrying way.

'You don't mind then if I have a stroll, do you?' he had asked, avoiding her gaze and knowing that she would be bound to say that of course he should go.

Within minutes of leaving, he had longed to return to the safety of her arms but he made himself walk on and on – the damp sand dragging at his trainers, so that his progress was slow – until he felt so tired that he believed his worries might be quietened for a time and allow him some peace.

*

Ian McEwan or Martin Amis?

Wendy grinned. She and Philip had been texting each other on and off all day about authors and books.

McEwan. I must have read everything he's ever written.
Me too. Oh, sorry. Marigold's just come home. Text you later.

She looked at her watch. Seven o'clock. She had not felt hungry at lunchtime, but now she was ravenous.

In the kitchen, she took a couple of eggs and a slice of ham out of the fridge. An omelette would be easy, with sourdough bread, and lots of sparkling water.

Having made her supper and eaten it, she glanced at her watch again and was amazed to find that only half an hour had passed since she had last checked the time. Perhaps she should put her feet up and read more of her book. She was halfway through *Conclave* by Robert Harris and was finding it deeply satisfying. But maybe she would have a bath first. She felt grubby, having spent time earlier clearing out her bedroom – amassing, in the process, two dustbin bags crammed with rubbish, and several

237

boxes of old clothes, vinyl records, CDs, books, posters and ornaments, which she would donate to a charity shop.

The only items she was saving were her school reports, her teenage diaries, the dress she had been christened in – just in case she ever became a grandmother – plus a *Bunty* annual and a copy of her favourite childhood book *The Silver Sword.*

It was not much to remind her of the years in which she had grown up here. But, as she had told Philip, she was not a nostalgic or sentimental person.

She ran upstairs to the bathroom and turned on the taps to fill the tub, and then padded along to her bedroom and sat down for a moment, freshly aware that before long the house would be sold, and this space belong to somebody else.

It felt strange, but not unpleasant, to be alone in the family home, she thought as she plucked an old dressing gown off a hook on the door and wandered back towards the bathroom. However, although there were still plenty of her parents' belongings in evidence, there was a sense already of them having moved on. For instance, the china cabinet which had stood in a niche on the landing for as long as she could remember, had been emptied of her mother's prized Capo di Monte figures. Presumably, her father had loaded them into the car yesterday to take to their new residence. Ever an optimist, he had hopes that once he and his wife were living together again – surrounded by more of their belongings – some of her memory might be restored. Would he be devastated when that failed to happen, as surely it must?

She felt her phone vibrate in her pocket. Fully expecting the message to be from Philip or Julian, she had to look twice at the display. It was from Francesca. That was weird. She breathed deeply, ignored the text, put the phone down on the empty cabinet and went into the bathroom and removed her clothes.

Sinking into water that was as hot as she could bear, she reminded herself that she could stay here for as long as she liked – relaxing her muscles and emptying her mind of all thoughts

– without any concern that someone else might want to use the bathroom, or need her to do something. This was, she thought, one of the significant benefits to being single.

But irritatingly, her mind refused to calm down, and instead returned to Fran. Had she and Robert gone away together? She was pretty sure that must be the case, but she would not think about it.

She squeezed her tummy and grimaced at the spare flesh that dwelled there. She must eat more sensibly, and ask Julian to advise her about exercise. They could be her resolutions for 2017; achievable ambitions that she could control, in a year that was bound to be full of uncertainties.

If Francesca and Robert had holidayed together, perhaps they had returned. Had Robert dropped her off at her gorgeous flat in Regent's Park and then disappeared from her life? It seemed likely. After all, even if he had considered his on-off lover to be good for company on a Christmas trip, she was never going to be a long-term prospect.

As Wendy emerged, pink from the bath and wrapped herself in a towel, she began to feel sorry for the other woman, so she sprinted out to the landing and picked up her phone.

The text was short. *I've sent you an email. Would appreciate you attend to it soonest.*

It would fit with Francesca's personality that she would be formal and slightly hectoring if she were upset. But surely someone else could help? She must have other friends to provide a listening ear; friends whose husbands she had not cheated with over decades.

The email could wait, Wendy decided. In any event, she had left her 'work' phone in London and the old one she had brought with her was very 'unsmart' and could not access the internet.

In her parents' lounge, she curled up on the sofa, flicked through the *Radio Times* and decided to watch the new *Sherlock*. But it would not start for forty-five minutes, so she sent a text to Hannah. She had felt a growing sense of embarrassment about how she had acted towards the young woman on Boxing Day. Nothing would ever reconcile her to being Richard Yateman's daughter, but she should have kept more of a lid on her emotions.

There was no immediate response, so she called Minty, but her phone went straight to voicemail.

'I hope you're all right, Minty,' Wendy said in her message. 'The other day was very upsetting but I don't think I behaved well. I'm sure this is difficult for you too. Probably you've gone away. I hope you're having a good time. Anyway, happy New Year.'

Could she text Philip if his wife was home? She risked it.

Are you OK?
Yes. Marigold came home. I asked her where she'd been and she said something about how I had an alternative life with Katie so she was having one too. Then she packed a suitcase and left again.
I'm sorry. Can I do anything?
Thanks, but I don't think so. What are you doing?
About to watch Sherlock.
I'll do the same then. Speak in the morning.

There were still twenty minutes to go till the programme so, despite her earlier intention, she gave into her curiosity about Francesca and made for the adjoining room and switched on her father's computer.

The ancient machine seemed to take an age to warm up, but eventually, after a series of unhealthy, grinding noises, it chugged into life and she was able to log into her internet provider's website.

There were a couple of dozen work-related emails, but she resisted dipping into them, and searched instead for Fran's email.

Wendy, hello.

I know you and Robert are finished so I don't feel bad about what I'm going to say. It's obvious you and he have never been right for each other. I mean, people don't keep being unfaithful if they are happy.

He and I have had a marvellous holiday – the first time we've been able to spend any sustained time as a couple since we met in 1994. We're now going to live together and get married once your divorce comes through.

Personally, I think his solicitors have been dragging their feet. This is not good for him. And not good for you either. You want to get on with your life, don't you? We've sacked them, and you'll be hearing from the new ones after the Christmas break.

Basically though, this is what we thought – and if you can agree, in principle, it will speed things up and cost us all less in legal fees. Robert and I want the Barbican flat. He loves it. I know he couldn't have afforded to buy you out, but I've got an estate agent selling my Regent's Park property and she says it'll go quickly and at such a good price I can hardly believe it. Let's hope she's right! So, we need to get a couple of valuations for your flat and draw up some figures.

Now – the business. I'm resigning. I've been on the career treadmill since I was 18 and now, at the age of 53, finding myself starting a new life, I want to be free of work, at least for now. You've always been the innovator and ideas person at BS&T, so as long as you get a good contracts manager/ accountant, you'll be fine. All I want is a year's salary, plus a leaving bonus. I think you'll find this fair. Details will come from the solicitor.

I know I'm supposed to give six months' notice, but I'd like to go much sooner. I also intend working from home till you've replaced me. I'm sure this will be easier for you too.

241

Robert says he loves that I'm so organised and practical! The only upsetting thing is that apparently your sons aren't happy about us. Still, they're intelligent boys and will have to get their heads around it. It's not like someone died. Perhaps you can talk sense into them.

Good luck for the future, Francesca.

'Oh my God!' Julian said to Joe, as he pocketed his mobile. 'You couldn't make it up!'

They were together in Joe's house, dining on the previous night's leftovers. Joe had worked a long shift at the nursing home and Julian had spent the day with his mother. She seemed brighter now that she had been told what was, almost certainly, wrong with her – and that something could be done to make her better. They had driven out in her old Vauxhall to Southwold and had had a New Year's Day pub lunch at The Sole Bay Inn.

Once she was in bed, he had joined Joe.

'Was that your friend Wendy on the phone?'

Julian nodded and explained the latest in her particular saga.

'Sounds like that Francesca is a real piece of work,' Joe said. 'I hope Wendy will pay her no mind.'

'Me too. I'm sure that most people would have had a breakdown with everything that's happened to her. I mean not only is she waiting to find out who her real father is, which – obviously – is a huge thing, but in the last six months, everything in her life that she thought was set up permanently has changed. Still, she always says she's a person who looks forward rather than back, so hopefully she'll be OK.'

'You'd think you and Wendy had known each other all your lives,' Joe commented as he helped himself to a second-helping of mango salad. 'You get on so well.'

'I know! That's why I'm so sure I'm her brother! I must see more of her when I'm in town, though of course I won't be there as often now.'

'You don't have to worry about being here for your mum,' Joe reassured him in his calm, slow voice. 'I'm sure she'll feel better soon, and she has me next door.'

Julian played with the bread roll on his plate and then tore off a piece and buttered it before looking up at Joe. 'I didn't exactly spell this out to the others last night, but it's not so much Mum,' he said tentatively, 'it's more to do with you. Normally, whenever I've been back in Gorleston, I've been counting the hours till I could leave, but now I find myself wanting to... well, to be with you, I suppose.'

Joe's smile was so broad that it seemed to stretch his entire face. 'Very flattering,' he murmured, but then he added, 'You'll feel differently, I bet, once you get back to London and all your city friends. I can't compete with all that. Sophistication's never been my strong point. Anyway, we're good as we are, aren't we? We don't need to make plans for life.'

'I suppose not.' Julian giggled. 'We could plan for tonight though. Is it OK if I stay over?'

'Of course – but just to sleep, right?'

'Oh God, yes. After last night I don't think I could raise a canter.'

They both laughed, then Joe remarked, 'Whoever thought it would come to this? You fancy someone like mad but you need to pace yourself. By the way, I'm going to be sixty-two next Saturday.'

'No! Well, you're very well-preserved, as I can testify!'

Joe reached over and hugged him. 'What about your mum if you sleep here?'

'She'll be fine. I'll go back next door first thing. I told her about us earlier. I hope you don't mind.'

'Was she shocked?'

'Good God, no! She's well past that with me,' Julian responded. 'She did say that she hadn't seen it coming though. But then neither did I!'

Chapter Seventeen

'This has just come in the post. What can it mean?'

Farid stared at the report that Hannah had thrust at him. He blinked and looked again. 'Well,' he said. 'I certainly never saw that coming.'

Wendy threw the letter into the bin. Was she surprised? Not really.

She would never tell anyone though – not outside of the group who had been at Minty's on Boxing Day.

It was horrendous, but she knew that she would come to view, and love, Minty as a half-sister, and Hannah as a niece. And, assuming the men's results were the same as hers, she felt sure that she would enjoy being related to them too.

But essentially, it was all about one solitary sperm. Was that what made a parent? Definitely not. Arthur Lawrence was named 'father' on her birth certificate, and that was how he would remain.

So, what did she feel for Richard Yateman? The words 'implacable hatred' came to mind, but she dismissed them. She would not dignify her biological link to the old doctor with such hot emotion. Indifference would be better.

'You're very quiet,' Michael reached over and patted Araminta's arm.

Having left the car in Dingle, they were taking a strenuous walk. Their guidebook claimed that the Conor Pass was the highest of its kind in Ireland. It certainly felt like it, Michael thought, as he struggled to catch his breath. Fortunately, as they rounded the next bend, they were confronted by such a dramatic waterfall that he felt justified in suggesting they stop to watch it.

Araminta sat down on a large, smooth rock next to Michael and absorbed herself in the mesmerising cascade of rushing water.

They remained silent for a while. Eventually, he asked, 'Are you all right, darling?'

She studied her walking shoes for a moment before replying, 'Today's the nineteenth anniversary of my mum's death.'

'I'm so sorry… I don't think you've mentioned her before.'

'That's probably right,' she murmured. 'It makes me cry to talk about her. She was only sixty-three.'

Michael nodded but said nothing, sensing that Araminta might want to open up now.

'She and my father were skiing in Austria,' she explained. 'Mum was a good skier, but she fell and broke her hip. She was taken to a hospital near Kitzbühel. Everything was fine. She was expected to recover well. But Dad took it into his head that she'd be better at home – I think he just wanted to get back to his practice – and he insisted on flying her back to England, and spent a ridiculous amount of money on a private plane. Two days later, she developed deep vein thrombosis, and died.' Tears coursed down Araminta's cheeks as she continued, 'It was a terrible time, because shortly after Mum died, Hilary – my wonderful godfather – had a break-down. And when he got better he retired from the library service in Ipswich, and moved to Cornwall. He'd been so much a part of my life and I really loved him. We had a special bond – I was even given 'Hilary' as my middle name – so it kind of felt like the end of the world to lose Mum and then, in a different way, Hilary too. Of course, I was married, with children who needed me, so I had to hold myself together, but it was incredibly painful.'

'That does sound really, really awful,' Michael whispered.

'It was. And I've never actually said this aloud before, but I've always felt that Dad killed Mum. I can't know for sure that she'd have lived if she'd been left in Austria till she was more mobile, but I think she would. My father's always been bossy. Thinks he knows it all. And now, because of what he's doing to us, I really, really hate him.'

She jumped up and strode away, indicating with a backward sweep of both arms that he should not follow.

Michael remained where he was, gazing at her till she disappeared from view. Several times since New Year, he had gone for a walk on his own. Now, he knew what it felt like for the other person, and it was not pleasant.

He could feel his heart beating faster, and a sliver of panic inserted itself between his ribs as he imagined that she might keep on walking and never come back. Breathing deeply, and urging his mind to think rationally, he surveyed the scenery all around him, observing that the sea, way below him, was a patchwork of different blues, greys and greens, like an Impressionist painting. Had he ever been here before, with his mother? He was unsure. Probably even if he had, he would not have noticed how stunning it was. More likely as a boy he would have run up the path, improvising a game of football by kicking loose stones, and quite oblivious to the steepness of the climb. He wanted to run now, run after Araminta and bring her back to him. Closing his eyes, he counted to ten. Then ten more. And when he opened them, she was sprinting down the track towards him, and he felt such a rush of gladness and relief that his eyes filled with tears.

He strode towards her and she threw herself into his arms. 'Sorry,' she cried.

'Don't be. Sounds like you've carried that particular burden for a long time.'

'Ever since we left Norwich,' she explained, 'I've been dwelling on my father and his meddling with patients' fertility. It's driving me crazy.'

'I understand that,' he reassured her. 'On the other hand, he may have given life to people who wouldn't have had it otherwise.'

She broke away from him and sat down again, shaking her head. 'I don't know what to think. I'm worried that I'm losing my mind. I'm anxious about you as well. I'm pretty sure you're having moments of severe panic about me, the priesthood, and who your father is. And that it might all get too much.'

He sank onto the rock beside her. 'I do have those moments. You're very perceptive.'

'Can I say something?'

He nodded.

'I think if we've got any chance at all as a couple that we have to talk about these sorts of feelings when they happen. From my point of view, feeling you slip away into your own private misery makes me very nervous. And I'm sure you feel shut out, and very uncomfortable, if I do something like I did just now, and walk away from you.'

He nodded again.

'Please – whatever you feel and whatever happens, remember that I love you, I want you, and I really need your company. I don't know how we're going to negotiate everything, but are you as sure as I am that you want to keep trying?'

'I'm surer,' he said. 'Please don't give up on me.'

'Never!'

'I think,' he ventured, 'we're both aware that by now, the others may know their DNA results. I think I should turn my phone on when we get back to the cottage and text Philip to find out.'

It had been a long day, and because Marigold was still away, Philip was deliberating whether to order a taxi and go out for supper or, yet again, rustle up something on toast.

He checked his phone. It was nine days since Michael and Araminta had left for Ireland; nine days with no communication.

He really missed his friend and wanted to talk to him about everything, including Marigold's strange behaviour.

Sweeping up the post from the table by the front door where his housekeeper always left it, he walked through to the snug and poured himself a drink. He discarded the inevitable junk mail about installing a stair lift, and was about to bin the latest Coopers catalogue but found himself flicking through its pages. Somewhere, some marketing person had chosen to define him as a man who needed a raised lavatory seat and orthotic insoles.

He winced as he tossed the little book away and turned his attention to an expensive-looking vellum envelope of the type favoured by the legal profession. Turning it over, he saw that it came from his father's solicitor in London. His pulse quickened as he anticipated what the contents might reveal, but the short letter simply requested him to make an appointment. Perhaps I'm to be disinherited, he thought.

The other two envelopes were identical, except that one was addressed to Michael, care of Hunsford Hall, and one to him.

So, this was it. He tore his envelope open. There was 'No Match'. He was not Dr Yateman's son. He sighed, as what felt like the greatest disappointment of his life settled on his shoulders.

Julian was on the phone to Wendy.

'I was so sure I was his son. Everything seemed to point to it. My mum's frolic with him. The fact that I was so unlike Pop. The way you and I immediately got on. The connection I felt to him when I was playing his piano. It just all felt so right. I'll never get over it... Are you OK?'

'I'll live, but I'd cheerfully swap fathers with you! Are you up to taking the choir tonight?'

'Darling, of course! Broken-hearted I may be, but the show must go on!'

*

'There's a text from Philip.'

Araminta stopped stirring the sauce she was making, and forced herself to turn to Michael and smile.

He was staring at his phone. 'Should I read it?'

She nodded but then turned away as he opened the message.

'Philip says the results have arrived in the post and is asking if I want him to open my envelope. Should I tell him to go ahead?'

'Yes,' she whispered.

Michael tapped out his text and pressed send. Almost immediately the reply sounded on his device.

'Wait!' she shouted as she ran to his side. 'Whatever it says, we are still going to get married, aren't we? We wouldn't be doing anything wrong, or hurting anyone.'

'Are you sure that's what you want?'

'Positive.'

'Thank you,' he answered softly. 'That's what I want too.' Then he clicked on the message, and all colour drained from his face.

All day, Wendy had wondered about Philip and whether or not he was her half-brother. It was late now. Was it possible that way out in the depths of Norfolk, his results had not arrived?

Eventually, just before she climbed into bed, she decided she could not sleep without asking him.

His reply was immediate.

No, alas. Not Richard's child. Are you?

Yes. Can't believe you're not.

I can't believe it either. I really wanted it to be true – mostly because I never had a sister before and thought you'd be a great one!

Wendy sat down on her bed, feeling – strangely – even bleaker about Philip's result than her own. She had been convinced that they must be siblings.

Julian's not Richard's son either. He's terribly upset. He said
if you and I were in touch, I should tell you.
Poor Jules. I'm seeing him on Saturday evening at Joe's
birthday dinner. But I'll text him tomorrow. Btw, Michael's
devastated because he IS Richard's son. He asked me
to tell you.
Oh God! Couldn't just one of these bloody results have turned
out happily?
Feels like some evil spirit has switched them around, so
that everyone is miserable. Makes me feel that 2017 is
going to be as awful as last year.
Don't say that.
Am coming to London soon to see my father's solicitor.
Could we have lunch?
Yes please.
Great. Are you OK?
Yes. I've had a good sing at the choir. That helped. Going
to bed now. You?
Going to bed too.

Sitting at a table for four in the Pier Hotel restaurant in Gorleston,
Philip watched Joe and Julian joshing with each other as they
finished enormous helpings of steak and chips.

'Penny for them.'

Vera, Julian's mother was staring at him. She was looking better
than when he had met her briefly on New Year's Eve. Then, she
had shared a drink with them but had pleaded exhaustion and
disappeared to bed about nine. Tonight, just a week later, she
seemed livelier and much more attractive; her hair was swept up
prettily, she was wearing a multicoloured kaftan and she jangled
every time she made a gesture, courtesy of the abundance of
metallic bracelets on her arms.

He leant towards her. 'Sorry, just thinking. Julian says that your
medication's beginning to make a difference already.'

250

'Well,' Vera smiled. 'I still get tired, and I need to lose the weight I put on, but I'm beginning to feel like me again. And there was I thinking I was on the way out!'

The sparkle in her eyes reminded him of the young Julian when he had been hatching some dodgy prank or other. It would have been good if they had turned out to be brothers.

'You look like a man with the world on his shoulders,' she said.

He shook his head. 'No, I'm fine. I've just got one of those faces… Ooh, here's the birthday cake. My goodness, Julian has pushed the boat out.'

But Vera was not to be deterred. 'Perhaps you need a holiday.'

Philip forced a smile. 'Possibly. I might go to Ireland to see my mother.'

'I've never been to the Emerald Isle. I'll come with you if you want company!'

'That's uncommonly decent of you, Vera,' he responded.

From across the table, Julian watched the two of them. It was a relief to see his mother in such good spirits. By contrast, Philip looked utterly woebegone – particularly when he thought that no one was watching him. The paternity test result had hit him badly. He had been a serious little boy. And now he was a serious adult, despite having what many people would regard as a charmed life.

'Cake?' Julian asked as he passed round plates with huge slices of chocolate and cream gateau on them.

Philip nodded his thanks and proceeded to make all the right noises about how delicious the meal had been, and how Joe most certainly did not look sixty-two, and how marvellous it was to be part of the celebration.

Julian walked round the table and leant over Philip so that he could speak softly to him.

'Why don't you stay over tonight? We've not had the chance to speak properly since meeting on Boxing Day. We used to know everything there was to know about each other and I want to bring you up to date with my exciting life!'

Philip patted Julian on the arm. 'I'll look forward to doing that at some point. But I need to get back tonight, for my dogs.'

'Can't I persuade you to change your mind? I'm sure Joe would like you to come and see the giant TV I bought him!'

Philip shook his head. 'Another time. To be honest, I think I might spoil the party.'

'Hello!' Wendy said cheerily on Hannah's voicemail. 'It's your auntie here! Good news! I've been in touch with one of my old colleagues at ITN and they'd like to see a showreel of you. I know you weren't thinking about appearing on screen, but nowadays they want to know that everyone in the newsroom can do everything. If you could come into BS&T one day, we could put something together. Have you heard from your mum? I've not been able to reach her since Boxing Day. Lots of love. Speak soon!'

Wendy replaced her handset and sighed. It was the evening of a very drizzly, and seemingly endless, Saturday. All day, she had done her best to keep occupied. This morning, she had walked from her flat to the river and across the Millennium 'wobbly' bridge and had had coffee and a sandwich in Tate Modern before retracing her steps to the Barbican. Then she had wandered into her local cinema, telling herself that there would be something she could see, and that it would be good if it was a movie outside of her normal comfort zone. But her heart had not been in it, so she had left, and returned home and spent the afternoon cleaning it.

Afterwards, she had spoken to her father. He had been enthusiastic about his new life in Wherry Haven. Now, on a whim, she rang her son, Rhys. Much to her delight, he picked up at the other end.

He was still in Boston with Daniel, he told her, but absolutely set on going to Canada with his twin. To her surprise he sounded older and very organised. It seemed he had fixed up an audition at the Toronto Conservatory for a conducting course. 'I can't play for choirs and ballet classes for the rest of my life, Mum. Danny's going to help with my course fees till I get on my feet because the salary the bank's going to pay him is obscene! They want him to be attached to them somehow from about April, I think, so it looks like he'll be going up there quite often before he finishes his MBA. He's already found an apartment in Toronto and we're going to live together. Should be fun.'

'I can give you money.'

'No, Mum, honestly, it's not necessary. You were the one who paid for everything when Dan and I were at university. I know it was because you earn more than Dad, but even so, you've done your bit. I've asked Dad for help – he's behaving so badly, he seriously owes me. If I could remember the number of his credit card I'd max out on that too, and it would serve him right.'

Wendy tried to placate Rhys by reminding him that Robert had always been a marvellous father, but her son was not interested in being reasonable and was adamant that he would never again speak to his dad unless he got rid of 'that woman'.

'But you didn't seem to mind when he was going out with his researcher.'

'I fucking did mind. But I didn't think it would last. Francesca's something else. She's ruthless. I can't believe Dad's been seeing her on and off since we were babies. I bloody hate her. Danny does too.'

Probably, she thought, as she ended the call and wandered into her immaculate kitchen to make a cup of tea, her two boys would end up with Canadian accents and marry Canadian girls and have Canadian children. She would visit, of course. But she would be alone forever.

As she surveyed the sparkling taps and polished worktops, she recalled how she used to wish for a tidy flat and more time to herself. She had both now, but it was not nearly as much fun as she had imagined.

'Would you prefer to be alone?' Araminta asked as they walked into the Catholic church. 'It's bound to be emotional for you to attend Mass.'

Though he had been full of indecision, Michael had shaken his head.

Inside, they found themselves enveloped in a palpably happy and welcoming atmosphere. Children wandered around throughout the service, but everyone seemed easy-going about it; there was a frown when needed, but more commonly a smile and occasionally a short chase to retrieve a toddler who was in danger of running too far away and annoying other people.

This is what I love, she mused, lots of warmth and relaxed people. There were, she acknowledged, bad bits about being a Catholic, but when it was good, like this, she was glad to belong to the club.

Afterwards, over coffee in the centre of Dingle, Michael seemed very upbeat.

'So, how did you feel in the church?' Araminta asked him.

'Jolly good! I enjoyed being in the congregation – and when I looked at the priest, I just thought that I didn't want to be that lonely guy at the front who would eventually drift off for his well-deserved lunch and then maybe a nap in his solitary bed. That's what I can't live with now. If I absolutely had to, I could manage without sex – though I don't want to! It's the aloneness I can't tolerate. I recognise that this is a major failing in me and I regret that, but I feel it was killing me.'

'So, you don't think you're doing the wrong thing in leaving the priesthood?'

'No. Though I sometimes worry how my mother might have reacted, had she still been alive.'

'But she's not alive, is she? And you very much are.'

His face broke into one of his carefree smiles that she loved so much, but had not seen recently.

'How about we go back to the cottage,' he suggested, 'and you make your famous roast chicken and I conjure up a pudding? I was thinking of having a crack at a crème brûlée!'

*

There was no doubt, thought Wendy, that she was more alert in the late afternoons since beginning her New Year fitness project – which was just as well because she had had a frantic day, and was planning to walk two and a half miles to Shaftesbury Avenue where she had arranged to meet Julian.

She changed her shoes, pulled on waterproof trousers, zipped herself into her jacket and wrestled her rucksack on to her back, laughing to herself at how different she looked compared with the businesslike self that she showed to clients.

Still, the new regime appeared to be working and it seemed to her that already some of her clothes felt looser round her waist than they had two weeks ago.

So, she was pleased about her energy levels and, she thought, as she set off from Hoxton Square, even more pleased about what had been accomplished today.

She had interviewed four applicants for the new post of Business Manager, and her choice had been made easy by the quality of the final candidate.

Melissa was American, and shortly to finish an MBA in London – which sounded remarkably similar to the one Daniel was completing in Boston. She had perfect teeth, a genuine smile, and the sort of shiny, tumbling, shoulder-length hair that Wendy had always yearned for, forlornly.

The girl was an impressive force of nature. Her original degree had been at Princeton, she had also done internships at a top theatrical agency as well as an international hotel group. And she was very frank about wanting to stay in Europe because of her passionate hatred for Donald Trump.

'The only thing is,' Wendy had said, 'I need someone *now*. And you won't complete your course till the summer.'

But Melissa had had an answer to that too. She could manage a twenty-hour week currently, she had said, and had explained how it was common for MBA students to start their new jobs before they finished studying. As her own son had told her much

255

the same about him beginning his employment at the Toronto bank before his course ended, Wendy had smiled her understanding and promptly welcomed Melissa to BS&T.

She found herself giggling as she remembered Melissa's excitement and how she had introduced herself exuberantly to the existing staff – and then persuaded the female ones, including Wendy, to join her the day after Trump's forthcoming inauguration, on the women's protest march through London.

But what an unpredictable world it was for all these young people, she reflected, and her mood instantly plummeted as she ruminated about the future of her multinational staff – and whether the UK was going to continue to extend a welcome and opportunities to those who came from Europe once it had severed its connection with the rest of the continent.

A text vibrated in her phone; it was a message from her solicitor saying they needed answers for 'the other side'. That was another anxiety but, unlike Brexit, it would pass.

In a surprisingly short time, she reached Shaftesbury Avenue, and began to look out for the landmarks that Julian had given her. Standing with her back to the Picturehouse cinema, she surveyed the busy street.

'Are you bored and lonely, dear?' He was standing watching her, from a traffic island. 'Just over here, love. I'll give you a good time,' he shouted.

No one gave him a second glance as she laughed and waved, and dodged between a taxi and a Number 38 bus to reach him.

They crossed to the other side of the street then he faced her, took hold of both her hands and stepped back to look at her. 'Are you taking this fitness lark a bit far, lovely lady?' he giggled. 'Where's the smart West-End executive with the designer handbag and briefcase? The high-heeled boots? The cashmere coat?'

Wendy looked down at her puffa jacket, waterproof trousers and trainers. 'Not very chic, I have to admit. But the thing is I need to get fitter and walking round London suits me better than making time for a gym. And if I'm going to do it, I need to carry stuff in a rucksack, so I can swing my arms. And walking in proper shoes cripples me. I've got them with me though. And a frock. Don't worry, I'm not going to a restaurant looking like this!'

He shook his head. 'I should hope not,' he said with mock severity. 'Got to keep up our standards, darling! Though actually I thought we might eat in.'

'Excellent. I can't wait to see your place.'

'Well, considering we've known each other since October, it's long overdue, but then I love coming to your flat because it's so much nicer!'

Upstairs, on the second floor, she walked around his home making appreciative noises about the view, the prints on the walls, the biggest cushions she had ever seen and the two Tom Merrifield sculptures of ballet characters.

Julian brought her a cup of tea and as she took it, she looked at him more carefully, her head on one side. 'Have you lost weight since last Thursday?'

'God, you're an observant woman,' he giggled. 'I have – three pounds! You're not the only one embarking on a new regime. Joe and I are on a healthy-eating kick. So, I'm doing more home cooking – as you'll find out later when I produce my latest culinary invention! And I haven't bought a takeaway pizza this month. Bella Italia's profits are going to plummet, because last year, I bought about four giant-sized ones per week.'

'I'm glad everything's working out so well for you,' she murmured.

He flashed a saucy smile at her. 'Well, getting the right man has been a long time coming – but just when I'd stopped looking, there he was. In Gorleston! Imagine!'

She grinned at him. 'Life is full of surprises. This flat is one of them, actually. It's like entering a secret kingdom when you come in from Shaftesbury Avenue. I can see why you've lived here all these years.'

'And I'd like to stay, though I'll have to see how the finances go. I've got quite a lot of work lined up at the moment. But if it dries up, I'll probably give notice to the landlord and just stay in a Travelodge whenever I need to be in town. But in the meantime, if you change your mind about fighting for your Barbican place, you can always lay your weary head here for as long as I've got it.

'I won't change my mind.' Her tone was uncompromising. 'So, if you ever have to give up your flat, you're welcome to stay with me when you're in town. We may not be brother and sister, but we'll always be the greatest of mates!'

The visit to Ronan and Maeve lived up to Araminta's expectations – which had been that the lunch would be delicious and the four of them would find plenty to laugh about.

As she and Maeve cleared away the remnants of the salad and River Laune trout, and then hovered in the kitchen till the coffee was brewed, she found herself chatting to the other woman as though they had known each other for years.

'Well, it won't be easy for you,' Maeve observed in response to Araminta's anxieties about becoming the wife of an ex-priest. 'For all he says it's behind him, he's bound to have days of doubt, isn't he? Thirty years is a long time. And I suppose you can't continue to live in his parish?'

'No, we've been thinking about that. I know you said the other night that we could live in Ireland, but we'd need jobs – and I have a daughter and an elderly father in England to consider.'

'It's early days.' Maeve's eyes looked serious but her mouth stretched into a smile. 'Can you carry the cheeseboard, and I'll bring the tray?'

Back in the dining room of the extensive bungalow, which stood on top of a hill, overlooking Lough Leane, Araminta gazed through the picture window and past the rambling garden with its palm trees and shrubbery at the water below.

'This is a wonderful spot.'

'It is, yes,' Maeve agreed. 'We found the location and then we had the house built. It took a while to get it just right!'

'Do you mean that no one lived here before you?' Araminta looked puzzled.

'Not a soul… now where are the men? Doing the grand tour I shouldn't wonder. Ronan would bore for Ireland about the solar panels and the wind turbine.'

'So, do you mind my asking, are either of you ill in any way?'

Maeve cut herself a slab of cheese and proceeded to nibble it enthusiastically. God, I love this. Milleens, it's called, and it's gorgeous. Here—' Maeve broke off a piece, 'do you want some?'

Araminta laughed. 'No, you carry on. I'm full of trout!'

'So,' Maeve said, 'you're wondering why we've built a house all on one level with disabled access and rails everywhere and wet rooms with no steps and a walk-in bath?'

'Yes, exactly.'

'Coffee?'

'Thanks.'

'Well, as doctors, we've seen elderly people moved into old people's homes they didn't want to be in. We've seen couples separated into different care places – or one of them in hospital and one of them stuck in their own house all alone. We've seen injuries from people falling down stairs. And we decided we'd do what we could to avoid all that. Our hope is that whatever happens to either of us – a stroke or broken hip or whatever – we'll be able to stay here.'

'Probably one does have to consider such things,' Araminta murmured.

'I think so, yes. But most people don't.' Maeve smiled at her. 'However, it's a good idea to give it some thought before either of you is disabled or gaga, and get things organised and funded while you can. Peace of mind, isn't it?'

*

259

> Can't wait to see you tomorrow. Have to meet my father's solicitor first. Would 1.30 be OK? I've booked a table at the rooftop restaurant of the National Portrait Gallery but can change if you'd sooner go somewhere else?

Wendy smiled at Philip's text. Why was he so uncertain? She guessed he must be quite a decisive person at work, but she had never seen that side of him.

> *Perfect! Funnily enough, am also seeing a solicitor tomorrow morning.*
> May have answers about all sorts of things by the time I see you. I've asked Michael to find out what's going on with Katie, so he's going to see my mother in Kerry this afternoon. I'm sure Ma is keeping something from me. But Michael should be good at getting at the truth. He's been trained for that kind of thing!

'It may be the most beautiful place I've ever been to,' Araminta ran to Michael and linked her arm through his as he emerged from the main entrance of The Fitzhenry Hotel. 'The grounds are magnificent and everywhere you look, there's a stunning view of the estuary. I know it's a sunny day today, but I can imagine that it's even more dramatic when there's a storm. And the shrubs and trees are absolutely exquisite.'

Michael smiled at her. 'I'm getting the impression you like it here!'

She punched him on the arm and laughed. 'Come and look at this!' She ran ahead and waited for him to catch up. 'There!' She pointed to the side door of the hotel and the lobby beyond.

Together, they surveyed the dozen pairs of wellington boots in varying sizes and colours – which were obviously provided for hotel guests – as well as the boxes on the shelves containing information about the trails through the extensive gardens, and guidebooks to the Iveragh Peninsula and the Ring of Kerry.

'Staying here would be like living with posh friends or relatives in an old country manor. I just love it!'

Michael put his arm around her and pulled her close. 'Come on, you'll love Nora, and she'll be wondering where I've got to. You can come in to the hotel with no worries because your ex-patient Katie left a week ago. It seems she's gone back to her ex-boyfriend and they're emigrating to Australia.'

Araminta's jaw dropped. 'Oh my God. How could she do that to Philip? I shouldn't talk about her really, but she was a pretty self-serving customer. How dreadful.'

'Apparently, Nora's been working up to telling him the whole story, but she's been worried that he'll take it very hard. However, I'm not sure she's right about that. I got the feeling that the attraction was waning.'

'Does Nora want you to tell Philip about Katie?'

'Seems like it.'

'But how will he see his child? And, bearing in mind that he's already lost a daughter, how will he cope with the baby being on the other side of the world?'

'Well that,' Michael responded, 'is the strangest thing of all. There *is* no baby. I wonder, in fact, if there ever was.'

Chapter Eighteen

As Araminta walked towards her, with Michael following behind, Nora stood and stretched out both hands in greeting. 'You're very welcome!' she exclaimed.

Araminta kissed the older woman on both cheeks and then stood back, taking in Nora's beautiful black business suit and immaculately blow-dried silver hair. Had she not known that the hotelier was in her eighties, she would have guessed her to be around sixty. She seemed to vibrate with energy.

'What an absolutely marvellous place you have here,' she said.

Nora beamed at her visitor's enthusiasm, and Araminta noticed that Philip's mother had the same enquiring and intelligent eyes as he had.

The three of them sat down in a lounge overlooking the gardens, and immediately, two waiters appeared bearing cakes and sandwiches on decorative stands, plus a huge pot of tea and jug of hot water.

Nora took Michael's hand and stroked it. 'I can't tell you, Araminta, how fantastic it is to meet the son of the lady who told me about Dr Richard. I never forgot her. And now, here – all grown up – is the baby she was carrying at the time. Now, if that's not a miracle, I don't know what is!' She reached up and tweaked Michael's cheek in a gesture of love bordering on ownership.

As her waiters backed away, Nora changed the subject to Katie, and launched into a heated explanation of how she had been duped and let down by 'that young woman' who had 'inveigled herself into my emotions and my household'.

'Awful for you,' Michael sympathised.

'And she must have known how thrilled I'd be to have another grandchild, having lost darling Emily. She certainly knew how to win me over; all that talk about learning how to become my right-hand help while the baby grew up here. All of it rubbish!'

'But surely she was pregnant, originally?' he asked.

'I wouldn't know,' Nora replied bitterly. 'But looking back at her drunken behaviour ever since she arrived at Christmas, my view is that she'd lost the baby – or taken steps to lose it – by then.'

Remembering her final session with Katie on Christmas Eve, Araminta recalled how her client had made no mention of her pregnancy.

'We won't talk about it any more,' Nora announced firmly, and she reached for a cucumber sandwich and motioned that the others should eat too. 'Just please tell Philip about it very gently. Will you be seeing him in person?'

Michael shook his head. 'No, sorry. We're staying in Kerry for a while yet. But I'll have a long talk with him on the phone, and we have mutual friends in England who'll support him.'

Nora turned to Araminta. 'So, are you thinking of moving to Ireland?'

Unsure what Michael might have said to Nora while she had remained in the grounds, she responded vaguely. 'It would be lovely... if we can.'

'Ah, sure if you put your mind to it, you can of course. But you want to be making some sensible decisions. Starting a new life in your fifties gives you the opportunity to think about needs you'll have later – and how you want to spend your last years. I suppose it's easy for me; I own a hotel! I can almost certainly end my days here. I have staff, and I could afford nursing care to come in if I needed it. You're young yet, but you'll come to understand how much this kind of thing matters. I mean, would you want to end up in some awful place with a bunch of dribbling and demented pensioners? You wouldn't! Not at all!'

Nora sprang up suddenly, excused herself, and – at some speed – left the room.

Michael leant over to whisper to Araminta. 'Nora would probably be thrilled to know you're Richard's daughter, shall I tell her?'

She shook her head vigorously. 'And I'm keeping quiet about having been Katie's therapist too,' she murmured as Nora returned waving a property supplement.

'Take this! It's the weekly segment from the local paper and it'll give you an idea of prices. You'll see that plenty of houses here are one-storey. Sure, when the Lord created the west coast of Ireland he made sure there was plenty of space – so builders here construct properties that their owners can grow old in! And you get a lot of square feet for your euros.'

'It's funny,' Araminta remarked to Michael later when they were driving away along the Ring of Kerry, 'how Nora was so keen to get us planning for our dotage. Maeve was talking about the same topic earlier.'

Michael nodded. 'Ronan too. It must play on people's minds. It never used to on mine, because till recently I'd always imagined ending up at the far end of a corridor in some presbytery or other! But I can see that since we're now faced with all this upheaval we ought to make long-term plans. I've seen too many parishioners end up in not-very-good care homes.'

'Funnily enough, going into a home was the thing I thought Dad would kick up a fuss about when it became obvious he couldn't remain in his own place. But once he managed to get two adjoining rooms in the Seastrand, which of course he's paying double for, he was OK. But then, he thinks he's coming back!'

'Coming back! Does he believe in reincarnation?'

'Not exactly. He's going to be cryogenically preserved. He believes that scientists will soon be able to regenerate life, and he wants to be in on it. It's fantastically expensive. He's arranged for an English-based company to prepare him after death then ship him to America, where he'll be stored. His house is mortgaged to the hilt to pay for it and the various other hair-brained schemes he's had in his life, which means he won't be leaving me anything. So I hope you're not marrying me thinking I'm a woman of substance!'

'Actually,' Michael admitted, 'I've been wondering how I could introduce the subject of money. It's kind of like the elephant we both know is there but never discuss.'

'I know. You're right, we must talk about it.'

'Well, obviously,' Michael sighed, 'I don't have much. Just a few ISAs and Premium Bonds. But my mother left me her house. I didn't, in fact, want her to do that. However, she insisted that I was to sell it when she was gone because I'd "need something to fall back on" – and she told me not to give it all away to CAFOD or the parish. I wonder now whether she realised that I was heading for some sort of crisis about the priesthood. Anyway, when I sold her place, I did actually give away half the proceeds to Catholic charities, but I've still got a hundred and twenty-five thousand pounds in fivers under my mattress.'

'Really?'

'No! It's in the bank – but making so little interest it might as well not be.'

'Well, we'll manage. I'll sell my house – there's a mortgage on it, but I'll probably come out with about double what you've got. It wouldn't buy anything very splendid in Norwich, but if we came here… Ooh, can we stop? Look!'

Michael pulled into the side of the road, and peered out of the window at the darkening landscape. There, in front of a large lake, stood a one-storey house with a *For Sale* board.

'That'll be in the newspaper Nora gave us, I bet,' Araminta said.

Michael switched on the car's interior light while she scrabbled in her bag for the supplement. She flicked through the pages. 'Is this it?'

Michael took the paper from her and stared at the tiny picture, first with his glasses on, and then without, before jumping out of the car to take a closer look.

'Mmmn,' he murmured as he returned. 'Can you smell the peat from someone's fire? I love that. It reminds me of being here as a kid. Anyway, yes, I'm sure that's it. What do the details say?'

She held the paper up near the light. 'Mountain and lake views, three bedrooms, large kitchen, two reception rooms, shower room, bathroom, just under two hundred and thirty thousand euros.' Not sure precisely what that is in sterling, but we could afford this.'

'We'd be way out in the country though. What sort of work could we do? Do you remember Ballynakilty, the little market town we liked on the way out here? Well, that's the nearest we'd be to any shops, and I doubt there'd be many jobs going.'

'Something will turn up!'

He grinned at her before switching off the light and restarting the car. 'Thank you, Mrs Micawber!'

Utterly Dickensian, thought Philip as he let himself out of the heavy door in the ancient building. He stood, breathing in the polluted air of Chancery Lane, which seemed positively fragrant after the fusty interior he had sat in for the past two hours.

The old lawyer seemed to have been left over from a bygone age with his ridiculous stiff collar and pince-nez. It was just amazing that he had written his notes with a Montblanc fountain pen rather than a quill.

Thank heavens it was almost time for his lunch with Wendy. He had a feeling that it was only by talking to her that he would make sense of it all.

*

266

Julian made the train to Norwich with less than a minute to spare. Being Friday lunchtime, it was crowded. As he passed groups of chattering passengers, he kept hearing the name 'Trump', which reminded him that the US Presidential Inauguration was taking place later. Not that he intended watching it. It was too tragic to contemplate. He walked on through five or six carriages until finally, in the quiet coach, he found a window seat.

It was funny, he thought, how much work he had all of a sudden. Soon, he would begin the Extra Chorus rehearsals for *Die Meistersinger* at the Opera House. And he had other bookings lined up – mostly modern compositions – in London, Edinburgh, Cambridge, Oxford, Dublin and Amsterdam. It was good, except that now he had Joe in his life he had anticipated spending more time with him in Norfolk.

He opened his *Guardian* and thumbed through the pages without really registering what he was reading. But then, on page seven, he stopped.

'No!'

He was unaware that he had yelled aloud till the woman in front of him – the only passenger nearby who was not wearing headphones – turned around. He raised his hand in apology.

There was a picture of the members of Chamber 28, an orchestra, formed in 2014, that he sometimes worked with. The musicians – all in their twenties and thirties and noted for their enthusiasm as well as their skill – were drawn from all over Europe. They specialised in unusual repertoire, and often used him as a soloist in pieces involving singers.

They were based in Cambridge, but, the report said, they were planning to move out of the UK because of Brexit; worried that their players would find it harder to travel freely once Britain withdrew from the EU.

His referendum vote last June – cast as a protest, and in solidarity with his ageing mother – came back to haunt him. 'Getting our country back' might have been a snappy slogan, but surely no one seriously wanted Brexit to sabotage cultural organisations?

For five minutes or so, he stared out of the train window, shaking his head from time to time. But then an idea occurred to him. It was probably too fanciful. Nonetheless, he picked up his phone and sent a text.

Wendy dropped into Pret a Manger by St Martin in the Fields for a quick coffee. She was early for her lunch with Philip and, after the morning she had spent with her solicitor, she was grateful to have time to think.

Her mobile rang. She was inclined to ignore it, but on noticing that the caller was Hannah, she answered.

'Wendy! I've been so rude. Sorry! We went skiing and since we came back so much has been going on – stuff I couldn't really talk about – so I avoided contacting you. But thanks so much for your offer of help with a showreel. I don't want you to think for one moment that I'm not grateful.'

'I don't! You're young. You're busy. It's fine.'

'Oh thanks, Wendy – so could I take you up on your offer?'

'Absolutely! I'll text you some possible dates and times.'

'Cool! By the way, you don't know where Mum is, do you?'

'No,' she replied. 'I've tried to call her a few times but it goes to voicemail.'

'Same thing's happening to me.' Hannah's voice sounded stressed. 'And I really need to speak to her. I've even been in touch with my uncle in Barbados. But he hasn't heard from her in years, let alone seen her. If she does contact you, can you let me know?'

'Of course. See you soon.'

As soon as Wendy was seated at their table in the rooftop restaurant, Philip told her all the news about Katie that he had learned the previous evening when Michael had rung from Ireland.

She stretched out a hand across the table and patted his arm. 'I'm so sorry, Philip. She's treated you appallingly. Odd about the baby though. I imagine that's the hardest bit.'

'Yes and no,' Philip murmured as he poured sparkling water into both their glasses. 'Are you sure you won't have wine? Don't let me inhibit you, just because I'm not drinking.'

'I am sure. I'm not much of a boozer these days – except at New Year obviously!' She laughed. 'I used to be able to drink most people under the table, even allowing for the prodigious amounts of alcohol everyone in the television industry imbibed in the eighties and nineties. But I can't do it now. Probably just as well! Anyway, I've got to write a script later. I'll need a clear head for that.'

'I thought with you being such a news junkie you'd be glued to the Trump inauguration this afternoon.'

'I can't bear to watch. In fact, I've never been more grateful that I no longer direct news bulletins. Everything's too awful.'

The waiter hovered. They both elected to begin with the Portland Crab, then she selected seabass as a main course, and he chose quail.

'That just proves how posh you are,' she teased him. 'Lesser mortals can't cope with all those fiddly bones; it's only people with breeding who order small game birds with confidence!'

He smiled but did not deny what she knew to be true.

'So,' she asked, 'what else did Michael say? Is he doing OK? Agonising over whether or not to leave the priesthood can't be easy.'

'I think he's done his agonising over that. It's the Richard Yateman thing for him – like you – that's so devastating.'

'I hadn't realised how strongly he felt about it.'

'Well, I mean he and Araminta now have a very difficult dilemma.'

'Minty? Do they?'

Philip gasped. 'I thought you knew their secret. Michael said that he and Araminta were each confiding in one person. He chose me and she chose you. You were talking together for ages on Boxing Day so I assumed she'd spilled the beans.'

'Gosh, now you mention it, she *was* trying to tell me something, before lunch... something she was finding difficult, but then Julian interrupted us. So, do you mean that she and Michael are having a relationship?'

'Yes – it only started properly at Christmas. Oh dear, now I feel I've betrayed their trust.'

'No, you haven't,' Wendy assured him. 'Not really. I can pretend to Minty that I don't know, till she officially tells me, which she will. Actually, now I come to think of it, I did notice something that day, but it went out of my head afterwards. They were standing very close together. It looked quite intimate. Well, that's lovely for them.'

'Only if everyone ignores the DNA result.'

'Oh gosh! I'm an idiot. That's incest, then, I suppose. Legally. But is it? They didn't grow up together. They're hardly going to have children. Surely it doesn't matter?'

'But Michael's a man of great conscience. I doubt if he's ever broken the tiniest law. And he probably doesn't think you can cherry pick the good ones and ignore anything that's inconvenient.'

Wendy sighed noisily, and shook her head. 'So,' she said after a pause, 'is Minty in Ireland too? With Michael?'

Philip nodded.

'Various things are beginning to make sense now – particularly the fact that Hannah hasn't been able to get hold of her mother. She called me earlier and sounded quite worried.'

'Araminta's phone has been switched off.' Philip reached for his own mobile. 'But Michael's checking his now, so if I text you his number, you can call him if you want – especially if you think they ought to contact Hannah.'

They fell silent while the waiter, who was Polish, brought their starters. His charm and efficiency propelled them into a conversation about their mutual horror of Brexit.

After they had both discussed their fears for their own companies, Philip told her how his mother was becoming increasingly keen that he should move to Ireland to help her with the hotel.

'And,' he confided, 'for the first time in my life – and possibly because of the political chaos here – I find the proposal more and more attractive.'

'But what about your wife? Now that Katie's out of the picture, can you recharge your marriage?'

Philip put down his knife and fork, and delicately wiped his mouth with the white starched napkin before responding. 'I really don't think so. Marigold still hasn't told me anything of what's going on in her life. But Bro – my brother-in-law – rang me a couple of days ago to tell me that she's seeing the guy she was engaged to before she married me. He's a viscount. She adored him. Or maybe she just adored his title! When they were going out years ago, he suddenly dumped her for a rich American. I got her on the rebound. But apparently, the viscount's wife has finally tired of him and our weather, and has gone back to Florida. Bro said that Marigold dropped in to comfort the old boy with indecent haste!'

'I can't believe that this is happening to you.'

'Well, it's no worse than what's happening to you, is it? Everything seems strange right now. I feel as if the world is spinning out of control.'

'Exactly!'

'But what's just occurred to me...' He paused as the waiter appeared between them to gather up their plates. '...is that you could move your company to Ireland. I know that I haven't thought this out, but just before you arrived, I had a text from Julian. He was telling me about a Cambridge-based chamber orchestra comprised of players from all over Europe. Apparently, they've decided to leave the UK in case the Brexit deal restricts their movement. Julian's solution was that I should invite them to base themselves in the conference complex at The Fitzhenry. He also thought we should mount an annual music festival.'

'That sounds like him!'

'But maybe he's right,' Philip went on. 'And the thing is, if I extended the facilities there, which I have the space to do, you could have an office and a studio. In fact, if we got good at music festivals, we could have media conferences there – television awards... all sorts of things. If Britain is looking inwards, Ireland would be mad if it didn't look outwards and seize these opportunities.'

He grinned at her and she noticed how boyish he looked when the strain temporarily left his features.

'Well, in the immortal words of Baldrick, "it's a cunning plan".'

'You can jest,' Philip retorted. 'But stranger things have happened. And if I run this past my ageing ma, who's an optimistic pragmatist of the first order, she'll be up for it.'

'Really?'

'Really. You'll have to meet her one day.'

Wendy was about to respond when the young waiter returned with their main courses and side dishes of vegetables.

Philip watched as she sampled her seabass. 'I nearly ordered that myself!' he told her.

'How can we not be siblings?' She sighed. 'That would have been great.'

His eyes met hers as he murmured sadly. 'I know.'

'Do you really think you'll move to Ireland, Philip? I know vast numbers of unhappy "Remainers" are applying for Irish passports.'

'Fortunately, courtesy of Ma, I've got one of those. I suppose I'm beginning to consider different options, now that the life I thought I had is in pieces.'

'I know the feeling. But, I mean, just supposing you're right and I should move my business to Ireland, I wouldn't have a clue how to begin, and how would I see my poor old parents in Norfolk?'

'It's only a hop across the water. There are plenty of flights from Kerry and Cork to Stansted. You could come over once a week.'

'Gosh, food for thought. Anyway, on a different tack, we've both been to solicitors this morning. How did yours go?'

'Totally unbelievable. But tell me about your morning first.'

So she did – and began by reminding Philip about Francesca and her demands.

'It's as if she wants to replace me. It's unsettling to think she may have been watching my life all these years, waiting in the hope that I'd give up on Robert so that she could waltz in and be a better version of me.'

He raised his eyebrows at her. 'No one could.'

'Anyway, the lawyer started going through everything that Robert says he wants, and what he'd pay me if I let him have the Barbican flat, and suddenly I began to add up in my head just what all the legal wrangling might cost – not just financially but in terms of time and effort. And I suddenly wondered *why* it was so important to keep the flat. And out of the blue, I got this surge of inspiration, or madness, and I realised that I could junk everything, and start again. Almost be a different person. Is that very strange? I think it may be. So, I interrupted my solicitor and said, "Agree to everything". He went quite pale. Then, he asked me if I understood what I was saying. I think for two pins he'd have referred me for a psychiatric assessment!' She laughed, then stopped, then laughed again so much that she had to put her cutlery down and cover her mouth with her napkin to muffle her merriment. Then she shook herself slightly and gazed at Philip, trying to interpret the expression in his eyes. If, she decided, he started looking as though he thought she were crazy she might have to accept that she was.

But his lips were quivering and his eyes lit up. 'Your solicitor had probably anticipated months of work, at five hundred pounds an hour or whatever! He'd probably already decided how he was going to spend your fee. Brilliant!'

'Thank you, Philip.'

He looked puzzled. 'For what?'

'For not thinking I'm going off my rocker!'

He beamed at her. 'You're one of the sanest people I've ever met,' he said. 'And I'm not trying to flatter you. It's just who you are.'

She shook her head, but smiled at the compliment.

'So, did you just get up and walk out of his office after you'd said that?' Philip asked.

'More or less; I did suggest he try and squeeze more money out of them for the flat, and get a reduction on what Fran wants as a pay-off. But I'm not going to prolong it. It's so draining.'

Philip nodded his understanding as a flurry of waiters arrived to clear their table and offer them the pudding menu, which they waved away.

'Coffee?'

'Please,' she answered. 'Black.'

'Two of those,' he ordered, then he leant back in his chair and chewed on his lip for a moment before saying, 'Shall I tell you about my morning?'

'I'd love to hear about it – if you want to tell me.'

'I definitely do,' he replied. And then he launched into a summary of his life with his father; a man, he told her, who from his birth had belittled and ignored him in equal measure. Then he explained how excited he had felt when it appeared he might be Richard Yateman's offspring – and how he had been in despair when he learned that he was not the doctor's son and that George Baldry must be his biological parent after all.

'Except...' He paused while the waiter delivered their coffees and retreated. 'Except,' he repeated, 'that apparently he isn't.'

'Sorry. Isn't what?'

'My father is not my father. That's what the solicitors told me this morning. I'm not his child. And to top it all, it seems he's known that since before I was born.'

'How?'

'Well it turns out that after he and my mother had been trying for a baby for a couple of years, he went to a doctor in Harley

274

Street and had his sperm tested – and he found out that he was infertile. The lawyer said he assumes it was because he had mumps badly as a boy. Needless to say, in typically self-interested fashion, he never told my mum that he was firing blanks, as it were.'

'So, what happened when she got the idea of going to Dr Yateman?'

'I suppose he saw it as a way in which he could father a child. I'm sure he was completely unaware that, when necessary, Richard contributed his own ejaculate. All he knew was that he was supposed to turn up with a fresh specimen, which the doc would inject into my mother. So, through the Harley Street medic that he'd seen, he bought the services of a suitable young man – a medical student, apparently – and paid him to come to Norwich and produce a sample on the appropriate day, which Pa presented at the surgery as his own. Obviously, it was then inseminated into my mother, presumably along with a donation from Richard, and I was the result.'

Wendy became aware that she had been stirring her coffee for the duration of Philip's explanation. She put the spoon in the saucer and then leant on the table.

'I… I can't honestly imagine how this must feel for you,' she said quietly. 'Does anyone know who your biological father was?'

'I asked, but apparently that was part of the deal. My father never knew. Didn't want to know. And now he's instructed the lawyer to tell me that he and I will have no further contact, but that he's signed over all his rights, shares and money in the company to me. In exchange for that, when he dies, everything else will be left to his nephews, which is obviously fine with me. The only proviso was that I had to sign an oath to say that I won't divulge the truth to anyone – and that includes Marigold. Obviously, I've broken the promise immediately by confiding in you! And doubtless I'll tell Michael, Araminta and Julian too. But that's all. Marigold, and all Pa's family and friends, will never know.'

'Are you glad that you're not his son?'

'Eventually, I'm sure the answer will be "yes". However, right now,' he sighed. 'I feel empty, and as if I don't know who I am, or what I am – which is ridiculous because I've got the best mother in the world. Probably, like you, I'm just drained by it all.'

It had, Philip reflected, been a productive week. In some peculiar way, the emptiness he had described to Wendy eight days ago had proved to be a blessing. He seemed to have been operating on autopilot, but had got through much more work than usual.

The brochures were well on their way to being finished. The revamped company website – with new images, products and copy – was up and running. There was a sense within his business that there were opportunities to be made from leaving Europe. He was allowing himself to be swept along with this notion, though he did not believe it.

He looked at his watch. Saturday stretched out before him. He had already walked the dogs. It was the coldest day they had had for a while, but he would go out again. It occurred to him suddenly that he might give his ancient three-wheeler a spin round the grounds.

He was going to see Wendy this evening, and Julian tomorrow. There was much to look forward to. So why was he so cast down by Marigold's letter, which had arrived an hour ago? What did it matter that she wanted a divorce? Did he want her back? No – so why did he mind that she had given up on him?

It would be pretty poor form to have a whisky when it was only midday – particularly since he had eschewed alcohol since New Year's Eve. But he yearned for comfort. He could have a glass or two. Sleep it off. Then see Wendy…

'It's just not like Philip,' Wendy said again.

She was on the phone to Julian.

'Don't worry, he'll be fine. Are you still in London?'

'No, I came up on the train first thing and now I'm out at Dad's new place about to have lunch with him and Mum. But I can't stop worrying about Philip. He was supposed to call by now and he hasn't.'

'Darling heart.' Julian's voice was, as ever, buoyant and reassuring. 'He's got acres of ground. Dogs to walk. A company to run. You weren't due to meet till this evening anyway.'

'Sorry, I'm being ridiculous. I'll have lunch and then maybe go for a walk with my dad. I don't mean to sound neurotic.'

Philip woke to find himself slumped in his favourite chair in the snug. It was dark. He reached for the switch on the table lamp beside him, then looked at his wrist watch and blinked. He looked again. How could it be five o'clock? Slowly, he got to his feet and, focusing extra hard, walked out of the room into the hallway. That was in darkness too. His feet were not obeying him for some reason, and he tumbled against the kitchen door as he tried to open it. Flicking on the lights, he stared at the huge clock that dominated the facing wall. Yes, it was five. Gone five, in fact. Carefully, he negotiated his way back to the snug and picked up the whisky bottle from the floor by his chair. Bemused, he gazed at it trying to compute how the full bottle he had opened was now empty. He leant over to feel if the carpet was damp. Perhaps he had spilled it. He almost fell, and as he tried to balance and return to an upright position, he hit his head against the leather chair.

He was due to see Wendy in a couple of hours. He must ring her, but perhaps he should get some fresh air first.

Outside, he made his way unsteadily to where his dogs were locked up in the stables. They started leaping up in their attempt to see him over the chest-high door.

He was about to let them out when he remembered his earlier idea of riding his three-wheeler. Having a drive would certainly get the air to his head. Realising suddenly that he was not wearing

277

his quilted jacket, he considered going back to the house to retrieve it, but everything felt such an effort and, since he would be outside for ten minutes at the most, he would be fine.

He wondered again about letting the dogs out, so that they could run around and exercise themselves, but decided they might get too near his ATV. Could be dangerous, he thought, as he opened the shed that housed the vehicle, and dragged the heavy tarpaulin off it.

He leant against the door for a moment. Really, he felt quite unsteady and very unfit and it took him a couple of attempts to haul himself onto the trike. Then the engine refused to start – but suddenly it thundered into life.

He took it slowly – very slowly – as he drove out of the court-yard and into the meadow, and headed in the direction of the lake at the bottom of the hill. It was difficult to see, as the lamps on the vehicle were not very bright and the security lights near the house did not illuminate this part of his land.

He would just do a circuit and get back to the house, and he would do it quickly as he was getting cold. Surprisingly cold.

Suddenly, he was bumping across the grass much faster than he had ever travelled over this terrain. It was what the vehicle was designed for, and really invigorating. Why had he never cranked up the speed before?

He was almost at the lake now. As he always did, he offered up a silent prayer for his daughter, then he found himself talking to her – shouting – over the noise of the engine.

'You were so beautiful, Emily. Such fun. I miss you.'

He heard a jarring sound as a wheel caught the crazy paving that surrounded the lake. He must be more careful...

'You're like a cat on a hot tin roof,' her father snapped. 'It's nice having you here, but it's almost like you're *not* here.'

She apologised. 'Sorry, Dad. I didn't mean to be rude.'

'Are you still going out tonight?'

'Well that's the thing. I don't know. Philip – my friend – was going to call. It's so unlike him not to.'

'Well, contact him.'

'I've tried. But I can't get him.'

'I hope this isn't another man who's going to let you down.' Her father began to walk away.

'Dad, stop, he's not like that. And the situation isn't what you think at all. We're like brother and sister. That's all.'

Her father turned towards her. She could see him selecting what he should say and was relieved when he settled for, 'Just don't like to see you upsetting yourself.'

Had he been lying here long? It was hard to tell, thought Philip.

He tried to pat his pockets to locate his phone, but he did not seem to be wearing his jacket. That might be why he was cold.

It was very dark. The lights on the vehicle had died. In fact, he could not see the trike, though he was sure he had not imagined riding it. It was, he realised, very misty. When had that happened? In a moment, he would make himself stand up and walk back to the house and ring Wendy. She would help him. He would probably shake off... whatever was stopping him... in a moment. Breathing hard with the effort, he tried to raise himself onto an elbow but a searing pain shot through his chest, winding him.

Just stay still a little longer, he counselled himself. Nothing to worry about. His teeth were chattering. Still, he was fine, wasn't he? He tried to move his right leg, which seemed quite numb. Then he reached his hand down his left leg as far as he could stretch without the agony exploding into life again. It seemed to be wet. Perhaps it had been raining. He felt something sharp, which made no sense.

Perhaps I might die here? This new concept sat in his mind for a while and he mentally hefted it around. Surely, he was just being dramatic? He felt much like his normal self. Just a bit cold. Still, his teeth were no longer chattering and the shivering seemed to have stopped too, which he assumed was good. He probably had injured something... Nothing crucial though. He had, he was sure, been riding his 'boy's toy' as Marigold referred to it. He must have fallen off.

He woke up again, or perhaps he was dreaming? He wondered if anyone might find him, and realised with a moment of panic – which quickly subsided to a sense of resignation – that it was most unlikely.

He seemed not to have been thinking anything for a while. Probably, it was time for him to try to work out what to do. But, he wondered, did I perhaps *mean* to have an accident? Or even to kill myself? It seemed unlikely, though he could not be sure. He had felt sad, and worthless. It was something else to be curious about.

He would be sorry to leave Julian and Michael... And Wendy... Wendy... Stupid way to die... How hopeless he was... Hopeless at life... Some people might miss him... for a while. Not long. The world would be better off without him. Poor Emily – what had gone through her mind in her last moments? Had she been terrified? Or really calm... calm like he was... Emily... Emily... It's Dad...

Chapter Nineteen

'Oh God, oh God...'

Wendy had borrowed her father's car even though it was not insured for her to drive, and now she was lost as well as panic-stricken. She elected to take the next turning – no matter whether it went to the left or the right – in the hope that, somehow, she would find herself at Philip's property.

Initially, she had tried to book a taxi, but when she had finally got through to the company, a somewhat ponderous woman had warned her that there was a wait of at least an hour.

'Everyone's going to the RNLI "do",' the taxi controller had explained, eager to chat. 'And they don't want to drive themselves now, do they? Not with it being such a frosty, rimy ol' evening.'

'OK, thanks.' Wendy had cut the woman short before shouting through to her father from his hallway, 'I've got to take your car, Dad. I'll be careful.' Then, without waiting for a response, she had swept up his keys and run out of the building.

'Concentrate, concentrate,' she urged herself, as she crashed the gears yet again.

She had been pleased that she had managed to get to Holt without too much difficulty – though there had been a really worrying moment when the nearside front tyre had clipped a kerb.

She had cursed herself at her ineptitude, and worried that she may have done some damage; a puncture now would be the absolute end.

But now that she had left the little market town, she realised she had no clue how to find Hunsford Hall. She wished she had taken more notice of her surroundings during her only previous visit, when Philip had picked her up at Sheringham station.

'Think,' she urged herself. 'You may be a lousy driver but you've got a good memory. Think!'

The road was bumpier now, and the mist denser.

Deciding she must be going in the wrong direction, she took the next turning on the left. Nothing looked familiar. But then the headlights picked up the shadowy image of a round-towered church. With a surge of relief, she sensed she had seen it before. Grabbing the torch her father kept in the glove compartment, she leapt out of the car and ran towards the noticeboard at the entrance to the graveyard.

'Letheringsett Church,' she read aloud.

Some thirty years ago, she had directed a programme for Anglia TV about historic churches in Norfolk. This had been one of them. As far as she could remember, she and Philip had not driven past it on their journey. She turned the car around and headed east, then took a gamble on the next tiny lane she came to. Suddenly, a small animal ran across the road right in front of her. Braking hard, she slid into a long skid. Practically choking with fear, she fought to regain control of the car. Her exhaled breath sounded like the death rattle of a character in a television drama. She was lucky not to have ended up in a ditch.

Suddenly, she came upon a red phone box. Was that promising? She rather thought so. 'Come on, come on,' she shouted, as she took a turning to the right. Something, possibly a wheel, was making a rasping, metallic noise, but she ignored it and carried on.

She was driving too fast to stop when, finally, she spied the Hunsford Hall sign at the end of Philip's drive. Screeching to a halt, and praying that no other car would be on this narrow, out-of-the-way road on such a night, she turned the vehicle around – with a five-point turn which would have ensured failure in the driving test – and set off through Philip's grounds towards his property.

Various security lights came on as she passed them. She swerved to a halt, grabbed her father's torch again and raced to the front door of the big house, and banged on it. No one came. She ran around towards the back of the building in the direction of the sound of dogs barking, but before she found them, she came upon a side door which was wide open.

Had Philip been burgled? Perhaps attacked? Might any intruder still be in his home? It seemed unlikely as there was no vehicle on the drive. She ran inside and sprinted around the ground floor till she came to the little room she had sat in with Philip on her previous visit. It was empty, but she did notice a discarded whisky bottle on the floor.

She ran outside again. The barking was louder now, and she found the dogs, locked in a stable, with one of those half-doors, jumping up and down in a frenzy.

They would help her find him. She wrestled with the bolt and as soon as she managed to push it back and the door began to open, the two Labradors rushed out, almost knocking her over, and disappeared. Directing the torch's beam beyond the courtyard, she ran in the direction they had taken, but could see nothing.

The mist swirled around her, but she could feel from the unevenness of the terrain that she was running on grass. She stumbled suddenly and hurt her ankle, but ignored the pain and hobbled on until she saw the dogs running in circles around a heap on the ground.

'Let me see!' she shouted at them as her torchlight picked out Philip's collapsed figure. He looked very peaceful. Too peaceful.

'No!' she screamed into the open air. 'No, no, no!'

She thought she saw his eyelids flicker.

'Philip, it's Wendy. Stay with me!' She touched his face. It was icy cold. One of the dogs pushed against her knee and looked up as if begging her to do something useful. Then he lay down across his master's chest, and started licking his face.

'That's a good idea,' she thought aloud. 'They can transmit body warmth.' She grabbed the other dog and with a few muttered commands that might or might not mean anything in canine language, she pushed him down so that he was lying alongside his master. It was only then she noticed that Philip's left leg had a jagged bone protruding from his skin. There was also a lot of blood, but she was relieved to find that it wasn't pumping out.

Uttering up yet another prayer that there would be a phone signal, she reached into a coat pocket for her mobile and rang 999.

She asked for an ambulance, and tried to give some clue as to where Hunsford Hall was. Then, attempting to suppress the panic she felt, she described Philip's injuries.

'Is he breathing?' the woman asked.

She heard a cry of terror escape from her throat as she leant over him, then she pushed her torch up against Philip's mouth, withdrew it, and looked to see if there was a mist of breath on it.

'To be honest, I don't know,' she answered.

'Put your cheek near his mouth and see if you can feel anything.'

She did as she was told. 'Sorry, it's so cold I can't really tell.'

'OK,' the operator said, 'is he on his back?'

'Yes.'

'Good, now make sure the airway is clear.'

'OK. I know how to do that. I'm just putting down the phone for a moment.'

She had once directed a video on first aid and could almost hear the commentary. 'Place one hand on the forehead of the patient and two fingers of your other hand under the chin and gently tilt the head back so that the chin is lifted.'

Picking up her phone again, she said, 'I've done that. Still not sure if he is breathing or not.'

'OK. Keep him as warm as you can. Do you know how to do CPR?'

'I think so,' Wendy answered. 'Should I do it? Even if he is breathing? Oh God, I'm being so useless.'

'If in doubt, do it. I'll stay on the line and talk you through it if you like.'

'No, it's OK, just please ask the ambulance to hurry.'

She threw her phone down, then shuffled herself out of her coat and covered Philip's legs. The dogs were eerily quiet as they watched her.

She pushed them away so she could sit at the side of Philip's torso, then she put one hand on top of the other, locked her fingers together and placed them on his chest and started pumping two beats to every second. 'OK, let's go!' she shouted to the heavens.

After a minute, she started to sing, '*Staying alive, staying alive.*'

She remembered that she was supposed to intersperse rescue breaths with the pumping, so she counted thirty compressions, and then leant over him, pinched his nose and put her lips to his and blew into his mouth, watching his chest rise and then fall. She did it once more, and then started pumping again. After a while, she stopped singing and instead cried out loudly. 'I've lost my cheating husband. I've lost my bloody flat. But I'll save you, Philip Baldry, if it's the last thing I do…'

Her upper arms were on fire. 'Breathe, Philip. Please breathe. Come on, help me, Philip. Help me. *Staying alive, staying alive.*' Her voice sounded weedy in the night air. 'You can't go, Philip. Your life isn't over. There's lots of stuff to do yet. *Staying alive, staying alive.*'

She had no idea how long she had been with him, all she knew was that she had to keep doing CPR and the rescue breaths. There was no one else to help. She had to save him.

'*Staying alive, staying alive.*'

Eventually, she thought she could hear an ambulance siren. She kept pumping. The dogs jumped up. 'It's good,' she reassured them. 'They're going to help us.'

A beam from the headlights told her that the paramedics were bringing the vehicle right up to them.

'OK,' she heard a reassuring male voice. 'We'll take over now.'

In a daze she sat back on her heels.

'Keep the dogs away,' warned a female voice.

Wendy patted one of the animals, and turned him around so she could hold his collar.

'Here,' she said firmly. 'Sit.'

Surprisingly, he did, and the other one came to her too, and lay down, making anxious snuffly sounds.

One of the paramedics was saying something. 'You've done well and he's breathing. We're going to get him into the ambulance in a minute. Are you OK?'

Wendy looked up into the concerned eyes of the young woman. But found she could not speak.

'We need to get you indoors. You're cold and exhausted. Can you get to your feet?'

Wendy stood up quickly. Her phone began to ring. She looked around wondering where it was. But then, everything started spinning, and her knees buckled. That's strange, she thought.

Driving along the Norwich ring road, Julian noticed in his mirror that Wendy was pushing herself into a sitting position on the back seat, and staring at the back of his head.

'Darling heart,' he said gleefully. 'You're back with us!'

'Is this the point where I ask weakly: "Where am I?".'

He laughed. 'You must be all right if you can make jokes. That's a relief. You gave me a terrible shock.'

'No but, honestly, where am I?'

'Almost at the hospital – which is where Philip must be by now. They went off like a bat out of hell.'

'Philip! Oh God.'

'It's fine. Well, truthfully, it may not be fine, but he's alive, which is entirely due to you.'

286

'I don't really understand where you fit in to all of this.'

'Your insistence that something was wrong got to me. So, as soon as Joe got home from his shift, we jumped into his car. I didn't know where Philip lived of course, and after reaching Holt we got completely lost, which is when we rang you. But you chose that moment to pass out, so the very nice paramedic answered your phone and gave us directions, and we arrived just as they were loading Philip into the ambulance.'

'How was he?'

'Well, pretty "mashed up" was how Joe described him. But hopefully they can put him back together again. Got to believe, haven't you?'

'And I was a bit vague, was I?'

'Sweetie, you were out cold. So we took you up to the house and when you came round, we made you some tea, which you didn't drink because you fell asleep. Then we fed the dogs and shut them back in the stable, found Philip's keys in his Barbour jacket by the side door, locked up the house and Joe carried you to his car. And here we are. By the way, you might notice you're wearing Philip's jacket. Your coat was covered in blood. It's in the boot.'

'But where's Joe?'

'He's stayed with your dad's old Rover. He was changing the wheel when we left. How you drove it with the puncture, I have no idea. The tyre was hanging off it. Anyway, if you can remember your father's address, I'll text Joe and he'll drive the car back to him.'

'Of course I can remember it, I'm fine.'

Julian pulled into the next lay-by, and she dictated the details to him.

'Good,' Julian said as he sent the text. 'Joe will take the car to your dad and explain everything, and I'll get you to A & E. The paramedics said you need to be checked over.'

'But I've told you I'm OK.'

'Great – but we're going anyway!'

'Julian, don't you think we should try and find how Philip is first? He can't go through this alone.'

'The paramedics told me there was no point in rushing. They also said the docs may do something complicated to do with Philip's blood – they withdraw it somehow, warm it up and put it back if someone's got extreme hypothermia. Then he's got to have a brain scan because they think he fell on his head. On top of that, apparently his left leg has a compound fracture, and he may have broken his hip too. He'll probably go to the operating theatre tonight and then be in Intensive Care. I don't think anyone will be allowed to see him.'

'I *must* see him,' she asserted. 'No question.'

'We'll sort it out when we get there,' he soothed her.

'OK. And I'd better ring my father. He'll be terribly worried. Where's my phone?'

'I've got it. Don't worry... Joe will be with him soon and tell him everything. You can call him later.'

He looked into his driving mirror expecting more protests from Wendy, but she had curled up on the back seat again and fallen asleep.

Michael shook her gently. 'Araminta! Sorry to wake you.'

She opened her eyes. 'What time is it?'

'7.15.'

'Dear boy, why are you up so early? You'll wear yourself out.'

'I've been walking on the beach. A very wise woman once told me you can do that at any time of the day or night and no one will think you're odd! But I woke you to tell you that Wendy left a voicemail on my mobile late last night to say that Philip's had an accident. I haven't liked to call her back this early, but the message said I really ought to go over and see him. Will you come too, or do you want to stay in Ireland and I'll get back as soon as I can?'

'I'll come.' She leapt out of bed and headed for the shower room, shouting over her shoulder as she went, 'What sort of accident? He's going to be all right, isn't he?'

'I think it's too early to say.'

She reappeared in the doorway. 'Oh, you mean it's really serious.'

He nodded and sank on to the bed.

To her horror, she saw that his eyes were full of tears. She ran over and sat beside him then pulled him to her, feeling his whole body juddering as he sobbed in her arms.

'Darling, I'm so sorry. Now listen, I'm going to make coffee and toast, and then I'm going to sort out how we can get to Norwich as quickly as possible.'

He slipped his arms around her then and hugged her so tightly it hurt. 'What would I do without you, Araminta?' he murmured.

'Don't worry,' she said as brightly as she could. 'You're never going to have to.'

'You're looking better,' Julian arrived in Wendy's room at the Maids Head Hotel in Norwich where she was toying with her room service breakfast.

'Blimey – I must have looked horrendous last night then! I'm going to need to buy something to wear today. I'd better pop round to Jarrolds when they open. I've got Philip's blood over all my own clothes – and I can't go into the hospital looking like a horror movie. I need to dress the part so I can persuade them to let us see him.'

Their efforts the previous evening to get anywhere near Philip had been thwarted by the need for various investigations and then surgery on their friend. It had not helped that neither of them had been able to claim they were 'next of kin'.

'I rang the hospital earlier,' Wendy went on. 'He's still in Intensive Care. They were pretty cagey, but they did say he might be moved to a private ward later.'

'You must have had a sixth sense about him yesterday. And thank God you did. When he's better, I'm going to tell him exactly how much he owes you.'

*

289

Araminta and Michael were in their car heading to Cork airport; the plan was to meet Nora there, before travelling with her on an early afternoon flight to Stansted where they had arranged to pick up a hire car for the rest of the journey.

'I think I'll text Hannah,' Araminta said suddenly. 'Now I've finally switched my phone on again, I can see that she's been trying to get hold of me for weeks. I'm just going to tell her I'll be at home tonight and will ring her. To be honest, I hadn't really clocked just how much I've been avoiding real life.'

Wendy sat watching Philip as he lay motionless and sedated on the high hospital bed in his dimly-lit room; his face virtually the colour of the icing-white pillow behind his head. There was a gash across his forehead with stitches in it. His right arm was punctured by various tubes. His left arm was in plaster, as was the whole of his left leg, which was also in traction, and his torso was strapped up to stabilise two broken ribs.

Throughout the day, she had asked numerous health professionals if Philip was going to live but the answers were vague, the best being a brusque 'Well, we certainly hope so'.

Word had spread among the staff that she was the person who had performed CPR on him and kept him alive, and this had seemed to effect an entrée for her, once he had been moved from Intensive Care.

Julian had wanted her to take a break and join him in the canteen for a cup of tea, but whenever she considered leaving Philip, she was filled with dread that he would die as soon as her back was turned.

She knew that Michael and Minty were on their way, and was expecting them in the next hour. But when the door opened, and the main light snapped on, she was surprised to see a tiny, lone figure.

'I'm Nora.'

Wendy struggled to her feet and blinked, then felt both her elbows grasped tightly as the woman with Philip's eyes reached up and kissed her on both cheeks. They stood, smiling at each other.

'I know you're Wendy,' Nora said quietly. 'I also know that you saved my poor boy's life. Thank you. Thank you.' And with that, she glided over to the bed and bent and kissed both of Philip's hands and stood there, stroking them.

Wendy swallowed. She should go. This was a private moment for mother and son. And yet, she continued standing and gazing at Philip.

Nora turned. 'You look absolutely awful.'

Wendy reeled back with a startled expression on her face.

'I mean that in the nicest possible way. You've been in this room all day. Last night you went through a terrible ordeal. You won't help Philip by getting ill yourself.'

Wendy nodded as though she were being admonished by a headmistress – albeit a kind one.

'I know it's crazy, Nora,' she whispered. 'But even though the omens are good, I have this sense of overwhelming terror that if I walk out of the door he'll die.'

'Of course you do,' Nora sympathised. 'You're in shock. You're not thinking straight. But I'm his mother…' She walked back to Wendy and held and stroked her hands just as she had her son's. 'Do you think I'm going to let anything bad happen to him now?'

Wendy shook her head.

'Araminta and Michael are in the waiting room down the corridor, and I know Michael is desperate to see Philip. Why don't you go and ask him to come in here to keep me company, and you and Araminta can have a chat and some tea. Your friend Julian's there too, though I think he said he was off to London later.'

Wendy felt bewildered that real life was going on outside of this particular room, but she smiled for the first time that day, and as she left the room, gave a little wave that embraced both Philip and his mother.

*

'I start rehearsals tomorrow morning for *Meistersinger*,' Julian told Araminta and Wendy. 'So I have to go to London, though I'd sooner stay here.'

'Of course you must go,' Wendy reassured him.

'What about you?' he asked. 'You could come and stay at my place and I could look after you.'

Wendy shook her head. 'No, I've already texted my staff and said they'll have to manage without me for a few days. I need to be here.'

'You ought to take it easy,' Julian warned. 'This is yet one more stress on top of loads of others.'

Araminta reached over and took Wendy's hand and held it tightly before turning to Julian. 'Don't worry,' she said to him. 'I know everything that's happened to Wendy over the past six months would have felled a lesser person, but I remember her in the TV control room when we were both much younger than we are today! She was made of steel. And that hasn't changed.'

All three of them laughed.

Then, suddenly serious again, Julian turned to Araminta. 'Obviously, I haven't seen you since Boxing Day, but in case you didn't know, I'm not your father's son, but I would have loved it if I had been. Still, I'm over it now – but Philip took the result much harder than me and I can't help wondering if perhaps he meant to kill himself. He has been quite low.'

'I don't think it will help anyone if we start thinking like that,' Wendy countered firmly. 'And unless Philip raises the subject, I don't think we should ever mention it.'

'I agree,' murmured Araminta. Then, as she remembered her former client's treatment of him, she added, 'But he has had a hell of a lot to cope with.'

Inside Philip's small room, Michael had been deep in thought for almost an hour.

Every now and again, he and Nora had exchanged a few words, but neither of them seemed to have the energy to start a real conversation.

As he watched Philip's broken body lying on the raised bed, he realised that it was the first time since his mother's death that, as a layman, he had visited someone who was dangerously ill. There had been a number of parishioners he had sat with as they left this world, but affecting though that had been, this was personal, and entirely different.

He glanced across at Nora. Her head was nodding and she looked exhausted. He stood up and walked over to her, and whispered that she ought to take a break and have some food. To his surprise, she was quick to agree.

As he sat down again, a nurse tiptoed in to do various checks – shining a light into his friend's eyes, and monitoring his pulse and blood pressure. Her demeanour gave nothing away and she slipped away quietly once her tasks were completed.

He sat watching Philip sleeping and found himself remembering all the long discussions they had had since they had met. He felt a wave of ineffable sadness sweep over him at the thought that he might never meet up with Philip again to talk or walk or eat.

Could his friend pull through this massive trauma? Did he even want to?

'Phil,' he whispered. 'Please get better. I'm not ready to let you go yet.'

Araminta drove the hire car back to her house on the south side of the city, very, very carefully. She was aware that she could pose a danger to herself or others on the road; she was overtired, distressed about Philip, desperately worried that Michael would not cope with being back in his erstwhile parish, and tearful about returning to Norwich. More than anything, right now, she longed to be walking on Inch Beach, and relishing the prospect of hearty, hot food in the beach café afterwards.

She parked outside her home and remained in the car for a few minutes. It was five weeks, all but two days, since she and Michael had left. Then, upset though they had been, they had still had a slim hope that the paternity test would come back negative.

'Come on,' she urged herself aloud. 'You've got to hold this together.'

The house, as she had expected, was icy cold, so she put the heating on and then raced around, turning all the radiators onto their highest settings before heading to the kitchen to make a pot of tea.

She was just pouring herself a cup, while wondering what she could produce as supper if Michael came back hungry, when she heard a key in the lock. Trying to suppress the panic that rose in her throat, she reassured herself that burglars tend to break in with crowbars not keys.

'Mum! Are you here?'

'Hannah!'

Her smiling daughter put her head round the kitchen door.

'Where did you spring from?' Araminta asked.

'Well, since you've finally turned your phone on, you've probably gathered I've been desperate to talk to you. So when you texted earlier to say you were on your way home, Farid drove me up here. He's gone off to get petrol because when you and I've chatted, I'm going straight back to London as we've both got early starts tomorrow.'

'This is so bizarre, I can't think straight. I've been hiding away in Ireland, but I realise now that I don't ever want to feel that distant from you again.'

'Well don't do it then,' Hannah sniggered.

'How was your holiday?'

'It was wonderful. We went skiing.'

'Skiing! After what happened to Granny!'

'Mum!' Hannah interrupted her. 'Don't go off on one about that!'

Araminta stared at her daughter, then her tense expression softened. 'Sorry, OK I won't. How was it?'

'Marvellous. If I say so myself, I'm really good at it! You could come next time!'

Araminta pursed her lips and shook her head vigorously. Then she shrugged her shoulders. 'Oh, I don't know... I don't know about anything... Tea?'

Hannah nodded.

'Sweetheart,' Araminta passed a mug to her daughter. 'I need to talk to you. When I left Ireland this morning, I wasn't sure what I was going to tell you about my situation. But now you're here, I realise I can't live a lie, and that's what it would mean if I didn't explain things.'

'Mum, you're being very opaque.'

'Good word! And you're right, but only because I'm working up to confessing something enormous. So, I need you to sit down because you're probably going to be extremely shocked.'

Wendy reached out and held Philip's hand. It was reassuringly warm. She stroked it lightly. He was still asleep. Was he out of danger? No one would say. But he seemed to have more colour in his face.

She had managed to book a room for his mother at the Maids Head. Both of them had protested to each other that they had no need of rest and would stay with Philip all night, but somehow a gentle compromise had been reached and Nora had agreed to go and sleep, leaving Wendy in sole charge now everyone else had left.

'Philip,' she whispered. 'I don't know if you can hear me. I was wondering if you'd like me to read to you?'

She opened her bag and withdrew her Kindle, and scrolled through the titles looking for something he might enjoy.

'*David Copperfield* or *Great Expectations*?' she asked. 'Hmmm – perhaps you're not sure on that one. OK, what about a Somerset Maugham short story, or one of Graham Greene's? Hmmn...

obviously I'm not hitting the spot here. Maybe we should do a little quiz. Um... holiday destinations – South of France or South of Spain? Not very interested in that, OK, here's something you'll have a view on, Theresa May or Jeremy Corbyn?'

'Caroline Lucas!'

The faint voice was so unlike Philip's that she wondered if she had imagined it.

She rose to her feet and peered at him more closely. Suddenly his lips moved.

'I suppose I'm in hospital.' His eyes opened, looked confused, and then closed again. But as she continued staring at him, they reopened slowly, and he attempted a smile.

'Are you OK?' she whispered.

'Wendy!'

She watched fearfully as he appeared to drift away again. But surely he could not be in too bad a way if he could recognise her? She sat down again, and breathed deeply. Should she go and tell the nurse that he had spoken?

'I think I am OK,' he mumbled slowly. 'Did someone run me over?'

'Something like that,' she answered. 'Can I get you anything?'

'I suppose a malt whisky's out of the question?'

She laughed too loudly in her relief.

'It's good, isn't it?' he muttered. 'A very good... good thing.'

Why was he rambling? That was a bad sign, surely?

'What's a good thing, Philip?'

He yawned, and his eyes closed again as he murmured, 'That you're not...'

'Not what?' she prompted.

But he had fallen asleep.

'I can't really believe what you're telling me,' Hannah cried. 'When did this all happen? I mean I knew you and Michael were becoming friendly, but... Oh my God – you're having sex!'

'Darling, I'm sorry. And with us being half-siblings we're…
well, it makes things almost impossible.'

'Oh, but hang on, Mum, that's the thing.'

The doorbell rang.

'That's going to be Michael,' Araminta said. 'Please be nice
to him. He's been through such a lot, and now Philip is desperately ill.'

'Philip!'

'Sweetheart, I'm sorry. I haven't had a chance to tell you.'
Araminta waved her hands in the air, in a gesture coupling apology
and helplessness, before leaving the room to open the front door.
She returned with Michael.

'Hannah!' he cried.

'Hello, Michael. God, you look exhausted. Mum's told me
everything – but you're just in time to hear why I've come to see
her.'

'Oh yes, what was that?' Araminta dragged her mind back to
why her daughter had felt the need to come all this way.

'Mum, you told me to sit down earlier, but I think you both
need to sit down now.' Hannah's tone was uncompromising.

Michael walked over and threw himself onto the old sofa.
Araminta looked at her daughter. What on earth was to be
revealed now?

'Darling,' Michael beckoned her to join him.

She sat beside him. 'OK,' she said, with contrived bravado, 'hit
me with it!'

'Thing is,' Hannah explained, 'I thought this was going to be
awful for you, Mum. And that it would be terribly upsetting, but
now I'm not sure. You know I took part in the paternity testing?'

The other two nodded.

'Well, the strangest thing, and this is incredibly hard to believe
– but it turns out that Grandad *isn't* my grandad.'

'Don't be ridiculous,' Araminta spluttered.

Michael took her hand and held it tightly.

297

'It's true, Mum. And obviously therefore you're not his daughter.'

'Hannah – you're talking rubbish. I would have known if I wasn't Richard Yateman's child. I definitely am. There can be no possible doubt.'

That's where you're wrong, Mum. I've been in touch with Uncle Nigel.'

'Nigel!'

'Yes, well, we needed another result to see what was going on. So, he got tested too and he *is* Grandad's son.'

'Well of course he is.'

'Yes, but he also believes he knows who your father was… Nigel seems to have been the sort of little boy who found out everything about everybody. I had a very interesting couple of phone calls with him. As a child, he was aware that Grandad had a soft spot for various children, including Michael and Philip, and he told me he found that, in his own words "bloody disturbing and fucking weird".'

'I never knew that.'

'I'm sure you didn't, Mum. But the thing is that now, actually, I think he feels a whole lot better. I had to tell him, obviously, about who has had a paternity test, and why. He was flabbergasted, but he said Grandad's methods were typical of his wish to play God. But when I asked if he had any idea who might have been your father, he immediately said it was Hilary.'

'Hilary!' Araminta's face broke into a huge smile. 'Hilary. My lovely godfather. He's my real dad?'

'Nigel says he's sure of it. Apparently, Hilary and Granny were very, very friendly. Nigel said that he often disturbed them in quiet parts of the house, sitting very close together. He even saw them kiss each other – like, properly.'

'Oh my goodness!' Araminta exclaimed. 'My mother. I can't believe it.'

'Well, that's what Nigel said. And he also told me something about Grandad and Granny's relationship. It seems they had to get married. Nigel was born only five months after the wedding and he thinks Grandad resented being tied down, and also that he wasn't very kind or supportive to Granny – and that that's probably why Granny took up with Hilary.'

'This is unbelievable,' Araminta said slowly. 'And yet, maybe not. I mean, Hilary would invite me to his house in Woodbridge in the holidays – but never Nigel. And he used to take me in with him to the library where he worked and let me help with the filing and so on. And of course, soon after Mum died, he had a breakdown. And then he suddenly retired to Cornwall.'

'We had some holidays with him, didn't we?' Hannah remembered. 'He was a sweet man.'

'Yes, he really was,' Araminta's voice trembled.

'So, that's it, Mum. We aren't who we thought we were at all.'

After a reflective pause, Araminta suddenly smiled broadly and announced, 'My goodness, this is wonderful news. It couldn't be better, could it? Quite apart from everything else, Hilary was a much more laudable character than Richard. An absolute gem of a man.'

'That's not very nice about Grandad.'

'I'm sorry, but it feels so right that I'm Hilary's child. Also, it's brilliant for us,' she turned to Michael, her eyes misty with happiness.

Michael looked hollow with fatigue, but he was smiling. 'Remind me again what relation Hilary was to Richard?'

'First cousins.'

'So,' he calculated, 'that means that you and I are only sort of second cousins. So, that's OK then, isn't it?'

'Far, far better than OK. It's fantastic!'

Michael put his arms around her. 'I'm thinking a wedding in early summer…'

'In Ireland?'

He nodded happily. 'At The Fitzhenry – where else!'

'Whoa!' Hannah interrupted. 'Isn't this all going rather too quickly?'

Michael reached out a hand in her direction. 'Hannah,' he pointed out with firmness in his voice but a sparkle in his eyes, 'I've been waiting about thirty-seven years for this!'

She grinned and ran to the sofa, then threw her arms around the two of them. 'Well, if you put it like that, can I be bridesmaid?'

Chapter Twenty

Wendy walked into the enchanting independent bookshop and café in the centre of Ballynakilty. It was her third visit since arriving in Ireland ten days previously, and she was looking forward to buying another collection of Irish short stories for Philip and some coffee for herself.

Tara, the manager, was chatting to a couple of small boys. Today, she was dressed in a vivid lime-green sweater with a long, navy denim skirt, lime and navy stripy tights, and blue suede boots. Her lustrous, auburn hair was gathered in a ponytail at the side of her head. Everything about her was delightful.

Wendy watched as the young woman agreed to read a story to the two children, and squatted down beside them in the Kids' Area. As she opened the book and began to speak, the boys' eyes grew wide with wonderment. Something about the duo reminded her of Rhys and Daniel when they were little.

Tara became aware of her gaze, and turned. 'Sorry! Were you wanting your usual coffee and scone?' she asked. 'I'm short-staffed today. But I can do it in five minutes.'

'Take your time; reading's much more important!' Wendy smiled and wandered over to a purple-painted table by the window and sank into the bright orange velvet chair beside it.

She had always loved bookshops – and being in this one was

particularly soothing, she thought, as she found herself reflecting on all the changes that had been precipitated by Philip's accident.

Back in the dying days of January, when his life had still hung in the balance, she and Nora had taken it in turns to sit with him in his hospital room. As he had gradually improved, she had found the hours while he slept to be surprisingly conducive to decision-making. First, she had come to the conclusion that she should adopt his suggestion of moving her company to the conference complex at Nora's hotel. And then she had had one of the best brainwaves of her life.

With sudden clarity, she had realised that she should invite Minty to work for BS&T. This would provide her friend with the career-change that she craved, and – once the organisation had moved to Kerry – would give her employment in the county where she and Michael wanted to buy a house. To top it all, Wendy had no doubt that Minty would be a huge asset to the company.

Before long, Philip's health had begun to improve, his mother had flown back to Ireland, and Wendy and Minty had settled into a routine where they met early every morning at Norwich station and travelled to and from the company headquarters in Hoxton. The short evenings were the only time they were apart – Minty in her home where Michael awaited her with a roaring fire and a hot meal, and she at the hospital, where she had read to Philip, or regaled him with stories of her day.

Over the next few weeks, she had taught Minty everything she needed to know about BS&T – and had brought her up to date with the technology which had changed completely since their days at Anglia television.

It felt like a bold new start for the business. With both Minty and the impressive American manager in place, she would not miss Francesca one bit.

Eventually, in the first week of March, Philip had been well enough to leave hospital, and he had pressed her to travel to

Ireland with him. They had done it in style, in a hired car with a chauffeur, a couple of suitcases each and two Labradors.

He had looked worryingly ill after the journey across to west Wales, a choppy sea crossing to Rosslare, and a four-hour drive from there to The Fitzhenry Hotel. However, after a couple of days and nights, he had rallied, and had then started intensive physiotherapy with dedicated determination.

She had taken a fortnight off work to be with him. But from next Monday, until the company-move, she would spend four days a week in Hoxton. It was all panning out so well.

A year ago, she could not have imagined living or working anywhere other than London. But now that she had vacated her Barbican flat, put most of her belongings in storage, and made her plans for relocating BS&T, she was ready for new pastures.

She sensed that her father regarded her schemes as some sort of hysterical over-reaction to her divorce. But if the last few months had taught her anything, it was that personal changes – as well as political ones – can happen overnight, and that the life you had assumed you would always have, could be wiped out in a moment. So, she had resolved to grasp options that filled her with hope, rather than force herself to stay in situations that no longer felt pleasant or relevant. It was as though she had torn up her orderly plan for life, thrown the pieces into the air and watched as they returned to earth in a totally unrecognisable pattern – but she found she liked the feeling.

There was a movement by her elbow, and she opened her eyes to find the young manager beside her.

'I'm terribly sorry,' Tara apologised. 'I've run out of scones, will this do?' She put a generous slice of iced carrot cake, as well as a large cappuccino, on the purple table.

Wendy grinned. 'I daresay I'll be able to force it down!'

The girl attempted a smile in return, but looked troubled.

Wendy reached out a hand. 'What's wrong?'

'I'm not supposed to say.'

Wendy looked around. There was nobody near them. 'I can keep a secret.'

Tara glanced behind her, before sitting in the chair opposite. 'I shouldn't burden you with this, but it's just so awful. The man who owned this shop died last December...'

'Oh! I'm sorry.'

'Yeah, he was lovely old fellow. He used to come in most days, but he encouraged me to run the place how I wanted. He even liked my weird colour schemes! But unfortunately, he left the shop to his son, who's a total bollocks and has probably never read a book in his life. And I heard today that this absolute bastard is determined to sell it. That's definitely not what his father would have wanted. This is such a wonderful, magical place... I know there are other jobs out there, but they could never compare to this one.'

And with that, the beautiful, normally serene, young woman began to sob.

Suddenly, Wendy realised how much Tara resembled her keen, energetic staff in London. And she found herself recalling the day she had gathered them together and asked how they would feel if she moved the company to Ireland. They had responded ecstatically, by whooping, cheering, crying and lining up to kiss her.

If only she could help Tara too.

So, that's that, Philip thought, as he sat in his room at the hotel and signed the papers that would transfer the ownership of Hunsford Hall to Marigold.

After weeks of work, his endlessly-patient housekeeper and her hired team of helpers had removed all his belongings from the house and outbuildings, and had had them transferred to a storage facility in Norwich. When he was more mobile, and had bought a property here, he would have them shipped over.

Had he always known that – eventually – he would make his home in Ireland? No. But now that he was going to, there was a pleasing symmetry to it. His holidays here had been the happiest times in his childhood, and Hibernia's emotional tentacles had never loosened their grip.

So, now he was looking ahead. Work was underway for transforming The Fitzhenry corporate complex to accommodate Wendy's company, and to modify the main auditorium, so that it could double as a concert hall and conference room.

Already, a sound-expert had advised on how to make it more acoustically favourable, and a designer had drawn up plans for new seats and lighting. As a result, Julian's pet orchestra would take up residence from the end of this year, and the first music festival was scheduled for eighteen months' time.

It had amazed him how easy it had been to change his life so completely.

Within days of his accident – which had left him scarred and broken but with an immense sense of good fortune at finding himself alive – he had seized the moment, and not only agreed to Marigold's terms for the divorce, but begun the process of extricating himself from the job he had never wanted to do.

He had sent for Geoff, his manager, and asked him to take over as CEO of Baldry's. His plan had been to leave his money in the company, but to take no part in running it. However, Geoff had returned a few days later with some dynamic suggestions of his own – including a plan for Philip to sell the company to a Shenyang businessman, who was a long-term customer, an Anglophile, and someone with the finance and vision to turn the business into a world brand.

The staff were happy with the arrangement, and Philip could not have been more thrilled at the prospect of being bought out.

It was almost time for coffee in the lounge and his daily phone chat with Michael, so he hauled himself to his feet and reached for his crutches, but as he did so, the divorce papers he had just signed, slipped to the floor. Cursing at the effort required, Philip struggled to keep his balance and gather them together. His left

305

wrist was still encased in plaster, and his ribs, though mending well, pained him when he leant over. So the task, which would have been so automatic prior to the accident, presented a considerable challenge and swiftly sapped his strength.

Being injured had opened his eyes to what it meant to be disabled. In the early hours of each morning, when discomfort tended to wake him, a wave of guilt and shame would sweep over him at the knowledge that he would make a full recovery – despite his own stupidity – while so many others were born to a life of struggle and immobility. Why had he been singled out to be a lucky survivor? He had no idea. Not only could he easily have died – he most certainly could have ended up brain damaged or in a wheelchair. He must have a guardian angel.

Julian was on the Norwich to Cambridge train bound for a rehearsal with Chamber 28, and a meeting with their committee about the orchestra's move to Kerry.

He had to hand it to Philip. Despite having almost died, once his friend had been well enough to talk to his accountant and make business plans for the future, he had decided that Julian's suggestions about the chamber orchestra and a music festival were not just viable, but hugely desirable as a tourism-boost for the area. Nora too was thrilled with the idea and talked about achieving the sort of success that Wexford Opera had long enjoyed.

The chamber orchestra, as the resident musicians, would provide much of the festival programme, but Julian, as newly-appointed Festival Director, was already booking a number of well-known soloists to participate in other concerts. Suddenly, all his years of networking in green rooms was bearing fruit. A festival in stunning surroundings – with ample accommodation for performers and their families – turned out to hold real appeal for frantically busy artists who spend their lives in airport lounges and anonymous hotels.

His biggest coup had been to persuade Britain's favourite baritone, Sir Bryn Terfel, to give a recital in 2019. He and the world-famous opera-knight were fellow alumni of the Guildhall School, and their paths had crossed on many occasions – most recently in Covent Garden's *Die Meistersinger*.

'He's just the same bloke he always was,' Julian had told Philip. 'Funny, lovely, down to earth. And once we announce that he's coming, the stars of the classical music world will be falling over each other to appear!'

So far, he was managing to combine his own singing commitments with his work on the festival. But it was a relief to know that he had a developing alternative career and income for the day when his voice gave out.

Almost everything in his life had taken a turn for the better. His only concern was Joe. No matter how much he encouraged and cajoled him, his boyfriend had no wish to travel to London to see him perform, or accompany him to Cambridge, or Ireland.

'We're fine when we're here, and it's just us,' Joe always insisted. 'And I can keep an eye on Vera when you're away. I'm not one for bright lights and the chattering classes.'

'I know. But we could be spending more time together... I mean, I'm not ready to be in Gorleston all the time. I need to carry on singing. Then there's the work in Ireland. I'm going to be there more and more.'

'That's your choice, Jules,' Joe had pointed out. 'But it's not for me.'

Did Joe have some sort of social anxiety, Julian wondered. It was possible, but obviously his lover did not regard it as a problem or as anything for which he should seek help. The other worry was the way Joe kept talking about the pull of Jamaica and his sister.

'But, Joe,' Julian had protested. 'You told me you left Jamaica so you could be free, sexually.'

'That's true. But I still have emotional ties there.'

Eventually, Julian had confided in Philip about Joe and their relationship. His pal had been quick to offer a constructive suggestion.

307

'I'm going to need a really expert carpenter to head up a team to work on the concert hall,' he had said. And he had gone on to explain that the acoustic specialist had suggested they incorporate much more natural wood into the design – which would be mellow on both the eye and ear.

'Joe could take charge of it,' Philip had said. 'It would be great to have him working here.'

So, one cosy evening in Gorleston, Julian had insinuated Philip's invitation into their conversation. But his partner had shaken his head.

'Wouldn't you love working with wood again? Philip would give you all the creative freedom you want in choice of materials and so on.'

There was another shake of the head. 'I'm sixty-two now,' Joe had said.

'That's still young,' Julian had protested.

'Not really,' Joe had smiled broadly, but his tone remained uncompromising.

Michael was becoming used to his new routine. But, strangely, now that he was, he was plagued with dreams about his days as a priest.

They all began the same way: he was in bed, but he could hear the organ playing so he knew he had overslept and was late for Mass. He leapt up and tried to dress, only to find that his clothes no longer fitted, so he had to run naked towards the church. But the floors of the presbytery slanted away from him and, as he attempted to progress along the corridor, it lengthened out, as if on giant elastic, to a far horizon which extended, infinitely.

He could not reach his congregation, and would never be forgiven.

Routinely, he disturbed Araminta as he woke, panic-stricken and breathless. She always held him to her, until he recognised that the nightmare, though terrifying, was not real.

She said it was common for people to feel panicky and to have bad dreams about a crisis in their lives, once that crisis was passed – and that his sleeping pattern would return to normal before long. He hoped she was right.

Other than that, life was sweet, and though they were impatient to move into their new house in Kerry, he and Araminta were enjoying what remained of their time in Norfolk – though they kept themselves to themselves most of the time so that he did not encounter former parishioners.

Every working day, they rose at six. He drove her to Norwich station. Then he returned to her house and assumed the role of cook and house-husband. With the chores done, and preparations for the evening meal completed, he spent the afternoons reading and studying. He had decided to train as a primary school teacher and he wanted to get into the habit of absorbing new information.

Meanwhile, Araminta was thrilled with her new career, and he was delighted that she was so happy and optimistic. The only aspect to her behaviour that he found less easy to deal with was her attitude to Dr Yateman.

Having discovered that she was not Richard's child, Araminta had decided that she had no need to visit him. More than that, she was full of rage about the way he had lived his life and the upheaval his unorthodox methods had caused.

However, for Michael, learning that Richard was his father had changed everything – and he felt a compelling urge to see him. He decided that this morning, when Philip called, he would ask his friend's advice.

Right on cue, his mobile rang.

'Top of the morning to you, good sir,' Philip said. 'I'm sitting in the lounge, looking over the estuary. God, it's so beautiful, I bet you wish you were here!'

'Sounds like everything's going swimmingly in your exciting life.' Michael laughed.

'Well, it *has* been quite exciting today. I've signed the divorce papers.'

'Goodness me, Phil. Things *are* moving fast. How do you feel?'

'Remarkably chipper.'

'But isn't it a huge wrench for you to give up Hunsford Hall?' Michael asked. 'You loved that place. It's even stranger that Marigold wanted it. I thought she hated being "buried in Norfolk". Wasn't that one of her phrases?'

'It was,' Philip agreed. 'But strangely, her wanting it has helped me. I suppose I feel she can't have loathed it so much after all. Obviously, she and old Batty Bertram won't live there – he's got an ancestral pile in Berkshire and a house in Eaton Square for starters – but I suppose it'll serve as a country retreat. And to be fair, maybe she wasn't ready to move away totally from the scene of Emily's death – whereas in my case, as I so nearly died in the same place, I am. Funny that the house was all she wanted from me, but then her intended is stinking rich!'

'Richer than you?'

Philip knew he was being teased but rather liked it. 'Completely different league! Talking of money, are you sure you won't let me contribute to your imminent property purchase?'

'Philip, you've done more than enough. And, as you know, I've got enough money – courtesy of my mother – to pay for my half of the new house. I hope Mum would be happy at the changes in my life. How does one know? But I'm pretty sure that she'd have been pleased I've decided to train as a teacher. It feels right that I'm going to end up doing the same job as she did.'

'Sounds as if everything's falling nicely into place.'

'Yes, mostly everything's great – but can I just tell you something that isn't?'

'Fire away.'

'Well, I'd really like to go and see Dr Yateman. After all, he's my biological father, and I'd like to meet him before his time runs out. But Araminta absolutely hates him now, and I don't want to upset her.'

'That *is* difficult…'

'I don't expect you to come up with an instant solution,' Michael assured him. 'But maybe you can have a think. Talk tomorrow?'

'Absolutely. Before you go, can I just mention Wendy's sixtieth birthday? She's planning to spend the actual day in north Norfolk with her parents, but I thought we could all have a celebration – perhaps at Araminta's house – the night before. That's the twenty-ninth. What do you think – a little surprise party?'

'Brilliant idea.'

Philip laughed. 'Mind you, that's the day Theresa May's going to trigger the Brexit process. I hope the evening won't turn into a wake!'

'It'll be fine. It's great that you're up to making the journey. And Araminta will do fantastic food. I know I could bore for England about how brilliant she is, but she really is Wonder Woman!'

'Well, I know another one. Wendy's been amazing. And she never seems to tire. She said the other day, she might look for a new project now that Araminta's established at BS&T. Frankly, I've never known anyone with more energy… Ooh, and here she is…'

There was a pause. Michael could just make out Wendy's voice, then Philip laughed loudly in his right ear.

'What's going on?' Michael found himself grinning in anticipation.

'I'll let your crazy half-sister tell you!' Philip replied.

'Hi, Michael,' Wendy was giggling. 'You're not going to believe this, but I've been trying to help a young woman who was worried about her job, and – well – I seem to have bought a bookshop!'

Chapter Twenty-One

The landline in the kitchen rang.

'Not now,' Araminta groaned in exasperation. She put down the tray of mimosa cocktails she had been about to carry through to her guests, so she could pick up the handset.

She had taken the day off so she could stay in Norwich and prepare the buffet for Wendy's birthday party, but she had been interrupted by a stream of calls from the estate agent, with a seemingly inexhaustible list of queries from the prospective buyer of her house. Surely there were no further questions now.

Michael appeared in the doorway as she started to speak to the caller. He blew her a kiss, picked up the tray, and signalled that he was going to take it to the sitting room.

Julian, Wendy and Philip were seated in easy chairs near the fireplace.

'OK, let the celebration commence!' Michael cried – and he handed each of them a drink.

Julian and Philip raised their glasses in Wendy's direction. 'Happy birthday for tomorrow!' they chorused.

She sipped from her glass. 'Gosh, that's delicious. Minty's such a talent. I hope she doesn't realise just how special she is and decide to open a bar or a restaurant – not now that I've got her working at BS&T. Having her there is the only way I'm going to find time to run my bookshop!'

Michael chuckled as he pulled up a chair and sat beside her. 'You and your new toy! I hope you'll let me come and help once you take it over!'

Wendy grinned. 'I may have a vacancy for a Saturday boy!'

'Do tell Michael and Julian about your other ideas,' Philip prompted her.

'Well, everything's pretty vague at this stage, but I was thinking that we might hold an annual literary festival at The Fitzhenry, and maybe an independent bookstore convention too?'

Philip, Julian and Michael raised their eyebrows at each other and then laughed.

'You may be the oldest here,' Michael remarked, 'and about to enter your seventh decade, but your energy levels put the rest of us to shame.'

'Coming back to The Fitzhenry,' Julian's eyes were sparkling, 'this morning, I've signed a young string quartet for next year's music festival. They've just won a major award in Switzerland and everyone says they're the next big thing in chamber music.'

'Cheers to The Fitzhenry Music Festival!' Philip raised his glass again.

Julian reached over and clinked glasses with him. 'Who'd have thought after everything that happened at the Boxing Day lunch here, that we'd be back three months later – having survived *major* turbulence – enjoying life and excited by new projects.'

Michael beamed at the group but kept glancing towards the door. 'Araminta's a long time on that call. I hope the buyer hasn't pulled out.'

'When are you supposed to move?' Wendy asked.

'Oh, not till the end of May. I expect it'll be OK.'

'Can be an awful stress, though. By the way,' Wendy leant towards him and lowered her normal volume, 'while Minty's not here, have you had any further ideas about whether or not we should try to trace the other two women who might be Dr Richard's offspring? Hannah keeps asking me to make a decision. Personally, I don't want to inflict what happened to us on anyone else. What purpose would it serve?'

'That bloody man!' Araminta burst through the door. 'Can you believe it? His past actions completely ruined Boxing Day. Now this! Apparently, he's about to die. Who's writing this script?'

Michael strode to her side and put his arm around her. 'Darling, start from the beginning, what's going on?'

'Give me a drink please. I'm not letting him ruin today; let's just carry on as if nothing has happened.'

'But what *has* happened?' Wendy asked.

'Richard's been taken to St Anne's hospice – you know the one in the lovely old building by the river? They thought they should tell me that they've sent for the cryogenic support team, because they don't expect him to last more than a few hours. I said I don't want to see him, but the woman on the phone asked me to reconsider. Well, I have – and I'm still not going!'

'Quite right!' Wendy joined in. 'I don't want to see him either. In fact, I don't want to think about him ever again.'

Philip sneaked a glance at Julian and Michael, who were both wearing uneasy expressions. He sipped from his drink and pondered how to voice what he knew he ought to say – aware, as he was, of Michael's gaze on him, pleading for help. Obviously, his friend wanted to see the man he knew to be his father, but was equally desperate to avoid distressing Araminta.

Then he realised that Julian was peering intently at Michael, and trying to make sense of the former priest's expression.

Suddenly, Julian cleared his throat and spoke. 'Richard Yateman has had a major influence on the five of us – one way or another. Would it help if I went up there to say our 'goodbyes'? I realise that the old doc doesn't believe he's dying in any final sense, but should he be left to face these last hours alone? I'm not sure that's right. And because he's not having a funeral, the only time to give him any kind of send-off is now.'

Both Wendy and Araminta glared at him, but he bestowed a gentle smile in their direction and did not flinch.

Michael walked over to the window and stared out onto the front drive.

'I agree with Julian,' Philip's voice broke the heavy silence. 'I don't remember exactly how I felt when I almost died in January, but I do have a lingering sense of how alone I was. To be honest, if Richard had turned out to be my father, I'd probably have visited him before now. So, I believe I should go too. That's me and Julian then. Anyone else?'

'I'll come!' Michael responded quickly. 'I *want* to see him. I haven't in any sense come to terms with our genetic link but maybe this will help. I can drive, as I haven't got round to having a drink yet.'

Julian walked over to Philip, handed him his stick, and helped him out of his chair. The three men glanced at the two women, and then left the room.

'I feel an absolute cow,' Wendy murmured to Minty. 'But I don't want to go. Do you think I should?'

'*I* should go. I mean he brought me up and, well, will I regret it if I don't?'

Wendy shrugged her shoulders. 'I'm the wrong person to ask.'

Michael put his head around the door. 'Is it all right if we leave now?' he asked, softly.

Araminta stood up. 'Of course, Michael, but maybe Wendy and I should tag along too, though we might stay in the car.'

Fifteen minutes later, Michael parked by the hospice building. Almost immediately, a nurse emerged from the doorway. As they all stepped out of the vehicle, she shook each of them by the hand as they introduced themselves.

On hearing Araminta's name, the nurse gently but firmly ushered her into the building and straight into the dimly-lit room where the dying doctor lay – his chest visibly trembling with every rasping breath.

Feeling it was expected of her, Araminta took hold of his hand, which was icy to the touch – as if, she thought irreverently, he was doing his bit to make the job of the cryogenics people that bit easier.

He was a shell of the man she had last seen in December, and as she gazed at him, she found herself grieving for Hilary, her biological father, and wishing desperately that she had known he was her parent before he died.

But then, while she watched Richard, her fury with him ebbed away. He had been a clever man, an energetic man, an interesting man if – frequently – an impossible one.

'Dad,' she found herself saying, 'it's Minty.'

She thought he tried to raise his head, but it was probably her imagination. Then she heard herself say, 'Go in peace.' And in that moment she knew she meant it, and also that she could draw a line under the complications of her parentage. She leant over and kissed his wrinkled cheek, then left.

In the relatives' room next door, she fell into Michael's arms. Clinging to him, she realised that she had never felt as grateful for anything as she did for the relationship she had with this loving and lovely man. She turned then to Philip and Julian, who were squeezed together on a low settee that looked far too small for them. 'Thank you.' She smiled at them both. 'You were so right about coming. Do you want to see him?'

Julian looked around as if he thought she must be speaking to someone else. 'Can I?' he asked.

She nodded.

'I just thought I'd tell him that he was once my mother's lover and that I rather wish he was my father. I don't really know what you're supposed to say to someone dying. So, do you think that's OK?'

Araminta chuckled, despite the gravity of the situation. 'I should think it would cheer him up no end, if he's conscious enough to understand. I don't think there are rules about what to say in this situation. If there are, I'm sure we should ignore them.'

Julian nodded and made his way towards Richard's room.

'Come and sit down,' Michael led Araminta to an easy chair. 'What should we do about Hannah?'

'Oh, I forgot to tell you. Back at the house, I rang her before I came in to tell you all about Dad. She said she wouldn't come. She's got an audition tomorrow – she was very secretive about where – and she's not prepared to lose sleep tonight by coming up here. I rang Nigel too, and left a message. I'll call him again later.'

Julian returned, and Philip looked enquiringly at Michael. 'Do you want to go in before me?'

Michael shook his head, so Philip reached for his walking stick, levered himself to his feet, then limped into Dr Yateman's room and – slowly – managed to manoeuvre himself into a seat by the dying man.

'I'm Philip,' he announced.

The elderly man's hands fluttered suddenly. Remembering how the doctor had engaged him in conversation as a child at Nigel's parties, it was entirely likely, he mused, that Richard had always assumed him to be his son. This would not, he felt, be a good moment to disabuse him. He gathered the papery, freezing hands into his and stroked them, before saying, 'Sir – I know I wouldn't be here if it hadn't been for your work, and I want to tell you how grateful I am.'

Richard's cracked lips seemed to be trying to mouth some words in response, but he had insufficient control or volume to make any sense. So Philip spoke again. 'Rest now. Your family are all with you. You gave life to a lot of people. It's... quite an achievement.' And with that, he pushed himself to a standing position and left the room, with tears streaming down his face.

As Philip returned to the other four, Michael gave Araminta a squeeze, before heading for the sick room door.

Just as he was about to push it open, he turned and caught Wendy's eye. She shook her head slowly, but something made him stretch out his arm in her direction. He could see her grappling with her decision. Suddenly, she grasped his hand and they entered their father's room together.

It took her a moment or two to make out the old man because the lighting was so low. Perhaps he was dead already? But then she heard Michael speaking to him. 'I'm Michael,' he said. 'You're my father. You gave me life and I have a very, very happy one. So I'm here to thank you for that.' Then he made the sign of the cross above the recumbent figure and said something in Latin.

Wendy watched her half-brother. He had obviously been present at the deaths of lots of people. He understood what one should do. His head was bowed now, in silent prayer. She knew she should do something, but what?

Trembling, she forced her unsteady legs to walk forward so that she could look closely at the frail and skeletal version of the man she had last seen before Christmas. 'Dr Yateman,' she said. 'It's Wendy.'

His eyes twitched, though they remained closed, then with a defiant and determined effort he raised his right arm and extended his forefinger. It was the same gesture he had made on the day she had met him at the nursing home. She could hear his voice in her head telling her: 'You were my Number One.' And, for the first time in over twenty years, she began to weep. She was indeed his first child. She knew that now; knew too that the only reason she was alive was that he had created her.

And then something else struck her. 'Oh my goodness, we've got the same hands.' Her tremulous voice took on a note of proud belonging, and she leant over to kiss him.

His breathing became quieter. And she felt herself drawn into an enveloping hug by her weeping brother, and together, they watched as their parent abandoned his struggle to survive, and life passed from him.

*

Julian paid off his taxi and sprinted up the short path to his mother's home.

It had been an extraordinary evening, but it had left him cheerful, optimistic and grateful – especially when Araminta had suddenly decided to give him Richard's piano. In fact, he thought, positively the only problem I have in my life right now, is where on earth to put it!

Inside the house, he was surprised to find his mother still awake and downstairs.

'Hey, Mum!' he said as he joined her in her lounge. 'You must be better. Still awake at 11.30!'

She jumped up and kissed him, then disappeared to put the kettle on, while he shrugged off his jacket, kicked off his shoes and threw himself onto the sofa.

'This reminds me of when I was little,' he murmured happily as his mother returned with two mugs of Horlicks and a plate of chocolate digestive biscuits. He patted the space beside him and as she sat, he moved closer to her and began to recount how Wendy's birthday has been overtaken by Richard's death – but how afterwards, they had gone back to Araminta's and had a bit of a party. 'And it finished off with me performing a couple of Noel Coward songs. All very convivial!'

'That's my boy,' said Vera.

'Actually, Philip described the evening as "a wake". But Michael used the word "reconciliation". Anyway, there was a lot of emotion sloshing around... Are you OK about Richard, Mum?'

She looked sad for a moment. 'Well, as you'll find out one day, it's a bit of a downer when you realise that most of the men you've slept with are dead. Still, that's something you can't control. Are you going back to London early tomorrow?'

'Yes. I've got my last chorus rehearsal before Easter, and I want to fit in a class at Pineapple before it... then it's the final *Meistersinger* on Friday. I'll be back on Saturday. Why?'

'Are you sober enough to have a conversation now?'

'What *are* you suggesting, Mum?'

They both giggled. 'No, stop,' she said, 'this is serious. I need to get something off my chest.'

Julian grinned at her. 'What have I done now?'

'It's not about you, Jules.'

And then she broke the news that she had been asked to move in with his sister in Yarmouth. He tried not to laugh at the preposterous idea. But then he realised that his mother was saying how it would mean that she could see more of her grandson, and that she would know where she was going to end up, and who was going to care for her, which made her feel secure.

'I bet she just wants a cheap babysitter,' he sneered. 'She and Hubby are so boring it would be too awful for words. You'll have to tell her it's out of the question. I mean, quite apart from the fact that I want to look after you, what about Joe? He adores you. He wouldn't be welcome there. He'd be too shy to go anyway. I wonder why she came up with this idea. I don't trust her!'

'You're talking about my daughter, Jules. And she does have a name!'

He was silent as he digested the obvious reprimand. 'OK, well, sorry. But, Mum, it's you and I who are close. And alike. She's like old buggerlugs – her dad. Not like you at all!'

'Jules, lovey, stop! You and I *are* alike and I love you. But Caroline's a good girl. And what you've never taken on board is that I love her too, just as much as I love you. And I love my grandson. Tyson's a great lad.'

'With a ridiculous name! How's he going to achieve anything in life called that?'

'Fuck off, Jules.' His mother stood up and moved herself to another chair on the far side of the room. 'You almost make me feel guilty for wanting to be with my own flesh and blood. You assume that I think the same way as you about everything, but I don't. I know I had my wild times but I'm older now. I want to feel settled, and I never would with you – because you're not a

320

very settled person. That's why you and Joe aren't working. You think you want to be here with him, but you only want it on your terms. You also want to be in Cambridge and London, and soon you'll be in Ireland – probably for months of every year. I hate to say this but you're one of the reasons that people like me voted to leave the EU. You're so busy living your arty-farty life you haven't a clue how other folk, who aren't like you, feel about the country changing and leaving them behind.'

'Well I voted to leave, in sympathy with you.'

'And I bet you've regretted it ever since. I imagine that with Brexit being triggered today, you and your lefty friends moaned on about what a disaster it was, whereas people like me and Caroline see it as a new beginning.'

He sighed loudly. 'Look, Mum, as you very well know, I wasn't born with a silver spoon in my mouth. So why should I apologise for having learned what I have about music and dance and art? It's what makes me tick. Makes life worth living. Surely, bettering oneself and opening one's mind can't be a bad thing? Everyone should want it.'

'But they don't, Jules. They want other things and you think those things are inferior – and these people know that you think that. So they see you as an arrogant snob, and you think they're lowlife. Neither of those things are true, actually. You're all just people doing your best. But you don't understand each other, and you don't *want* to understand each other. I've made my choice, Jules. I need you to be nice about it and to come and see me at Caroline's and be polite. And I'll come to London sometimes and meet up with you. I'll even come over to your festival in Ireland, if you invite me. And I'm certainly going to accept Joe's invitation to spend a couple of months every winter with him in Jamaica, now he's going back.'

'What! No! He isn't!'

'Oh Lord, now I've done it. I thought the two of you would have had this conversation by now.'

'What conversation?'

'Jules, he decided weeks ago. It was the day an old lady died in his care home – the one who had absolutely no friends and no relations. Joe was very cut up about that. You were away in Cambridge, so he talked to me and he said his mind was made up and that he was going back to Jamaica to be with his sister. It's not just her though; he basically wants to die in his own country.'

'Die! But he's got years left in him yet. And we're so good together. *He* says that.'

'Does he?'

'Well, he says we're good together when we're here. I get it that he doesn't want to come to Cambridge or London or Kerry.'

'Do you, because he really doesn't want any of that? But he believes you think that – given time – he'll come round to your way of thinking.'

'Is that really what I'm like?'

'Yes, it is. You love what you love, and you absolutely cannot imagine how other people might not love the same things.'

'But I thought he was my "happy-ever-after".'

'Did *he* think that? Possibly not.'

'God, Mum, you really know how to go for the jugular once you get going!'

'Perhaps it's long overdue, son,' she responded quietly. Then she took a deep breath and said more loudly, 'I'm selling the house by the way. And Joe's selling his. And there's a developer interested in buying them both, knocking them together and turning them into maisonettes. By the way, Joe knew I was going to talk to you tonight. He said he'd be waiting up for you and he hoped you'd come over.'

'Well, I don't want to,' Julian protested, with a slight toss of the head.

'Oh yes you do,' his Mum corrected him.

And of course, she was right.

*

322

'So,' Michael asked when she returned to the sitting room, 'how was Nigel?'

Araminta sank into the chair next to his and picked up the wine glass she had been drinking from before the phone had rung.

'I think,' she reflected, 'that we've probably just had the best conversation of our lives. He says he's smoking a spliff or two, and has opened a very special bottle of Piedmont Barolo – which probably means it costs well over two hundred quid! I get the feeling he won't live to be the age that Richard achieved, but he's not going to change now.'

'It's strange how now that he knows you're not his full sister you get on better. I just don't really understand why he hated Richard so much.'

'He told me he feels better about Dad now. He said that Hannah's unearthing of Richard's diaries explained everything. You see, it seems he went through his childhood mystified about why his father was always insisting that he invite kids whom he hardly knew to his parties. He hated it when, as he put it, Dad then "fawned all over them", and as he grew older he became convinced Richard was a paedophile.'

Michael sighed. 'What a mess.'

'And, as Hannah told us the night we got back from Ireland, I think he sussed out very early that Mum and Hilary were very close. He suspected I was their daughter – and he thought it was unfair that Richard seemed to like me more than him. I don't think he did actually. It's just that Nigel was trouble. Always. Still, he probably had his reasons.'

Michael nodded, reached for her hand and squeezed it.

'Oh, and something else,' she continued. 'I hope you're going to be OK about this. I just found a text that Hannah sent earlier. She said that since you and Wendy couldn't make up your mind about whether or not to seek out the two women who might also have been Richard's children, she decided to shred Dad's diaries. She said the secrets should die with him.'

'That's probably the right solution,' Michael said quietly, and then he leant back in his chair and closed his eyes.

After a moment or two, she asked gently, 'Are you all right, love?'

Michael opened his eyes, and stared, vaguely, into the distance. 'Actually, I feel... peaceful... Something about being with Richard as he died seems to have calmed my mind.'

With her free hand she reached across and stroked his cheek. 'My dear, dear boy.'

'I really love you, Araminta.'

'And I really love you... more and more each day.'

'It'll be your birthday in under an hour,' Philip pointed out, as Wendy helped him down the steps into a quiet seating area of the Maids Head Hotel. 'Sixty! Quite a landmark!'

'Don't!'

She watched as he made himself comfortable, then sat down herself.

'You certainly don't look sixty,' he went on. 'And you very, very definitely don't act it! Do you want a drink?'

'No, I've had enough... It was a surprisingly good evening, wasn't it? Watching Richard as he died really helped to reconcile me to him and what he did. But then it was such a great atmosphere at Minty's afterwards. I wouldn't have believed it possible after all that emotion at the hospice. And wasn't Julian hysterical? Those Noel Coward songs are so funny, and he did them so well.'

Philip grinned. 'He keeps amazing me. And I can't tell you how pleased I am that he's working so hard on the festival, and that it's going to happen. Having lost touch with him for decades, it's phenomenal that he's become such a big part of my life.'

Wendy leaned over and patted his hand. 'I've been thinking...'

Philip burst out laughing.

'What?' she demanded. 'What's funny?'

'You are,' he answered. 'You just fizz with ideas. Go on, what is it this time?'

She grinned. 'It was Julian doing his 'Mad About the Boy' rendition. I suddenly thought that when we have the various festivals at The Fitzhenry, we should have an after-hours festival club, and we could have a cabaret – and Julian could do an act sometimes, and we could book stand-up comedians and maybe a local Irish band.'

'You and your projects – you're a genius! But, would you believe it, I've got a scheme of my own? My daughter would have been twenty-one next month and I'd been wondering how to mark that anniversary. So how about this? Maybe we could hold a catering school at the hotel a couple of times a year, which would be free for interested kids from Kerry and Cork. They could learn basic cooking and all about nutrition and eating well. But naturally the hope would be that some of them might be inspired to go into catering.'

Wendy gazed at him, her eyes wide and happy. 'I'm sure your daughter would be proud – and it'll be a lasting and lovely legacy… And maybe we could make a programme about it? Or podcasts for schools?'

His smile broadened. 'I knew you'd understand, and run with it. Is it any wonder that I really, really love you?'

'Well, I love you too, Philip. You're a great person and a wonderful friend.'

'No, but I mean, I *love* you!'

Wendy wrinkled her nose in puzzlement.

'Do you understand?' He pressed her.

She continued to look bewildered for a moment, then she raised her eyebrows as she considered a new option. 'Do you mean, like, in italics?'

His face creased into the grin that she had become so fond of. 'Yes, exactly. Not just as in "I love this smoked salmon drizzled with lime juice".'

'Mmmn, but that sounds really good. So, you mean you love me more than that?'

'I do, actually. And in a rather lustful way.'

'Lustful! But I'm sixty in…' she looked at her watch, 'forty minutes. Surely not? Are you drunk?'

'Not at all.'

'But do you really mean what you're saying?'

He nodded. 'Totally.'

'Gosh!'

'Are you surprised?'

'Flabbergasted. I mean, we're the two who're well aware that we're hopeless at sex, and even worse at relationships.'

'Perhaps we could try to push that assumption into the past tense?'

Her eyes glinted with fun. 'Do you mean what I think you mean?'

'I imagine so.'

She giggled. 'Well, I'm game to give it a go, if that doesn't sound too impossibly romantic!' Leaning towards him, she gave him a tentative kiss on the cheek. 'Your room or mine?'

'You choose,' he said.

'OK, mine. Here's your stick. Can you manage the stairs, or do we need the lift?'

'Do you mind if we take the lift? Sorry, but I want to conserve my strength.' He sighed as he rose to his feet. 'Wendy, I'm hardly love's young dream.'

'I'm the one who's about to be sixty! We'll just do our best, shall we?'

'I might have to experiment to find a position where my ribs or my leg don't hurt, or my wrist doesn't give way!'

She took his arm. 'If you don't shut up you're going to talk yourself out of this, just when I'm getting keen on the idea!'

Chapter Twenty-Two

Wendy crossed her fingers as she padded over to the window. Was it going to be fine for Michael and Minty's wedding? Her heart sank as she drew back the curtains and saw that it was what Nora called 'a grand, soft day'. In other words, it was raining torrentially, and the views she loved were obscured by a dense mist. She shivered and returned to bed.

It felt strange to have a break from travelling to London this week. For the last three months, she had spent Sundays, Mondays and Tuesdays in her Ballynakilty bookshop, but early every Wednesday had taken a taxi to Cork airport and flown to Heathrow. She had worked by day at her company, and spent the nights at Julian's flat. Most weeks, she had also fitted in a brief visit to her parents in Norfolk, before returning to Ireland on Saturdays.

It was a mad schedule, but it would not go on much longer.

Meanwhile, Minty had flown to London every Monday morning and returned late on Thursdays. She was, as Wendy had hoped, an absolute godsend to BS&T. And everything was working out very well, in a crazy sort of way. However, both women were counting the days till the company moved to its new headquarters at The Fitzhenry.

Never having even been to Ireland before this year, it had been a bold move to base herself here. But though she had a few qualms that some of her staff might miss the buzz of a big city when they arrived in this quiet part of Kerry, she knew she would never regret the relocation of her business. She continued to hate the idea of Brexit, which seemed unstoppable regardless of the recent General Election, with its inconclusive outcome. And the London Bridge terror attack at the beginning of the month had filled her with such horror she could not help but feel relieved that soon her young employees would be here, out of harm's way.

As she looked fondly at the sleeping man beside her, she acknowledged that there would be another bonus to being in Ireland most of the time.

After a few moments, Philip seemed to sense she was staring at him and opened his eyes. Smiling, he levered himself up on his elbows so that he could lean across and kiss her.

'You couldn't have done that a few weeks ago,' she congratulated him. 'Your ribs must be fully mended now.'

'You've been so patient with this old wreck. I suppose you wouldn't care to marry me?'

'That might be going a bit far!' She giggled.

'I'm going to keep asking till I get the answer I want!'

'You'll regret it if I agree.'

'Never! How can I convince you I'm serious?'

'I know you *think* you're serious,' Wendy indulged him, 'but once you're fully fit I'm sure you'll go looking for someone younger and more glamorous. But till that happens, I'm enjoying all the horizontal exercise we're getting. Funny that we've found out we're better at it than we realised!'

She gave him a comically lascivious stare over her naked right shoulder.

'Stay here,' he said. 'I'm going to make you a cup of tea.'

'Gosh, I may have to marry you after all!'

She listened as he walked down the winding staircase, enjoying a glow of pleasure at how much his mobility had improved. Most of the time, at least indoors, he managed without a stick. Nora thought it was a miracle, and perhaps indeed it was.

He had brought her to look at the old barn in early April. It had been a complete mess. Someone else, they learned, had purchased it and begun the conversion, but run out of money. Once he saw it, Philip had been determined to buy it. She had loved it as much as he had, but had worried that he would find it difficult to negotiate his way around what was, in some areas, little more than a building site.

She could hear him whistling as he laid a tray. He was a happy man – and she was happy too.

Smiling to herself, she reached for her phone. Unusually, both of her twins had texted her. Perhaps they were worried that she might be upset about Robert's nuptials. It was an odd coincidence that he and Francesca had wed yesterday, and that Minty and Michael were marrying today.

The boys had refused to cross the Atlantic to attend their father's wedding. She supposed they would accept his situation eventually. As yet, she had not told them that she too had someone new.

Both boys' messages ended by asking when she was going to come to Canada to visit them, and as she began to text a reply, a spark of an idea ignited in her brain. She could go, maybe, while her company was relocating to Ireland. There would be no clients to deal with over that period, and no studio work – just all the hassle of moving staff and equipment, and getting everything to work this side of the water. It was bound to be chaotic. Minty, with her marvellous organisational skills, would be in heaven. But surely everyone would be better off if she herself stayed away? As for her other pet project, maybe Michael could do more days at the bookshop while she was abroad. He loved it there as much as she did. She would miss him once he started his teacher-training in Cork and had to reduce his hours with her.

Philip returned with a tray of tea and a plate of her favourite oat biscuits from the local farm shop.

'You are spoiling me, Excellency!'

'Will you marry me then?'

'No. But would you like a holiday in Canada in about six weeks? I want to see my boys – and it'd be so much nicer if you came too.'

'Do you mean it?'

She took a sip of tea before nodding.

'What if your sons don't like me?'

'How could they not?'

'Lots of reasons. You don't think we should get married first?'

'Not really, I was thinking more like when the barn is finished.'

'If I get more men on the job, it might get done by November. We could have a Christmas wedding.'

'That seems a bit soon. What about on your sixtieth birthday?'

'That's not for four years!'

'I'm sure it'll go quickly. Meantime, we can keep practising you-know-what!'

'Grilled seabass fillets and creamy mash for everyone then?' Maeve queried.

The two doctors were in ebullient form when Araminta and Michael turned up at the waterfront restaurant in Ballynakilty for their pre-wedding lunch.

'Sweetheart, surely the bride and groom should be choosing?' Ronan protested.

'It's the best thing they do here,' his wife overruled him, 'and the ideal meal when you're feeling a little bit nervy and queasy.'

'But I'm not!' Michael laughed.

'I was thinking about your fiancée,' Maeve countered.

The other three looked at Araminta, who winced slightly. 'I am a bit anxious. I don't know why. Trivial things – such as whether Hannah will try to make me look too glamorous, or too young, when she does my hair and make-up, and whether I chose the right dress. As a result, I think I've lost my appetite.'

Maeve laughed. 'Not you! You just need to eat something sensible and you'll be fine.'

Ronan poured out sparkling water for them all before picking up a bottle of Pinot Grigio and waving it in Michael's direction.

'No wine for me. Not till after the ceremony!'

'It'd be very relaxing,' Ronan urged him.

'I *am* relaxed,' Michael insisted. 'Never better.'

'Araminta?'

'No thanks, Ronan, just water.'

'Now,' Maeve faced the two men and her voice took on a commanding tone, 'why don't you two boys go outside and take stock of the weather? I'm sure the forecast said it would improve.'

They looked reluctant to move, but Maeve waved them away. 'That's better,' she murmured once they had gone. 'Now what's got into you?'

Araminta shook her head. 'I don't know.'

'The Fitzhenry are marvellous at weddings. It's going to go like a dream.'

'Yes, I'm sure you're right.'

'Not having second thoughts?'

'About Michael? Of course not. In fact, I was just thinking how different getting married feels when you know you're doing it for the right reasons. I was pregnant on my first wedding day, and to be honest, though I tried to make the best of it, I knew I was making a mistake. I've felt guilty, actually, a few times recently because I couldn't help but feel glad that Simon had died and left me free to marry again. Don't tell anyone. It's awful.'

'Not that awful,' Maeve assured her. 'I've never told anyone else this, but Ronan's mother was very opposed to me. She thought I was too career-minded and would never look after her beloved boy properly. She wanted him to marry a distant cousin of his who was very religious. It would never have worked. Anyway, I used to literally pray that something bad would happen to his mother. And it did! She got pneumonia and it carried her off. Such a relief. She never liked me.'

'Oh my God!'

'You're not shocked are you?'

'N– no. I don't think so. But how soon after you prayed for her to, uh, die, did she oblige?'

'About twenty-seven years!'

Minty choked on the water she was drinking, and began to cough and laugh at the same time. 'Maeve,' she managed at last. 'You are too much. Thank God we know you.'

'Better now?'

'Yes. Last minute nerves I expect. But you don't think that Michael will have any regrets about marrying me or giving up the priesthood? Or feel he could have done better?'

Maeve pulled Araminta to her and kissed the top of her head. 'Look for yourself!' She pointed to Michael and Ronan as they returned to the room, brushing raindrops off their jackets, and beaming at each other, and then at the women. 'If that's not the picture of a man who knows exactly what he's doing, sure I don't know what is.'

'You must be tired.' Nora was standing in the storm porch of her house as Julian parked his hire car. '*And* you must have left at the crack of dawn. That journey from Dublin takes forever. I haven't driven it myself for years. But I remember how you lose the will to live!'

Julian had been performing Poulenc's rarely heard cantata *Le Bal Masqué* at the National Concert Hall, the night before.

'I'm fine! Anyway, I couldn't possibly miss lunch with my favourite girl, or a chance to see where you hide away when you're not at the hotel! What a wonderful place this is.'

He stood, gazing at the lush, green fields all around him and then, down the hill to the Kenmare River, several hundred feet below.

'Come in, come in. God, it's a good job you weren't here earlier – it was like living in a cold potato soup. Couldn't see a thing. It's a different day now altogether – and I've asked all my Catholic friends to pray for a sunny afternoon, so I'm sure it'll be grand!'

Julian followed Nora through the hall and into a large sitting room with huge windows which overlooked the water.

'Gin and tonic? Sherry?'

'Would it be awful to ask for a cup of tea?'

'Not at all. Sure, I'd sooner have one of those myself anyway.'

'Do you manage this house yourself? It's bigger than I imagined.'

'I have a cleaner twice a week, but to be fair, living alone – and being at the hotel most of the time – it doesn't get very untidy or dirty!'

'Well, I think you're amazing; it's a lot to cope with.'

'I like plenty of space, and when I first returned to Ireland after my divorce, Philip came for all the school holidays, and so it was a well-used house. But it's too big for me now.'

They wandered through to the spacious kitchen and Julian leant against an old, polished dresser while Nora laid out two mugs, produced a pot of tea and took cling film off a plate of crusty, generously filled cheese and tomato sandwiches which she had prepared before he arrived.

'You don't mind a light lunch, do you?'

Julian laughed. 'It doesn't look very light to me!'

'Ah, but it is for a big boy like you. Still, we both need to keep a lot of space for the wedding buffet at the hotel later. Jesus, the chefs have gone mental!'

Julian chuckled as he picked up the tray and followed Nora back into the sitting room.

He loved talking to her. When they had met at the hospital during the dark days of Philip's incarceration there, he had seen it as his duty to take his friend's mother out for a meal and look after her. But within minutes, he had realised what a pleasure it was to spend time with this funny and dynamic older woman. And on his two previous trips to Ireland, she had been a constant source of fun and information. 'I'm like your Irish mammy,' she had declared, and he had felt cheered and validated by her warmth towards him.

As they ate, they talked about Philip and Wendy. He had wondered if Nora had any reservations about the two of them becoming so close, but it seemed the reverse was true.

'I just hope they'll get married before I get too old to dance at their wedding,' she told him, before adding, 'Till now, Philip's always been hopeless with women – always going for the sort who treated him poorly. I'm sure George Baldry had a lot to do with that. He put Philip down from the day he was born.'

It occurred to Julian that Philip may have decided to keep from his mother the news that Baldry senior was not his biological parent, so he said nothing.

'But,' Nora continued, 'when Wendy sat up with him in the hospital night after night, I saw someone who valued and loved him for who he is. I'm sure they didn't realise they were falling for each other at the time. Not sure she quite realises it now! But she's perfect. And they're made for each other.'

'It's nice you feel that way.'

'How could I not?' She indicated he should take another sandwich before continuing. 'Now, I don't want you to feel sad this afternoon.'

'Sad! Why would I?'

'I get the feeling sometimes that you think you're less important to the other four than they are to you.'

'Wow!' Julian exhaled so sharply that his breath created a little channel in the curls on his forehead.

'But,' Nora continued, 'I've seen a lot of what goes on, and I want you to know you should never feel that. I know the others are now two sets of pairs, but you really, really matter to them.'

'In what way?'

'Well, Philip remembers you as a boy who befriended him when he was lonely at school, and who made him laugh – and he

334

also knows that you came searching for him the night of his accident. And Wendy's told me how you bolstered her confidence when her marriage ended, and how you cheered her up, and got her singing, and became a friend she could really rely on. And Michael and Araminta told me it was you who insisted that you should all go and see Richard as he was dying, and they said that without your wisdom and support, they might never have made it to today as a couple. You're like the glue in this quintet – it's just you don't know it. So, I thought I'd tell you!'

Julian felt tears stinging his eyes. 'I'm sure you're exaggerating.'

'No, I'm not. And both Wendy and Araminta have said how lovely it is to stay in your flat when they're working in London, and how you keep treating them to wine and food and won't take any rent.'

'Honestly, it's the other way around. They stock up the fridge and cook properly – well, Araminta does! Sometimes I'm not there anyway, but it's great to have them around.'

'Still, I'm sure it's not easy for you with the other four pairing off, especially now that your partner's going back to Jamaica.'

Julian sighed and took a sip of his tea. 'Well, I think I'm over that disappointment. Joe and I are good together and we really like each other. But we're not soulmates. He's seeing his old age roll out in front of him and wants to go home. It's partly his sister, and not wanting her to struggle on her own. I think it's also the upheaval that's happening in the UK. He's very sensitive to how this has loosened some people's tongues so they feel they can make racist comments. I know he gets a bit of that from the old folk in the care home, which I find too horrible for words. Most of all though, he feels a real pull from the island he was born in. You can't fight that. And on top of that, I'm a selfish sod!' Julian smiled wryly.

'I'm sure you're not.'

'I am though. I've been on my own too long. I like my life. I love my friends. I enjoy the freedom I have. And I'm thrilled that we're all involved in starting something wonderful here – music festival, book festival and so on – I couldn't turn my back on that now and stay in Gorleston all the time, let along go to Jamaica.'

'Well it's grand that you know that. Not all of us are built for coupledom, are we? I've been a million times happier since I stopped being a wife!'

'Did you never consider marrying again?'

'Certainly not! I like my own way too much.'

'Boyfriends?'

'Don't be a cheeky lad!' She grinned at him, her eyes twinkling. 'To be honest, I don't care for the sex thing. Very messy.'

They both giggled.

'Now, if you're sitting comfortably I want to ask you something.'

'Go ahead!'

'What would look good in that corner?' Nora had a huge smile on her face as she gestured to the far end of the long room where there was no furniture.

He knew he looked surprised, but thought it was probably a trick question.

'A grand piano!' she announced. 'It would be perfect.'

'That's a very good idea,' he agreed.

'Good! Because I understand that you've come by one that used to belong to Dr Richard, but you don't have anywhere to put it.'

His face brightened. 'That's true. You mean you wouldn't mind having it here? And I could play it when I was over?'

'Well that would be one option.'

He looked puzzled again.

'Would you like to hear my plan, which is a bit different?'

'Absolutely!'

'Well, you're going to spend more and more time in Ireland, aren't you? I mean there's the festival, but there's also the fact that your four closest friends are here and, as I've tried to explain, they want you to be around as much as possible. I know you like to go to dance classes – but there are good teachers in Cork and

Killarney. Of course you're still doing a lot of singing, but we're not far from London – as Wendy and Araminta have found out – and also you perform in other parts of Europe which you can get to easily from here.'

Unconsciously, he pushed his bottom lip over his top one while he considered what Nora was saying.

'I was just wondering,' she went on, 'if you would consider spending more time in Ireland and regarding this house as your home? I'd really love the company. As you see for yourself, I'm rattling around here on my own. And when I shuffle off the old mortal coil, which I hope won't be for ages by the way, Philip won't need this place. He'll inherit the hotel... he's got money... he's got a house... So, I just wanted to ask you if I could leave this place to you? It would be a weight off my mind. And if I'm doing that, to me it makes good sense for you to enjoy it right away, rather than wait till I'm gone. That's my plan. What do you say?'

Can I ask you something?' Hannah caught up with Julian as the wedding guests filed out of the small, formal room where the ceremony had taken place into the large dining room which over-looked the hotel swimming pool.

'Of course, dear heart.'

'I was wondering if you'd like to be my honorary uncle?'

Julian chortled. What an extraordinary day this was turning out to be. 'Excellent idea, but why?

'Well, you and Mum and Michael and Philip and Wendy are like a family. And the thing is that Michael's my stepdad now, and Wendy's something like my second half-cousin once removed, though I think of her as an aunt. And it stands to reason that Philip therefore will be my sort of uncle when they get married. I know she's playing hard to get, but you can see they're never going to be parted – which means that you're the only one who's not related to me and I really wish you were. So, how about it?'

'Sounds great. How about getting your uncle another drink when I finish this one? One won't even touch the sides, not with all this emotion! Where's the happy couple anyway?' Julian turned around to try to see them among the jostling crowd.

'Probably they're still signing things, or having photos,' Hannah suggested. 'They both looked wonderful, didn't they? Michael was the biggest shock in his electric blue suit. Nice to see him out of black! I must get some pictures on my phone when they turn up.'

'You should. I've never seen your mum look more divine than she does today in that Paul Costello dress. Coral is absolutely her colour and I loved those flared sleeves. As for her hair and make-up – I know that's all down to you. Loved the flowers pinned to the top of that French pleat. Honestly, is there anything you *can't* do?'

Hannah blushed. 'Loads of stuff.'

'I don't believe it! By the way,' Julian bent down to whisper in her ear, 'your man's looking particularly striking today.' He nodded in the direction of Farid who was wearing a dark plum coloured brocade jacket.

Her expression became proprietorial and proud. 'Yes, isn't he?'

'It'll be your wedding next, I expect.'

Hannah shook her head. 'Oh no. We haven't known each other that long and now I've got my job at Morse TV, we're not even able to live together. And because Farid works long hours too, we hardly seem to meet.'

'Methinks you do protest too much, fair lady. But not a bad idea to wait!'

Turning again he spied Philip and Wendy deep in conversation. 'Come over here, you two!' His voice cut through the hubbub. 'May I,' he indicated Hannah as they arrived, 'introduce you to my niece.'

'You're mad.' Wendy leant over and gave him a hug.

'Not at all. Hannah's given me honorary status. And, what I haven't had time to tell you is that Nora has asked me to live with her.'

'Wow!' Hannah exclaimed. 'I told you on Boxing Day you should all live in one big house together… it's kind of happening… you're already all in the same vicinity. Cool!'

'Yes, we can all end up in the same care home!' Wendy chuckled.

Philip looked slightly pained. 'I was thinking more of us all being in the hotel!'

Wendy and Julian exchanged a grin. 'Now you're talking!'

Hannah beamed at the three of them. 'Does anyone other than Uncle Julian want a top-up?' she asked.

'Definitely!' Philip answered. 'All of us need one. And bring drinks for your mum and stepdad. They can't be much longer!'

Hannah gave them a little salute and disappeared.

'Now she's gone,' Julian said. 'Do tell me, what on earth is Morse TV?'

'Oh,' Wendy replied. 'I forgot that this particular development may not have reached you. It's your fault for being so busy singing all over the place.'

Julian looked pleased but said, 'It's only all this modern stuff that the chamber orchestra specialise in. But it's great for me, because there's not much long legato singing and I can keep the vibrato in check.'

Wendy slapped his arm. 'Stop – your voice is wonderful. Don't do that self-denigration thing… Anyway, yes, Morse. It's a very go-ahead young local TV channel in Oxford and I'm guessing they partly called it Morse because Oxford was the home of the detective, but rather more because they do lots of breaking news in brief, really sassy and upbeat clips so I suppose it's like a modern Morse code. Anyway, she's presenting and promoting and editing… I don't think she ever sleeps, but she's in her element. My guess is that she'll be snapped up by Sky or ITN before long. Let's hope so!'

'Nice for her that you've got all these contacts.'

'But she got Morse herself. I'd never heard of them.'

339

Hannah returned with a waiter in tow just as Araminta and Michael entered the room, hand in hand and flushed with excitement and joy.

The young man dispensed champagne to all of them and retreated.

Hannah rummaged in her tiny bag for her phone, and before the others had time to pose or protest, or pull funny faces, she quickly took a succession of images. Then she flicked through them, her head on one side, intent on finding the best one to show them.

'Here we go! This one's great.'

'I don't think we've ever had a picture of the five of us before,' Philip mused. 'Let's have a look.'

There was silence while they crowded round Hannah's phone.

'Well, *you* all look marvellous,' said Wendy. 'And we do all look very happy!'

'You look magnificent,' Philip assured her. 'Really lovely. What don't you like?'

She grimaced. 'Well, the ruched effect on the front of my frock doesn't camouflage my tummy as much as I'd hoped!'

'And,' Araminta joined in, 'I was just thinking that my neck's a lot older than it was when I got married last time!'

'You all look jolly good,' Michael grinned. 'But I did think I had a bit more hair!'

'Hmmn. I thought I'd lost that gaunt expression,' Philip muttered. 'Obviously not. I look ancient.'

'Darlings!' Julian broke in. 'You're all wildly lovely and glamorous. I, on the other hand, have jowls taking over my entire face!'

Hannah, smiling to herself, surveyed the interchange and waited for them to finish. 'Well,' she said eventually. 'I think it's a good picture. You lot are awfully picky. You've had a year of challenges, to say the least. You've saved the jobs of the people at BS&T by moving the company away from the UK. You've rescued an entire chamber orchestra. You've prevented a lovely independent

340

bookshop from closing. You're bringing more tourism and employment to this part of Ireland by starting all these festivals. You've uprooted yourselves and come here – in a kind of "Five Leave Brexit Island" sort of a way despite your ages, commitments and baggage. *And* you're all in good health and looking great. Honestly, you're totally mad and impossible and never satisfied.'

Julian winked at the others. 'Hannah's right – it takes a lot to satisfy us. But maybe that's good. Anyway,' he shrugged his shoulders and laughed. 'It's who we are!'

About the Author

Christine Webber originally trained as an opera singer but had to re-think her career plans when her voice professor told her: 'Your voice is OK, but your legs are very much better!'

Musical theatre beckoned. There was some success. But not much.

In 1979, she became a news presenter for Anglia TV. At last she had found something she enjoyed that other people thought she was good at. It was such a happy relief that she stayed for 12 years. Towards the end of that period, *In Honour Bound*, her first novel, was published.

After leaving Anglia Television, she became an agony aunt for various publications including *TV Times, Best, Dare* and *BBC Parenting*. And she wrote a relationship advice column for *The Scotsman* and one for *Woman*, called Sexplanations. She also regularly broadcast advice on *Trisha, The Good Sex Guide… Late* and from the BBC's *Breakfast* sofa.

During her 'problem page' years, she decided to train as a psycho-therapist. This led to her having a practice in Harley Street.

Christine has written twelve non-fiction books including *How to Mend a Broken Heart* and *Too Young to Get Old*. She has also ghosted and consulted on several celebrity books. But her intention was always to find time to return to writing fiction. In 2016, she published a novel about romance in mid-life called *Who'd Have Thought It?* – this new novel also explores what it is to be fifty-something (or older) in today's turbulent world.

Book Club Questions

1. We are living in very unsettling times – how much does this impact on your friendships or family life?

2. As you grow older, which do you value more – support from your friends, or support from your family?

3. How easy – or difficult – is it to maintain friendships in mid-life? Or to make new ones?

4. Secrets tend to be uncovered as our parents become infirm or die. How have you coped with discovering new truths about you or your family?

5. Do you identify with any particular character in *It's Who We Are*? If so, which one?

6. Is it realistic for mid-life people to respond to difficult circumstances by making radical alterations to their lives?

7. Do you ever dream of a completely different life? Can you see any way of making it happen?

8. More and more people are finding love in later life – how do you feel relationships differ then, compared with early romance?